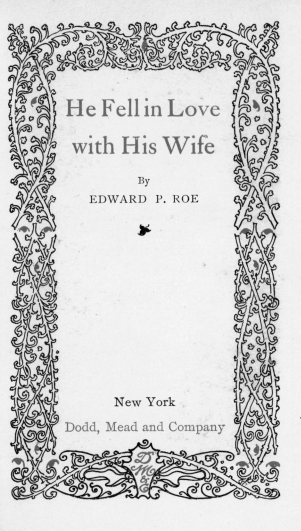

He Fell in Love
with His Wife

By

EDWARD P. ROE

New York

Dodd, Mead and Company

CONTENTS.

HE FELL IN LOVE WITH HIS WIFE.

CHAPTER I.

LEFT ALONE.

THE dreary March evening is rapidly passing from murky gloom to obscurity. Gusts of icy rain and sleet are sweeping full against a man who, though driving, bows his head so low that he cannot see his horses. The patient beasts, however, plod along the miry road, unerringly taking their course to the distant stable door. The highway sometimes passes through a grove on the edge of a forest, and the trees creak and groan as they writhe in the heavy blasts. In occasional groups of pines there is sighing and moaning almost human in suggestiveness of trouble. Never had Nature been in a more dismal mood, never had she been more prodigal of every element of discomfort, and never had the hero of my story been more cast down in heart and hope than on this chaotic day which, even to his dull fancy, appeared closing in harmony with his feelings and fortune. He is going home, yet the thought brings no assurance of welcome and comfort. As he cowers upon the seat of his market wagon, he is to the reader what he is in the fading light—a mere dim outline of a man. His progress is so slow that there will be plenty of time to relate some facts about him which will make the scenes and events to follow more intelligible.

James Holcroft is a middle-aged man and the owner of a small, hilly farm. He had inherited his rugged acres from his father, had always lived upon them, and the feeling had grown strong with the lapse of time that he could live nowhere else. Yet he knew that he was, in the vernacular of the region, "going down hill." The small savings of years were slowly melting away, and the depressing feature of this truth was that he did not see how he could help himself. He was not a sanguine man, but rather one endowed with a hard, practical sense which made it clear that the down-hill process had only to continue sufficiently long to leave him landless and penniless. It was all so distinct on this dismal evening that he groaned aloud.

"If it comes to that, I don't know what I'll do—crawl away on a night like this and give up, like enough."

Perhaps he was right. When a man with a nature like his "gives up," the end has come. The low, sturdy oaks that grew so abundantly along the road were types of his character—they could break, but not bend. He had little suppleness, little power to adapt himself to varied conditions of life. An event had occurred a year since, which, for months, he could only contemplate with dull wonder and dismay. In his youth he had married the daughter of a small farmer. Like himself, she had always been accustomed to toil and frugal living. From childhood she had been impressed with the thought that parting with a dollar was a serious matter, and to save a dollar one of the good deeds rewarded in this life and the life to come. She and her husband were in complete harmony on this vital point. Yet not a miserly trait entered into their humble thrift. It was a necessity entailed by their meager resources ; it was inspired by the wish for an honest independence in their old age.

There was to be no old age for her. She took a heavy cold, and almost before her husband was aware of her danger, she had left his side. He was more than grief-stricken, he was appalled. No children had blessed their union, and they had become more and more to each other in their simple home life. To many it would have seemed a narrow and even a sordid life. It could not have been the latter, for all their hard work, their petty economies and plans to increase the hoard in the savings bank were robbed of sordidness by an honest, quiet affection for each other, by mutual sympathy and a common purpose. It undoubtedly was a meager life, which grew narrower with time and habit. There had never been much romance to begin with, but something that often wears better—mutual respect and affection. From the first, James Holcroft had entertained the sensible hope that she was just the girl to help him make a living from his hillside farm, and he had not hoped for or even thought of very much else except the harmony and good comradeship which bless people who are suited to each other. He had been disappointed in no respect ; they had toiled and gathered like ants ; they were confidential partners in the homely business and details of the farm ; nothing was wasted, not even time. The little farmhouse abounded in comfort, and was a model of neatness and order. If it and its surroundings were devoid of grace and ornament, they were not missed, for neither of its occupants had ever been accustomed to such things. The years which passed so uneventfully only cemented the union and increased the sense of mutual dependence

They would have been regarded as exceedingly matter-of-fact and undemonstrative, but they were kind to each other and understood each other. Feeling that they were slowly yet surely getting ahead, they looked forward to an old age of rest and a sufficiency for their simple needs. Then, before he could realize the truth, he was left alone at her wintry grave; neighbors dispersed after the brief service, and he plodded back to his desolate home. There was no relative to step in and partially make good his loss. Some of the nearest residents sent a few cooked provisions until he could get help, but these attentions soon ceased. It was believed that he was abundantly able to take care of himself, and he was left to do so. He was not exactly unpopular, but had been much too reticent and had lived too secluded a life to find uninvited sympathy now. He was the last man, however, to ask for sympathy or help; and this was not due to misanthropy, but simply to temperament and habits of life. He and his wife had been sufficient for each other, and the outside world was excluded chiefly because they had no time or taste for social interchanges. As a result, he suffered serious disadvantages; he was misunderstood and virtually left to meet his calamity alone.

But, indeed, he could scarcely have met it in any other way. Even to his wife, he had never formed the habit of speaking freely of his thoughts and feelings. There had been no need, so complete was the understanding between them. A hint, a sentence, revealed to each other their simple and limited processes of thought. To talk about her now to strangers was impossible. He had no language by which to express the heavy, paralyzing pain in his heart.

For a time he performed necessary duties in a dazed, mechanical way. The horses and live stock were fed regularly, the cows milked; but the milk stood in the dairy room until it spoiled. Then he would sit down at his desolate hearth and gaze for hours into the fire, until it sunk down and died out. Perhaps no class in the world suffer from such a terrible sense of loneliness as simple-natured country people, to whom a very few have been all the company they required.

At last Holcroft partially shook off his stupor, and began the experiment of keeping house and maintaining his dairy with hired help. For a long year he had struggled on through all kinds of domestic vicissitude, conscious all the time that things were going from bad to worse. His house was isolated, the region sparsely settled, and good help difficult to be obtained under favoring auspices. The few respectable women in the neighborhood who occasionally "lent a hand" in other homes than their own would not compromise themselves, as they expressed it, by "keepin' house for a widower." Servants obtained from the neighboring town either could not endure the loneliness, or else were so wasteful and ignorant that the farmer, in sheer desperation, discharged them. The silent, grief-stricken, rugged-featured man was no company for anyone. The year was but a record of changes, waste, and small pilferings. Although he knew he could not afford it, he tried the device of obtaining two women instead of one, so that they might have society in each other; but either they would not stay or else he found that he had two thieves to deal with instead of one—brazen, incompetent creatures who knew more about whisky than milk, and who made his home a terror to him.

Some asked good-naturedly, "Why don't you marry again?" Not only was the very thought repugnant, but he knew well that he was not the man to thrive on any such errand to the neighboring farmhouses. Though apparently he had little sentiment in his nature, yet the memory of his wife was like his religion. He felt that he could not put an ordinary woman into his wife's place, and say to her the words he had spoken before. Such a marriage would be to him a grotesque farce, at which his soul revolted.

At last he was driven to the necessity of applying for help to an Irish family that had recently moved into the neighborhood. The promise was forbidding, indeed, as he entered the squalid abode in which were huddled men, women, and children. A sister of the mistress of the shanty was voluble in her assurances of unlimited capability.

"Faix I kin do all the wourk, in doors and out, so I takes the notion," she had asserted.

There certainly was no lack of bone and muscle in the big, red-faced, middle-aged woman who was so ready to preside at his hearth and glean from his diminished dairy a modicum of profit; but as he trudged home along the wintry road, he experienced strong feelings of disgust at the thought of such a creature sitting by the kitchen fire in the place once occupied by his wife.

During all these domestic vicissitudes he had occupied the parlor, a stiff, formal, frigid apartment, which had been rarely used in his married life. He had no inclination for the society of his help; in fact, there had been none with whom he could associate. The better class of those who went out to service could find places much more to their taste than the lonely farmhouse. The kitchen had been the one cozy, cheerful room of the house, and, driven from it, the farmer was an exile in his own home. In the parlor he could at least brood over the happy past, and that was about all the solace he had left.

Bridget came and took possession of her domain with a *sangfroid* which appalled Holcroft from the first. To his directions and suggestions, she curtly informed him that she knew her business and "didn't want no mon around, orderin' and interferin'."

In fact, she did appear, as she had said, capable of any amount of work, and usually was in a mood to perform it : but soon her male relatives began to drop in to smoke a pipe with her in the evening. A little later on, the supper-table was left standing for those who were always ready to "take a bite." The farmer had never heard of the camel who first got his head into the tent, but it gradually dawned upon him that he was half supporting the whole Irish tribe down at the shanty. Every evening, while he shivered in his best room, he was compelled to hear the coarse jests and laughter in the adjacent apartment. One night his bitter thoughts found expression : "I might as well open a free house for the keeping of man and beast."

He had endured this state of affairs for some time simply because the woman did the essential work in her offhand, slapdash style, and left him unmolested to his brooding as long as he did not interfere with her ideas of domestic economy. But his impatience and the sense of being wronged were producing a feeling akin to desperation. Every week there was less and less to sell from the dairy ; chickens and eggs disappeared, and the appetites of those who dropped in to "kape Bridgy from bein' a bit lonely" grew more voracious.

Thus matters had drifted on until this March day when he had taken two calves to market. He had said to the kitchen potentate that he would take supper with a friend in town and therefore would not be back before nine in the evening. This friend was the official keeper of the poorhouse and had been a crony of Holcroft's in early life. He had taken to politics instead of farming, and now had attained to what he and his acquaintances spoke of as a "snug berth." Holcroft had maintained with this man a friendship based partly on business relations, and the well-to-do purveyor for paupers always gave his old playmate an honest welcome to his private supper table, which differed somewhat from that spread for the town's pensioners.

On this occasion the gathering storm had decided Holcroft to return without availing himself of his friend's hospitality, and he is at last entering the lane leading from the highway to his doorway. Even as he approaches his dwelling he hears the sound of revelry and readily guesses what is taking place.

Quiet, patient men, when goaded beyond a certain point, are capable of terrible ebullitions of anger, and Holcroft was no exception. It seemed to him that night that the God he had worshiped all his life was in league with man against him. The blood rushed to his face, his chilled form became rigid with a sudden, passionate protest against his misfortunes and wrongs. Springing from the wagon, he left his team standing at the barn door and rushed to the kitchen window. There before him sat the whole tribe from the shanty, feasting at his expense. The table was loaded with coarse profusion, Roast fowls alternated with fried ham and eggs, a great pitcher of milk was flanked by one of foaming cider, while the post of honor was occupied by the one con-tribution of his self-invited guests—a villanous-looking jug.

They had just sat down to the repast when the weazen-faced patriarch of the tribe remarked, by way of grace, it may be supposed, "Be jabers, but isn't ould Holcroft givin' us a foine spread the noight! Here's bad luck to the glowerin' ould skinflint!" and he poured out a bumper from the jug.

The farmer waited to see and hear no more. Hasten-ing to a parlor window, he raised it quietly and clambered in; then taking his rusty shotgun, which he kept loaded for the benefit of the vermin that prowled about his hen-roost, he burst in upon the startled group.

"Be off!" he shouted. "If you value your lives, get out of that door, and never show your faces on my place again. I'll not be eaten out of house and home by a lot of jackals!"

His weapon, his dark, gleaming eyes, and desperate aspect taught the men that he was not to be trifled with a moment, and they slunk away.

Bridget began to whine. "Yez wouldn't turn a woman out in the noight and storm."

"You are not a woman!" thundered Holcroft, "you are a jackal, too! Get your traps and begone! I warn the whole lot of you to beware! I give you this chance to get off the premises, and then I shall watch for you all, old and young!"

There was something terrible and flame-like in his anger, dismaying the cormorants, and they hastened away with such alacrity that Bridget went down the lane screaming, "Sthop, I tell yees, and be afther waitin' for me!"

Holcroft hurled the jug after them with words that sounded like an imprecation, He next turned to the viands on the table with an expression of loathing, gathered them up, and carried them to the hog-pen. He seemed possessed by a feverish impatience to banish every vestige of those whom he had driven forth, and to restore the apartment as nearly as possible to the aspect it had worn in former happy years. At last, he sat down where his wife had been accustomed to sit, unbuttoned his waistcoat and flannel shirt, and from against his naked breast took an old, worn daguerreotype. He looked a moment at the plain, good face reflected there, then, bowing his head upon it, strong, convulsive sobs shook his frame, though not a tear moistened his eyes.

How long the paroxysm would have lasted it were hard to say, had not the impatient whinnying of his horses, still exposed to the storm, caught his attention. The lifelong habit of caring for the dumb animals in his charge asserted itself. He went out mechanically, unharnessed and stabled them as carefully as ever before in his life, then returned and wearily prepared himself a pot of coffee, which, with a crust of bread, was all the supper he appeared to crave.

CHAPTER II.

FOR the next few days, Holcroft lived alone. The weather remained inclement and there was no occasion for him to go farther away than the barn and outbuildings. He felt that a crisis in his life was approaching, that he would probably be compelled to sell his property for what it would bring, and begin life again under different auspices.

" I must either sell or marry," he groaned, " and one's about as hard and bad as the other. Who'll buy the place and stock at half what they're worth, and where could I find a woman that would look at an old fellow like me, even if I could bring myself to look at her ? "

The poor man did indeed feel that he was shut up to dreadful alternatives. With his ignorance of the world, and dislike for contact with strangers, selling out and going away was virtually starting out on an unknown sea without rudder or compass. It was worse than that—it was the tearing up of a life that had rooted itself in the soil whereon he had been content from childhood to middle age. He would suffer more in going, and in the memory of what he had parted with, than in any of the vicissitudes which might overtake him. He had not much range of imagination or feeling, but within his limitations his emotions were strong and his convictions unwavering. Still, he thought it might be possible to

live in some vague, unknown place, doing some kind of
work for people with whom he need not have very much
to do. "I've always been my own master, and done
things in my own way," he muttered, "but I suppose I
could farm it to suit some old, quiet people, if I could
only find 'em. One thing is certain, anyhow—I couldn't
stay here in Oakville, and see another man living in
these rooms, and plowing my fields, and driving his
cows to my old pasture lots. That would finish me like
a galloping consumption."

Every day he shrunk with a strange dread from the
wrench of parting with the familiar place and with all
that he associated with his wife. This was really the
ordeal which shook his soul, and not the fear that he
would be unable to earn his bread elsewhere. The
unstable multitude, who are forever fancying that they
would be better off somewhere else or at something else,
can have no comprehension of this deep-rooted love of
locality and the binding power of long association. They
regard such men as Holcroft as little better than plod-
ding oxen. The highest tribute which some people can
pay to a man, however, is to show that they do not and
cannot understand him. But the farmer was quite
indifferent whether he was understood or not. He gave
no thought to what people said or might say. What
were people to him? He only had a hunted, pathetic
sense of being hedged in and driven to bay. Even to
his neighbors, there was more of the humorous than the
tragic in his plight. It was supposed that he had a
goodly sum in the bank, and gossips said that he and
his wife thought more of increasing this hoard than of
each other, and that old Holcroft's mourning was chiefly
for a business partner. His domestic tribulations evoked

mirth rather than sympathy; and as the news spread from farmhouse to cottage of his summary bundling of Bridget and her satellites out of doors, there were both hilarity and satisfaction.

While there was little commiseration for the farmer, there was decided disapprobation of the dishonest Irish tribe, and all were glad that the gang had received a lesson which might restrain them from preying upon others.

Holcroft was partly to blame for his present isolation. Remote rural populations are given to strong prejudices, especially against those who are thought to be well-off from an oversaving spirit, and who, worse still, are unsocial. Almost anything will be forgiven sooner than " thinking one's self better than other folks"; and that is the usual interpretation of shy, reticent people. But there had been a decided tinge of selfishness in the Holcrofts' habit of seclusion ; for it became a habit rather than a principle. While they cherished no active dislike to their neighbors, or sense of superiority, these were not wholly astray in believing that they had little place in the thoughts or interests of the occupants of the hill farm. Indifference begat indifference, and now the lonely, helpless man had neither the power nor the disposition to bridge the chasm which separated him from those who might have given him kindly and intelligent aid. He was making a pathetic effort to keep his home and to prevent his heart from being torn bleeding away from all it loved. His neighbors thought that he was merely exerting himself to keep the dollars which it had been the supreme motive of his life to accumulate.

Giving no thought to the opinions of others, Holcroft only knew that he was in sore straits—that all which made his existence a blessing was at stake.

At times, during these lonely and stormy March days, he would dismiss his anxious speculations in regard to his future course. He was so morbid, especially at night, that he felt that his wife could revisit the quiet house. He cherished the hope that she could see him and hear what he said, and he spoke in her viewless presence with a freedom and fullness that was unlike his old reticence and habit of repression. He wondered that he had not said more endearing words and given her stronger assurance of how much she was to him. Late at night, he would start out of a long reverie, take a candle, and, going through the house, would touch what she had touched, and look long and fixedly at things associated with her. Her gowns still hung in the closet, just as she had left them ; he would take them out and recall the well-remembered scenes and occasions when they were worn. At such times, she almost seemed beside him, and he had a consciousness of companionship which soothed his perturbed spirit. He felt that she appreciated such loving remembrance, although unable to express her approval. He did not know it, but his nature was being softened, deepened, and enriched by these deep and unwonted experiences ; the hard materiality of his life was passing away, rendering him capable of something better than he had ever known.

In the morning all the old, prosaic problems of his life would return, with their hard, practical insistence, and he knew that he must decide upon something very soon. His lonely vigils and days of quiet had brought h m to the conclusion that he could not hunt up a wife as a matter of business. He would rather face the "ever angry bears " than breathe the subject of matrimony to any woman that he could ever imagine himself marrying.

He was therefore steadily drifting toward the necessity of selling everything and going away. This event, however, was like a coral reef to a sailor, with no land in view beyond it. The only thing which seemed certain was the general breaking up of all that had hitherto made his life.

The offer of help came from an unexpected source. One morning Holcroft received a call from a neighbor who had never before shown any interest in his affairs. On this occasion, however, Mr. Weeks began to display so much solicitude that the farmer was not only surprised, but also a little distrustful. Nothing in his previous knowledge of the man had prepared the way for such very kindly intervention.

After some general references to the past, Mr. Weeks continued, " I've been saying to our folks that it was too bad to let you worry on alone without more neighborly help. You ought either to get married or have some thoroughly respectable and well-known middle-aged woman keep house for you. That would stop all talk, and there's been a heap of it, I can tell you. Of course, I and my folks don't believe anything's been wrong."

" Believing that something was wrong is about all the attention my neighbors have given me, as far as I can see," Holcroft remarked bitterly.

" Well, you see, Holcroft, you've kept yourself so inside your shell that people don't know what to believe. Now, the thing to do is to change all that. I know how hard it is for a man, placed as you be, to get decent help. My wife was a-wondering about it the other day, and I shut her up mighty sudden by saying, ' You're a good manager, and know all the country side, yet how often you're a-complaining that you can't get a girl that's worth her salt to help in haying and other busy times when we have to board a lot of men.' Well, I won't beat around the bush any more. I've come to act the part of a good neighbor. There's no use of you're trying to get along with such haphazard help as you can pick up here and in town. You want a respectable woman for house-keeper, and then have a cheap, common sort of a girl to work under her. Now, I know of just such a woman, and it's not unlikely she'd be persuaded to take entire charge of your house and dairy. My wife's cousin, Mrs. Mumpson——" At the mention of this name Holcroft gave a slight start, feeling something like a cold chill run down his back.

Mr. Weeks was a little disconcerted but resumed, " I believe she called on your wife once ? "

" Yes," the farmer replied laconically. " I was away and did not see her."

" Well, now," pursued Mr. Weeks, " she's a good soul. She has her little peculiarities ; so have you and me, a lot of 'em ; but she's thoroughly respectable, and there isn't a man or woman in the town that would think of saying a word against her. She has only one child, a nice, quiet little girl who'd be company for her mother and make everything look right, you know."

" I don't see what there's been to look wrong," growled the farmer.

" Nothing to me and my folks, of course, or I wouldn't suggest the idea of a relation of my wife coming to live with you. But you see people will talk unless you stop their mouths so they'll feel like fools in doing it. I know yours has been a mighty awkward case, and here's a plain way out of it. You can set yourself right and have everything looked after as it ought to be, in twenty-four hours. We've talked to Cynthy—that's Mrs. Mumpson—and she takes a sight of interest. She'd do well by you and straighten things out, and you might do a plaguey sight worse than give her the right to take care of your indoor affairs for life."

"I don't expect to marry again," said Holcroft curtly.

"Oh, well! many a man and woman has said that and believed it, too, at the time. I'm not saying that my wife's cousin is inclined that way herself. Like enough, she isn't at all, but then, the right kind of persuading does change women's minds sometimes, eh? Mrs. Mumpson is kinder alone in the world, like yourself, and if she was sure of a good home and a kind husband there's no telling what good luck might happen to you. But there'll be plenty of time for considering all that on both sides. You can't live like a hermit."

"I was thinking of selling out and leaving these parts," Holcroft interrupted.

"Now look here, neighbor, you know as well as I do that in these times you couldn't give away the place. What's the use of such foolishness? The thing to do is to keep the farm and get a good living out of it. You've got down in the dumps and can't see what's sensible and to your own advantage."

Holcroft was thinking deeply, and he turned his eyes wistfully to the upland slopes of his farm. Mr. Weeks had talked plausibly, and if all had been as he represented, the plan would not have been a bad one. But the widower did not yearn for the widow. He did not know much about her, but had very unfavorable impressions. Mrs. Holcroft had not been given to speaking ill of anyone, but she had always shaken her head with a peculiar significance when Mrs. Mumpson's name was mentioned.

The widow had felt it her duty to call and counsel against the sin of seclusion and being too much absorbed in the affairs of this world.

" You should take an interest in everyone," this self-appointed evangelist had declared, and in one sense she lived up to her creed. She permitted no scrap of information about people to escape her, and was not only versed in all the gossip of Oakville, but also of several other localities in which she visited.

But Holcroft had little else to deter him from employing her services beyond an unfavorable impression. She could not be so bad as Bridget Malony, and he was almost willing to employ her again for the privilege of remaining on his paternal acres. As to marrying the widow—a slight shudder passed through his frame at the thought.

Slowly he began, as if almost thinking aloud, " I suppose you are right, Lemuel Weeks, in what you say about selling the place. The Lord knows I don't want to leave it. I was born and brought up here, and that counts with some people. If your wife's cousin is willing to come and help me make a living, for such wages as I can pay, the arrangement might be made. But I want to look on it as a business arrangement. I have quiet ways of my own, and things belonging to the past to think about, and I've got a right to think about 'em. I aint one of the marrying kind, and I don't want people to be a-considering such notions when I don't. I'd be kind and all that to her and her little girl, but I should want to be left to myself as far as I could be."

" Oh, certainly," said Mr. Weeks, mentally chuckling over the slight prospect of such immunity, " but you must remember that Mrs. Mumpson isn't like common help——"

"That's where the trouble will come in," ejaculated the perplexed farmer, "but there's been trouble enough with the other sort."

"I should say so," Mr. Weeks remarked emphatically. "It would be a pity if you couldn't get along with such a respectable, conscientious woman as Mrs. Mumpson, who comes from one of the best families in the country."

Holcroft removed his hat and passed his hand over his brow wearily as he said, "Oh, I could get along with anyone who would do the work in a way that would give me a chance to make a little, and then leave me to myself."

"Well, well," said Mr, Weeks, laughing, "you needn't think that because I've hinted at a good match for you I'm making one for my wife's. cousin. You may see the day when you'll be more hot for it than she is. All I'm trying to do is to help you keep your place, and live like a man ought and stop people's mouths."

"If I could only fill my own and live in peace, it's all I ask. When I get to plowing and planting again I'll begin to take some comfort."

These words were quoted against Holcroft, far and near. "Filling his own mouth and making a little money are all he cares for," was the general verdict. And thus people are misunderstood. The farmer had never turned anyone hungry from his door, and he would have gone to the poorhouse rather than have acted the part of the man who misrepresented him. He had only meant to express the hope that he might be able to fill his mouth—earn his bread, and get it from his native soil. "Plowing and planting"—working where he had toiled since a child—would be a solace in itself, and not a grudged means to a sordid end.

Mr. Weeks was a thrifty man also, and in nothing was he more economical than in charitable views of his neighbors' motives and conduct. He drove homeward with the complacent feeling that he had done a shrewd, good thing for himself and "his folks" at least. His wife's cousin was not exactly embraced in the latter category, although he had been so active in her behalf. The fact was, he would be at much greater pains could he attach her to Holcroft or anyone else and so prevent further periodical visits. He regarded her and her child as barnacles with such appalling adhesive powers that even his ingenuity at "crowding out" had been baffled. In justice to him, it must be admitted that Mrs. Mumpson was a type of the poor relation that would tax the long-suffering of charity itself. Her husband had left her scarcely his blessing, and if he had fled to ills he knew not of, he believed that he was escaping from some of which he had a painfully distinct consciousness. His widow was one of the people who regard the "world as their oyster," and her scheme of life was to get as much as possible for nothing. Arrayed in mourning weeds, she had begun a system of periodical descents upon his relatives and her own. She might have made such visitations endurable and even welcome, but she was not shrewd enough to be sensible. She appeared to have developed only the capacity to talk, to pry, and to worry people. She was unable to rest or to permit others to rest, yet her aversion to any useful form of activity was her chief characteristic. Wherever she went she took the ground that she was "company," and, with a shawl hanging over her sharp, angular shoulders, she would seize upon the most comfortable rocking chair in the house, and mouse for bits of news about everyone of whom she had ever heard. She was quite as ready to tell all she knew also, and for the sake of her budget of gossip and small scandal, her female relatives tolerated her after a fashion for a time ; but she had been around so often, and her scheme of obtaining subsistence for herself and child had become so offensively apparent, that she had about exhausted the patience of all the kith and kin on whom she had the remotest claim. Her presence was all the more unwelcome by reason of the faculty for irritating the men of the various households which she invaded. Even the most phlegmatic or the best-natured lost their self-control, and as their wives declared, " felt like flying all to pieces" at her incessant rocking, gossiping, questioning, and, what was worse still, lecturing. Not the least endurable thing about Mrs. Mumpson was her peculiar phase of piety. She saw the delinquencies and duties of others with such painful distinctness that she felt compelled to speak of them ; and her zeal was sure to be instant out of season.

When Mr. Weeks had started on his ominous mission to Holcroft his wife remarked to her daughter confidentially, " I declare, sis, if we don't get rid of Cynthy soon, I believe Lemuel will fly off the handle."

To avoid any such dire catastrophe, it was hoped and almost prayed in the Weeks household that the lonely occupant of the hill farm would take the widow for good and all.

CHAPTER III.

MRS. MUMPSON NEGOTIATES AND YIELDS.

MR. WEEKS, on his return home, dropped all diplomacy in dealing with the question at issue. "Cynthy," he said in his own vernacular, "the end has come, so far as me and my folks are concerned—I never expect to visit you, and while I'm master of the house, no more visits will be received. But I haint taken any such stand onconsiderately," he concluded. "I've given up the whole forenoon to secure you a better chance of living than visiting around. If you go to Holcroft's you'll have to do some work, and so will your girl. But he'll hire someone to help you, and so you won't have to hurt yourself. Your trump card will be to hook him and marry him before he finds you out. To do this, you'll have to see to the house and dairy, and bestir yourself for a time at least. He's pretty desperate off for lack of woman-folks to look after indoor matters, but he'll sell out and clear out before he'll keep a woman, much less marry her, if she does nothing but talk. Now remember, you've got a chance which you won't get again, for Holcroft not only owns his farm, but has a snug sum in the bank. So you had better get your things together, and go right over while he's in the mood."

When Mrs. Mumpson reached the blank wall of the inevitable, she yielded, and not before. She saw that th. Weeks mine was worked out completely, and she knew that this exhaustion was about equally true of all similar mines, which had been bored until they would yield no further returns.

But Mr. Weeks soon found that he could not carry out his summary measures. The widow was bent on negotiations and binding agreements. In a stiff, cramped hand, she wrote to Holcroft in regard to the amount of " salary " he would be willing to pay, intimating that one burdened with such responsibilities as she was expected to assume " ort to be compansiated proposhundly."

Weeks groaned as he dispatched his son on horse-back with this first epistle, and Holcroft groaned as he read it, not on account of its marvelous spelling and construction, but by reason of the vista of perplexities and trouble it opened to his boding mind. But he named on half a sheet of paper as large a sum as he felt it possible to pay and leave any chance for himself, then affixed his signature and sent it back by the messenger.

The widow Mumpson wished to talk over this first point between the high contracting powers indefinitely, but Mr. Weeks remarked cynically, " It's double what I thought he'd offer, and you're lucky to have it in black and white. Now that everything's settled, Timothy will hitch up and take you and Jane up there at once."

But Mrs. Mumpson now began to insist upon writing another letter in regard to her domestic status and that of her child. They could not think of being looked upon as servants. She also wished to be assured that a girl would be hired to help her, that she should have all the church privileges to which she had been accustomed and

the right to visit and entertain her friends, which meant
every farmer's wife and all the maiden sisters in Oakville. "And then," she continued, "there are always
little perquisites which a housekeeper has a right to look
for——" Mr. Weeks irritably put a period to this phase
of diplomacy by saying, "Well, well, Cynthy, the stage
will be along in a couple of hours. We'll put you and
your things aboard, and you can go on with what you
call your negotiations at Cousin Abiram's. I can tell
you one thing though—if you write any such letter to
Holcroft, you'll never hear from him again."

Compelled to give up all these preliminaries, but inwardly resolving to gain each point by a nagging persistence of which she was a mistress, she finally declared that
she "must have writings about one thing which couldn't
be left to any man's changeful mind. He must agree
to give me the monthly salary he names for at least a
year."

Weeks thought a moment, and then, with a shrewd
twinkle in his eyes, admitted, "It would be a good
thing to have Holcroft's name to such an agreement.
Yes, you might try that on, but you're taking a risk. If
you were not so penny-wise and pound-foolish you'd go
at once and manage to get him to take you for 'better
or worse.'"

"You misjudge me, Cousin Lemuel," replied the
widow, bridling and rocking violently. "If there's any
such taking to be done, he must get me to take him."

"Well, well, write your letter about a year's engage-
ment. That 'll settle you for a twelvemonth, at least."

Mrs. Mumpson again began the slow, laborious construction of a letter in which she dwelt upon the uncer-
tainties of life, her "duty to her offspring," and the evils

of "vicissitude." "A stable home is woman's chief desire," she concluded, "and you will surely agree to pay me the salary you have said for a year."

When Holcroft read this second epistle he so far yielded to his first impulse that he half tore the sheet, then paused irresolutely. After a few moments he went to the door and looked out upon his acres. "It 'll soon be plowing and planting time," he thought. "I guess I can stand her—at least I can try it for three months. I'd like to turn a few more furrows on the old place," and his face softened and grew wistful as he looked at the bare, frost-bound fields. Suddenly it darkened and grew stern as he muttered, "But I'll put my hand to no more paper with that Weeks tribe."

He strode to the stable, saying to Timothy Weeks, as he passed, "I'll answer this letter in person."

Away cantered Timothy, and soon caused a flutter of expectancy in the Weeks household, by announcing that "Old Holcroft looked black as a thundercloud and was comin' himself."

"I tell you what 'tis, Cynthy, it's the turn of a hair with you now," growled Weeks. "Unless you agree to whatever Holcroft says, you haven't the ghost of a chance."

The widow felt that a crisis had indeed come. Cousin Abiram's was the next place in the order of visitation, but her last experience there left her in painful doubt as to a future reception. Therefore she tied on a new cap, smoothed her apron, and rocked with unwonted rapidity. "It 'll be according to the ordering of Providence——"

"Oh, pshaw!" interrupted Cousin Lemuel, "it 'll be according to whether you've got any sense or not."

Mrs. Weeks had been in a pitiable state of mind all

day. She saw that her husband had reached the limit
of his endurance—that he had virtually already " flown
off the handle." But to have her own kin actually
bundled out of the house—what would people say ?
Acceptance of Holcroft's terms, whatever they might be,
was the only way out of the awkward predicament, and
so she began in a wheedling tone, " Now, Cousin Cynthy,
as Lemuel says, you've got a first-rate chance. Holcroft's
had an awful time with women, and he'll be glad enough
to do well by anyone who does fairly well by him.
Everybody says he's well off, and once you're fairly
there and get things in your own hands, there's no telling what may happen. He'll get a girl to help you, and
Jane's big enough now to do a good deal. Why, you'll
be the same as keeping house like the rest of us."

Further discussion was cut short by the arrival of the
victim. He stood awkwardly in the door of the Weeks
sitting room for a moment, seemingly at a loss how to
state his case.

Mr. and Mrs. Weeks now resolved to appear neutral
and allow the farmer to make his terms. Then, like
other superior powers in the background, they proposed
to exert a pressure on their relative and do a little
coercing. But the widow's course promised at first to
relieve them of all further effort. She suddenly seemed
to become aware of Holcroft's presence, sprang up, and
gave him her hand very cordially.

" I'm glad to see you, sir," she began. " It's very
considerate of you to come for me. I can get ready in
short order, and as for Jane, she's never a bit of trouble.
Sit down, sir, and make yourself to home while I get our
things together and put on my bonnet ; " and she was
about to hasten from the room.

She, too, had been compelled to see that Holcroft's farmhouse was the only certain refuge left, and while she had rocked and waited the thought had come into her scheming mind, "I've stipulated to stay a year, and if he says nothing against it, it's a bargain which I can manage to keep him to in spite of himself, even if I don't marry him."

But the straightforward farmer was not to be caught in such a trap. He had come himself to say certain words and he would say them. He quietly, therefore, stood in the door and said, "Wait a moment, Mrs. Mumpson. It's best to have a plain understanding in all matters of business. When I've done, you may conclude not to go with me, for I want to say to you what I said this morning to your cousin, Lemuel Weeks. I'm glad he and his wife are now present, as witnesses. I'm a plain man, and all I want is to make a livin' off the farm I've been brought up on. I'll get a girl to help you with the work. Between you, I'll expect it to be done in a way that the dairy will yield a fair profit. We'll try and see how we get on for three months and not a year. I'll not bind myself longer than three months. Of course, if you manage well, I'll be glad to have this plain business arrangement go on as long as possible, but it's all a matter of business. If I can't make my farm pay, I'm going to sell or rent and leave these parts."

"Oh, certainly, certainly, Mr. Holcroft! You take a very senserble view of affairs. I hope you will find that I will do all that I agree to and a great deal more. I'm a little afraid of the night air and the inclement season, and so will hasten to get myself and my child ready," and she passed quickly out.

Weeks put his hand to his mouth to conceal a grin as he thought, " She hasn't agreed to do anything that I know on. Still, she's right ; she'll do a sight more than he expects, but it won't be just what he expects."

Mrs. Weeks followed her relative to expedite matters, and it must be confessed that the gathering of Mrs. Mumpson's belongings was no heavy task. A small hair trunk, that had come down from the remote past, held her own and her child's wardrobe and represented all their worldly possessions.

Mr. Weeks, much pleased at the turn of affairs, became very affable, but confined his remarks chiefly to the weather, while Holcroft, who had an uneasy sense of being overreached in some undetected way, was abstracted and laconic. He was soon on the road home, however, with Mrs. Mumpson and Jane. Cousin Lemuel's last whispered charge was, " Now, for mercy's sake, do keep your tongue still and your hands busy."

Whatever possibilities there may be for the Ethiopian or the leopard, there was no hope that Mrs. Mumpson would materially change any of her characteristics. The chief reason was that she had no desire to change. A more self-complacent person did not exist in Oakville. Good traits in other people did not interest her. They were insipid, they lacked a certain pungency which a dash of evil imparts ; and in the course of her minute investigations she had discerned or surmised so much that was reprehensible that she had come to regard herself as singularly free from sins of omission and commission. " What have I ever done ? " she would ask in her self-communings. The question implied so much truth of a certain kind that all her relatives were in gall and bitterness as they remembered the weary months during which she had rocked idly at their firesides. With her, talking was as much of a necessity as breathing; but during the ride to the hillside farm she, in a sense, held her breath, for a keen March wind was blowing.

She was so quiet that Holcroft grew hopeful, not realizing that the checked flow of words must have freer course later on. A cloudy twilight was deepening fast when they reached the dwelling. Holcroft's market wagon served for the general purposes of conveyance, and he drove as near as possible to the kitchen door. Descending from the front seat, which he had occupied alone, he turned and offered his hand to assist the widow to alight, but she nervously poised herself on the edge of the vehicle and seemed to be afraid to venture. The wind fluttered her scanty draperies, causing her to appear like a bird of prey about to swoop down upon the unprotected man. " I'm afraid to jump so far——" she began.

" There's the step, Mrs. Mumpson."

" But I can't see it. Would you mind lifting me down ? "

He impatiently took her by the arms, which seemed in his grasp like the rounds of a chair, and put her on the ground.

" Oh ! " she exclaimed, in gushing tones, " there's nothing to equal the strong arms of a man."

He hastily lifted out her daughter, and said, " You had better hurry in to the fire. I'll be back in a few minutes," and he led his horses down to the barn, blanketed and tied them. When he returned, he saw two dusky figures standing by the front door which led to the little hall separating the kitchen from the parlor.

" Bless me ! " he exclaimed. " You haven't been standing here all this time ? "

"It's merely due to a little oversight. The door is locked, you see, and——"

"But the kitchen door is not locked."

"Well, it didn't seem quite natural for us to enter the dwelling, on the occasion of our first arrival, by the kitchen entrance, and——"

Holcroft, with a grim look, strode through the kitchen and unlocked the door.

"Ah!" exclaimed the widow. "I feel as if I was coming home. Enter, Jane, my dear. I'm sure the place will soon cease to be strange to you, for the home feeling is rapidly acquired when——"

"Just wait a minute, please," said Holcroft, "and I'll light the lamp and a candle." This he did with the deftness of a man accustomed to help himself, then led the way to the upper room which was to be her sleeping apartment. Placing the candle on the bureau, he forestalled Mrs. Mumpson by saying, "I'll freshen up the fire in the kitchen and lay out the ham, eggs, coffee, and other materials for supper. Then I must go out and unharness and do my night work. Make yourselves to home. You'll soon be able to find everything," and he hastened away.

It would not be their fault if they were not soon able to find everything. Mrs. Mumpson's first act was to take the candle and survey the room in every nook and corner. She sighed when she found the closet and bureau drawers empty. Then she examined the quantity and texture of the bedding of the "couch on which she was to repose," as she would express herself. Jane followed her around on tiptoe, doing just what her mother did, but was silent. At last they shivered in the fireless apartment, threw off their scanty wraps, and went down to the kitchen. Mrs. Mumpson instinctively looked around for a rocking chair, and as none was visible she hastened to the parlor, and, holding the candle aloft, surveyed this apartment. Jane followed in her wake as before, but at last ventured to suggest, " Mother, Mr. Holcroft 'll be in soon and want his supper."

" I suppose he'll want a great many things," replied Mrs. Mumpson with dignity, " but he can't expect a lady of my connections to fly around like a common servant. It is but natural, in coming to a new abode, that I should wish to know something of that abode. There should have been a hired girl here ready to receive and get supper for us. Since there is not one to receive us, bring that rocking chair, my dear, and I will direct you how to proceed."

The child did as she was told, and her mother was soon rocking on the snuggest side of the kitchen stove, interspersing her rather bewildering orders with various reflections and surmises.

Sketching the child Jane is a sad task, and pity would lead us to soften every touch if this could be done in truthfulness. She was but twelve years of age, yet there was scarcely a trace of childhood left in her colorless face. Stealthy and catlike in all her movements, she gave the impression that she could not do the commonest thing except in a sly, cowering manner. Her small greenish-gray eyes appeared to be growing nearer together with the lease of time, and their indirect, furtive glances suggested that they had hardly, if ever, seen looks of frank affection bent upon her. She had early learned, on the round of visits with her mother, that so far from being welcome she was scarcely tolerated, and she reminded one of a stray cat that comes to a dwelling and seeks to maintain existence there in a lurking, deprecatory manner. Her kindred recognized this feline trait, for they were accustomed to remark, "She's always snoopin' around."

She could scarcely do otherwise, poor child! There had seemed no place for her at any of the firesides. She haunted halls and passage-ways, sat in dusky corners, and kept her meager little form out of sight as much as possible. She was the last one helped at table when she was permitted to come at all, and so had early learned to watch, like a cat, and when people's backs were turned, to snatch something, carry it off, and devour it in secret. Detected in these little pilferings, to which she was almost driven, she was regarded as even a greater nuisance than her mother.

The latter was much too preoccupied to give her child attention. Ensconced in a rocking chair in the best room, and always in full tide of talk if there was anyone present, she rarely seemed to think where Jane was or what she was doing. The rounds of visitation gave the child no chance to go to school, so her developing mind had little other pabulum than what her mother supplied so freely. She was acquiring the same consuming curiosity, with the redeeming feature that she did not talk. Listening in unsuspected places, she heard much that was said about her mother and herself, and the pathetic part of this experience was that she had never known enough of kindness to be wounded. She was only made to feel more fully how precarious was her foothold in her transient abiding place, and therefore was rendered more furtive, sly, and distant in order to secure toleration by keeping out of everyone's way. In her prowlings, however, she managed to learn and understand all that was going on even better than her mother, who, becoming aware of this fact, was acquiring the habit of putting her through a whispered cross-questioning when they retired for the night. It would be hard to imagine a child beginning life under more unfavorable auspices and still harder to predict the outcome.

In the course of her close watchfulness she had observed how many of the domestic labors had been performed, and she would have helped more in the various households if she had been given a chance; but the housewives had not regarded her as sufficiently honest to be trusted in the pantries, and also found that, if there was a semblance of return for such hospitality as they extended, Mrs. Mumpson would remain indefinitely. Moreover, the homely, silent child made the women nervous, just as her mother irritated the men, and they did not want her around. Thus she had come to be but the specter of a child, knowing little of the good in the world and as much of the evil as she could understand.

She now displayed, however, more sense than her mother. The habit of close scrutiny had made it clear that Holcroft would not long endure genteel airs and inefficiency, and that something must be done to keep this shelter. She did her best to get supper, with the aid given from the rocking chair, and at last broke out sharply, "You must get up and help me. He'll turn us out of doors if we don't have supper ready when he comes in."

Spurred by fear of such a dire possibility, Mrs. Mumpson was bustling around when Holcroft entered. "We'll soon be ready," she gushed, " we'll soon place our evening repast upon the table."

"Very well," was the brief reply, as he passed up the stairs with the small hair trunk on his shoulder.

CHAPTER IV.

DOMESTIC BLISS.

HOLCROFT had been given a foretaste of the phase of torment which he was destined to endure in his domestic relations, and was planning to secure a refuge into which he could not be pursued. He had made himself a little more presentable for supper, instinctively aware that nothing would escape the lynx-eyed widow, and was taking some measurements from the floor to a stovepipe hole leading into the chimney flue, when he became aware that someone was in the doorway. Turning, he saw Jane with her small catlike eyes fixed intently upon him. Instantly he had the feeling that he was being watched and would be watched.

"Supper's ready," said the girl, disappearing.

Mrs. Mumpson smiled upon him—if certain contortions of her thin, sharp face could be termed a smile—from that side of the table at which his wife had sat so many years, and he saw that the low rocking chair, which he had preserved jealously from his former "help," had been brought from the parlor and established in the old familiar place. Mrs. Mumpson folded her hands and assumed a look of deep solemnity; Jane, as instructed, also lowered her head, and they waited for him to say "grace." He was in far too bitter a mood for any such pious farce, and stolidly began to help them to the ham and eggs, which viands had been as nearly spoiled as was possible in their preparation. The widow raised her head with a profound sigh which set Holcroft's teeth on edge, but he proceeded silently with his supper. The biscuits were heavy enough to burden the lightest conscience ; and the coffee, simply grounds swimming around in lukewarm water. He took a sip, then put down his cup and said, quietly, " Guess I'll take a glass of milk to-night. Mrs. Mumpson, if you don't know how to make coffee, I can soon show you."

" Why ! isn't it right ? How strange ! Perhaps it would be well for you to show me just exactly how you like it, for it will afford me much pleasure to make it to your taste. Men's tastes differ so ! I've heard that no two men's tastes were alike ; and, after all, everything is a matter of taste. Now Cousin Abiram doesn't believe in coffee at all. He thinks it is unwholesome. Have *you* ever thought that it might be unwholesome ? "

" I'm used to it, and would like it good when I have it at all."

" Why, of course, of course ! You must have it exactly to your taste. Jane, my dear, we must put our minds on coffee and learn precisely how Mr. Holcroft likes it, and when the hired girl comes we must carefully superintend her when she makes it. By the way, I suppose you will employ my assistant to-morrow, Mr. Holcroft."

" I can't get a girl short of town," was the reply, " and there is so much cream in the dairy that ought to be churned at once that I'll wait till next Monday and take down the butter."

Mrs. Mumpson put on a grave, injured air, and said, " Well," so disapprovingly that it was virtually saying that it was not well at all. Then, suddenly remembering that this was not good policy, she was soon all smiles and chatter again. "How cozy this is!" she cried, "and how soon one acquires the home feeling! Why, anyone looking in at the window would think that we were an old established family, and yet this is but our first meal together. But it won't be the last, Mr. Holcroft. I cannot make it known to you how your loneliness, which Cousin Lemuel has so feelingly described to me, has affected my feelings. Cousin Nancy said but this very day that you have had desperate times with all kinds of dreadful creatures. But all that's past. Jane and me will give a look of stability and respecterbility to every comer."

"Well, really, Mrs. Mumpson, I don't know who's to come."

"Oh, you'll see!" she replied, wrinkling her thin, blue lips into what was meant for a smile, and nodding her head at him encouragingly. "You won't be so isolated no more. Now that I'm here, with my offspring, your neighbors will feel that they can show you their sympathy. The most respecterble people in town will call, and your life will grow brighter and brighter; clouds will roll away, and——"

"I hope the neighbors will not be so ill-mannered as to come without being invited," remarked Mr. Holcroft, grimly. "It's too late in the day for them to begin now."

"*My* being here with Jane will make all the difference in the world," resumed Mrs. Mumpson, with as saccharine an expression as she could assume. "They will come out of pure kindness and friendly interest, with the wish to encourage——"

"Mrs. Mumpson," said Holcroft, half desperately, "if

anyone comes it 'll be out of pure curiosity, and I don't want such company. Selling enough butter, eggs, and produce to pay expenses will encourage me more than all the people of Oakville, if they should come in a body. What's the use of talking in this way? I've done without the neighbors so far, and I'm sure they've been very careful to do without me. I shall have nothing to do with them except in the way of business, and as I said to you down at Lemuel Weeks's, business must be the first consideration with us all," and he rose from the table.

"Oh, certainly, certainly!" the widow hastened to say, "but then business is like a cloud, and the meetings and greetings of friends is a sort of silver lining, you know. What would the world be without friends—the society of those who take an abiding interest? Believe me, Mr. Holcroft," she continued, bringing her long, skinny finger impressively down on the table, "you have lived alone so long that you are unable to see the crying needs of your own constitution. As a Christian man, you require human sympathy and——"

Poor Holcroft knew little of centrifugal force; but at that moment he was a living embodiment of it, feeling that if he did not escape he would fly into a thousand atoms. Saying nervously, "I've a few chores to do," he seized his hat, and hastening out, wandered disconsolately around the barn. "I'm never going to be able to stand her," he groaned. "I know now why my poor wife shook her head whenever this woman was mentioned. The clack of her tongue would drive any man living crazy, and the gimlet eyes of that girl Jane would bore holes through a saint's patience. Well, well! I'll put a stove up in my room, then plowing and planting time

will soon be here, and I guess I can stand it at meal-
times for three months, for unless she stops her foolishness she shan't stay any longer."

Jane had not spoken during the meal, but kept her
eyes on Holcroft, except when he looked toward her, and
then she instantly averted her gaze. When she was
alone with her mother, she said abruptly, "We aint a-
goin' to stay here long, nuther."

"Why not?" was the sharp, responsive query.

"'Cause the same look's comin' into his face that was
in Cousin Lemuel's and Cousin Abiram's and all the rest
of 'em. 'Fi's you I'd keep still now. 'Pears to me they
all want you to keep still and you won't."

"Jane," said Mrs. Mumpson in severe tones, "you're
an ignorant child. Don't presume to instruct *me!* Besides, this case is entirely different. Mr. Holcroft must
be made to understand from the start that I'm not a
common woman—that I'm his equal, and in most
respects his superior. If he aint made to feel this, it 'll
never enter his head—but law! there's things which you
can't and oughtn't to understand."

"But I do," said the girl shortly, "and he won't
marry you, nor keep you, if you talk him to death."

"Jane!" gasped Mrs. Mumpson, as she sank into the
chair and rocked violently.

The night air was keen and soon drove Holcroft into
the house. As he passed the kitchen window, he saw
that Mrs. Mumpson was in his wife's rocking chair and
that Jane was clearing up the table. He kindled a fire
on the parlor hearth, hoping, but scarcely expecting, that
he would be left alone.

Nor was he very long, for the widow soon opened the
door and entered, carrying the chair. "Oh, you are

here," she said sweetly. "I heard the fire crackling, and I do so love open wood fires. They're company in themselves, and they make those who bask in the flickering blaze inclined to be sociable. To think of how many long, lonely evenings you have sat here when you had persons in your employ with whom you could have no affinity whatever! I don't see how you stood it. Under such circumstances life must cloud up into a dreary burden." It never occurred to Mrs. Mumpson that her figures of speech were often mixed. She merely felt that the sentimental phase of conversation must be very flowery. But during the first evening she had resolved on prudence. "Mr. Holcroft shall have time," she thought, "for the hope to steal into his heart that his housekeeper may become something more to him than housekeeper—that there is a nearer and loftier relation."

Meanwhile she was consumed with curiosity to know something about the "persons" previously employed and his experiences with them. With a momentary, and, as she felt, a proper pause before descending to ordinary topics, she resumed, "My dear Mr. Holcroft, no doubt it will be a relief to your overfraught mind to pour into a symperthetic ear the story of your troubles with those—er—those peculiar females that—er—that——"

"Mrs. Mumpson, it would be a much greater relief to my mind to forget all about 'em," he replied briefly.

"*Indeed!*" exclaimed the widow. "Was they as bad as that? Who'd 'a' thought it! Well, well, well; what people there is in the world! And you couldn't abide 'em, then?"

"No, I couldn't."

"Well now; what hussies they must have been! And

to think you were here all alone, with no better company! It makes my heart bleed. They *do* say that Bridget Malony is equal to anything, and I've no doubt but that she took things and did things."

" Well, she's taken herself off, and that's enough." Then he groaned inwardly, " Good Lord! I could stand her and all her tribe better'n this one."

" Yes, Mr. Holcroft," pursued Mrs. Mumpson, sinking her voice to a loud, confidential whisper, "and I don't believe you've any idea how much she took with her. I fear you've been robbed in all these vicissitudes. Men never know what's in a house. They need caretakers; respecterble women, that would sooner cut out their tongues than purloin. How happy is the change which has been affected! How could you abide in the house with such a person as that Bridget Malony? "

" Well, well, Mrs. Mumpson! she abode with herself. I at least had this room in peace and quietness."

" Of course, of course! A person so utterly unrespecterble would not think of entering *this* apartment; but then you had to meet her, you know. You could not act as if she was not, when she was, and there being so much of her, too. She was a monstrous-looking person. It's dreadful to think that such persons belong to our sex. I don't wonder you feel as you do about it all. I can understand you perfectly. All your senserbleness was offended. You felt that your very home had become sacrilegious. Well, now, I suppose she said awful things to you? "

Holcroft could not endure this style of inquisition and comment another second longer, He rose and said, " Mrs. Mumpson, if you want to know just what she said and did, you must go and ask her. I'm very tired. I'll go out and see that the stock's all right, and then go to bed."

"Oh, certainly, certainly!" ejaculated the widow. "Repose is nature's sweet rester, says the poet. I can see how recalling those dreadful scenes with those peculiar females——" But he was gone.

In passing out, he caught sight of Jane whisking back into the kitchen. "She's been listening," he thought. "Well, I'll go to town to-morrow afternoon, get a stove for my room upstairs, and stuff the keyhole."

He went to the barn and looked with envy at the placid cows and quiet horses. At last, having lingered as long as he could, he returned to the kitchen. Jane had washed and put away the supper dishes after a fashion, and was now sitting on the edge of a chair in the farthest corner of the room.

"Take this candle and go to your mother," he said curtly. Then he fastened the doors and put out the lamp. Standing for an instant at the parlor entrance, he added, "Please rake up the fire and put out the light before you come up. Good-night."

"Oh, certainly, certainly! we'll look after everything just as if it was our own. The sense of strangeness will soon pass——" But his steps were halfway up the stairs.

Mother and daughter listened until they heard him overhead, then, taking the candle, they began a most minute examination of everything in the room.

Poor Holcroft listened also; too worried, anxious, and nervous to sleep until they came up and all sounds ceased in the adjoining apartment.

CHAPTER V.

THE next morning Holcroft awoke early. The rising sun flooded his plain little room with mellow light. It was impossible to give way to dejection in that radiance, and hope, he scarcely knew why, sprung up in his heart. He was soon dressed, and having kindled the kitchen fire, went out on the porch. There had been a change in the wind during the night, and now it blew softly from the south. The air was sweet with the indefinable fragrance of spring. The ethereal notes of bluebirds were heard on every side. Migratory robins were feeding in the orchard, whistling and calling their noisy congratulations on arriving at old haunts. The frost was already oozing from the ground, but the farmer welcomed the mud, knowing that it indicated a long advance toward plowing and planting time.

He bared his head to the sweet, warm air and took long, deep breaths. "If this weather holds," he muttered, "I can soon put in some early potatoes on that warm hillside yonder. Yes, I can stand even her for the sake of being on the old place in mornings like this. The weather 'll be getting better every day and I can be out of doors more. I'll have a stove in my room to-night; I would last night if the old air-tight hadn't given out completely. I'll take it to town this afternoon and sell it for old iron. Then I'll get a bran'-new one and put it up in my room. They can't follow me there and they can't follow me outdoors, and so perhaps I can live in peace and work most of the time."

Thus he was murmuring to himself, as lonely people so often do, when he felt that someone was near, Turning suddenly, he saw Jane half-hidden by the kitchen door. Finding herself observed, the girl came forward and said in her brief, monotonous way :

"Mother'll be down soon. If you'll show me how you want the coffee and things, I guess I can learn."

"I guess you'll have to, Jane. There'll be more chance of your teaching your mother than of her teaching you, I fear. But we'll see, we'll see ; it's strange people can't see what's sensible and best for 'em when they see so much."

The child made no reply, but watched him intently as he measured out and then ground half a cup of coffee.

"The first thing to do," he began kindly, "is to fill the kettle with water fresh drawn from the well. Never make coffee or tea with water that's been boiled two or three times. Now, I'll give the kettle a good rinsing, so as to make sure you start with it clean."

Having accomplished this, he filled the vessel at the well and placed it on the fire, remarking as he did so, "Your mother can cook a little, can't she ? "

"I s'pose so," Jane replied. "When father was livin' mother said she kept a girl. Since then, we've visited round. But she'll learn, and if she can't, I can."

"What on earth—but there's no use of talking. When the water boils—bubbles up and down, you know—call me. I suppose you and your mother can get the rest of the breakfast ? Oh, good-morning, Mrs. Mumpson! I was just showing Jane about the coffee. You two can go on and do all the rest, but don't touch the coffee till the kettle boils, and then I'll come in and show you my way, and, if you please, I don't wish it any other way."

" Oh, certainly, certainly ! " began Mrs. Mumpson, but Holcroft waited to hear no more.

" She's a woman," he muttered, " and I'll say nothing rude or ugly to her, but I shan't listen to her talk half a minute when I can help myself ; and if she won't do any thing but talk—well, we'll see, we'll see ! A few hours in the dairy will show whether she can use anything besides her tongue."

As soon as they were alone Jane turned sharply on her mother and said, " Now you've got to do something to help. At Cousin Lemuel's and other places they wouldn't let us help. Anyhow, they wouldn't let me. He 'spects us both to work, and pays you for it. I tell you agin, he won't let us stay here unless we do. I won't go visitin' round any more, feelin' like a stray cat in every house I go to. You've got to work, and talk less."

" Why, Jane ! how *you* talk ! "

" I talk sense. Come, help me get breakfast."

" Do you think that's a proper way for a child to address a parent ? "

" No matter what I think. Come and help. You'll soon know what he thinks if we keep breakfast waitin'."

" Well, I'll do such menial work until he gets a girl, and then he shall learn that he can't expect one with such respecterble connections——"

" Hope I may never see any of 'em agin," interrupted Jane shortly, and then she relapsed into silence while her mother rambled on in her characteristic way, making singularly inapt efforts to assist in the task before them.

As Holcroft rose from milking a cow he found Jane beside him. A ghost could not have come more silently, and again her stealthy ways gave him an unpleasant sensation. " Kettle is boilin'," she said, and was gone.

He shook his head and muttered, " Queer tribe, these Mumpsons! I've only to get an odd fish of a girl to help, and I'll have something like a menagerie in the house." He carried his pails of foaming milk to the dairy, and then entered the kitchen.

" I've only a minute," he began hastily, seeking to forestall the widow. " Yes, the kettle's boiling all right. First scald out the coffeepot—put three-quarters of a cup of ground coffee into the pot, break an egg into it, so ; pour on the egg and coffee half a cup of cold water and stir it all up well, this way. Next pour in about a pint of boiling water from the kettle, set the pot on the stove and let it—the coffee, I mean—cook twenty minutes, remember, not less than twenty minutes. I'll be back to breakfast by that time. Now you know just how I want my coffee, don't you ? " looking at Jane.

Jane nodded, but Mrs. Mumpson began, "Oh, certainly, certainly ! Boil an egg twenty minutes, add half a cup of cold water, and——"

" I know," interrupted Jane, " I can always do as you did."

Holcroft again escaped to the barn, and eventually returned with a deep sigh. " I'll have to face a good deal of her music this morning," he thought, " but I shall have at least a good cup of coffee to brace me."

Mrs. Mumpson did not abandon the suggestion that grace should be said,—she never abandoned anything,— but the farmer, in accordance with his purpose to be civil, yet pay no attention to her obtrusive ways, gave no heed to her hint. He thought Jane looked apprehensive, and soon learned the reason. His coffee was at least hot, but seemed exceedingly weak.

"I hope now that it's just right," said Mrs. Mumpson complacently, "and feeling sure that it was made just to suit you, I filled the coffeepot full from the kettle. We can drink what we desire for breakfast and then the rest can be set aside until dinner time and warmed over. Then you'll have it just to suit you for the next meal, and we, at the same time, will be practicing econermy. It shall now be my great aim to help you econermize. Any coarse, menial hands can work, but the great thing to be considered is a caretaker ; one who, by thoughtfulness and the employment of her mind, will make the labor of others affective."

During this speech, Holcroft could only stare at the woman. The rapid motion of her thin jaw seemed to fascinate him, and he was in perplexity over not merely her rapid utterance, but also the queries, Had she maliciously spoiled the coffee ? or didn't she know any better ? "I can't make her out," he thought, "but she shall learn that I have a will of my own," and he quietly rose, took the coffeepot, and poured its contents out of doors ; then went through the whole process of making his favorite beverage again, saying coldly, "Jane, you had better watch close this time. I don't wish anyone to touch the coffeepot but you."

Even Mrs. Mumpson was a little abashed by his manner, but when he resumed his breakfast she speedily recovered her complacency and volubility. "I've always heard," she said, with her little cackling laugh, "that men would be extravergant, especially in some things.

There are some things they're fidgety about and will have just so. Well, well, who has a better right than a well-to-do, fore-handed man? Woman is to complement the man, and it should be her aim to study the great—the great—shall we say reason, for her being? which is adaptation," and she uttered the word with feeling, assured that Holcroft could not fail of being impressed by it. The poor man was bolting such food as had been prepared in his haste to get away.

"Yes," continued the widow, "adaptation is woman's mission and——"

"Really, Mrs. Mumpson, your and Jane's mission this morning will be to get as much butter as possible out of the cream and milk on hand. I'll set the old dog on the wheel, and start the churn within half an hour," and he rose with the thought, "I'd rather finish my breakfast on milk and coffee by and by than stand this." And he said, "Please let the coffee be until I come in to show you about taking out and working the butter."

The scenes in the dairy need not be dwelt upon. He saw that Jane might be taught, and that she would probably try to do all that her strength permitted. It was perfectly clear that Mrs. Mumpson was not only ignorant of the duties which he had employed her to perform, but that she was also too preoccupied with her talk and notions of gentility ever to learn. He was already satisfied that in inducing him to engage her, Lemuel Weeks had played him a trick, but there seemed no other resource than to fulfill his agreement. With Mrs. Mumpson in the house, there might be less difficulty in securing and keeping a hired girl who, with Jane, might do the essential work. But the future looked so unpromising that even the strong coffee could not sustain his spirits.

The hopefulness of the early morning departed, leaving nothing but dreary uncertainty.

Mrs. Mumpson was bent upon accompanying him to town and engaging the girl herself. "There would be great propriety in my doing so," she argued at dinner, "and propriety is something that adorns all the human race. There would be no danger of my getting any of the peculiar females such as you have been afflicted with. As I am to superintend her labors, she will look up to me with respect and humility if she learns from the first to recognize in me a superior on whom she will be dependent for her daily bread. No shiftless hussy would impose upon *me*. I would bring home—how sweet the word sounds!—a model of industry and patient endurance. She would be deferential, she would know her place, too. Everything would go like clockwork in our home. I'll put on my things at once and——"

"Excuse me, Mrs. Mumpson. It would not be right to leave Jane here alone. Moreover, I'd rather engage my own help."

"But, my dear Mr. Holcroft, you don't realize—men never do realize—that you will have a long, lonely ride with a female of unknown—unknown antercedents. It will be scarcely respecterble, and respecterbility should be man and woman's chief aim. Jane is not a timid child, and in an emergency like this, even if she was, she would gladly sacrifice herself to sustain the proprieties of life. Now that your life has begun under new and better auspicies, I feel that I ought to plead with you not to cloud your brightening prospects by a thoughtless unregard of what society looks upon as proper. The eyes of the commnuity will now be upon us——"

"You must excuse me, Mrs. Mumpson. All I ask of

the community is to keep their eyes on their own business, while I attend to mine in my own way. The
probabilities are that the girl will come out on the stage
Monday," and he rose from the dinner table and hastily
made his preparations for departure. He was soon
driving rapidly away, having a sort of nervous apprehension lest Jane, or the widow, should suddenly appear on
the seat beside him. A basket of eggs and some inferior
butter, with the burnt-out stove, were in his wagon and
his bank book was in his pocket. It was with sinking
heart that he thought of making further inroads on his
small accumulations.

Before he was out of sight Mrs. Mumpson betook herself to the rocking chair and began to expatiate on the
blindness and obduracy of men in general and of Mr.
Holcroft in particular. "They are all much alike," she
complained, "and are strangely neglectful of the proprieties of life. My dear, deceased husband, your father,
was becoming gradually senserble of my value in guiding
him in this respect, and indeed, I may add in all respects,
when, in the very prime of his expanding manhood, he
was laid low. Of course, my happiness was buried
then and my heart can never throb again, but I have a
mission in the world—I feel it—and here is a desolate
home bereft of female influence and consolation and
hitherto painfully devoid of respecterbility. I once
called on the late Mrs. Holcroft, and—I must say it—I
went away depressed by a sense of her lack of ability to
develop in her husband those qualities which would make
him an ornament to society. She was a silent woman,
she lacked mind and ideas. She had seen little of the
world and knew not what was swaying people. Therefore, her husband, having nothing else to think of, became

absorbed in the accumulation of dollars. Not that I object to dollars,—they have their proper place,—but minds should be fixed on all things. We should take a deep personal interest in our fellow-beings, and thus we grow broad. As I was saying, Mr. Holcroft was not developed by his late spouse. He needs awakening, arousing, stimulating, drawing out, and such I feel to be my mission. I must be patient; I cannot expect the habits of years to pass away under a different kind of female influence, at once."

Jane had been stolidly washing and putting away dishes during this partial address to herself and partial soliloquy, but now remarked, "You and me will pass away in a week if you go on as you've begun. I can see it comin'. Then, where 'll we go to?"

"Your words, Jane, only show that you are an ignorant, short-sighted child. Do you suppose that a woman of my years and experience would make no better provision for the future than a man's changeful mind—a warped and undeveloped mind, at that? No; I have an agreement with Mr. Holcroft. I shall be a member of his household for three months at least, and long before that he will begin to see everything in a new light. It will gradually dawn upon him that he has been defrauded of proper female influence and society. Now, he is crude, he thinks only of work and accumulating; but when the work is done by a menial female's hands and his mind is more at rest, there will begin to steal in upon him the cravings of his mind. He will see that material things are not all in all."

"P'raps he will. I don't half know what you're talkin' about. 'Fi's you, I'd learn to work and do things as he wants 'em. That's what I'm going to do. Shall I go now and make up his bed and tidy his room?"

"I think I will accompany you, Jane, and see that your task is properly performed."

"Of course you want to see everythin' in the room, just as I do."

"As housekeeper, I should see everything that is under my care. That is the right way to look at the matter."

"Well, come and look then."

"You are becoming strangely disrerspectful, Jane."

"Can't help it," replied the girl, "I'm gettin' mad. We've been elbowed around long's I can remember, at least I've been, and now we're in a place where we've a right to be, and you do nothin' but talk, talk, talk, when he hates talk. Now you'll go up in his room and you'll see everythin' in it, so you could tell it all off to-morrow. Why, can't you see he hates talk and wants somethin' done?"

"Jane," said Mrs. Mumpson, in her most severe and dignified manner, "you are not only disrerspectful to your parent, but you're a time-server. What Mr. Holcroft wants is a very secondary matter; what is *best* for him is the chief consideration. But I have touched on things far above your comprehension. Come, you can make up the bed, and I shall inspect as becomes my station."

CHAPTER VI.

A MARRIAGE?

IN a quiet side street of the market town in which Mr. Holcroft was accustomed to dispose of his farm produce was a three-story tenement house. A family occupied each floor, those dwelling in the first two stories being plain, respectable people of the mechanic class. The rooms in the third story were, of course, the cheapest, but even from the street might be seen evidences that more money had been spent upon them than could have been saved in rent. Lace curtains were looped aside from the windows, through which were caught glimpses of flowers that must have come from a greenhouse. We have only to enter these apartments to find that the suggestion of refined taste is amply fulfilled. While nothing is costly, there is a touch of grace, a hint of beauty in everything permitting simple adornment. The mistress of these rooms is not satisfied with neatness and order merely; it is her instinct to add something to please the eye—a need essential to her, yet too often conspicuously absent in rented quarters of a similar character.

It is remarkable to what a degree people's abodes are a reflex of themselves. Mrs. Alida Ostrom had been brought to these rooms a happy bride but a few months since. They were then bare and not very clean. Her husband had seemed bent on indulging her so far as his

limited means permitted. He had declared that his income was so modest that he could afford nothing better
than these cheap rooms in an obscure street, but she had
been abundantly content, for she had known even the
extremity of poverty.

Alida Ostrom had passed beyond the period of girlhood, with its superficial desires and ambitions. When
her husband first met her she was a woman of thirty, and
had been chastened by deep sorrows and some bitter experiences. Years before, she and her mother had come
to this town from a New England city in the hope of bet-
tering their circumstances. They had no weapons other
than their needles with which to fight life's battle, but
they were industrious and frugal—characteristic traits
which won the confidence of the shopkeepers for whom
they worked. All went as well, perhaps, as they could
expect, for two or three years, their secluded lives passing
uneventfully and, to a certain extent, happily. They had
time to read some good books obtained at a public
library ; they enjoyed an occasional holiday in the country ; and they went to church twice every Sunday when
it was not stormy. The mother usually dozed in the
obscure seat near the door which they occupied, for she
was getting old, and the toil of the long week wearied
her. Alida, on the contrary, was closely attentive. Her
mind seemed to crave all the sustenance it could get from
every source, and her reverential manner indicated that
the hopes inspired by her faith were dear and cherished.
Although they lived such quiet lives and kept themselves
apart from their neighbors, there was no mystery about
them which awakened surmises. " They've seen better
days," was the common remark when they were spoken
of ; and this was true. While they had no desire to be

social with the people among whom they lived, they di
not awaken prejudices by the assertion of superiority
Indeed, it was seen that the two women had all the
could do to earn their livelihood, and they were left to d
this in peace.

When Alida Armstrong—for that was her maide
name—carried her own and her mother's work to an
from the shops, she often encountered admiring glances
She was not exactly pretty, but she had the good, refine
face which is often more attractive than the merely pretty
one, and she possessed a trim, rounded figure which sh
knew how to clothe with taste from the simplest and mos
inexpensive materials. Nor did she seek to dress abov
her station. When passing along the street, any discern
ing person would recognize that she was a working girl
only the superficial would look upon her as a common
place girl. There was something in her modest air an
graceful, elastic carriage which suggested the thought t
many observers, " She has seen better days."

The memory of these days, which had promised immu
nity from wearing toil, anxiety, and poverty, was a barrie
between the two women and their present world. Deatl
had bereft them of husband and father, and such property
as he had left had been lost in a bad investment. Learn
ing that they were almost penniless, they had patientl
set about earning honest bread. This they had succeeded
in doing as long as the mother kept her usual health
But the infirmities of age were creeping upon her. One
winter she took a heavy cold and was very ill. She
rallied only temporarily in the milder days of spring. In
the summer's heat her strength failed, and she died.

During her mother's long illness Alida was devotion
itself. The strain upon her was severe indeed, for she

not only had to earn food for both, but there were also doctor's bills, medicines, and delicacies to pay for. The poor girl grew thin from work by day, watching by night, and from fear and anxiety at all times. Their scanty savings were exhausted; articles were sold from their rooms; the few precious heirlooms of silver and china were disposed of; Alida even denied herself the food she needed rather than ask for help or permit her mother to want for anything which ministered to their vain hopes of renewed health.

What she should have done she scarcely knew, had not an unexpected friend interested himself in her behalf. In one of the men's clothing stores was a cutter from whom she obtained work. Soon after he appeared in this shop he began to manifest signs of interest in her. He was about her own age, he had a good trade, and she often wondered why he appeared so reticent and moody, as compared with others in similar positions. But he always spoke kindly to her, and when her mother's illness first developed, he showed all the leniency permitted to him in regard to her work. His apparent sympathy, and the need of explaining why she was not able to finish her tasks as promptly as usual, led her gradually to reveal to him the sad struggle in which she was engaged. He promised to intercede in her behalf with their mutual employers, and asked if he might come to see her mother.

Recognizing how dependent she was upon this man's good will, and seeing nothing in his conduct but kindness and sympathy, she consented. His course and his words confirmed all her good impressions and awakened on her side corresponding sympathy united with a lively gratitude, He told her that he also was a stranger in the town, that he had but few acquaintances and no friends, that he had lost relatives and was in no mood to go about like other young men. His manner was marked apparently by nothing more than interest and a wish to help her, and was untinged by gallantry ; so they gradually became good friends. When he called Sunday afternoons the mother looked at him wistfully, in the hope that her daughter would not be left without a protector. At last the poor woman died, and Alida was in sore distress, for she had no means with which to bury her. Ostrom came and said in the kindest tones :

" You must let me lend you what you need and you can pay me back with interest, if you wish. You won't be under any obligation, for I have money lying idle in the bank. When you have only yourself to support it will not take you long to earn the sum."

There seemed nothing else for her to do and so it was arranged. With tear-blinded eyes she made her simple mourning, and within a week after her mother's death was at work again, eager to repay her debt. He urged her not to hasten—to take all the rest she could while the hot weather lasted, and few evenings passed that he did not come to take her out for a walk through the quieter streets.

By this time he had won her confidence completely, and her heart overflowed with gratitude. Of course she was not so unsophisticated as not to know whither all this attention was tending, but it was a great relief to her mind that his courtship was so quiet and undemonstrative. Her heart was sore and grief-stricken, and she was not conscious of any other feeling toward him than the deepest gratitude and wish to make such return as was within her power. He was apparently very frank in regard to his past life, and nothing was said which excited her suspicions. Indeed, she felt that it would be disloyalty to think of questioning or surmising evil of one who had proved himself so true a friend in her sore need. She was therefore somewhat prepared for the words he spoke one warm September day, as they sat together in a little shaded park.

"Alida," he said, a little nervously, "we are both strangers and alone in this world, but surely we are no longer strangers to each other. Let us go quietly to some minister and be married. That is the best way for you to pay your debt and keep me always in debt to you."

She was silent a moment, then faltered, "I'd rather pay all my debt first."

"What debts can there be between husband and wife? Come now, let us look at the matter sensibly. I don't want to frighten you. Things will go on much the same. We can take quiet rooms, I will bring work to you instead of your having to go after it. It's nobody's business but our own. We've not a circle of relations to consult or invite. We can go to some parsonage, the minister's family will be the witnesses; then I'll leave you at your room as usual, and no one will be any the wiser till I've found a place where we can go to housekeeping. That won't be long, I can tell you."

He placed the matter in such a simple, natural light that she did not know how to refuse.

"Perhaps I do not love you as much as you ought to be loved, and deserve to be in view of all your kindness," she tried to explain. "I feel I ought to be very truthful and not deceive you in the least, as I know you would not deceive me." So strong a shiver passed through his

frame that she exclaimed, "You are taking cold or you
don't feel well."

"Oh, it's nothing!" he said hastily, "only the night
air; and then a fellow always feels a little nervous, I suppose, when he's asking for something on which his happiness depends. I'm satisfied with such feeling and
good will as you have for me, and will be only too glad to
get you just as you are. Come, before it is too late in
the evening."

"Is your heart bent on this, after what I have said,
Wilson?"

"Yes, yes, indeed!" clasping her hand and drawing her
to her feet.

"It would seem very ungrateful in me to refuse, after
all you have done for me and mother, if you think it's
right and best. Will you go to the minister whose
church I attended, and who came to see mother?"

"Certainly, anyone you like," and he put her hand on
his arm and led her away.

The clergyman listened sympathetically to her brief
history of Ostrom's kindness, then performed a simple
ceremony which his wife and daughters witnessed. As
they were about to depart he said, "I will send you a
certificate."

"Don't trouble yourself to do that," said the groom,
"I'll call for it some evening soon."

Never had she seen Ostrom in such gay spirits as on
their return; and, woman-like, she was happy chiefly
because she had made him happy. She also felt a glad
sense of security. Her mother's dying wish had been
fulfilled; she had now a protector, and would soon have
a home instead of a boarding place among strangers.

Her husband speedily found the rooms to which the

reader has been introduced. The street on which they were located was no thoroughfare. Its farther end was closed by a fence and beyond were fields. With the exception of those who dwelt upon it or had business with the residents, few people came thither. To this locality, Ostrom brought his bride, and selected rooms whose windows were above those of the surrounding houses. So far from regretting this isolation and remoteness from the central life of the town, Alida's feelings sanctioned his choice. The sense of possessing security and a refuge was increased, and it was as natural for her to set about making the rooms homelike as it was to breathe. Her husband appeared to have exhausted his tendencies toward close economy in the choice of apartments, and she was given more money than she desired with which to furnish and decorate. He said, " Fix everything up to suit your mind, and I'll be satisfied."

This she did with such skill, taste, and good management that she returned a large portion of the sum he had given her, whereupon he laughingly remarked that she had already saved more than she owed him. He seemed disinclined to accompany her in the selection of their simple outfit, but professed himself so pleased with her choice of everything that she was gratified and happy in the thought of relieving him from trouble.

Thus their married life began under what appeared to her the most promising and congenial circumstances. She soon insisted on having work again, and her busy fingers did much to increase his income.

Alida was not an exacting woman, and recognized from the beginning that her husband would naturally have peculiar ways of his own. Unlike Mrs. Mumpson, she never expatiated on " adaptation," but Ostrom soon

learned, with much inward relief, that his wife would
accept unquestioningly what appeared to be his habits
and preferences. He went early to his place of work,
taking the nice little lunch which she prepared, and
returned in the dusk of the evening when he always
found a warm dinner in readiness. After this he was
ready enough to walk with her, but, as before, chose the
least frequented streets. Places of amusement and resort
seemed distasteful. On Sundays he enjoyed a ramble in
the country as long as the season permitted, and then
showed a great disinclination to leave the fireside. For
a time he went with her in the evening to church, but
gradually persuaded her to remain at home and read or
talk to him.

His wife felt that she had little cause to complain of his
quiet ways and methodical habits. He had exhibited
them before marriage and they were conducive to her
absolute sense of proprietorship in him—an assurance so
dear to a woman's heart. The pleasures of his home and
her society appeared to be all that he craved. At times she
had wondered a little at a certain air of apprehensiveness
in his manner when steps were heard upon the stairs, but
as the quiet days and weeks passed, such manifestations
of nervousness ceased. Occasionally, he would start
violently and mutter strange words in his sleep, but nothing disturbed the growing sense of security and satisfaction in Alida's heart. The charm of a regular, quiet life
grows upon one who has a nature fitted for it, and this
was true to an unusual degree of Alida Ostrom. Her
content was also increased by the fact that her husband
was able each month to deposit a goodly portion of their
united earnings in a savings bank.

Every day, every week, was so like the preceding ones

that it seemed as if their happy life might go on forever. She was gladly conscious that there was more than gratitude and good will in her heart. She now cherished a deep affection for her husband and felt that he had become essential to her life.

"Oh, how happy mother would be if she knew how safe and protected I am!" she murmured one March evening, as she was preparing her husband's dinner. "Leaving me alone in the world was far worse to her than dying."

At that very moment a gaunt-looking woman, with a child in her arms, stood in the twilight on the opposite side of the street, looking up at the windows.

CHAPTER VII.

FROM HOME TO THE STREET.

As the shadows of the gloomy March evening deepened Alida lighted the lamp, and was then a little surprised to hear a knock at the door. No presentiment of trouble crossed her mind ; she merely thought that one of her neighbors on the lower floors had stepped up to borrow something.

"Come in !" she cried, as she adjusted the shade of the lamp.

A tall, thin, pale woman entered, carrying a child that was partly hidden by a thin shawl, their only outer protection against the chill winds which had been blustering all day. Alida looked at the stranger inquiringly and kindly, expecting an appeal for charity. The woman sank into a chair as if exhausted, and fixed her dark hollow eyes on Mrs. Ostrom. She appeared consumed by a terrible curiosity.

Alida wondered at the strange chill of apprehension with which she encountered this gaze. It was so intent, so searching, yet so utterly devoid of a trace of good will. She began gently, "Can I do anything for you ?"

For a moment or two longer there was no response other than the same cold, questioning scrutiny, as if, instead of a sweet-faced woman, something monstrously unnatural was present. At last, in slow, icy utterance, came the words, "So you are—*her !*"

" Is this woman insane?" thought Alida. " Why else does she look at me so? Oh, that Wilson would come! I'm sorry for you, my good woman," she began kindly. " You are laboring under some mistake. My husband——"

" *Your* husband!" exclaimed the stranger, with an indescribable accent of scorn and reproach.

" Yes," replied Alida with quiet dignity. " *My* husband will be home soon and he will protect me. You have no right to enter my rooms and act as you do. If you are sick and in trouble, I and my husband——"

" Please tell me, miss, how he became *your* husband?"

" By lawful marriage, by my pastor."

" We'll soon see how *lawful* it was," replied the woman, with a bitter laugh. " I'd like you to tell me how often a man can be married lawfully."

" What do you mean?" cried Alida, with a sudden flash in her blue eyes. Then, as if reproaching herself, she added kindly, " Pardon me. I see you are not well. You do not realize what you are saying or where you are. Take a seat nearer the fire, and when Mr. Ostrom comes from his work he'll take you to your friends."

All the while she was speaking the woman regarded her with a hard, stony gaze; then replied, coldly and decisively, " You are wrong, miss "—how that title grated on Alida's ears!—" I am neither insane nor drunk. I do know what I am saying and where I am. You are playing a bold game or else you have been deceived, and very easily deceived, too. They say some women are so eager to be married that they ask no questions, but jump at the first chance. Whether deceived or deceiving, it doesn't matter now. But you and he shall learn that there is a law in the land which will protect an honest

woman in her sacred rights.   You needn't look so shocked
and bewildered.   You are not a young, giddy girl if I
may judge from your face.   What else could you expect
when you took up with a stranger you knew nothing
about?   Do you know that likeness?" and she drew
from her bosom a daguerreotype.

Alida waved it away as she said indignantly, "I won't
believe ill of my husband.   I——"

"No, miss," interrupted the woman sternly, "you are
right for once.   You won't indeed believe ill of *your* husband, but you'll have to believe ill of *mine*.   There's no
use of your putting on such airs any longer.   No matter
how rash and silly you may have been, if you have a
spark of honesty you'll be open to proof.   If you and he
try to brazen it out, the law will open both your eyes.
Look at that likeness, look at these letters; and I have
other proof and witnesses which can't be disputed.   The
name of the man you are living with is not Wilson
Ostrom.   His name is Henry Ferguson.   I am Mrs.
Ferguson, and I have my marriage certificate, and——
What! are you going to faint?   Well, I can wait till you
recover and till *he* comes," and she coolly sat down again.

Alida had glanced at the proofs which the woman had
thrust into her hands, then staggered back to a lounge
that stood near.   She might have fainted, but at that
awful moment she heard a familiar step on the stairs.
She was facing the door; the terrible stranger sat at one
side, with her back toward it.

When Ostrom entered he first saw Alida looking pale
and ill.   He hastened toward her exclaiming, "Why, Lida,
dear, what is the matter?   You are sick!"

Instinctively she sprung to his arms, crying, "Oh, thank
God! you've come.   Take away this awful woman!"

"Yes, Henry Ferguson; it's very proper you should take me away from a place like this."

As the man who had called himself Wilson Ostrom heard that voice he trembled like an aspen; his clasp of Alida relaxed, his arms dropped to his side, and, as he sunk into a chair and covered his face with his hands, he groaned, "Lost!"

"Found out, you mean," was the woman's reply.

Step by step, with horror-stricken eyes, Alida retreated from the man to whose protection and embrace she had flown. "Then it's true?" she said in a hoarse whisper.

He was speechless.

"You are willfully blind now, miss, if you don't see it's true," was the stranger's biting comment.

Paying no heed to her, Alida's eyes rested on the man whom she had believed to be her husband. She took an irresolute step toward him. "Speak, Wilson!" she cried. "I gave you my whole faith and no one shall destroy it but yourself. Speak, explain! show me that there's some horrible mistake."

"Lida," said the man, lifting his bloodless face, "if you knew all the circumstances——"

"She shall know them!" half shrieked the woman, as if at last stung to fury. "I see that you both hope to get through this affair with a little high tragedy, then escape and come together again in some other hiding place. As for this creature, she can go where she pleases, after hearing the truth; but you, Henry Ferguson, have got to do your duty by me and your child or go to prison. Let me tell you, miss, that this man was also married to me by a minister. I have my certificate and can produce witnesses. There's one little point you'll do well to consider," she continued, in bitter sarcasm, " he married me first. I suppose you are not so young and innocent as not to know where this fact places *you*. He courted and won me as other girls are courted and married. He promised me all that he ever promised you. Then, when I lost my rosy cheeks— when I became sick and feeble from child-bearing—he deserted and left me almost penniless. You needn't think you will have to take my word for this. I have proof enough. And now, Henry Ferguson, I've a few words for you, and then you must take your choice. You can't escape. I and my brother have tracked you here. You can't leave these rooms without going to prison. You'd be taken at the very door. But I give you one more chance. If you will promise before God to do your duty by me and your child, I'll forgive as far as a wronged woman can forgive. Neither I nor my brother will take proceedings against you. What this woman will do I don't know. If she prosecutes you, and you are true to me, I'll stand by you, but I won't stand another false step or a false word from you."

Ferguson had again sunk into his chair, buried his face in his hands, and sat trembling and speechless. Never for an instant had Alida taken her eyes from him ; and now, with a long, wailing cry, she exclaimed, " Thank God, thank God ! mother's dead."

This was now her best consolation. She rushed into her bedchamber, and a moment later came out, wearing her hat and cloak. Ferguson started up and was about to speak, but she silenced him by a gesture, and her tones were sad and stern as she said, " Mr. Ferguson, from your manner more truly than from this woman, I learn the truth. You took advantage of my misfortunes, my sorrow and friendlessness, to deceive me. You know how false are your wife's words about my eagerness to be deceived and married. But you have nothing to fear from me. I shall not prosecute you as she suggests, and I charge you before God to do your duty by your wife and child and never to speak to me again." Turning, she hastened toward the door.

"Where are you going?" Ferguson exclaimed, seeking to intercept her.

She waved him off. "I don't know," she replied. "I've no right to be here," and she fled down the stairway and out into the darkness.

The child had not wakened. It was well that it had not looked upon such a scene, even in utter ignorance of its meaning.

CHAPTER VIII.

HOLCROFT'S VIEW OF MATRIMONY.

HOLCROFT was indeed very lonely as he drove through the bare March fields and leafless woods on his way to town. The sky had clouded again, like his prospects, and he had the dreary sense of desolation which overwhelms a quiet, domestic man who feels that his home and all to which he clings are slipping from him. His lot was hard enough at best, and he had a bitter sense of being imposed upon and wronged by Lemuel Weeks. It was now evident enough that the widow and her daughter had been an intolerable burden to his neighbor, who had taken advantage of his need and induced him to assume the burden through false representations. To a man of Holcroft's simple, straightforward nature, any phase of trickery was intensely repugnant, and the fact that he had been overreached in a matter relating to his dearest hopes galled him to the quick. He possessed the strong common sense of his class; his wife had been like him in this respect, and her influence had intensified the trait. Queer people with abnormal manners excited his intense aversion. The most charitable view that he could take of Mrs. Mumpson was that her mind—such as she had—was unbalanced, that it was an impossibility for her to see any subject or duty in a sensible light or its right proportions. Her course, so prejudicial to her own interests, and her incessant and stilted talk, were proof to his mind of a certain degree of insanity, and he had heard that people in this condition often united to their unnatural ways a wonderful degree of cunning. Her child was almost as uncanny as herself and gave him a shivering sense of discomfort whenever he caught her small, greenish eyes fixed upon him.

"Yet she'll be the only one who'll earn her salt. I don't see how I'm going to stand 'em—I don't, indeed, but suppose I'll have to for three months, or else sell out and clear out."

By the time he reached town a cold rain had set in. He went at once to the intelligence office, but could obtain no girl for Mrs. Mumpson to "superintend," nor any certain promise of one. He did not much care, for he felt that the new plan was not going to work. Having bartered all his eggs for groceries, he sold the old stove and bought a new one, then drew from the bank a little ready money. Since his butter was so inferior, he took it to his friend Tom Watterly, the keeper of the poorhouse.

Prosperous Tom slapped his old friend on the back and said, "You look awfully glum and chopfallen, Jim. Come now, don't look at the world as if it was made of tar, pitch, and turpentine. I know your luck's been hard, but you make it a sight harder by being so set in all your ways. You think there's no place to live on God's earth but that old up-and-down-hill farm of yours that I wouldn't take as a gift. Why, man alive, there's a dozen things you can turn your hand to; but if you will stay there, do as other men do. Pick out a smart, handy woman that can make butter yaller as gold, that 'll bring

gold, and not such limpsy-slimsy, ghostly-looking stuff as
you've brought me. Bein' it's you, I'll take it and give
as much for it as I'd pay for better, but you can't run
your old ranch in this fashion."

"I know it, Tom," replied Holcroft ruefully. "I'm
all at sea; but, as you say, I'm set in my ways, and I'd
rather live on bread and milk and keep my farm than
make money anywhere else. I guess I'll have to give it
all up, though, and pull out, but it's like rooting up one
of the old oaks in the meadow lot. The fact is, Tom,
I've been fooled into one of the worst scrapes I've got
into yet."

"I see how it is," said Tom heartily and complacently, "you want a practical, foresighted man to talk
straight at you for an hour or two and clear up the fog
you're in. You study and brood over little things out
there alone until they seem mountains which you can't
get over nohow, when, if you'd take one good jump out,
they'd be behind you. Now, you've got to stay and take
a bite with me, and then we'll light our pipes and
untangle this snarl. No backing out! I can do you
more good than all the preachin' you ever heard. Hey,
there, Bill!" shouting to one of the paupers who was
detailed for such work, "take this team to the barn and
feed 'em. Come in, come in, old feller! You'll find that
Tom Watterly allus has a snack and a good word for an
old crony."

Holcroft was easily persuaded, for he felt the need of
cheer, and he looked up to Tom as a very sagacious,
practical man. So he said, "Perhaps you can see farther
into a millstone than I can, and if you can show me a
way out of my difficulties you'll be a friend sure enough."

"Why, of course I can. Your difficulties are all here

and here," touching his bullet head and the region of his heart. "There aint no great difficulties in fact, but, after you've brooded out there a week or two alone, you think you're caught as fast as if you were in a bear-trap. Here, Angy," addressing his wife, "I've coaxed Holcroft to take supper with us. You can hurry it up a little, can't you?"

Mrs. Watterly gave their guest a cold, limp hand and a rather frigid welcome. But this did not disconcert him. "It's only her way," he had always thought. "She looks after her husband's interests as mine did for me, and she don't talk him to death."

This thought, in the main, summed up Mrs. Watterly's best traits. She was a commonplace, narrow, selfish woman, whose character is not worth sketching. Tom stood a little in fear of her, and was usually careful not to impose extra tasks, but since she helped him to save and get ahead, he regarded her as a model wife.

Holcroft shared in his opinion and sighed deeply as he sat down to supper. "Ah, Tom!" he said, "you're a lucky man. You've got a wife that keeps everything in-doors up to the mark, and gives you a chance to attend to your own proper business. That's the way it was with mine. I never knew what a lopsided, helpless creature a man was until I was left alone. You and I were lucky in getting the women we did, but when my partner left me, she took all the luck with her. That aint the worst. She took what's more than luck and money and everything. I seemed to lose with her my grit and interest in most things. It 'll seem foolishness to you, but I can't take comfort in anything much except working that old farm that I've worked and played on ever since I can remember anything. You're not one of those fools, Tom, that have to learn from their own experience. Take a bit from mine, and be good to your wife while you can. I'd give all I'm worth—I know that aint much—if I could say some things to my wife and do some things for her that I didn't do."

Holcroft spoke in the simplicity of a full and remorseful heart, but he unconsciously propitiated Mrs. Watterly in no small degree. Indeed, she felt that he had quite repaid her for his entertainment, and the usually taciturn woman seconded his remarks with much emphasis.

"Well now, Angy," said Tom, "if you averaged up husbands in these parts I guess you'd find you were faring rather better than most women-folks. I let you take the bit in your teeth and go your own jog mostly. Now, own up, don't I?"

"That wasn't my meaning, exactly, Tom," resumed Holcroft. "You and I could well afford to let our wives take their own jog, for they always jogged steady and faithful and didn't need any urging and guiding. But even a dumb critter likes a good word now and then and a little patting on the back. It doesn't cost us anything and does them a sight of good. But we kind of let the chances slip by and forget about it until like enough it's too late."

"Well," replied Tom, with a deprecatory look at his wife, "Angy don't take to pettin' very much. She thinks it's a kind of foolishness for such middle-aged people as we're getting to be."

"A husband can show his consideration without blarneying," remarked Mrs. Watterly coldly. "When a man takes on in that way, you may be sure he wants something extra to pay for it."

After a little thought Holcroft said, "I guess it's a good way to pay for it between husband and wife."

"Look here, Jim, since you're so well up on the matrimonial question, why in thunder don't you marry again? That would settle all your difficulties," and Tom looked at his friend with a sort of wonder that he should hesitate to take this practical, sensible course.

"It's very easy for you to say, 'Why don't you marry again?' If you were in my place you'd see that there are things in the way of marrying for the sake of having a good butter-maker and all that kind of thing."

"Mr. Watterly wouldn't be long in comforting himself," remarked his wife. "His advice to you makes the course he'd take mighty clear."

"Now, Angy!" said Tom reproachfully. "Well," he added with a grin, "you're forewarned. So you've only to take care of yourself and not give me a chance."

"The trouble is," Holcroft resumed, "I don't see how an honest man is going to comfort himself unless it all comes about in some natural sort of way. I suppose there are people who can marry over and over again, just as easy as they'd roll off a log. It aint for me to judge 'em, and I don't understand how they do it. You are a very practical man, Tom, but just you put yourself in my shoes and see what you'd do. In the first place, I don't know of a woman in the world that I'd think of marrying. That's saying nothing against the women,—there's lots too good for me,—but I don't know 'em and I can't go around and hunt 'em up. Even if I could, with my shy, awkward ways, I wouldn't feel half so nervous starting out on a bear hunt. Here's difficulty right at the beginning. Supposing I found a nice, sensible woman, such as I'd be willing to marry, there isn't one chance in a hundred she'd look at an old fellow like me. Another difficulty : Supposing she would ; suppose she looked me square in the eyes and said, ' So you truly want a wife ? ' what in thunder would I say then ?   I don't want a wife, I want a housekeeper, a butter-maker, one that would look after my interests as if they were her own ; and if I could hire a woman that would do what I wish, I'd never think of marrying.   I can't tell a woman that I love her when I don't.   If I went to a minister with a woman I'd be deceiving him, and deceiving her, and perjuring myself promiscuously.   I married once according to law and gospel and I was married through and through, and I can't do the thing over again in any way that would seem to me like marrying at all.   The idea of me sitting by the fire and wishing that the woman who sat on the t'other side of the stove was my first wife !   Yet I couldn't help doing this any more than breathing.   Even if there was any chance of my succeeding I can't see anything square or honest in my going out and hunting up a wife as a mere matter of business.   I know other people do it and I've thought a good deal about it myself, but when it comes to the point of acting I find I can't do it."

The two men now withdrew from the table to the fireside and lighted their pipes.   Mrs. Watterly stepped out for a moment and Tom, looking over his shoulder to make sure she was out of ear-shot, said under his breath, " But suppose you found a woman that you could love and obey, and all that ? "

" Oh, of course, that would make everything different. I wouldn't begin with a lie then, and I know enough of my wife to feel sure that she wouldn't be a sort of dog in the manger after she was dead.   She was one of those good souls that if she could speak her mind this minute she would say, 'James, what's best and right for you *is* best and right.' But it's just because she was such a good wife that I know there's no use of trying to put any-one in her place. Where on earth could I find anybody, and how could we get acquainted so that we'd know anything about each other? No, I must just scratch along for a short time as things are and be on the look-out to sell or rent."

Tom smoked meditatively for a few moments, and then remarked, "I guess that's your best way out."

"It aint an easy way, either," said Holcroft. "Find-ing a purchaser or tenant for a farm like mine is almost as hard as finding a wife. Then, as I feel, leaving my place is next to leaving the world."

Tom shook his head ruefully and admitted, "I declare, Jim, when a feller comes to think it all over, you *are* in a bad fix, especially as you feel. I thought I could talk you over into practical common sense in no time. It's easy enough, when one don't know all the bearin's of a case, to think carelessly, 'Oh, he aint as bad off as he thinks he is. He can do this and that and the t'other thing.' But when you come to look it all over, you find he can't, except at a big loss. Of course, you can give away your farm on which you were doing well and get-ting ahead, though how you did it, I don't see. You'd have to about give it away if you forced a sale, and where on earth you'll find a tenant who'll pay anything worth considering—— But there's no use of croaking. I wish I could help you, old feller. By jocks! I believe I can. There's an old woman here who's right smart and handy when she can't get her bottle filled. I believe she'd be glad to go with you, for she don't like our board and lodging over much."

" Do you think she'd go to-nighl ? "

" Oh, yes! guess so.   A little cold water 'll be a good change for her."

Mrs. Wiggins was seen, and, feeling that any change would be for the better, readily agreed to go for very moderate wages. Holcroft looked dubiously at the woman's heavy form and heavier face, but felt that it was the best he could do. Squeezing Mrs. Watterly's cold, limp hand in a way that would have thawed a lump of ice, he said " good-by "; and then declaring that he would rather do his own harnessing for a night ride, he went out into the storm. Tom put on his rubber coat and went to the barn with his friend, toward whom he cherished honest good-will.

" By jocks ! " he ejaculated sympathetically, " but you have hard lines, Jim. What in thunder would I do with two such widdy women to look after my house! "

CHAPTER IX.

MRS. MUMPSON ACCEPTS HER MISSION.

As Holcroft drove through the town Mrs. Wiggins, who, as matters were explained to her, had expressed her views chiefly by affirmative nods, now began to use her tongue with much fluency.

" Hi 'ave a friend 'erehabouts," she said, "an' she's been a-keepin' some of my things. Hi'll be be'olden to ye, master, hif ye'll jes stop a bit hat the door whiles hi gets 'em. Hif ye'll hadvance me a dollar or so on me wages hit 'll be a long time hafore I trouble ye hagain."

The farmer had received too broad a hint not to know that Mrs. Wiggins was intent on renewing her acquaintance with her worst enemy. He briefly replied, therefore, " It's too late to stop now. I'll be coming down soon again and will get your things."

In vain Mrs. Wiggins expostulated, for he drove steadily on. With a sort of grim humor, he thought of the meeting of the two " widdy women," as Tom had characterized them, and of Mrs. Mumpson's dismay at finding in the " cheap girl " a dame of sixty, weighing not far from two hundred. " If it wasn't such awfully serious business for me," he thought, " it would be better'n going to a theater to see the two go on. If I haven't got three 'peculiar females' on my hands now, I'd like to hear of the man that has."

When Mrs. Wiggins found that she could not gain her point, she subsided into utter silence. It soon became evident in the cloudy light of the moon that she was going to sleep, for she so nodded and swayed about that the farmer feared she would tumble out of the wagon. She occupied a seat just back of his and filled it, too. The idea of stepping over, sitting beside her, and holding her in, was inexpressibly repugnant to him. So he began talking to her, and finally shouting at her, to keep her awake.

His efforts were useless. He glanced with rueful dismay over his shoulder as he thought, " If she falls out, I don't see how on earth I'll ever get her back again."

Fortunately the seat slipped back a little, and she soon slid down into a sort of mountainous heap on the bottom of the wagon, as unmindful of the rain as if it were a lullaby. Now that his mind was at rest about her falling out, and knowing that he had a heavy load, Holcroft let the horses take their own time along the miry highway.

Left to her own devices by Holcroft's absence, Mrs. Mumpson had passed what she regarded as a very eventful afternoon and evening. Not that anything unusual had happened, unless everything she said and did may be looked upon as unusual; but Mrs. Mumpson justly felt that the critical periods of life are those upon which definite courses of action are decided upon. In the secret recesses of her heart—supposing her to possess such an organ—she had partially admitted to herself, even before she had entered Holcroft's door, that she might be persuaded into marrying him; but the inspection of his room, much deliberate thought, and prolonged soliloquy, had convinced her that she ought to "enter into nuptial relations," as her thought formulated itself

It was a trait of Mrs. Mumpson's active mind, that when it once entered upon a line of thought, it was hurried along from conclusion to conclusion with wonderful rapidity.

While Jane made up Mr. Holcroft's bed her mother began to inspect, and soon suffered keenly from a very painful discovery. The farmer's meager wardrobe and other belongings were soon rummaged over, but one large closet and several bureau drawers were locked. "These are the recepterctles of the deceased Mrs. Holcroft's affects," she said with compressed lips. "They are moldering useless away. Moth and rust will enter, while I, the caretaker, am debarred. I should not be debarred. All the things in that closet should be shaken out, aired, and carefully put back. Who knows how useful they may be in the future! Waste is wicked. Indeed, there are few things more wicked than waste. Now I think of it, I have some keys in my trunk."

"He won't like it," interposed Jane.

"In the responserble persition I have assumed," replied Mrs. Mumpson with dignity, "I must consider, not what he wants, but what is best for him and what may be best for others."

Jane had too much curiosity herself to make further objection, and the keys were brought. It was astonishing what a number of keys Mrs. Mumpson possessed, and she was not long in finding those which would open the ordinary locks thought by Holcroft to be ample protection.

"I was right," said Mrs. Mumpson complacently. "A musty odor exudes from these closed receptercles. Men have no comprehension of the need of such caretakers as I am."

Everything that had ever belonged to poor Mrs. Hol-croft was pulled out, taken to the window, and examined, Jane following, as usual, in the wake of her mother and putting everything to the same tests which her parent applied. Mrs. Holcroft had been a careful woman, and the extent and substantial character of her wardrobe proved that her husband had not been close in his allow-ances to her. Mrs. Mumpson's watery blue eyes grew positively animated as she felt of and held up to the light one thing after another. " Mrs. Holcroft was evidently unnaturally large," she reflected aloud, "but then these things could be made over, and much material be left to repair them, from time to time. The dresses are of somber colors, becoming to a lady somewhat advanced in years and of subdued taste."

By the time that the bed and all the chairs in the room were littered with wearing apparel, Mrs. Mumpson said, " Jane, I desire you to bring the rocking chair. So many thoughts are crowding upon me that I must sit down and think."

Jane did as requested, but remarked, " The sun is get-tin' low, and all these things 'll have to be put back just as they was or he'll be awful mad."

" Yes, Jane," replied Mrs. Mumpson abstractedly and rocking gently, "you can put them back. Your mind is not burdened like mine, and you haven't offspring and the future to provide for," and, for a wonder, she relapsed into silence. Possibly she possessed barely enough of womanhood to feel that her present train of thought had better be kept to herself. She gradually rocked faster and faster, thus indicating that she was rapidly approach-ing a conclusion.

Meanwhile, Jane was endeavoring to put things back

as they were before and found it no easy task. As the light declined she was overcome by a sort of panic, and, huddling the things into the drawers as fast as possible, she locked them up. Then, seizing her mother's hand and pulling the abstracted woman to her feet, she cried, "If he comes and finds us here and no supper ready, he'll turn us right out into the rain!"

Even Mrs. Mumpson felt that she was perhaps reaching conclusions too fast and that some diplomacy might be necessary to consummate her plans. Her views, however, appeared to her so reasonable that she scarcely thought of failure, having the happy faculty of realizing everything in advance, whether it ever took place or not.

As she slowly descended the stairs with the rocking chair, she thought, "Nothing could be more suiterble. We are both about the same age; I am most respecterbly connected—in fact, I regard myself as somewhat his superior in this respect; he is painfully undeveloped and irreligious and thus is in sore need of female influence; he is lonely and down-hearted, and in woman's voice there is a spell to banish care; worst of all, things are going to waste. I must delib'rately face the great duty with which Providence has brought me face to face. At first, he may be a little blind to this great oppertunity of his life—that I must expect, remembering the influence he was under so many years—but I will be patient and, by the proper use of language, place everything eventually before him in a way that will cause him to yield in glad submission to my views of the duties, the priviliges, and the responserbilities of life."

So active was Mrs. Mumpson's mind that this train of thought was complete by the time she had ensconced her self in the rocking chair by the fireless kitchen stove. Once more Jane seized her hand and dragged her up. "You must help," said the child. "I 'spect him every minnit and I'm scart half to death to think what he'll do, 'specially if he finds out we've been rummagin'."

"Jane," said Mrs. Mumpson severely, "that is not a proper way of expressing yourself. I am housekeeper here, and I've been inspecting."

"Shall I tell him you've been inspectin'?" asked the girl keenly.

"Children of your age should speak when they are spoken to," replied her mother, still more severely. "You cannot comprehend my motives and duties, and I should have to punish you if you passed any remarks upon my actions."

"Well," said Jane apprehensively, "I only hope we'll soon have a chance to fix up them drawers, for if he should open 'em we'd have to tramp again, and we will anyway if you don't help me get supper."

"You are mistaken, Jane," responded Mrs. Mumpson with dignity. "We shall not leave this roof for three months, and that will give me ample time to open his eyes to his true interests. I will condescend to these menial tasks, until he brings a girl who will yield the deference due to my years and station in life."

Between them, after filling the room with smoke, they kindled the kitchen fire. Jane insisted on making the coffee and then helped her mother to prepare the rest of the supper, doing, in fact, the greater part of the work. Then they sat down to wait, and they waited so long that Mrs. Mumpson began to express her disapproval by rocking violently. At last, she said severely, "Jane, we will partake of supper alone."

" I'd ruther wait till he comes."

" It's not proper that we should wait. He is **not** showing me due respect. Come, do as I command."

Mrs. Mumpson indulged in lofty and aggrieved remarks throughout the meal and then returned to her rocker. At last, her indignant sense of wrong reached such a point that she commanded Jane to clear the table and put away the things.

" I won't," said the child.

" What ! will you compel me to chastise you ? "

" Well, then, I'll tell him it was all your doin's."

" I shall tell him so myself. I shall remonstrate with him. The idea of his coming home alone at this time of night, with an unknown female ! "

" One would think you was his aunt, to hear you talk," remarked the girl sullenly.

" I am a respecterble woman and most respecterbly connected. My character and antercedents render me irrerproachful. This could not be said of a hussy, and a hussy he'll probably bring—some flighty, immerture female that will tax even *my* patience to train."

Another hour passed, and the frown on Mrs. Mumpson's brow grew positively awful. " To think," she muttered, " that a man whom I have deemed it my duty to marry should stay out so and under such peculiar circumstances. He must have a lesson which he can never forget." Then aloud, to Jane, " Kindle a fire on the parlor hearth and let this fire go out. He must find us in the most respecterble room in the house—a room befitting my station."

" I declare, mother, you aint got no sense at all ! " exclaimed the child, exasperated beyond measure.

" I'll teach you to use such unrerspectful language ! "

cried Mrs. Mumpson, darting from her chair like a hawk and pouncing upon the unhappy child.

With ears tingling from a cuffing she could not soon forget, Jane lighted the parlor fire and sat down sniffling in the farthest corner.

" There shall be only one mistress in this house," said Mrs. Mumpson, who had now reached the loftiest plane of virtuous indignation, " and its master shall learn that his practices reflect upon even me as well as himself."

At last the sound of horses' feet was heard on the wet, oozy ground without.   The irate widow did not rise, but merely indicated her knowledge of Holcroft's arrival by rocking more rapidly.

" Hello, there, Jane!" he shouted, " bring a light to the kitchen."

" Jane, remain !" said Mrs. Mumpson, with an awfu look.

Holcroft stumbled through the dark kitchen to the parlor door and looked with surprise at the group before him,—Mrs. Mumpson apparently oblivious and rocking as if the chair was possessed, and the child crying in a corner.

" Jane, didn't you hear me call for a light ? " he asked a little sharply.

Mrs. Mumpson rose with great dignity and began, " Mr. Holcroft, I wish to remonstrate——"

" Oh, bother ! I've brought a woman to help you, and we're both wet through from this driving rain."

" You've brought a strange female at this time of——"

Holcroft's patience gave way, but he only said quietly, " You had better have a light in the kitchen within two minutes. I warn you both. I also wish some hot coffee."

Mrs. Mumpson had no comprehension of a man who could be so quiet when he was angry, and she believed that she might impress him with a due sense of the enormity of his offense. " Mr. Holcroft, I scarcely feel that I can meet a girl who has no more sense of decorum than to——" But Jane, striking a match, revealed the fact that she was speaking to empty air.

Mrs. Wiggins was at last so far aroused that she was helped from the wagon and came shivering and dripping toward the kitchen. She stood a moment in the doorway and filled it, blinking confusedly at the light. There was an absence of celerity in all Mrs. Wiggins' movements, and she was therefore slow in the matter of waking up. Her aspect and proportions almost took away Mrs. Mumpson's breath. Here certainly was much to superintend, much more than had been anticipated. Mrs. Wiggins was undoubtedly a " peculiar female," as had been expected, but she was so elderly and monstrous that Mrs. Mumpson felt some embarrassment in her purpose to overwhelm Holcroft with a sense of the impropriety of his conduct.

Mrs. Wiggins took uncertain steps toward the rocking chair, and almost crushed it as she sat down. " Ye gives a body a cold velcome," she remarked, rubbing her eyes.

Mrs. Mumpson had got out of her way as a minnow would shun a leviathan. " May I ask your name ? " she gasped.

" Viggins, Mrs. Viggins."

" Oh, indeed ! You are a married woman ? "

" No, hi'm a vidder. What's more, hi'm cold, an' drippin', an' 'ungry. Hi might 'a' better stayed at the poor-us than come to a place like this."

" What ! " almost screamed Mrs. Mumpson, " are you a pauper ?

" Hi tell ye hi'm a vidder, an' good as you be, for hall he said," was the sullen reply.

" To think that a respecterbly connected woman like me——" But for once Mrs. Mumpson found language inadequate. Since Mrs. Wiggins occupied the rocking chair, she hardly knew what to do and plaintively declared, " I feel as if my whole nervous system was giving way."

" No 'arm 'll be done hif hit does," remarked Mrs. Wiggins, who was not in an amiable mood,

" This from the female I'm to superintend ! " gasped the bewildered woman.

Her equanimity was still further disturbed by the entrance of the farmer, who looked at the stove with a heavy frown.

" Why in the name of common sense isn't there a fire ? " he asked, " and supper on the table ? Couldn't you hear that it was raining and know we'd want some supper after a long, cold ride ?

" Mr. Holcroft," began the widow, in some trepidation, " I don't approve—such irregular habits——"

" Madam," interrupted Holcroft sternly, " did I agree to do what you approved of ? Your course is so peculiar that I scarcely believe you are in your right mind. You had better go to your room and try to recover your senses. If I can't have things in this house to suit me I'll have no one in it. Here, Jane, you can help."

Mrs. Mumpson put her handkerchief to her eyes and departed. She felt that this display of emotion would touch Holcroft's feelings when he came to think the scene all over.

Having kindled the fire, he said to Jane, " You and Mrs. Wiggins get some coffee and supper in short order, and have it ready when I come in," and he hastened out to care for his horses. If the old woman was slow, she knew just how to make every motion effective, and a good supper was soon ready.

" Why didn't you keep up a fire, Jane ? " Holcroft asked.

" She wouldn't let me. She said how you must be taught a lesson," replied the girl, feeling that she must choose between two potentates, and deciding quickly in favor of the farmer. She had been losing faith in her mother's wisdom a long time, and this night's experience had banished the last shred of it.

Some rather bitter words rose to Holcroft's lips, but he restrained them. He felt that he ought not to disparage the mother to the child. As Mrs. Wiggins grew warm, and imbibed the generous coffee, her demeanor thawed perceptibly and she graciously vouchsafed the remark, " Ven you're hout late hag'in hi'll look hafter ye."

Mrs. Mumpson had not been so far off as not to hear Jane's explanation, as the poor child found to her cost when she went up to bed.

CHAPTER X.

A NIGHT OF TERROR.

As poor, dazed, homeless Alida passed out into the
street, after the revelation that she was not a wife and
never had been, she heard a voice say, " Well, Hanne
wasn't long in bouncing the woman. I guess we'd bet
ter go up now. Ferguson will need a lesson that h
won't soon forget."

The speaker of these words was Mrs. Ferguson'
brother, William Hackman, and his companion was a
detective. The wife had laid her still sleeping chil
down on the lounge and was coolly completing Alida'
preparations for dinner. Her husband had sunk bac
into a chair and again buried his face in his hands
He looked up with startled, bloodshot eyes as his brother
in-law and the stranger entered, and then resumed hi
former attitude.

Mrs. Ferguson briefly related what had happened, an
then said, " Take chairs and draw up."

"I don't want any dinner," muttered the husband.

Mr. William Hackman now gave way to his irritation
Turning to his brother, he relieved his mind as follows
" See here, Hank Ferguson, if you hadn't the best wife i
the land, this gentleman would now be giving you a prom
enade to jail. I've left my work for weeks, and spent
sight of money to see that my sister got her rights, and

by thunder! she's going to have 'em. We've agreed to give you a chance to brace up and be a man. If we find out there isn't any man in you, then you go to prison and hard labor to the hull extent of the law. We've fixed things so you can't play any more tricks. This man is a private detective. As long as you do the square thing by your wife and child, you'll be let alone. If you try to sneak off, you'll be nabbed. Now, if you aint a scamp down to your heel-taps, get up out of that chair like a man, treat your wife as she deserves for letting you off so easy, and don't make her change her mind by acting as you, and not her, was the wronged person."

At heart Ferguson was a weak, cowardly, selfish creature, whose chief aim in life was to have things to suit himself. When they ceased to be agreeable, he was ready for a change, without much regard for the means to his ends. He had always foreseen the possibility of the event which had now taken place, but, like all self-indulgent natures, had hoped that he might escape detection. Alida, moreover, had won a far stronger hold upon him than he had once imagined possible. He was terribly mortified and cast down by the result of his experiment, as he regarded it. But the thought of a prison and hard labor speedily drew his mind away from this aspect of the affair. He had been fairly caught, his lark was over, and he soon resolved that the easiest and safest way out of the scrape was the best way. He therefore raised his head and came forward with a penitent air, as he said: "It's natural I should be overwhelmed with shame at the position in which I find myself. But I see the truth of your words, and I'll try to make it all right, as far as I can. I'll go back with you and Hannah to my old home. I've got money in the bank, I'll sell out everything here,

and I'll pay you, William, as far as I can, what you've
spent. Hannah is mighty good to let me off so easy, and
she won't be sorry. This man is witness to what I say,"
and the detective nodded.

"Why, Ferguson," said Mr. Hackman effusively
"now you're talking like a man. Come and kiss him,
Hanner, and make it all up."

"That's the way with you men," said the woman bitterly. "These things count for little. Henry Ferguson
must prove he's honest in what he says by deeds, no
words. I'll do as I've said if he acts square, and that's
enough to start with."

"All right," said Ferguson, glad enough to escape the
caress. "I'll do as I say."

He did do all he promised, and very promptly, too.
He was not capable of believing that a woman wronged
as Alida had been would not prosecute him, and he was
eager to escape to another State, and, in a certain measure, again to hide his identity under his own actual name.

Meanwhile, how fared the poor creature who had fled,
driven forth by her first wild impulse to escape from a
false and terrible position? With every step she took
down the dimly lighted street, the abyss into which she
had fallen seemed to grow deeper and darker. She was
overwhelmed with the magnitude of her misfortune. She
shunned the illumined thoroughfares with a half-crazed
sense that every finger would be pointed at her. Her
final words, spoken to Ferguson, were the last clear
promptings of her womanly nature. After that, everything grew confused, except the impression of remedile
disaster and shame. She was incapable of forming a
correct judgment concerning her position. The thought
of her pastor filled her with horror. He, she thought

would take the same view which the woman had so brutally expressed—that in her eagerness to be married, she had brought to the parsonage an unknown man and had involved a clergyman in her own scandalous record. It would all be in the papers, and her pastor's name mixed up in the affair. She would rather die than subject him to such an ordeal. Long after, when he learned the facts in the case, he looked at her very sadly, as he asked: "Didn't you know me better than that? Had I so failed in my preaching that you couldn't come straight to me?"

She wondered afterward that she had not done this, but she was too morbid, too close upon absolute insanity, to do what was wise and safe. She simply yielded to the wild impulse to escape, to cower, to hide from every human eye, hastening through the darkest, obscurest streets, not caring where. In the confusion of her mind she would retrace her steps, and soon was utterly lost, wandering she knew not whither. As it grew late casual passers-by looked after her curiously, rough men spoke to her, and others jeered. She only hastened on, driven by her desperate trouble like the wild, ragged clouds that were flying across the stormy March sky.

At last a policeman said gruffly, "You've passed me twice. You can't be roaming the streets at this time of night. Why don't you go home?"

Standing before him and wringing her hands, she moaned, "I have no home?"

"Where did you come from?"

"Oh, I can't tell you! Take me to any place where a woman will be safe."

"I can't take you to any place now but the station house."

"But can I be alone there? I won't be put with anybody?"

"No, no; of course not! You'll be better off there. Come along. 'Taint far."

She walked beside him without a word.

"You'd better tell me something of your story. Perhaps I can do more for you in the morning."

"I can't. I'm a stranger. I haven't any friends in town."

"Well, well, the sergeant will see what can be done in the morning. You've been up to some foolishness, I suppose, and you'd better tell the whole story to the sergeant."

She soon entered the station house and was locked up in a narrow cell. She heard the grating of the key in the lock with a sense of relief, feeling that she had at least found a temporary place of refuge and security. A hard board was the only couch it possessed, but the thought of sleep did not enter her mind. Sitting down, she buried her face in her hands and rocked back and forth in agony and distraction until day dawned. At last, someone—she felt she could not raise her eyes to his face—brought her some breakfast and coffee. She drank the latter, but left the food untasted. Finally, she was led to the sergeant's private room and told that she must give an account of herself. "If you can't or won't tell a clear story," the officer threatened, "you'll have to go before the justice in open court, and he may commit you to prison. If you'll tell the truth now, it may be that I can discharge you. You had no business to be wandering about the streets like a vagrant or worse; but if you were a stranger or lost and hadn't sense enough to go where you'd be cared for, I can let you go."

"Oh!" said Alida, again wringing her hands and looking at the officer with eyes so full of misery and fear that he began to soften, "I don't know where to go."

"Haven't you a friend or acquaintance in town?"

"Not one that I can go to!"

"Why don't you tell me your story? Then I'll know what to do, and perhaps can help you. You don't look like a depraved woman."

"I'm not. God knows I'm not!"

"Well, my poor woman, I've got to act in view of what I know, not what God knows."

"If I tell my story, will I have to give names?"

"No, not necessarily. It would be best, though."

"I can't do that, but I'll tell you the truth. I will swear it on the Bible. I married someone. A good minister married us. The man deceived me. He was already married, and last night his wife came to my happy home and proved before the man whom I thought my husband that I was no wife at all. He couldn't, didn't deny it. Oh! oh! oh!" and she again rocked back and forth in uncontrollable anguish. "That's all," she added brokenly. "I had no right to be near him or her any longer, and I rushed out. I don't remember much more. My brain seemed on fire. I just walked and walked till I was brought here."

"Well, well!" said the sergeant sympathetically, "you have been treated badly, outrageously; but you are not to blame unless you married the man hastily and foolishly."

"That's what everyone will think, but it don't seem to me that I did. It's a long story, and I can't tell it."

"But you ought to tell it, my poor woman. You ought to sue the man for damages and send him to State prison."

"No, no!" cried Alida passionately. "I don't want to see him again, and I won't go to a court before people unless I am dragged there."

The sergeant looked up at the policeman who had arrested her and said, "This story is not contrary to anything you saw?"

"No, sir; he was wandering about and seemed half out of her mind."

"Well, then, I can let you go."

"But I don't know where to go," she replied, looking at him with hunted, hollow eyes. "I feel as if I were going to be sick. Please don't turn me into the streets. I'd rather go back to the cell.

"That won't answer. There's no place that I can send you to except the poorhouse. Haven't you any money?"

"No, sir. I just rushed away and left everything when I learned the truth."

"Tom Watterly's hotel is the only place for her," said the policeman with a nod.

"Oh, I can't go to a hotel."

"He means the almshouse," explained the sergeant. "What is your name?"

"Alida—that's all now. Yes, I'm a pauper and I can't work just yet. I'll be safe there, won't I?"

"Certainly, safe as in your mother's house."

"Oh, mother, mother; thank God, you are dead!"

"Well, I *am* sorry for you," said the sergeant kindly. "'Taint often we have so sad a case as yours. If you say so, I'll send for Tom Watterly, and he and his wife will take charge of you. After a few days, your mind will get quieter and clearer, and then you'll prosecute the man who wronged you."

"I'll go to the poorhouse until I can do better," she replied wearily. "Now, if you please, I'll return to my cell, where I can be alone."

"Oh, we can give you a better room than that," said the sergeant. "Show her into the waiting room, Tim. If you prosecute, we can help you with our testimony. Good-by, and may you have better days!"

Watterly was telegraphed to come down with a conveyance, for the almshouse was in a suburb. In due time he appeared, and was briefly told Alida's story. He swore a little at the "mean cuss," the author of all the trouble, and then took the stricken woman to what all his acquaintances facetiously termed his "hotel."

CHAPTER XI.

BAFFLED.

IN the general consciousness Nature is regarded as feminine, and even those who love her most will have to adopt Mrs. Mumpson's oft-expressed opinion of the sex and admit that she is sometimes a "peculiar female." During the month of March, in which our story opens, there was scarcely any limit to her varying moods. It would almost appear that she was taking a mysterious interest in Holcroft's affairs; but whether it was a kindly interest or not, one might be at a loss to decide. When she caught him away from home, she pelted him with the coldest of rain and made his house, with even Mrs. Mumpson and Jane abiding there, seem a refuge. In the morning after the day on which he had brought, or in a sense had carted, Mrs. Wiggins to his domicile, Nature was evidently bent on instituting contrasts between herself and the rival phases of femininity with which the farmer was compelled to associate. It may have been that she had another motive and was determined to keep her humble worshiper at her feet, and to render it impossible for him to make the changes toward which he had felt himself driven.

Being an early riser he was up with the sun, and the sun rose so serenely and smiled so benignly that Holcroft's clouded brow cleared in spite of all that had happened or could take place. The rain, which had brought such discomfort the night before, had settled the ground and made it comparatively firm to his tread. The southern breeze which fanned his cheek was as soft as the air of May. He remembered that it was Sunday, and that beyond feeding his stock and milking he would have nothing to do. He exulted in the unusual mildness and thought, with an immense sense of relief, " I can stay outdoors nearly all day." He resolved to let his help kindle the fire and get breakfast as they could, and to keep out of their way. Whatever changes the future might bring, he would have one more long day in rambling about his fields and in thinking over the past. Feeling that there need be no haste about anything, he leisurely inhaled the air, fragrant from springing grass. and listened with a vague, undefined pleasure to the ecstatic music of the bluebirds, song-sparrows, and robins. If anyone had asked him why he liked to hear them he would have replied, " I'm used to 'em. When they come I know that plowing and planting time is near."

It must be admitted that Holcroft's enjoyment of spring was not very far removed from that of the stock in his barnyard. All the animal creation rejoices in the returning sun and warmth. A subtle, powerful influence sets the blood in more rapid motion, kindles new desires, and awakens a glad expectancy. All that is alive becomes more thoroughly alive and existence in itself is a pleasure. Spring had always brought to the farmer quickened pulses, renewed activity and hopefulness, and he was pleased to find that he was not so old and cast down that its former influence had spent itself. Indeed, it seemed that never before had his fields, his stock, and outdoor work—and these comprised Nature to him—

been so attractive. They remained unchanged amid the sad changes which had clouded his life, and his heart clung more tenaciously than ever to old scenes and occupations. They might not bring him happiness again, but he instinctively felt that they might insure a comfort and peace with which he could be content.

At last he went to the barn and began his work, doing everything slowly, and getting all the solace he could from the tasks. The horses whinnied their welcome and he rubbed their noses caressingly as he fed them. The cows came briskly to the rack in which he foddered them in pleasant weather, and when he scratched them between the horns they turned their mild, Juno-like eyes upon him with undisguised affection. The chickens, clamoring for their breakfast, followed so closely that he had to be careful where he stepped. Although he knew that all this good will was based chiefly on the hope of food and the remembrance of it in the past, nevertheless it soothed and pleased him. He was in sympathy with this homely life; it belonged to him and was dependent on him; it made him honest returns for his care. Moreover, it was agreeably linked with the past. There were quiet cows which his wife had milked, clucking biddies which she had lifted from nests with their downy broods. He looked at them wistfully, and was wondering if they ever missed the presence that he regretted so deeply, when he became conscious that Jane's eyes were upon him. How long she had been watching him he did not know, but she merely said, "Breakfast's ready," and disappeared.

With a sigh he went to his room to perform his ablutions, remembering with a slight pang how his wife always had a basin and towel ready for him in the kitchen. In the breaking up of just such homely customs, he was continually reminded of his loss.

On awakening to the light of this Sabbath morning Mrs. Mumpson had thought deeply and reasoned everything out again. She felt that it must be an eventful day and that there was much to be accomplished. In the first place there was Mrs. Wiggins. She disapproved of her decidedly. "She isn't the sort of person that I would prefer to superintend," she remarked to Jane while making a toilet which she deemed befitting the day, "and the hour will assuredly come when Mr. Holcroft will look upon her in the light that I do. He will eventually realize that I cannot be brought in such close relationship with a pauper. Not that the relationship is exactly close, but then I shall have to speak to her—in brief, to superintend her. My eyes will be offended by her vast proportions and uncouth appearance. The floor creaks beneath her tread and affects my nerves seriously. Of course, while she is here, I shall zealously, as befits one in my responserble position, try to render useful such service as she can perform. But then, the fact that I disapprove of her must soon become evident. When it is discovered that I only tolerate her, there will be a change. I cannot show my disapproval very strongly to-day, for this is a day set apart for sacred things, and Mrs. Wiggins, as she called herself,—I cannot imagine a Mr. Wiggins, for no man in his senses could have married such a creature,—as I was saying, Mrs. Wiggins is not at all sacred, and I must endeavor to abstract my mind from her till to-morrow, as far as posserble. My first duty to-day is to induce Mr. Holcroft to take us to church. It will give the people of Oakville such a pleasing impression to see us driving to church. Of course, I may fail.

Mr. Holcroft is evidently a hardened man. All th
influences of his life have been adverse to spiritual dev
opment, and it may require some weeks of my influen
to soften him and awaken yearnings for what he ha
not yet known."

"He may be yearnin' for breakfast," Jane remarke
completing her toilet by tying her little pigtail bra
with something that had once been a bit of black ribbo
but was now a string. "You'd better come down soo
and help."

"If Mrs. Viggins cannot get breakfast, I would like
know what she is here for" continued Mrs. Mumpso
loftily, and regardless of Jane's departure. "I sha
decline to do menial work any longer, especially on th
sacred day, and after I have made my toilet for churc
Mr. Holcroft has had time to think. My disapprov
was manifest last night and it has undoubtedly occurre
to him that he has not conformed to the proprieties
life. Indeed, I almost fear I shall have to teach hi
what the proprieties of life are. He witnessed my em
tion when he spoke as he should not have spoken to *m*
But I must make allowances for his unregenerate stat
He was cold, and wet, and hungry last night, and me
are unreasonerble at such times. I shall now heap coa
of fire upon his head. I shall show that I am a mee
forgiving Christian woman, and he will relent, soften, an
become penitent. Then will be my opportunity," an
she descended to the arena which should witness he
efforts.

During the period in which Mrs. Mumpson ha
indulged in these lofty reflections and self-communing
Mrs. Wiggins had also arisen. I am not sure wheth
she had thought of anything in particular or not. Sh

ay have had some spiritual longings which were not
ecoming to any day of the week. Being a woman of
eeds, rather than of thought, probably not much else
ccurred to her beyond the duty of kindling the fire and
etting breakfast. Jane came down, and offered to assist,
ut was cleared out with no more scruple than if Mrs.
Viggins had been one of the much-visited relatives.

"The hidee," she grumbled, "of 'avin' sich a little
ollop round hunder my feet!"

Jane, therefore, solaced herself by watching the "cheap
rl" till her mother appeared.

Mrs. Mumpson sailed majestically in and took the
ocking chair, mentally thankful that it had survived the
ushing weight imposed upon it the evening before.
Irs. Wiggins did not drop a courtesy. Indeed, not a
gn of recognition passed over her vast, immobile face.
Irs. Mumpson was a little embarrassed. "I hardly
now how to comport myself toward that female," she
ought. "She is utterly uncouth. Her manners are
nmistakerbly those of a pauper. I think I will ignore
er to-day. I do not wish my feelings ruffled or put out
harmony with the sacred duties and motives which
ctuate me."

Mrs. Mumpson therefore rocked gently, solemnly, and,
range to say, silently, and Mrs. Wiggins also proceeded
ith her duties, but not in silence, for everything in the
om trembled and clattered at her tread. Suddenly she
rned on Jane and said, "'Ere, you little baggage, go
d tell the master breakfast's ready."

Mrs. Mumpson sprung from her chair, and with a voice
oked with indignation, gasped, "Do you dare address
y offspring thus?"

"Yer vat?"

"My child, my daughter, who is not a pauper, but the offspring of a most respecterble woman and respecterbly connected. I'm amazed, I'm dumfoundered, I'm——"

"Ye're a bit daft, hi'm a-thinkin'." Then to Jane, "Vy don't ye go an' hearn yer salt?"

"Jane, I forbid——" But it had not taken Jane half a minute to decide between the now jarring domestic powers, and henceforth she would be at Mrs. Wiggins' beck and call. "She can do somethin'," the child muttered, as she stole upon Holcroft.

Mrs. Mumpson sunk back in her chair, but her mode of rocking betokened a perturbed spirit. " I will restrain myself till to-morrow, and then——" She shook her head portentously and waited till the farmer appeared, feeling assured that Mrs. Wiggins would soon be taught to recognize her station. When breakfast was on the table she darted to her place behind the coffeepot, for she felt that there was no telling what this awful Mrs. Wiggins might not assume during this day of sacred restraint. But the ex-pauper had no thought of presumption in her master's presence, and the rocking chair again distracted Mrs. Mumpson's nerves as it creaked under an unwonted weight.

Holcroft took his seat in silence. The widow again bowed her head devoutly, and sighed deeply when observing that the farmer ignored her suggestion.

"I trust that you feel refreshed after your repose," she said benignly.

"I do."

"It is a lovely morning—a morning, I may add, befitting the sacred day. Nature is at peace, and suggests that we and all should be at peace."

" There's nothing I like more, Mrs. Mumpson, unless it is quiet."

" I feel that way, myself. You don't know what restraint I have put upon myself that the sacred quiet of this day might not be disturbed. I have had strong provercation since I entered this apartment. I will forbear to speak of it till to-morrow, in order that there may be quietness and that our minds may be prepared for worship. I feel that it would he unseemly for us to enter a house of worship with thoughts of strife in our souls. At precisely what moment do you wish me to be ready for church ? "

" I am not going to church, Mrs. Mumpson."

" Not going to church ! I—I—scarcely understand. Worship is such a sacred duty——"

" You and Jane certainly have a right to go to church, and since it is your wish, I'll take you down to Lemuel Weeks' and you can go with them."

" I don't want to go to Cousin Lemuel's, nor to church, nuther," Jane protested.

" Why, Mr. Holcroft," began the widow sweetly, " after you've once harnessed up it will take but a little longer to keep on to the meeting house. It would appear so seemly for us to drive thither, as a matter of course. It would be what the communerty expects of us. This is not our day, that we should spend it carnally. We should be spiritually-minded. We should put away things of earth. Thoughts of business and any unnecessary toil should be abhorrent. I have often thought that here was too much milking done on Sunday among armers. I know they say it is essential, but they all seem so prone to forget that but one thing is needful. feel it borne in upon my mind, Mr. Holcroft, that I should plead with you to attend divine worship and seek an uplifting of your thoughts. You have no idea how differently the day may end, or what emotions may be aroused if you place yourself under the droppings of the sanctuary."

"I'm like Jane, I don't wish to go," said Mr. Holcroft nervously.

"But, my dear Mr. Holcroft,"—the farmer fidgeted under this address,—"the very essence of true religion is to do what we don't wish to do. We are to mortify the flesh and thwart the carnal mind. The more thorny the path of self-denial is, the more certain it's the right path. I've already entered upon it," she continued, turning a momentary glare upon Mrs. Wiggins. "Never before was a respecterble woman so harrowed and outraged; but I am calm; I am endeavoring to maintain a frame of mind suiterble to worship, and I feel it my bounden duty to impress upon you that worship is a necessity to every human being. My conscience would not acquit me if I did not use all my influence——"

"Very well, Mrs. Mumpson, you and your conscience are quits. You have used all your influence. I will do as I said—take you to Lemuel Weeks'—and you can go to church with his family," and he rose from the table.

"But Cousin Lemuel is also painfully blind to his spiritual interests——"

Holcroft did not stay to listen and was soon engaged in the morning milking. Jane flatly declared that she would not go to Cousin Lemuel's or to church. "It don' do me no good, nor you, nuther," she sullenly declared to her mother.

Mrs. Mumpson now resolved upon a different line of tactics. Assuming a lofty, spiritual air, she commanded

Jane to light a fire in the parlor, and retired thither with the rocking chair. The elder widow looked after her and ejaculated, " Vell, hif she haint the craziest loon hi hever 'eard talk. Hif she vas blind she might 'a' seen that the master didn't vant hany sich lecturin' clack."

Having kindled the fire, the child was about to leave the room when her mother interposed and said solemnly, " Jane, sit down and keep Sunday."

" I'm going to help Mrs. Wiggins, if she'll let me."

" You will not so demean yourself. I wish you to have no relations whatever with that female in the kitchen. If you had proper self-respect you would never speak to her again."

" We aint visitin' here. If I can't work indoors I'll tell him I'll work out-doors."

" It's not proper for you to work to-day. I want you to sit there in the corner and learn the Fifth Commandment."

" Aint you goin' to Cousin Lemuel's?"

" On mature reflection, I have decided to remain at home."

" I thought you would if you had any sense left. You know well enough we aint wanted down there. I'll go tell him not to hitch up."

" Well, I will permit you to do so. Then return to your Sunday task."

" I'm goin' to mind him," responded the child. She passed rapidly and apprehensively through the kitchen, but paused on the doorstep to make some overtures to Mrs. Wiggins. If that austere dame was not to be propitiated, a line of retreat was open to the barn. " Say," she began, to attract attention.

"Vell, young-un," replied Mrs. Wiggins, rendered more pacific by her breakfast.

"Don't you want me to wash up the dishes and put 'em away? I know how."

"Hi'll try ye. Hif ye breaks hanythink——" and the old woman nodded volumes at the child.

"I'll be back in a minute," said Jane. A moment later she met Holcroft carrying two pails of milk from the barnyard. He was about to pass without noticing her, but she again secured attention by her usual preface, "Say," when she had a somewhat extended communication to make.

"Come to the dairy room, Jane, and say your say there," said Holcroft not unkindly.

"She aint goin' to Cousin Lemuel's," said the girl, from the door.

"What is she going to do."

"Rock in the parlor. Say, can't I help Mrs. Wiggins wash up the dishes and do the work?"

"Certainly; why not?"

"Mother says I must sit in the parlor 'n' learn Commandments 'n' keep Sunday."

"Well, Jane, which do you think you ought to do?"

"I think I oughter work, and if you and Mrs. Wiggins will let me, I will work in spite of mother."

"I think that you and your mother both should help do the necessary work to-day. There won't be much."

"If I try and help Mrs. Wiggins mother 'll bounce out at me. She shook me last night after I went upstairs, and she boxed my ears 'cause I wanted to keep the kitchen fire up last night."

"I'll go with you to the kitchen and tell Mrs. Wiggins

to let you help, and I won't let your mother punish you again unless you do wrong."

Mrs. Wiggins, relying on Jane's promise of help, had sat down to the solace of her pipe for a few minutes, but was about to thrust it hastily away on seeing Holcroft. He reassured her by saying good-naturedly, "No need of that, my good woman. Sit still and enjoy your pipe. I like to smoke myself. Jane will help clear away things and I wish her to. You'll find she's quite handy. By the way, have you all the tobacco you want?"

"Vell, now, master, p'raps ye know the 'lowance down hat the poor-us vasn't sich as ud keep a body in vat ye'd call satisfyin' smokin'. Hi never 'ad henough ter keep down the 'ankerin'.''

"I suppose that's so. You shall have half of my stock, and when I go to town again, I'll get you a good supply. I guess I'll light my pipe, too, before starting for a walk."

"Bless yer 'art, master, ye makes a body comf'terble. Ven hi smokes hi feels more hat 'ome and kind o' contented like. An hold 'ooman like me haint got much left to comfort 'er but 'er pipe."

"Jane!" called Mrs. Mumpson sharply from the parlor. As there was no answer, the widow soon appeared in the kitchen door. Smoking was one of the unpardonable sins in Mrs. Mumpson's eyes; and when she saw Mrs. Wiggins puffing comfortably away and Holcroft lighting his pipe, while Jane cleared the table, language almost failed her. She managed to articulate, "Jane, this atmosphere is not fit for you to breathe, on this sacred day. I wish you to share my seclusion."

"Mrs. Mumpson, I have told her to help Mrs. Wiggins in the necessary work," Holcroft interposed.

"Mr. Holcroft, you don't realize—men never do—Jane is my offspring, and——"

"Oh, if you put it that way, I shan't interfere between mother and child. But I suppose you and Jane came here to work."

"If you will enter the parlor, I will explain to you fully my views, and——"

"Oh, please excuse me!" said Holcroft, hastily passing out. "I was just starting for a walk—I'm bound to have one more day to myself on the old place," he muttered, as he bent his steps toward an upland pasture.

Jane, seeing that her mother was about to pounce upon her, ran behind Mrs. Wiggins, who slowly rose and began a progress toward the irate widow, remarking as she did so, "Hi'll just shut the door 'twixt ye and yer hoffspring, and then ye kin say yer prayers hon the t'other side."

Mrs. Mumpson was so overcome at the turn affairs had taken on this day, which was to witness such progress in her plans and hopes, as to feel the absolute necessity of a prolonged season of thought and soliloquy, and she relapsed, without further protest, into the rocking chair.

CHAPTER XII.

JANE.

HOLCROFT was not long in climbing to a sunny nook whence he could see not only his farm and dwelling, but also the Oakville valley, and the little white spire of the distant meeting house. He looked at this last-named object wistfully and very sadly. Mrs. Mumpson's tirade about worship had been without effect, but the memories suggested by the church were bitter-sweet indeed. It belonged to the Methodist denomination, and Holcroft had been taken, or had gone thither, from the time of his earliest recollection. He saw himself sitting between his father and mother, a round-faced urchin to whom the sermon was unintelligible, but to whom little Bessie Jones in the next pew was a fact, not only intelligible, but very interesting. She would turn around and stare at him until he smiled, then she would giggle until her mother brought her right-about-face with considerable emphasis. After this, he saw the little boy—could it have been himself?—nodding, swaying, and finally slumbering peacefully, with his head on his mother's lap, until shaken into sufficient consciousness to be half dragged, half led, to the door. Once in the big, springless farm wagon he was himself again, looking eagerly around to catch another glimpse of Bessie Jones. Then he was a big, irreverent boy, shyly and awkwardly bent on mischief in the same old meeting house. Bessie Jones no longer turned and stared at him, but he exultingly discovered that he could still make her giggle on the sly. Years passed, and Bessie was his occasional choice for a sleigh-ride when the long body of some farm wagon was placed on runners, and boys and girls— young men and women, they almost thought themselves— were packed in like sardines. Something like self-reproach smote Holcroft even now, remembering how he had allowed his fancy much latitude at this period, paying attention to more than one girl besides Bessie, and painfully undecided which he liked best.

Then had come the memorable year which had opened with a protracted meeting. He and Bessie Jones had passed under conviction at the same time, and on the same evening had gone forward to the anxious seat. From the way in which she sobbed, one might have supposed that the good, simple-hearted girl had terrible burdens on her conscience; but she soon found hope, and her tears gave place to smiles. Holcroft, on the contrary, was terribly cast down and unable to find relief. He felt that he had much more to answer for than Bessie; he accused himself of having been a rather coarse, vulgar boy; he had made fun of sacred things in that very meeting house more times than he liked to think of, and now for some reason could think of nothing else. He could not shed tears or get up much emotion; neither could he rid himself of the dull weight at heart. The minister, the brethren and sisters, prayed for him and over him, but nothing removed his terrible inertia. He became a familiar form on the anxious seat, for there was a dogged persistence in his nature which prevented him from giving up; but at the close of each meeting he went home in a state of deeper dejection. Sometimes, in returning, he was Bessie Jones' escort, and her happiness added to his gall and bitterness. One moonlight night they stopped under the shadow of a pine near her father's door, and talked over the matter a few moments before parting. Bessie was full of sympathy which she hardly knew how to express. Unconsciously, in her earnestness—how well he remembered the act!—she laid her hand on his arm as she said, "James, I guess I know what's the trouble with you. In all your seeking you are thinking only of yourself—how bad you've been, and all that. I wouldn't think of myself and what I was any more, if I was you. You aint so awful bad, James, that I'd turn a cold shoulder to you; but you might think I was doing just that if ye stayed away from me and kept saying to yourself, 'I aint fit to speak to Bessie Jones.'"

Her face had looked sweet and compassionate, and her touch upon his arm had conveyed the subtle magic of sympathy. Under her homely logic, the truth had burst upon him like sunshine. In brief, he had turned from his own shadow and was in the light. He remembered how in his deep feeling he had bowed his head on her shoulder and murmured, "Oh, Bessie, Heaven bless you! I see it all."

He no longer went to the anxious seat. With this young girl, and many others, he was taken into the church on probation. Thereafter, his fancy never wandered again, and there was no other girl in Oakville for him but Bessie. In due time, he had gone with her to yonder meeting house to be married. It had all seemed to come about as a matter of course. He scarcely knew when he became formally engaged. They "kept company" together steadfastly for a suitable period, and that seemed to settle it in their own and everybody else's mind.

There had been no change in Bessie's quiet, constant soul. After her words under the shadow of the pine tree she seemed to find it difficult to speak of religious subjects, even to her husband; but her simple faith had been unwavering, and she had entered into rest without fear or misgiving.

Not so her husband. He had his spiritual ups and downs, but, like herself, was reticent. While she lived, only a heavy storm kept them from "going to meeting," but with Holcroft worship was often little more than a form, his mind being on the farm and its interests. Parents and relatives had died, and the habit of seclusion from neighborhood and church life had grown upon them gradually and almost unconsciously.

For a long time after his wife's death Holcroft had felt that he did not wish to see anyone who would make references to his loss. He shrunk from formal condolences as he would from the touch of a diseased nerve. When the minister called, he listened politely but silently to a general exhortation; then muttered, when left alone, "It's all as he says, I suppose; but somehow his words are like the medicines Bessie took—they don't do any good."

He kept up the form of his faith and a certain vague hope until the night on which he drove forth the Irish revelers from his home. In remembrance of his rage and profanity on that occasion, he silently and in dreary misgiving concluded that he should not, even to himself, keep up the pretense of religion any longer. "I've fallen from grace—that is, if I ever had any"—was a thought which did much to rob him of courage to meet his other trials. Whenever he dwelt on these subjects, doubts, perplexities, and resentment at his misfortunes so thronged his mind that he was appalled ; so he strove to occupy himself with the immediate present,

To-day, however, in recalling the past, his thoughts would question the future and the outcome of his experiences. In accordance with his simple, downright nature, he muttered, " I might as well face the truth and have done with it. I don't know whether I'll ever see my wife again or not ; I don't know whether God is for me or against me. Sometimes, I half think there isn't any God. I don't know what will become of me when I die. I'm sure of only one thing—while I do live I could take comfort in working the old place."

In brief, without ever having heard of the term, he was an agnostic, but not one of the self-complacent, superior type who fancy that they have developed themselves beyond the trammels of faith and are ever ready to make the world aware of their progress.

At last he recognized that his long reverie was leading to despondency and weakness ; he rose, shook himself half angrily, and strode toward the house. "I'm here, and here I'm going to stay," he growled. " As long as I'm on my own land, it's nobody's business what I am or how I feel. If I can't get decent, sensible women help, I'll close up my dairy and live here alone. I certainly can make enough to support myself."

Jane met him with a summons to dinner, looking apprehensively at his stern, gloomy face. Mrs. Mumpson did not appear. " Call her," he said curtly.

The literal Jane returned from the parlor and said unsympathetically, " She's got a hank'chif to her eyes and says she don't want no dinner."

"Very well," he replied, much relieved.

Apparently he did not want much dinner, either, for he soon started out again. Mrs. Wiggins was not utterly wanting in the intuitions of her sex, and said nothing to break in upon her master's abstraction.

In the afternoon Holcroft visited every nook and corner of his farm, laying out, he hoped, so much occupation for both hands and thoughts as to render him proof against domestic tribulations.

He had not been gone long before Mrs. Mumpson called in a plaintive voice, "Jane!"

The child entered the parlor warily, keeping open a line of retreat to the door. "You need not fear me," said her mother, rocking pathetically. "My feelings are so hurt and crushed that I can only bemoan the wrongs from which I suffer. You little know, Jane, you little know a mother's heart."

"No," assented Jane. "I dunno nothin' about it."

"What wonder, then, that I weep, when even my child is so unnatural!"

"I dunno how to be anything else but what I be," replied the girl in self-defense.

"If you would only yield more to my guidance and influence, Jane, the future might be brighter for us both. If you had but stored up the Fifth Commandment in memory—but I forbear. You cannot so far forget your duty as not to tell me how *he* behaved at dinner."

"He looked awful glum, and hardly said a word."

"Ah-h!" exclaimed the widow, "the spell is working."

"If you aint a-workin' to-morrow, there'll be a worse spell," the girl remarked.

"That will do, Jane, that will do. You little understand—how should you? Please keep an eye on him, and let me know how he looks and what he is doing, and whether his face still wears a gloomy or a penitent aspect. Do as I bid you, Jane, and you may unconsciously secure your own well-being by obedience.''

Watching anyone was a far more congenial task to the child than learning the Commandments, and she hastened to comply. Moreover, she had the strongest curiosity in regard to Holcroft herself. She felt that he was the arbiter of her fate. So untaught was she that delicacy and tact were unknown qualities. Her one hope of pleasing was in work. She had no power of guessing that sly espionage would counterbalance such service. Another round of visiting was dreaded above all things ; she was, therefore, exceedingly anxious about the future. '' Mother may be right,'' she thought. '' P'raps she can make him marry her, so we needn't go away any more. P'raps she's taken the right way to bring a man around and get him hooked, as Cousin Lemuel said. If I was goin' to hook a man though, I'd try another plan than mother's. I'd keep my mouth shut and my eyes open. I'd see what he wanted and do it, even 'fore he spoke. 'Fi's big anuf I bet I could hook a man quicker'n she can by usin her tongue 'stead of her hands.''

Jane's scheme was not so bad a one but that it might be tried to advantage by those so disposed. Her matrimonial prospects, however, being still far in the future, it behooved her to make her present existence as tolerable as possible. She knew how much depended on Holcroft, and was unaware of any other method of learning his purposes except that of watching him. Both fearing and fascinated, she dogged his steps most of the afternoon, but saw nothing to confirm her mother's view that any spell was working. She scarcely understood why he looked so long at field, thicket, and woods, as if he saw something invisible to her.

In planning future work and improvements, the farmer had attained a quieter and more genial frame of mind. When, therefore, he sat down and in glancing about saw Jane crouching behind a low hemlock, he was more amused than irritated. He had dwelt on his own interests so long that he was ready to consider even Jane's for a while. "Poor child!" he thought, "she doesn't know any better and perhaps has even been taught to do such things. I think I'll surprise her and draw her out a little "Jane, come here," he called.

The girl sprang to her feet, and hesitated whether to fly or obey. "Don't be afraid," added Holcroft. "I won't scold you. Come!"

She stole toward him like some small, wild, fearful animal in doubt of its reception. "Sit down there on that rock," he said.

She obeyed with a sly, sidelong look, and he saw that she kept her feet gathered under her so as to spring away if he made the slightest hostile movement.

"Jane, do you think it's right to watch people so? he asked gravely.

"She told me to.'

"Your mother?"

The girl nodded.

"But do you think it's right yourself?"

"Dunno. 'Taint best if you get caught."

"Well, Jane," said Holcroft, with something like smile lurking in his deep-set eyes, "I don't think it right at all. I don't want you to watch me any more, no matter who tells you to. Will you promise not to?"

The child nodded. She seemed averse to speaking when a sign would answer.

"Can I go now?" she asked after a moment.

"Not yet. I want to ask you some questions. Was anyone ever kind to you?"

"I dunno. I suppose so,"

"What would you call being kind to you?"

"Not scoldin' or cuffin' me."

"If I didn't scold or strike you, would you think I was kind, then?"

She nodded; but after a moment's thought, said, "And if you didn't look as if you hated to see me round."

"Do you think I've been kind to you?"

"Kinder'n anybody else. You sorter look at me sometimes as if I was a rat. I don't s'pose you can help it, and I don't mind. I'd ruther stay here and work than go a-visitin' again. Why can't I work out-doors when there's nothin' for me to do in the house?"

"Are you willing to work—to do anything you can?"

Jane was not sufficiently politic to enlarge on her desire for honest toil and honest bread; she merely nodded. Holcroft smiled as he asked, "Why are you so anxious to work?"

"'Cause I won't feel like a stray cat in the house then. I want to be some'ers where I've a right to be."

"Wouldn't they let you work down at Lemuel Weeks'?" She shook her head.

"Why not?" he asked.

"They said I wasn't honest; they said they couldn't trust me with things, 'cause when I was hungry I took things to eat."

"Was that the way you were treated at other places?"

"Mostly."

"Jane," asked Holcroft very kindly, "did anyone ever kiss you?"

"Mother used to 'fore people. It allus made me kinder sick."

Holcroft shook his head as if this child was a problem beyond him, and for a time they sat together in silence. At last he arose and said, "It's time to go home. Now, Jane, don't follow me; walk openly at my side, and when you come to call me at any time, come openly, make a noise, whistle or sing as a child ought. As long as you are with me never do anything on the sly, and we'll get along well enough."

She nodded and walked beside him. At last, as if emboldened by his words, she broke out, "Say, if mother married you, you couldn't send us away, could you?"

"Why do you ask such a question?" said Holcroft, frowning.

"I was a-thinkin' ——"

"Well," he interrupted sternly, "never think or speak of such things again."

The child had a miserable sense that she had angered him; she was also satisfied that her mother's schemes would be futile, and she scarcely spoke again that day.

Holcroft was more than angry; he was disgusted. That Mrs. Mumpson's design upon him was so offensively open that even this ignorant child understood it, and was expected to further it, caused such a strong revulsion in his mind that he half resolved to put them both in his market wagon on the morrow and take them back to their relatives. His newly awakened sympathy for Jane quickly vanished. If the girl and her mother had been repulsive from the first they were now hideous, in view of their efforts to fasten themselves upon him permanently. Fancy, then, the climax in his feelings when, as they passed the house, the front door suddenly opened and Mrs. Mumpson emerged with clasped hands and the exclamation, "Oh, how touching! just like father and child!"

Without noticing the remark he said coldly, as he passed, "Jane, go help Mrs. Wiggins get supper."

His anger and disgust grew so strong, as he hastily did his evening work, that he resolved not to endanger his self-control by sitting down within earshot of Mrs. Mumpson. As soon as possible, therefore, he carried the new stove to his room and put it up. The widow tried to address him as he passed in and out, but he paid no heed to her. At last, he only paused long enough at the kitchen door to say, "Jane, bring me some supper to my room. Remember, you only are to bring it."

Bewildered and abashed, Mrs. Mumpson rocked nervously. "I had looked for relentings this evening, a general softening," she murmured, "and I don't understand his bearing toward me." Then a happy thought struck her. "I see, I see," she cried softly and ecstatically: "he is struggling with himself; he finds that he must either deny himself my society or yield at once. The end is near."

A little later she, too, appeared at the kitchen door and said, with serious sweetness, "Jane, you can also bring me *my* supper to the parlor."

Mrs. Wiggins shook with mirth in all her vast portions as she remarked, "Jane, ye can bring me *my* supper from the stove to the table 'ere, and then vait hon yeself."

CHAPTER XIII.

NOT WIFE, BUT WAIF.

TOM WATTERLY'S horse was the pride of his heart. It was a bobtailed, rawboned animal, but, as Tom complacently remarked to Alida, "He can pass about anything on the road"—a boast that he let no chance escape of verifying. It was a terrible ordeal to the poor woman to go dashing through the streets in an open wagon, feeling that every eye was upon her. With head bowed down, she employed her failing strength in holding herself from falling out, yet almost wishing that she might be dashed against some object that would end her wretched life. It finally occurred to Tom that the woman at his side might not, after her recent experience, share in his enthusiasm, and he pulled up, remarking, with a rough effort at sympathy, "It's a cussed shame you've been treated so, and as soon as you're ready, I'll help you get even with the scamp."

"I'm not well, sir," said Alida humbly. "I only ask for a quiet place where I can rest till strong enough to do some kind of work."

"Well, well," said Tom kindly, "don't lose heart. We'll do the best by you we can. That aint saying very much, though, for we're full and running over."

He soon drew rein at the poorhouse door and sprang out. "I—I—feel strange," Alida gasped.

Tom caught the fainting woman in his arms and
outed, "Here, Bill, Joe! you lazy loons, where are
ou?"

Three or four half wrecks of men shuffled to his assist-
ce, and together they bore the unconscious woman to
e room which was used as a sort of hospital. Some
d crones gathered around with such restoratives as they
d at command. Gradually the stricken woman revived,
t as the whole miserable truth came back, she turned
r face to the wall with a sinking of heart akin to
spair. At last, from sheer exhaustion, feverish sleep
sued, from which she often started with moans and low
ies. One impression haunted her—she was falling,
er falling into a dark, bottomless abyss.

Hours passed in the same partial stupor, filled with
antoms and horrible dreams. Toward evening, she
oused herself mechanically to take the broth Mrs.
atterly ordered her to swallow, then relapsed into the
me lethargy. Late in the night, she became conscious
at someone was kneeling at her bedside and fondling
r. She started up with a slight cry.

"Don't be afraid; it's only me, dear," said a quavering
ice.

In the dim rays of a night lamp, Alida saw an old
oman with gray hair falling about her face and on her
ght-robe. At first, in her confused, feverish impres-
ons, the poor waif was dumb with superstitious awe,
d trembled between joy and fear. Could her mother
ve come to comfort her in her sore extremity?

"Put yer head on me ould withered breast," said the
parition, "an' ye'll know a mither's heart niver changes.
ve been a-lookin' for ye and expectin' ye these long,
eary years. They said ye wouldn't come back—that

I'd niver find ye ag'in ; but I knowed I wud, and here ye
are in me arms, me darlint. Don't draw away from yer
ould mither. Don't ye be afeard or 'shamed loike. No
matter what ye've done or where ye've been or who ye've
been with, a mither's heart welcomes ye back jist the
same as when yes were a babby an' slept on me breast.
A mither's heart ud quench the fires o' hell. I'd go inter
the burnin' flames o' the pit an' bear ye out in me arms.
So niver fear. Now that I've found ye, ye're safe. Ye'l
not rin away from me ag'in. I'll hould ye—I'll hould ye
back," and the poor creature clasped Alida with such
conclusive energy that she screamed from pain and
terror.

" Ye shall not get away from me, ye shall not go back
to evil ways. Whist, whist ! be aisy and let me plead wid
ye. Think how many long, weary years I've looked for
ye and waited for ye. Niver have I slept noight or day
in me watchin'. Ye may be so stained an' lost an' ruined
that the whole wourld will scorn ye, yet not yer mither
not yer ould mither. Oh, Nora, Nora, why did ye rin
away from me ? Wasn't I koind ? No, no ; ye cannot
lave me ag'in," and she threw herself on Alida, whose
disordered mind was tortured by what she heard.
Whether or not it was a more terrible dream than had yer
oppressed her, she scarcely knew, but in the excess of her
nervous horror she sent out a cry that echoed in every
part of the large building. Two old women rushed in
and dragged Alida's persecutor screaming away.

" That's allus the way o' it," she shrieked. " As soor
as I find me Nora they snatches me and carries me off
and I have to begin me watchin' and waitin' and lookin
ag'in."

Alida continued sobbing and trembling violently. One

of the awakened patients sought to assure her by saying, " Don't mind it so, miss. It's only old crazy Kate. Her daughter ran away from her years and years ago—how many no one knows—and when a young woman's brought here she thinks it's her lost Nora. They oughtn't 'a' let her get out, knowin' you was here."

For several days Alida's reason wavered. The nervous shock of her sad experiences had been so great that it did not seem at all improbable that she, like the insane mother, might be haunted for the rest of her life by an overwhelming impression of something lost. In her morbid, shaken mind she confounded the wrong she had received with guilt on her own part. Eventually, she grew calmer and more sensible. Although her conscience acquitted her of intentional evil, nothing could remove the deep-rooted conviction that she was shamed beyond hope of remedy. For a time she was unable to rally from nervous prostration ; meanwhile, her mind was preternaturally active, presenting every detail of the past until she was often ready to cry aloud in her despair.

Tom Watterly took an unusual interest in her case and exhorted the visiting physician to do his best for her. She finally began to improve, and with the first return of strength sought to do something with her feeble hands. The bread of charity was not sweet.

Although the place in which she lodged was clean, and the coarse, unvarying fare abundant, she shrunk shuddering, with each day's clearer consciousness, from the majority of those about her. Phases of life of which she had scarcely dreamed were the common topics of conversation. In her mother she had learned to venerate gray hairs, and it was an awful shock to learn that so many of the feeble creatures about her were coarse,

wicked, and evil-disposed. How could their withered
lips frame the words they spoke? How could they dwell
on subjects that were profanation, even to such wrecks
of womanhood as themselves?

Moreover, they persecuted her by their curiosity. The
good material in her apparel had been examined and
commented on; her wedding ring had been seen and its
absence soon noted, for Alida, after gaining the power to
recall the past fully, had thrown away the metal lie, feeling that it was the last link in a chain binding her to a
loathed and hated relationship. Learning from their
questions that the inmates of the almshouse did not know
her history, she refused to reveal it, thus awakening endless surmises. Many histories were made for her, the
beldams vying with each other in constructing the worst
one. Poor Alida soon learned that there was public
opinion even in an almshouse, and that she was under
its ban. In dreary despondency she thought, "They've
found out about me. If such creatures as these think
I'm hardly fit to speak to, how can I ever find work
among good, respectable people?"

Her extreme depression, the coarse, vulgar, and un-
charitable natures by which she was surrounded, retarded
her recovery. By her efforts to do anything in her power
for others she disarmed the hostility of some of the
women, and those that were more or less demented
became fond of her; but the majority probed her wound
by every look and word. She was a saint compared with
any of these, yet they made her envy their respectability.
She often thought, "Would to God that I was as old and
ready to die as the feeblest woman here, if I could only
hold up my head like her!"

One day a woman who had a child left it sleeping in

its rude wooden cradle and went downstairs. The babe wakened and began to cry. Alida took it up and found a strange solace in rocking it to sleep again upon her breast. At last the mother returned, glared a moment into Alida's appealing eyes, then snatched the child away with the cruel words, "Don't ye touch my baby ag'in! To think it ud been in the arms o' the loikes o' ye!"

Alida went away and sobbed until her strength was gone. She found that there were some others ostracised like herself, but they accepted their positions as a matter of course—as if it belonged to them and was the least of their troubles.

Her strength was returning, yet she was still feeble when she sent for Mrs. Watterly and asked, "Do you think I'm strong enough to take a place somewhere?"

"You ought to know that better than me," was the chilly reply.

"Do you—do you think I could get a place? I would be willing to do any kind of honest work not beyond my strength."

"You hardly look able to sit up straight. Better wait till you're stronger. I'll tell my husband. If applications come, he'll see about it," and she turned coldly away.

A day or two later Tom came and said brusquely, but not unkindly, "Don't like my hotel, hey? What can you do?"

"I'm used to sewing, but I'd try to do almost anything by which I could earn my living."

"Best thing to do is to prosecute that scamp and make him pay you a good round sum."

She shook her head decidedly. "I don't wish to see him again. I don't wish to go before people and have the—the—past talked about. I'd like a place with some kind, quiet people who keep no other help. Perhaps they wouldn't take me if they knew ; but I would be so faithful to them, and try so hard to learn what they wanted——"

" That's all nonsense, their not taking you. I'll find you a place some day, but you're not strong enough yet. You'd be brought right back here. You're as pale as a ghost—almost look like one. So don't be impatient, but give me a chance to find you a good place. I feel sorry for you, and don't want you to get among folks that have no feelings. Don't you worry now ; chirk up, and you'll come out all right."

" I—I think that if—if I'm employed, the people who take me ought to know," said Alida with bowed head.

" They'll be blamed fools if they don't think more of you when they do know," was his response. " Still, that shall be as you please. I've told only my wife, and they've kept mum at the police station, so the thing hasn't got into the papers."

Alida's head bowed lower still as she replied, " I thank you. My only wish now is to find some quiet place in which I can work and be left to myself."

" Very well," said Tom good-naturedly. " Cheer up ! I'll be on the lookout for you."

She turned to the window, near which she was sitting, to hide the tears which his rough kindness evoked. " He don't seem to shrink from me as if I wasn't fit to be spoken to," she thought ; " but his wife did. I'm afraid people won't take me when they know."

The April sunshine poured in at the window ; the grass was becoming green ; a robin alighted on a tree near by and poured out a jubilant song. For a few moments hope, that had been almost dead in her heart, revived. As she looked gratefully at the bird, thanking it in her heart for the song, it darted upon a string hanging on an adjacent spray and bore it to a crotch between two boughs. Then Alida saw it was building a nest. Her woman's heart gave way. " Oh," she moaned, " I shall never have a home again ! no place shared by one who cares for me. To work, and to be tolerated for the sake of my work, is all that's left."

CHAPTER XIV.

A PITCHED BATTLE.

IT was an odd household under Holcroft's roof on the evening of the Sunday we have described. The farmer, in a sense, had " taken sanctuary " in his own room, that he might escape the maneuvering wiles of his tormenting housekeeper. If she would content herself with general topics he would try to endure her foolish, high-flown talk until the three months expired; but that she should speedily and openly take the initiative in matrimonial designs was proof of such an unbalanced mind that he was filled with nervous dread. "Hanged if one can tell what such a silly, hairbrained woman will do next!" he thought, as he brooded by the fire. "Sunday or no Sunday, I feel as if I'd like to take my horsewhip and give Lemuel Weeks a piece of my mind."

Such musings did not promise well for Mrs. Mumpson, scheming in the parlor below; but, as we have seen, she had the faculty of arranging all future events to her mind. That matters had not turned out in the past as she had expected, counted for nothing. She was one who could not be taught, even by experience. The most insignificant thing in Holcroft's dwelling had not escaped her scrutiny and pretty accurate guess as to value, yet she could not see or understand the intolerable disgust and irritation which her ridiculous conduct excited. In weak mind egotism and selfishness, beyond a certain point, pass into practical insanity. All sense of delicacy, of the fitness of things, is lost; even the power to consider the rights and feelings of others is wanting. Unlike poor Holcroft, Mrs. Mumpson had few misgivings in regard to coming years. As she rocked unceasingly before the parlor fire, she arranged everything in regard to his future as well as her own.

Jane, quite forgotten, was oppressed with a miserable presentiment of evil. Her pinched but intense little mind was concentrated on two facts—Holcroft's anger and her mother's lack of sense. From such premises it did not take her long to reason out but one conclusion—"visitin' again"; and this was the summing up of all evils. Now and then a tear would force its way out of one of her little eyes, but otherwise she kept her troubles to herself.

Mrs. Wiggins was the only complacent personage in the house, and she unbent with a garrulous affability to Jane, which could be accounted for in but one way— Holcroft had forgotten about his cider barrel, thereby unconsciously giving her the chance to sample its contents freely. She was now smoking her pipe with much content, and indulging in pleasing reminiscences which the facts of her life scarcely warranted.

"Ven hi vas as leetle a gal as ye are," she began, and then she related experiences quite devoid of the simplicity and innocence of childhood. The girl soon forgot her fears and listened with avidity until the old dame's face grew heavier, if possible, with sleep, and she stumbled off to bed.

Having no wish to see or speak to her mother again, the child blew out the candle and stole silently up the stairway. At last Mrs. Mumpson took her light and went noisily around, seeing to the fastenings of doors and windows. "I know he is listening to every sound from me, and he shall learn what a caretaker I am," she murmured softly.

Once out of doors in the morning, with his foot on the native heath of his farm, Holcroft's hopefulness and courage always returned. He was half angry with himself at his nervous irritation of the evening before. "If she becomes so cranky that I can't stand her, I'll pay the three months' wages and clear her out," he had concluded, and he went about his morning work with a grim purpose to submit to very little nonsense.

Cider is akin to vinegar, and Mrs. Wiggins' liberal potations of the evening before had evidently imparted a marked acidity to her temper. She laid hold of the kitchen utensils as if she had a spite against them, and when Jane, confiding in her friendliness shown so recently, came down to assist, she was chased out of doors with language we forbear to repeat. Mrs. Mumpson, therefore, had no intimation of the low state of the barometer in the region of the kitchen. "I have taken time to think deeply and calmly," she murmured. "The proper course has been made clear to me. He is somewhat uncouth; he is silent and unable to express his thoughts and emotions—in brief, undeveloped; he is awfully irreligious. Moth and rust are busy in this house; much that would be so useful is going to waste. He must learn to look upon me as the developer, the caretaker, a patient and healthful embodiment of female influence. I will now begin actively my mission of making him an ornerment to society. That mountainous Mrs. Viggins must be replaced by a deferential girl who will naturally look up to me. How can I be a true caretaker—how can I bring repose and refinement to this dwelling with two hundred pounds of female impudence in my way? Mr. Holcroft shall see that Mrs. Viggins is an unseemly and jarring discord in our home," and she brought the rocking chair from the parlor to the kitchen, with a serene and lofty air. Jane hovered near the window, watching.

At first, there was an ominous silence in respect to words. Portentous sounds increased, however, for Mrs. Wiggins strode about with martial tread, making the boards creak and the dishes clatter, while her red eyes shot lurid and sanguinary gleams. She would seize a dipper as if it were a foe, slamming it upon the table again as if striking an enemy. Under her vigorous manipulation, kettles and pans resounded with reports like firearms.

Mrs. Mumpson was evidently perturbed; her calm superiority was forsaking her; every moment she rocked faster—a sure indication that she was not at peace. At last she said, with great dignity: " Mrs. Viggins, I must request you to perform your tasks with less clamor. My nerves are not equal to this peculiar way of taking up and laying down things."

" Vell, jes' ye vait a minute, han hi'll show ye 'ow hi kin take hup things han put 'em down hag'in hout o' my vay," and before Mrs. Mumpson could interfere, she found herself lifted, chair and all bodily, and carried to the parlor. Between trepidation and anger, she could only gasp during the transit, and when left in the middle of the parlor floor she looked around in utter bewilderment.

It so happened that Holcroft, on his way from the barn, had seen Jane looking in at the window, and, suspecting something amiss, had arrived just in time for the spectacle. Convulsed with laughter, he returned hastily to the barn ; while Jane expressed her feelings, whatever they were, by executing something like a hornpipe before the window.

Mrs. Mumpson, however, was not vanquished. She had only made a compulsory retreat from the scene of hostilities ; and, after rallying her shattered faculties, advanced again with the chair. " How dared you, you disreputerble female ? " she began.

Mrs. Wiggins turned slowly and ominously upon her. " Ye call me a disrupterbul female hag'in, han ye vont find hit 'ealthy."

Mrs. Mumpson prudently backed toward the door before delivering her return fire.

"Woman!" she cried, " are you out of your mind ? Don't you know I'm housekeeper here, and that it's my duty to superintend you and your work ? "

" Vell, then, hi'll double ye hup hand put ye hon the shelf hof the dresser han' lock the glass door hon ye. From hup there ye kin see all that's goin' hon and sup'intend to yer 'eart's content," and she started for her superior officer.

Mrs. Mumpson backed so precipitately with her chair that it struck against the door-case, and she sat down hard. Seeing that Mrs. Wiggins was almost upon her, she darted back into the parlor, leaving the chair as a trophy in the hands of her enemy. Mrs. Wiggins was somewhat appeased by this second triumph, and with the hope of adding gall and bitterness to Mrs. Mumpson's defeat, she took the chair to her rival's favorite rocking place, lighted her pipe, and sat down in grim complacency. Mrs. Mumpson warily approached to recover a support which, from long habit, had become moral as well as physical, and her indignation knew no bounds when she saw it creaking under the weight of her foe. It must be admitted, however, that her ire was not so great that she did not retain the " better part of valor," for she stepped back, unlocked the front door, and set it ajar. On returning, she opened with a volubility that awed even Mrs. Wiggins for a moment. " You miserable, mountainous pauper ; you interloper ; you unrefined, irresponserble, unregenerate female, do you know what you have done in thus outraging *me ?* I'm a respecterble woman, respecterbly connected. I'm here in a responserble station. When Mr. Holcroft appears he'll drive you from the dwelling which you vulgarize. Your presence makes this apartment a den. You are a wild beast——"

" Hi'm a vile beastes, ham hi ? " cried Mrs. Wiggins, at last stung into action, and she threw her lighted pipe at the open mouth that was discharging high-sounding epithets by the score.

It struck the lintel over the widow's head, was shattered, and sent down upon her a shower of villainously smelling sparks. Mrs. Mumpson shrieked and sought frantically to keep her calico wrapper from taking fire. Meanwhile, Mrs. Wiggins rose and took a step or two that she might assist should there be any positive danger, for she had not yet reached a point of malignity which would lead her to witness calmly an *auto-da-fé*. This was Jane's opportunity. Mrs. Wiggins had alienated this small and hitherto friendly power, and now, with a returning impulse of loyalty, it took sides with the weaker party. The kitchen door was on a crack ; the child pushed it noiselessly open, darted around behind the stove, and withdrew the rocking chair.

Mrs. Wiggins' brief anxiety and preoccupation passed, and she stepped backward again to sit down. She did sit down, but with such terrific force that the stove and nearly everything else in the room threatened to fall with her. She sat helplessly for a bewildered moment, while Jane, with the chair, danced before her exclaiming, tauntingly, "That's for chasing me out as if I was a cat!"

"Noo hi'll chase ye both hout," cried the ireful Wiggins, scrambling to her feet. She made good her threat, for Holcroft, a moment later, saw mother and daughter, the latter carrying the chair, rushing from the front door, and Mrs. Wiggins, armed with a great wooden spoon, waddling after them, her objurgations mingling with Mrs. Mumpson's shrieks and Jane's shrill laughter. The widow caught a glimpse of him standing in the barn door, and, as if borne by the wind, she flew toward him, crying, "He shall be my protector!"

He barely had time to whisk through a side door and close it after him. The widow's impetuous desire to pant out the story of her wrongs carried her into the midst of the barnyard, where she was speedily confronted by an unruly young heifer that could scarcely be blamed for hostility to such a wild-looking object.

The animal shook its head threateningly as it advanced. Again the widow's shrieks resounded. This time Holcroft was about to come to the rescue, when the beleaguered woman made a dash for the top of the nearest fence, reminding her amused looker-on of the night of her arrival when she had perched like some strange sort of bird on the wagon wheel.

Seeing that she was abundantly able to escape alone, the farmer remained in concealment. Although disgusted and angry at the scenes taking place, he was scarcely able to restrain roars of laughter. Perched

upon the fence, the widow called piteously for him to lift
her down, but he was not to be caught by any such device. At last, giving up hope and still threatened by the
heifer, she went over on the other side. Knowing that she
must make a detour before reaching the dwelling, Holcroft went thither rapidly with the purpose of restoring
order at once. "Jane," he said sternly, "take that chair
to the parlor and leave it there. Let there be no more
such nonsense."

At his approach, Mrs. Wiggins had retreated sullenly
to the kitchen. "Come," he ordered good-naturedly,
" hasten breakfast and let there be no more quarreling."

"Hif hi vas left to do me work hin peace——" she
began.

"Well, you shall do it in peace."

At this moment Mrs. Mumpson came tearing in, quite
oblivious of the fact that she had left a goodly part of
her calico skirt on a nail of the fence. She was rushing
toward Holcroft, when he said sternly, and with a repel-
lent gesture, "Stop and listen to me. If there's any
more of this quarreling like cats and dogs in my house,
I'll send for the constable and have you all arrested. If
you are not all utterly demented and hopeless fools, you
will know that you came here to do my work, and nothing else." Then catching a glimpse of Mrs. Mumpson's
dress, and fearing he should laugh outright, he turned
abruptly on his heel and went to his room, where he
was in a divided state between irrepressible mirth and
vexation.

Mrs. Mumpson also fled to her room. She felt that
the proper course for her at this juncture was a fit of
violent hysterics; but a prompt douche from the water
pitcher, administered by the unsympathetic Jane, effectu-

ally checked the first symptoms. "Was ever a respecterble woman ——"

"You aint respectable," interrupted the girl, as she departed, "you look like a scarecrow. 'Fi's you I'd begin to show some sense now."

CHAPTER XV.

" WHAT *IS* TO BECOME OF ME ? "

HOLCROFT'S reference to a constable and arrest, though scarcely intended to be more than a vague threat, had the effect of clearing the air like a clap of thunder. Jane had never lost her senses, such as she possessed, and Mrs. Wiggins recovered hers sufficiently to apologize to the farmer when he came down to breakfast. " But that Mumpson's hawfully haggravatin', master, as ye know yeself, hi'm a-thinkin'. Vud ye jis tell a body vat she is 'ere, han 'ow hi'm to get hon vith 'er. Hif hi'm to take me horders from 'er hi'd ruther go back to the poor-'us."

" You are to take your orders from me and no one else. All I ask is that you go on quietly with your work and pay no attention to her. You know well enough that I can't have such goings on. I want you to let Jane help you and learn her to do everything as far as she can. Mrs. Mumpson can do the mending and ironing, I suppose. At any rate, I won't have any more quarreling and uproar. I'm a quiet man and intend to have a quiet house. You and Jane can get along very well in the kitchen, and you say you understand the dairy work."

" Vell hi does, han noo hi've got me horders hi'll go right along."

Mrs. Mumpson was like one who had been rudely

shaken out of a dream, and she appeared to have sense enough to realize that she couldn't assume so much at first as she anticipated. She received from Jane a cup of coffee, and said feebly, " I can partake of no more after the recent trying events."

For some hours she was a little dazed, but her mind was of too light weight to be long cast down. Jane rehearsed Holcroft's words, described his manner, and sought with much insistence to show her mother that she must drop her nonsense at once. " I can see it in his eye," said the girl, " that he won't stand much more. If yer don't come down and keep yer hands busy and yer tongue still, we'll tramp. As to his marrying you, bah ! he'd jes' as soon marry Mrs. Wiggins."

This was awful prose, but Mrs. Mumpson was too bewildered and discouraged for a time to dispute it, and the household fell into a somewhat regular routine. The widow appeared at her meals with the air of a meek and suffering martyr ; Holcroft was exceedingly brief in his replies to her questions, and paid no heed to her remarks. After supper and his evening work, he went directly to his room. Every day, however, he secretly chafed, with ever-increasing discontent, over this tormenting presence in his house. The mending and such work as she attempted was so wretchedly performed that it would better have been left undone. She was also recovering her garrulousness, and mistook his toleration and her immunity in the parlor for proof of a growing consideration. " He knows that my hands were never made for such coarse, menial tasks as that Viggins does," she thought, as she darned one of his stockings in a way that would render it almost impossible for him to put his foot into it again. " The events of last Monday morning were un-

fortunate, unforeseen, unprecedented. I was unprepared
for such vulgar, barbarous, unheard-of proceedings—
taken off my feet, as it were; but now that he's had
time to think it all over, he sees that I am not a common
woman like Viggins,"—Mrs. Mumpson would have suffered rather than have accorded her enemy the prefix of
Mrs., ——"who is only fit to be among pots and kettles.
He leaves me in the parlor as if a refined apartment became me and I became it. Time and my influence will
mellow, soften, elevate, develop, and at last awaken a
desire for my society, then yearnings. My first error
was in not giving myself time to make a proper impression. He will soon begin to yield like the earth without.
First it is hard and frosty, then it is cold and muddy, if I
may permit myself so disagreeable an illustration. Now
he is becoming mellow, and soon every word I utter will
be like good seed in good ground. How aptly it all fits!
I have only to be patient."

She was finally left almost to utter idleness, for Jane
and Mrs. Wiggins gradually took from the incompetent
hands even the light tasks which she had attempted.
She made no protest, regarding all as another proof that
Holcroft was beginning to recognize her superiority and
unfitness for menial tasks. She would maintain, however, her character as the caretaker and ostentatiously
inspected everything; she also tried to make as much
noise in fastening up the dwelling at night as if she were
barricading a castle. Holcroft would listen grimly, well
aware that no house had been entered in Oakville during
his memory. He had taken an early occasion to say at
the table that he wished no one to enter his room except
Jane, and that he would not permit any infringement of
this rule. Mrs. Mumpson's feelings had been hurt at

first by this order, but she soon satisfied herself that it
had been meant for Mrs. Wiggins' benefit and not her
own. She found, however, that Jane interpreted it liter-
ally. "If either of you set foot in that room I'll tell him,"
she said flatly. "I've had my orders and I'm a-goin' to
obey. There's to be no more rummagin'. If you'll give
me the keys I'll put things back in order ag'in."

"Well, I won't give you the keys. I'm the proper
person to put things in order if you did not replace them
properly. You are just making an excuse to rummage
yourself. My motive for inspecting is very different from
yours."

"Shouldn't wonder if you was sorry some day," the
girl had remarked, and so the matter had dropped and
been forgotten.

Holcroft solaced himself with the fact that Jane and Mrs.
Wiggins served his meals regularly and looked after the
dairy with better care than it had received since his wife
died. "If I had only those two in the house I could get
along first-rate," he thought. "After the three months
are up I'll try to make such an arrangement. I'd pay the
mother and send her off now, but if I did, Lemuel Weeks
would put her up to a lawsuit."

April days brought the longed-for plowing and planting, and the farmer was so busy and absorbed in his
work that Mrs. Mumpson had less and less place in his
thoughts, even as a thorn in the flesh. One bright afternoon, however, chaos came again unexpectedly. Mrs.
Wiggins did not suggest a volatile creature, yet such,
alas! she was. She apparently exhaled and was lost,
leaving no trace. The circumstances of her disappearance permit of a very matter-of-fact and not very credit-
able explanation. On the day in question she prepared

an unusually good dinner, and the farmer had enjoyed it
in spite of Mrs. Mumpson's presence and desultory
remarks. The morning had been fine and he had made
progress in his early spring work. Mrs. Wiggins felt
that her hour and opportunity had come. Following him
to the door, she said in a low tone and yet with a decisive
accent, as if she was claiming a right, "Master, hi'd
thank ye for me two weeks' wages."

He unsuspectingly and unhesitatingly gave it to her,
thinking, "That's the way with such people. They want
to be paid often and be sure of their money. She'll work
all the better for having it."

Mrs. Wiggins knew the hour when the stage passed
the house; she had made up a bundle without a very
close regard to *meum* or *tuum*, and was ready to flit.
The chance speedily came.

The "caretaker" was rocking in the parlor and would
disdain to look, while Jane had gone out to help plant
some early potatoes on a warm hillside. The coast was
clear. Seeing the stage coming, the old woman waddled
down the lane at a remarkable pace, paid her fare to
town, and the Holcroft kitchen knew her no more. That
she found the "friend" she had wished to see on her way
out to the farm, and that this friend brought her quickly
under Tom Watterly's care again, goes without saying.

As the shadows lengthened and the robins became
tuneful, Holcroft said, "You've done well, Jane. Thank
you. Now you can go back to the house."

The child soon returned in breathless haste to the field
where the farmer was covering the potato pieces she had
dropped, and cried, "Mrs. Wiggins 's gone!"

Like a flash the woman's motive in asking for her
wages occurred to him, but he started for the house to

assure himself of the truth. "Perhaps she's in the cellar," he said, remembering the cider barrel, "or else she's out for a walk."

"No, she aint," persisted Jane. "I've looked everywhere and all over the barn, and she aint nowhere. Mother haint seen her, nuther."

With dreary misgivings, Holcroft remembered that he no longer had a practical ally in the old Englishwoman, and he felt that a new breaking up was coming. He looked wistfully at Jane, and thought, "I *could* get along with that child if the mother was away. But that can't be; *she'd* visit here indefinitely if Jane stayed."

When Mrs. Mumpson learned from Jane of Mrs. Wiggins' disappearance, she was thrown into a state of strong excitement. She felt that her hour and opportunity might be near also, and she began to rock very fast. "What else could he expect of such a female?" she soliloquized. "I've no doubt but she's taken things, too. He'll now learn my value and what it is to have a caretaker who will never desert him."

Spirits and courage rose with the emergency; her thoughts hurried her along like a dry leaf caught in a March gale. "Yes," she murmured, "the time has come for me to act, to dare, to show him in his desperate need and hour of desertion what might be, may be, must be. He will now see clearly the difference between these peculiar females who come and go, and a respecterble woman and a mother who can be depended upon—one who will never steal away like a thief in the night."

She saw Holcroft approaching the house with Jane; she heard him ascend to Mrs. Wiggins' room, then return to the kitchen and ejaculate, "Yes, she's gone, sure enough."

" Now, *act!* " murmured the widow, and she rushed toward the farmer with clasped hands, and cried with emotion, " Yes, she's gone; but I'm not gone. You are not deserted. Jane will minister to you; I will be the caretaker, and our home will be all the happier because that monstrous creature is absent. Dear Mr. Holcroft, don't be so blind to your own interests and happiness, don't remain undeveloped ! Everything is wrong here if you would but see it. You are lonely and desolate. Moth and rust have entered, things in unopened drawers and closets are molding and going to waste. Yield to true female influence and——"

Holcroft had been rendered speechless at first by this onslaught, but the reference to unopened drawers and closets awakened a sudden suspicion. Had she dared to touch what had belonged to his wife ? " What ! " he exclaimed sharply, interrupting her ; then with an expression of disgust and anger, he passed her swiftly and went to his room. A moment later came the stern summons, " Jane, come here ! "

" Now you'll see what 'll come of that rummagin'," whimpered Jane. " You aint got no sense at all to go at him so. He's jes' goin' to put us right out," and she went upstairs as if to execution.

" Have I failed ? " gasped Mrs. Mumpson, and retreating to the chair, she rocked nervously.

" Jane," said Holcroft in hot anger, " my wife's things have been pulled out of her bureau and stuffed back again as if they were no better than dishcloths. Who did it ? "

The child now began to cry aloud.

" There, there ! " he said, with intense irritation, " I can't trust you either."

"I haint—touched 'em—since you told me—told me —not to do things on the sly," the girl sobbed brokenly; but he had closed the door upon her and did not hear.

He could have forgiven her almost anything but this. Since she only had been permitted to take care of his room he naturally thought that she had committed the sacrilege, and her manner had confirmed this impression. Of course the mother had been present and probably had assisted; but he had expected nothing better of her.

He took the things out, folded and smoothed them as carefully as he could with his heavy hands and clumsy fingers. His gentle, almost reverent touch was in strange contrast with his flushed, angry face and gleaming eyes. "This is the worst that's happened yet," he muttered. "Oh, Lemuel Weeks! it's well you are not here now, or we might both have cause to be sorry. It was you who put these prying, and for all I know, thieving creatures into my house, and it was as mean a trick as ever one man played another. You and this precious cousin of yours thought you could bring about a marriage; you put her up to her ridiculous antics. Faugh! the very thought of it all makes me sick."

"Oh, mother, what shall I do?" Jane cried, rushing into the parlor and throwing herself on the floor, "he's goin' to put us right out."

"He can't put me out before the three months are up," quavered the widow.

"Yes, he can. We've been a-rummagin' where we'd no bizniss to be. He's mad enough to do anything; he jes looks awful; I'm afraid of him."

"Jane," said her mother plaintively, "I feel indisposed. I think I'll retire.

"Yes, that's the way with *you*," sobbed the child. "You got me into the scrape and now you retire."

Mrs. Mumpson's confidence in herself and her schemes was terribly shaken. "I must act very discreetly. I must be alone that I may think over these untoward events. Mr. Holcroft has been so warped by the past female influences of his life that there's no counting on his action. He taxes me sorely," she explained, and then ascended the stairs.

"Oh! oh!" moaned the child, as she writhed on the floor, "mother aint got no sense at all. What *is* goin' to become of me? I'd ruther hang about his barn than go back to Cousin Lemuel's or any other cousin's."

Spurred by one hope, she at last sprung up and went to the kitchen. It was already growing dark, and she lighted the lamp, kindled the fire, and began getting supper with breathless energy.

As far as he could discover, Holcroft was satisfied that nothing had been taken. In this respect he was right. Mrs. Mumpson's curiosity and covetousness were boundless, but she would not steal. There are few who do not draw the line somewhere.

Having tried to put the articles back as they were before, he locked them up, and went hastily down and out, feeling that he must regain his self-control and decide upon his future action at once. "I will then carry out my purposes in a way that will give the Weeks tribe no chance to make trouble."

As he passed the kitchen windows he saw Jane rushing about as if possessed, and he stopped to watch her. It soon became evident that she was trying to get his supper. His heart relented at once in spite of himself. "The poor, wronged child!" he muttered. "Why should I be so hard on her for doing what she's been brought up to do? Well, well, it's too bad to send her away, but I can't help it. I'd lose my own reason if the mother were here much longer, and if I kept Jane, her idiotic mother would stay in spite of me. If she didn't there'd be endless talk and lawsuits, too, like enough, about separating parent and child. Jane's too young and little, anyway, to be here alone and do the work. But I'm sorry for her, I declare I am, and I wish I could do something to give her a chance in the world. If my wife was only living we'd take and bring her up, disagreeable and homely as she is; but there's no use of my trying to do anything alone. I fear, after all, that I shall have to give up the old place and go—I don't know where. What is to become of her?"

CHAPTER XVI.

MRS. MUMPSON'S VICISSITUDES.

HAVING completed her preparations for supper, Jane stole timidly up to Holcroft's room to summon him. Her first rap on his door was scarcely audible, then she ventured to knock louder and finally to call him, but there was no response. Full of vague dread she went to her mother's room and said, "He won't answer me; he's so awful mad that I don't know what he'll do."

"I think he has left his apartment," her mother moaned from the bed.

"Why couldn't yer tell me so before?" cried Jane. "What yer gone to bed for? If you'd only show some sense and try to do what he brought you here for, like enough he'd keep us yet."

"My heart's too crushed, Jane——"

"Oh, bother, bother!" and the child rushed away. She looked into the dark parlor and called, "Mr. Holcroft!" Then she appeared in the kitchen again, the picture of uncouth distress and perplexity. A moment later she opened the door and darted toward the barn.

"What do you wish, Jane?" said Holcroft, emerging from a shadowy corner and recalling her.

"Sup—supper's—ready," sobbed the child.

He came in and sat down at the table, considerately appearing not to notice her until she had a chance to recover composure. She vigorously used the sleeves of both arms in drying her eyes, then stole in and found a seat in a dusky corner.

"Why don't you come to supper?" he asked quietly.

"Don't want any."

"You had better take some up to your mother."

"She oughtn't to have any."

"That doesn't make any difference. I want you to take up something to her, and then come down and eat your supper like a sensible girl."

"I aint been sensible, nor mother nuther."

"Do as I say, Jane." The child obeyed, but she couldn't swallow anything but a little coffee.

Holcroft was in a quandary. He had not the gift of speaking soothing yet meaningless words, and was too honest to raise false hopes. He was therefore almost as silent and embarrassed as Jane herself. To the girl's furtive scrutiny he did not seem hardened against her, and she at last ventured, "Say, I didn't touch them drawers after you told me not to do anything on the sly."

"When were they opened? Tell me the truth, Jane."

"Mother opened them the first day you left us alone. I told her you wouldn't like it, but she said she was housekeeper; she said how it was her duty to inspect everything. I wanted to inspect, too. We was jes' rummagin'—that's what it was. After the things were all pulled out, mother got the rocker and wouldn't do anything. It was gettin' late, and I was frightened and poked 'em back in a hurry. Mother wanted to rummage ag'in the other day and I wouldn't let her: then she wouldn't let me have the keys, so I could fix 'em up."

"But the keys were in my pocket, Jane."

" Mother has a lot of keys. I've told you jes' how it all was."

" Nothing was taken away ? "

" No. Mother aint got sense, but she never takes things. I nuther 'cept when I'm hungry. Never took anything here. Say, are you goin' to send us away ? "

" I fear I shall have to, Jane. I'm sorry for *you*, for I believe you would try to do the best you could if given a chance, and I can see you never had a chance."

" No," said the child, blinking hard to keep the tears out of her eyes. " I aint had no teachin'. I've jes' kinder growed along with the farm hands and rough boys. Them that didn't hate me teased me. Say, couldn't I stay in your barn and sleep in the hay ? "

Holcroft was sorely perplexed and pushed away his half-eaten supper. He knew himself what it was to be friendless and lonely, and his heart softened toward this worse than motherless child.

" Jane," he said kindly, " I'm just as sorry for you as I can be, but you don't know the difficulties in the way of what you wish, and I fear I can't make you under- stand them. Indeed, it would not be best to tell you all of them. If I could keep you at all, you should stay in the house, and I'd be kind to you, but it can't be. I may not stay here myself. My future course is very uncertain. There's no use of my trying to go on as I have. Perhaps some day I can do something for you, and if I can, I will. I will pay your mother her three months' wages in full in the morning, and then I want you both to get your things into your trunk, and I'll take you to your Cousin Lemuel's."

Driven almost to desperation, Jane suggested the only scheme she could think of. " If you stayed here and I run away and came back, wouldn't you keep me? I'd work all day and all night jes' for the sake of stayin'."

"No, Jane," said Holcroft firmly, "you'd make me no end of trouble if you did that. If you'll be a good girl and learn how to do things, I'll try to find you a place among kind people some day when you're older and can act for yourself."

"You're afraid 'fi's here mother'd come a-visitin'," said the girl keenly.

"You're too young to understand half the trouble that might follow. My plans are too uncertain for me to tangle myself up. You and your mother must go away at once, so I can do what I must do before it's too late in the season. Here's a couple of dollars which you can keep for yourself," and he went up to his room, feeling that he could not witness the child's distress any longer.

He fought hard against despondency and tried to face the actual condition of his affairs. "I might have known," he thought, "that things would have turned out somewhat as they have, with such women in the house, and I don't see much chance of getting better ones. I've been so bent on staying and going on as I used to that I've just shut my eyes to the acts." He got out an old account book and pored over it a long time. The entries therein were blind enough, but at last he concluded, "It's plain that I've lost money on the dairy ever since my wife died, and the prospects now are worse than ever. That Weeks tribe will set the whole town talking against me and it will be just about impossible to get a decent woman to come here. I might as well have an auction and sell all the cows but one. at once. After that, if I find I can't make out living alone,

'll put the place in better order and sell or rent. I can
get my own meals after a fashion, and old Jonathan
ohnson's wife will do my washing and mending. It's
ime it was done better than it has been, for some of my
lothes make me look like a scarecrow. I believe
onathan will come with his cross dog and stay here too,
vhen I must be away. Well, well, it's a hard lot for a
nan; but I'd be about as bad off, and a hundred-fold
nore lonely, if I went anywhere else. I can only feel my
vay along and live a day at a time. I'll learn what can
e done and what can't be. One thing is clear; I can't
o on with this Mrs. Mumpson in the house a day
onger. She makes me creep and crawl all over, and the
rst thing I know I shall be swearing like a bloody
irate unless I get rid of her. If she wasn't such a hope-
ess idiot I'd let her stay for the sake of Jane, but I won't
ay her good wages to make my life a burden a day
onger," and with like self-communings he spent the
vening until the habit of early drowsiness overcame
im.

The morning found Jane dispirited and a little sulllen,
s older and wiser people are apt to be when disappointed.
he employed herself in getting breakfast carelessly and
anguidly, and the result was not satisfactory.

"Where's your mother?" Holcroft asked when he
ame in.

"She told me to tell you she was indisposed."

"Indisposed to go to Lemuel Weeks'?"

"I 'spect she means she's sick."

He frowned and looked suspiciously at the girl.
Here was a new complication, and very possibly a
rick.

"What's the matter with her?"

"Dunno."

"Well, she had better get well enough to go by this afternoon," he remarked, controlling his irritation with difficulty, and nothing more was said.

Full of his new plans he spent a busy forenoon and then came to dinner. It was the same old story. He went up and knocked at Mrs. Mumpson's door, saying that he wished to speak with her.

"I'm too indisposed to transact business," she replied feebly.

"You must be ready to-morrow morning," he called. "I have business plans which can't be delayed," and he turned away muttering rather sulphurous words.

"He will relent; his hard heart will soften at last——" But we shall not weary the reader with the long soliloquies with which she beguiled her politic seclusion, as she regarded it. Poor, unsophisticated Jane made matters worse. The condition of life among her much-visited relatives now existed again. She was not wanted, and her old sly, sullen, and furtive manner reasserted itself. Much of Holcroft's sympathy was thus alienated, yet he partially understood and pitied her. It became, however, all the more clear that he must get rid of both mother and child, and that further relations with either of them could only lead to trouble.

The following morning only Jane appeared. "Is your mother really sick?" he asked.

"S'pose so," was the laconic reply.

"You haven't taken much pains with the breakfast, Jane."

"'Taint no use."

With knitted brows he thought deeply, and silently ate the wretched meal which had been prepared. Then, remarking that he might do some writing, he went up to a small attic room which had been used occasionally by a hired man. It contained a covered pipe-hole leading into the chimney flue. Removing the cover, he stopped up the flue with an old woolen coat. " I suppose I'll have to meet tricks with tricks," he muttered.

Returning to his own apartment, he lighted a fire in the stove and laid upon the kindling blaze some dampened wood, then went out and quietly hitched his horses to the wagon.

The pungent odor of smoke soon filled the house. The cover over the pipe-hole in Mrs. Mumpson's room was not very secure, and thick volumes began to pour in upon the startled widow. " Jane ! " she shrieked.

If Jane was sullen toward Holcroft she was furious at her mother, and paid no heed at first to her cry.

" Jane, Jane, the house is on fire ! "

Then the child did fly up the stairway. The smoke seemed to confirm the words of her mother, who was dressing in hot haste. " Run and tell Mr. Holcroft ! " she cried.

" I won't," said the girl. " If he won't keep us in the house I don't care if he don't have any house."

" No, no, tell him ! " screamed Mrs. Mumpson. " If we save his house he will relent. Gratitude will overwhelm him. So far from turning us away, he will sue, he will plead for forgiveness for his former harshness ; his home saved will be our home won. Just put our things in the trunk first. Perhaps the house can't be saved, and you know we must save *our* things. Help me, quick ! There, there ; now, now "—both were sneezing and choking in a half-strangled manner. " Now let me lock it ; my hand trembles so ; take hold and draw it out; drag it downstairs; no matter how it scratches things!"

Having reached the hall below, she opened the door and shrieked for Holcroft; Jane also began running toward the barn. The farmer came hastily out, and shouted, "What's the matter?"

"The house is on fire!" they screamed in chorus.

To carry out his ruse, he ran swiftly to the house. Mrs. Mumpson stood before him wringing her hands and crying, "Oh, dear Mr. Holcroft, can't I do anything to help you? I would so like to help you and——"

"Yes, my good woman, let me get in the door and see what's the matter. Oh, here's your trunk. That's sensible. Better get it outside," and he went up the stairs two steps at a time and rushed into his room.

"Jane, Jane," ejaculated Mrs. Mumpson, sinking on a seat in the porch, "he called me his good woman!" But Jane was busy dragging the trunk out of doors. Having secured her own and her mother's worldly possessions, she called, "Shall I bring water and carry things out?"

"No," he replied, "not yet. There's something the matter with the chimney," and he hastened up to the attic room, removed the clog from the flue, put on the cover again, and threw open the window. Returning, he locked the door of the room which Mrs. Mumpson had occupied and came downstairs. "I must get a ladder and examine the chimney," he said as he passed.

"Oh, my dear Mr. Holcroft!" the widow began.

"Can't talk with you yet," and he hastened on.

"As soon as he's sure the house is safe, Jane, all will be well." But the girl had grown hopeless and cynical. She had not penetrated his scheme to restore her mothe to health, but understood the man well enough to be sure that her mother's hopes would end as they had in the past. She sat down apathetically on the trunk to see what would happen next.

After a brief inspection Holcroft came down from the roof and said, " The chimney will have to be repaired," which was true enough and equally so of other parts of the dwelling. The fortunes of the owner were reflected in the appearance of the building.

If it were a possible thing Holcroft wished to carry out his ruse undetected, and he hastened upstairs again, ostensibly to see that all danger had passed, but in reality to prepare his mind for an intensely disagreeable interview. " I'd rather face a mob of men than that one idiotic woman," he muttered. " I could calculate the actions of a setting hen with her head cut off better than I can this widow's. But there's no help for it," and he came down looking very resolute. " I've let the fire in my stove go out, and there's no more danger," he said quietly, as he sat down on the porch opposite Mrs. Mumpson.

" Oh-h," she exclaimed, with a long breath of relief, " we've saved the dwelling. What would we have done if it had burned down ! We would have been homeless."

" That may be my condition soon, as it is," he said coldly. " I am very glad, Mrs. Mumpson, that you are so much better. As Jane told you, I suppose, I will pay you the sum I agreed to give you for three months' service——"

" My dear Mr. Holcroft, my nerves have been too shaken to talk business this morning," and the widow leaned back and looked as if she were going to faint. " I'm only a poor lone woman," she added feebly, " and you cannot be so lacking in the milk of human kindness as to take advantage of me."

"No, madam, nor shall I allow you and Lemuel Weeks to take advantage of me. This is my house and I have a right to make my own arrangements."

"It might all be arranged so easily in another way," sighed the widow.

"It cannot be arranged in any other way——" he began.

"Mr. Holcroft," she cried, leaning suddenly forward with clasped hands and speaking effusively, "you but now called me your good woman. Think how much those words mean. Make them true, now that you've spoken them. Then you won't be homeless and will never need a caretaker."

"Are you making me an offer of marriage?" he asked with lowering brow.

"Oh, no, indeed!" she simpered. "That wouldn't be becoming in me. I'm only responding to your own words."

Rising, he said sternly, "No power on earth could induce me to marry you, and that would be plain enough if you were in your right mind. I shall not stand this foolishness another moment. You must go with me at once to Lemuel Weeks'. If you will not I'll have you taken to an insane asylum."

"To an insane asylum! What for?" she half shrieked, springing to her feet.

"You'll see," he replied, going down the steps. "Jump up, Jane! I shall take the trunk to your cousin's. If you are so crazy as to stay in a man's house when he don't want you and won't have you, you are fit only for an asylum."

Mrs. Mumpson was sane enough to perceive that she was at the end of her adhesive resources. In his possession of her trunk, the farmer also had a strategic advantage which made it necessary for her to yield. She did so, however, with very bad grace. When he drove up, she bounced into the wagon as if made of india rubber, while Jane followed slowly, with a look of sullen apathy. He touched his horses with the whip into a smart trot, scarcely daring to believe in his good fortune. The lane was rather steep and rough, and he soon had to pull up lest the object of his unhappy solicitude should be jolted out of the vehicle. This gave the widow her chance to open fire. "The end has not come yet, Mr. Holcroft," she said vindictively. "You may think you are going to have an easy triumph over a poor, friendless, unfortunate, sensitive, afflicted woman and a fatherless child, but you shall soon learn that there's a law in the land. You have addressed improper words to me, you have threatened me, you have broken your agreement. I have writings, I have a memory, I have language to plead the cause of the widow and the fatherless. I have been wronged, outraged, trampled upon, and then turned out of doors. The indignant world shall hear my story, the finger of scorn will be pointed at you. Your name will become a byword and a hissing. Respecterble women, respecterbly connected, will stand aloof and shudder."

The torrent of words was unchecked except when the wheels struck a stone, jolting her so severely that her jaws came together with a click as if she were snapping at him.

He made no reply whatever, but longed to get his hands upon Lemuel Weeks. Pushing his horses to a

high rate of speed, he soon reached that intereste
neighbor's door, intercepting him just as he was starting
to town.

He looked very sour as he saw his wife's relatives, and
demanded harshly, " What does this mean ? "

" It means," cried Mrs. Mumpson in her high, cackling
tones, " that he's said things and done things too awfu
to speak of ; that he's broken his agreement and turned
us out of doors."

" Jim Holcroft," said Mr. Weeks, blustering up to the
wagon, "you can't carry on with this high hand. Take
these people back to your house where they belong, or
you'll be sorry."

Holcroft sprung out, whirled Mr. Weeks out of his
way, took out the trunk, then with equal expedition and
no more ceremony lifted down Mrs. Mumpson and Jane.

" Do you know what you're about ? " shouted Mr.
Weeks in a rage. " I'll have the law on you this very
day."

Holcroft maintained his ominous silence as he hitched
his horses securely. Then he strode toward Weeks, who
backed away from him. " Oh, don't be afraid ! you
sneaking, cowardly fox," said the farmer bitterly. " If
I gave you your deserts, I'd take my horsewhip to you.
You're going to law me, are you ? Well, begin to-day,
and I'll be ready for you. I won't demean myself by
answering that woman, but I'm ready for you in any
way you've a mind to come. I'll put you and your wife
on the witness stand. I'll summon Cousin Abiram, as
you call him, and his wife, and compel you all under oath
to give Mrs. Mumpson a few testimonials. I'll prove the
trick you played on me and the lies you told. I'll prove
that this woman, in my absence, invaded my room, and

with keys of her own opened my dead wife's bureau and pulled out her things. I'll prove that she hasn't earned her salt and can't, and may prove something more. Now, if you want to go to law, begin. Nothing would please me better than to show up you and your tribe. I've offered to pay this woman her three months' wages in full and so have kept my agreement. She has not kept hers, for she's only sat in a rocking chair and made trouble. Now, do as you please. I'll give you all the law you want. I'd like to add a horsewhipping, but that would give you a case and now you haven't any."

As Holcroft uttered these words sternly and slowly, like a man angry indeed but under perfect self-control, the perspiration broke out on Weeks' face. He was aware that Mrs. Mumpson was too well known to play the rôle of a wronged woman, and remembered what his testimony and that of many others would be under oath. Therefore, he began, "Oh, well, Mr. Holcroft! there's no need of your getting in such a rage and threatening so; I'm willing to talk the matter over and only want to do the square thing."

The farmer made a gesture of disgust as he said, "I understand you, Lemuel Weeks. There's no talking needed and I'm in no mood for it. Here's the money I agreed to pay. I'll give it to Mrs. Mumpson when she has signed this paper, and you've signed as witness of her signature. Otherwise, it's law. Now decide quick. I'm in a hurry."

Objections were interposed, and Holcroft, returning the money to his pocket, started for his team, without a word. "Oh, well!" said Weeks in strong irritation, "I haven't time for a lawsuit at this season of the year. You are both cranks, and I suppose it would be best for me and my folks to be rid of you both. It's a pity, though, you couldn't be married and left to fight it out."

Holcroft took the whip from his wagon and said quietly, "If you speak another insulting word, I'll horse-whip you and take my chances."

Something in the man's look prevented Weeks from uttering another unnecessary remark. The business was soon transacted, accompanied with Mrs. Mumpson's venomous words, for she had discovered that she could stigmatize Holcroft with impunity. He went to Jane and shook her hand as he said good-by. "I am sorry for *you*, and I won't forget my promise;" then drove rapidly away.

"Cousin Lemuel," said Mrs. Mumpson plaintively, "won't you have Timothy take my trunk to our room?"

"No, I won't," he snapped. "You've had your chance and have fooled it away. I was just going to town, and you and Jane will go along with me," and he put the widow's trunk into his wagon.

Mrs. Weeks came out and wiped her eyes ostentatiously with her apron as she whispered, "I can't help it, Cynthy. When Lemuel goes off the handle in this way, it's no use for me to say anything."

Mrs. Mumpson wept hysterically as she was driven away. Jane's sullen and apathetic aspect had passed away in part, for Holcroft's words had kindled something like hope.

CHAPTER XVII.

A MOMENTOUS DECISION.

IT must be admitted that Holcroft enjoyed his triumph over Lemuel Weeks very much after the fashion of the aboriginal man. Indeed, he was almost sorry he had not been given a little more provocation, knowing well that, had this been true, his neighbor would have received a fuller return for his interested efforts. As he saw his farmhouse in the shimmering April sunlight, as the old churning dog came forward, wagging his tail, the farmer said, " This is the only place which can ever be home to me. Well, well! it's queer about people. Some, when they go, leave you desolate ; others make you happy by their absence. I never dreamed that silly Mumpson could make me happy, but she has. Blessed if I don't feel happy ! The first time in a year or more !" and he began to whistle old " Coronation " in the most lively fashion as he unharnessed his horses.

A little later, he prepared himself a good dinner and ate it in leisurely enjoyment, sharing a morsel now and then with the old dog. " You're a plaguey sight better company than she was," he mused. " That poor little stray cat of a Jane ! What will become of her ? Well, well ! soon as she's old enough to cut loose from her mother I'll try to give her a chance, if it's a possible thing."

After dinner, he made a rough draught of an auction bill, offering his cows for sale, muttering as he did so "Tom Watterly 'll help me put it in better shape." Then he drove a mile away to see old Mr. and Mrs. Johnson. The former agreed for a small sum to mount guard with his dog during the farmer's occasional absences, and the latter readily consented to do the washing and mending

"What do I want of any more 'peculiar females,' as that daft widow called 'em?" he chuckled on his return. "Blamed if she wasn't the most peculiar of the lot. Think of me marrying her!" and the hillside echoed to his derisive laugh. "As I feel to-day, there's a better chance of my being struck by lightning than marrying, and I don't think any woman could do it in spite of me. I'll run the ranch alone."

That evening he smoked his pipe cheerfully beside the kitchen fire, the dog sleeping at his feet. "I declare," he said smilingly, "I feel quite at home."

In the morning, after attending to his work, he went for old Jonathan Johnson and installed him in charge of the premises; then drove to the almshouse with all the surplus butter and eggs on hand. Tom Watterly arrived at the door with his fast-trotting horse at the same time and cried, "Hollo, Jim! just in time. I'm a sort of grass widower to-day—been taking my wife out to see her sister. Come in and take pot-luck with me and keep up my spirits."

"Well, now, Tom," said Holcroft, shaking hands. "I'm glad, not that your wife's away, although it does make me downhearted to contrast your lot and mine, but I'm glad you can give me a little time, for I want to use that practical head of yours—some advice, you know."

"All right. Nothing to do for an hour or two but eat

dinner and smoke my pipe with you. Here, Bill! take this team and feed 'em."

"Hold on," said Holcroft. "I'm not going to sponge on you. I've got some favors to ask, and I want you to take in return some butter half spoiled in the making and this basket of eggs. They're all right."

"Go to thunder, Holcroft! what do you take me for? When you've filled your pipe after dinner will you pull an egg out of your pocket and say, 'That's for a smoke'? No, no, I don't sell any advice to old friends like you. I'll buy your butter and eggs at what they're worth and have done with 'em. Business is one thing, and sitting down and talking over an old crony's troubles is another. I'm not a saint. Jim, as you know—a man in politics can't be—but I remember when we were boys together, and somehow thinking of those old days always fetches me. Come in, for dinner is a-waiting, I guess."

"Well, Tom, saint or no saint, I'd like to vote for you for gov'nor."

"This aint an electioneering trick, as you know. I can play them off as well as the next feller when there's need, kiss the babies and all that."

Dinner was placed on the table immediately, and in a few moments the friends were left alone. Then Holcroft related in a half comic, half serious manner his tribulations with the help. Tom sat back in his chair and roared at the account of the pitched battle between the two widows and the final smoking out of Mrs. Mumpson, but he reproached his friend for not having horsewhipped Lemuel Weeks. "Don't you remember, Jim, he was a sneaking, tricky chap when we were at school together? I licked him once, and it always does me good to think of it."

" I own it takes considerable to rile me to the point of striking a man, especially on his own land. His wife was looking out the window, too. If we'd been out in the road or anywhere else—but what's the use? I'm glad now it turned out as it has, for I've too much on my mind for lawsuits, and the less one has to do with such cattle as Weeks the better. Well, you see I'm alone again, and I'm going to go it alone. I'm going to sell my cows and give up the dairy, and the thing I wanted help in most is the putting this auction bill in shape; also advice as to whether I had better try to sell here in town or up at the farm,"

Tom shook his head dubiously and scarcely glanced at the paper. " Your scheme don't look practical to me," he said. " I don't believe you can run that farm alone without losing money. You'll just keep on going behind till the first thing you know you'll clap a mortgage on it. Then you'll soon be done for. What's more, you'll break down if you try to do both outdoor and indoor work. Busy times will soon .come, and you won't get your meals regularly ; you'll be living on coffee and anything that comes handiest ; your house will grow untidy and not fit to live in. If you should be taken sick, there'd be no one to do for you. Lumbermen, hunters, and such fellows can rough it alone awhile, but I never heard of a farm being run by man-power alone. Now as to selling out your stock, look at it. Grazing is what your farm's good for mostly. It's a pity you're so bent on staying there. Even if you didn't get very much for the place, from sale or rent, you'd have something that was sure. A strong, capable man like you could find something to turn your hand to. Then you could board in some respectable family, and not have to live like Robinson Crusoe. I've thought it over since we talked last, and if I was you I'd sell or rent."

"It's too late in the season to do either," said Holcroft dejectedly. "What's more, I don't want to, at least not this year. I've settled that, Tom. I'm going to have one more summer on the old place, anyway, if I have to live on bread and milk."

"You can't make bread."

"I'll have it brought from town on the stage."

"Well, it's a pity some good, decent woman—— There, how should I come to forget all about *her* till this minute? I don't know whether it would work. Perhaps it would. There's a woman here out of the common run. She has quite a story, which I'll tell you in confidence. Then you can say whether you'd like to employ her or not. If you *will* stay on the farm, my advice is that you have a woman to do the housework, and me and Angy must try to find you one, if the one I have in mind won't answer. The trouble is, Holcroft, to get the right kind of a woman to live there alone with you, unless you married her. Nice women don't like to be talked about, and I don't blame 'em. The one that's here, though, is so friendless and alone in the world that she might be glad enough to get a home almost anywheres."

"Well, well! tell me about her," said Holcroft gloomily. "But I'm about discouraged in the line of women help."

Watterly told Alida's story with a certain rude pathos which touched the farmer's naturally kind heart, and he quite forgot his own need in indignation at the poor woman's wrongs. "Its a —— shame!" he said excitedly, pacing the room. "I say, Tom, all the law in the land wouldn't keep me from giving that fellow a whipping or worse."

"Well, she won't prosecute; she won't face the public; she just wants to go to some quiet place and work for her bread. She don't seem to have any friends, or else she's too ashamed to let them know."

"Why, of course I'd give such a woman a refuge till she could do better. What man wouldn't?"

"A good many wouldn't. What's more, if she went with you her story might get out, and you'd both be talked about."

"I don't care that for gossip," with a snap of his fingers. "You know I'd treat her with respect."

"What I know, and what other people would say, are two very different things. Neither you nor anyone else can go too strongly against public opinion. Still, it's nobody's business," added Tom thoughtfully. 'Perhaps it's worth the trial. If she went I think she'd stay and do the best by you she could. Would you like to see her?"

"Yes."

Alida was summoned and stood with downcast eyes in the door. "Come in and take a chair," said Tom kindly. "You know I promised to be on the lookout for a good place for you. Well, my friend here, Mr. Holcroft, whom I've known ever since I was a boy, wants a woman to do general housework and take care of the dairy."

She gave the farmer one of those swift, comprehensive glances by which women take in a personality, and said in a tone of regret, "But I don't understand dairy work."

"Oh, you'd soon learn. It's just the kind of a place you said you wanted, a lonely, out-of-the-way farm and no other help kept. What's more, my friend Holcroft is a kind, honest man. He'd treat you right. He knows all about your trouble and is sorry for you."

If Holcroft had been an ogre in appearance, he would have received the grateful glance which she now gave him as she said, "I'd be only too glad to work for you, sir, if you think I can do, or learn to do, what is required."

Holcroft, while his friend was speaking, had studied closely Alida's thin, pale face, and he saw nothing in it not in harmony with the story he had heard. "I am sorry for you," he said kindly. "I believe you never meant to do wrong and have tried to do right. I will be perfectly honest with you. My wife is dead, the help I had has left me, and I live alone in the house. The truth is, too, that I could not afford to keep two in help, and there would not be work for them both."

Alida had learned much in her terrible adversity, and had, moreover, the instincts of a class superior to the position she was asked to take. She bowed low to hide the burning flush that crimsoned her pale cheeks as she faltered, "It may seem strange to you, sirs, that one situated as I am should hesitate, but I have never knowingly done anything which gave people the right to speak against me. I do not fear work, I would humbly try to do my best, but——" She hesitated and rose as if to retire.

"I understand you," said Holcroft kindly, "and I don't blame you for doing what you think is right."

"I'm very sorry, sir," she replied, tears coming into her eyes as she went out of the room.

"There it is, Holcroft," said Tom. "I believe she's just the one for you, but you can see she isn't of the common kind. She knows as well as you and me how people would talk, especially if her story came out, as like enough it will."

"Hang people!" snarled the farmer.

"Yes, a good lot of 'em deserve hanging, but it wouldn't help you any just now. Perhaps she'd go with you if you got another girl or took an old woman from the house here to keep her company."

"I'm sick to death of such hags," said the farmer with an impatient gesture. Then he sat down and looked at his friend as if a plan was forming in his mind of which he scarcely dare speak.

"Well, out with it!" said Tom.

"Have you ever seen a marriage ceremony performed by a justice of the peace?" Holcroft asked slowly.

"No, but they do it often enough. What! are you going to offer her marriage?"

"You say she is homeless and friendless?"

"Yes."

"And you believe she is just what she seems—just what her story shows her to be?"

"Yes. I've seen too many frauds to be taken in. She isn't a fraud. Neither does she belong to that miserable, wishy-washy, downhill class that sooner or later fetches up in a poorhouse. They say we're all made of dust, but some seem made of mud. You could see she was out of the common; and she's here on account of the wrong she received and not the wrong she did. I say all this in fairness to her; but when it comes to marrying her, that's another question."

"Tom, as I've told you, I don't want to marry. In fact, I couldn't go before a minister and promise what I'd have to. But I could do something like this. I could give this woman an honest name and a home. It would would be marriage before the law. No one could ever say a word against either of us. I would be true and kind to her and she should share in my fortunes. That's all. You have often advised me to marry, and you know if I did it couldn't be anything else but a business affair. Then it ought to be done in a businesslike way. You say I can't get along alone, and like enough you're right. I've learned more from this woman's manner than I have in a year why I can't get and keep the right kind of help, and I now feel if I could find a good, honest woman who would make my interests hers, and help me make a living in my own home, I'd give her my name and all the security which an honest name conveys. Now, this poor woman is in sore need and she might be grateful for what I can do, while any other woman would naturally expect me to promise more than I honestly can. Anyhow, I'd have to go through the form, and I can't and won't go and say sacred words—just about what I said when I married my wife—and know all the time I was lying."

"Well, Holcroft, you're a queer dick and this is a queer plan of yours. You're beyond my depth now and I can't advise."

"Why is it a queer plan? Things only seem odd because they are not common. As a matter of fact, you advise a business marriage. When I try to follow your advice honestly and not dishonestly, you say I'm queer."

"I suppose if everybody became honest, it would be the queerest world ever known," said Tom, laughing. "Well, you might do worse than marry this woman. I can tell you that marrying is risky business at best. You know a justice will tie you just as tight as a minister, and while I've given you my impression about this woman, I *know* little about her and you know next to nothing."

"I guess that would be the case, anyhow. If you set

out to find a wife for me, where is there a woman that you actually do know more about? As for my going here and there, to get acquainted, it's out of the question. All my feelings rise up against such a course. Now, I feel sorry for this woman. She has at least my sympathy. If she is as friendless, poor, and unhappy as she seems, I might do her as great a kindness as she would do for me if she could take care of my home. I wouldn't expect very much. It would be a comfort just to have some-one in the house that wouldn't rob or waste, and who, knowing what her station was, would be content. Of course I'd have to talk it over with her and make my purpose clear. She might agree with you that it's too queer to be thought of. If so, that would be the end of it."

"Well, Jim, you always finish by half talking me over to your side of a question. Now, if my wife was home, I don't believe she'd listen to any such plan."

"No, I suppose she wouldn't. She'd believe in people marrying and doing everything in the ordinary way. But neither I nor this woman is in ordinary circumstances. Do you know of a justice?"

"Yes, and you know him, too; Justice Harkins."

"Why, certainly. He came from our town and I knew him when he was a boy, although I haven't seen much of him of late years."

"Well, shall I go and say to this woman—Alida Armstrong is her name now, I suppose—that you wish to see her again?"

"Yes, I shall tell her the truth. Then she can decide."

CHAPTER XVIII.

HOLCROFT GIVES HIS HAND.

ALIDA was seated by a window with some of the mending in which she assisted, and, as usual, was apart by herself. Watterly entered the large apartment quietly, and at first she did not observe him. He had time to note that she was greatly dejected, and when she saw him she hastily wiped tears from her eyes.

"You are a good deal cast down, Alida," he said, watching her closely.

"I've reason to be. I don't see any light ahead at all."

"Well, you know the old saying, 'It's darkest before day.' I want you to come with me again. I think I've found a chance for you."

She arose with alacrity and followed. As soon as they were alone, he turned and looked her squarely in the face as he said gravely, "You have good common sense, haven't you?"

"I don't know, sir," she faltered, perplexed and troubled by the question.

"Well, you can understand this much, I suppose. As superintendent of this house I have a responsible position, which I could easily lose if I allowed myself to be mixed up with anything wrong or improper. To come right to the point, you don't know much about me and next to nothing of my friend Holcroft, but can't you see that even if I was a heartless, good-for-nothing fellow, it wouldn't be wise or safe for me to permit anything that wouldn't bear the light ? "

" I think you are an honest man, sir. It would be strange if I did not have confidence when you have judged me and treated me so kindly. But, Mr. Watterly, although helpless and friendless, I must try to do what I think is best. If I accepted Mr. Holcroft's position it might do him harm. You know how quick the world is to misjudge. It would seem to confirm everything that has been said against me," and the same painful flush again overspread her features.

" Well, Alida, all that you have to do is to listen patiently to my friend. Whether you agree with his views or not, you will see that he is a good-hearted, honest man. I want to prepare you for this talk by assuring you that I've known him since he was a boy, that he has lived all his life in this region and is known by many others, and that I wouldn't dare let him ask you to do anything wrong, even if I was bad enough."

" I'm sure, sir, you don't wish me any harm," she again faltered in deep perplexity.

" Indeed I don't. I don't advise my friend's course ; neither do I oppose it. He's certainly old enough to act for himself. I suppose I'm a rough counselor for a young woman, but since you appear to have so few friends I'm inclined to act as one. Just you stand on the question of right and wrong, and dismiss from your mind all foolish notions of what people will say. As a rule, all the people in the world can't do as much for us as somebody in particular. Now you go in the parlor and listen like a sensible woman. I'll be reading the paper, and the girl will be clearing off the table in the next room here."

Puzzled and trembling, Alida entered the apartment where Holcroft was seated. She was so embarrassed that she could not lift her eyes to him.

"Please sit down," he said gravely, "and don't be troubled, much less frightened. You are just as free to act as ever you were in your life."

She sat down near the door and compelled herself to look at him, for she felt instinctively that she might gather more from the expression of his face than from his words.

"Alida Armstrong is your name, Mr. Watterly tells me ?"

"Yes, sir."

"Well, Alida, I want to have a plain business talk with you. That's nothing to be nervous and worried about, you know. As I told you, I've heard your story. It has made me sorry for you instead of setting me against you. It has made me respect you as a right-minded woman, and I shall give you good proof that my words are true. At the same time, I shan't make any false pretenses to what isn't true and couldn't be true. Since I've heard your story, it's only fair you should hear mine, and I ought to tell it first."

He went over the past very briefly until he came to the death of his wife. There was simple and homely pathos in the few sentences with which he referred to this event. Then more fully he enlarged upon his efforts and failure to keep house with hired help. Unconsciously, he had taken the best method to enlist her sympathy. The secluded cottage and hillside farm became realities to her fancy. She saw how the man's heart clung to his home, and his effort to keep it touched her deeply.

"Oh!" she thought, "I do wish there was some way

for me to go there. The loneliness of the place which drove others away is the chief attraction for me. Then it would be pleasant to work for such a man and make his home comfortable for him. It's plain from his words and looks that he's as honest and straightforward as the day is long. He only wants to keep his home and make his living in peace."

As he had talked her nervous embarrassment passed away, and the deep sense of her own need was pressing upon her again. She saw that he also was in great need. His business talk was revealing deep trouble and perplexity. With the quick intuitions of a woman, her mind went far beyond his brief sentences and saw all the difficulties of his lot. His feeling reference to the loss of his wife proved that he was not a coarse-natured man. As he spoke so plainly of his life during the past year, her mind was insensibly abstracted from everything but his want and hers, and she thought his farmhouse afforded just the secluded refuge she craved. As he drew near the end of his story and hesitated in visible embarrassment, she mustered courage to say timidly, "Would you permit a suggestion from me ?"

" Why, certainly."

" You have said, sir, that your business and means would not allow you to keep two in help, and as you have been speaking I have tried to think of some way. The fact that your house is so lonely is just the reason why I should like to work in it. As you can understand, I have no wish to meet strangers. Now, sir, I am willing to work for very little ; I should be glad to find such a quiet refuge for simply my board and clothes, and I would do my very best and try to learn what I did not know. It seems to me that if I worked for so little you might think

ou could afford to hire some elderly woman also ? " and
he looked at him in the eager hope that he would accept
er proposition.

He shook his head as he replied, " I don't know of any
uch person. I took the best one in this house, and you
now how she turned out."

" Perhaps Mr. Watterly may know of someone else,"
he faltered. She was now deeply troubled and per-
lexed again, supposing that he was about to renew his
irst proposition that she should be his only help.

" If Mr. Watterly did know of anyone I would make
he trial, but he does not. Your offer is very considerate
nd reasonable, but "—and he hesitated again, scarcely
nowing how to go on.

" I am sorry, sir," she said, rising, as if to end the
nterview.

" Stay," he said, " you do not understand me yet. Of
ourse I should not make you the same offer that I did at
irst, after seeing your feeling about it, and I respect you
ll the more because you so respect yourself. What I
ad in mind was to give you my name, and it's an honest
ame. If we were married it would be perfectly proper
or you to go with me, and no one could say a word
gainst either of us."

" Oh ! " she gasped, in strong agitation and surprise.

" Now don't be so taken aback. It's just as easy for
ou to refuse as it is to speak, but listen first. What
eems strange and unexpected may be the most sensible
hing for us both. You have your side of the case to
hink of just as truly as I have mine ; and I'm not for-
getting, and I don't ask you to forget, that I'm still talk-
ng business. You and I have both been through too
much trouble and loss to say any silly nonsense to each

other. You've heard my story, yet I'm almost a stranger to you as you are to me. We'd both have to take considerable on trust. Yet I know I'm honest and well-meaning, and I believe you are. Now look at it. Here we are, both much alone in the world—both wishing to live a retired, quiet life. I don't care a rap for what people say as long as I'm doing right, and in this case they'd have nothing to say. It's our own business. I don't see as people will ever do much for you, and a good many would impose on you and expect you to work beyond your strength. They might not be very kind or considerate, either. I suppose you've thought of this?"

"Yes," she replied with bowed head. "I should meet coldness, probably harshness and scorn."

"Well, you'd never meet anything of the kind in my house. I would treat you with respect and kindness. At the same time, I'm not going to mislead you by a word. You shall have a chance to decide in view of the whole truth. My friend, Mr. Watterly, has asked me more'n once, 'Why don't you marry again?' I told him I had been married once, and that I couldn't go before a minister and promise the same things over again when they wasn't true. I can't make to you any promises or say any words that are not true, and I don't ask or expect you to do what I can't do. But it has seemed to me that our condition was out of the common lot—that we could take each other for just what we might be to each other and no more. You would be my wife in name, and I do not ask you to be my wife in more than name. You would thus secure a good home and the care and protection of one who would be kind to you, and I would secure a housekeeper—one that would stay with me and make my interests hers. It would be a fair, square arrangement between ourselves, and nobody else's business. By taking this course, we don't do any wrong to our feelings or have to say or promise anything that isn't true."

" Yet I can't help saying, sir," she replied, in strong, yet repressed agitation, "that your words sound very strange; and it seems stranger still that you can offer marriage of any kind to a woman situated as I am. You know my story, sir," she added, crimsoning, "and all may soon know it. You would suffer wrong and injury."

" I offer you open and honorable marriage before the world, and no other kind. Mr. Watterly and others—as many as you pleased—would witness it, and I'd have you given a certificate at once. As for your story, it has only awakened my sympathy. You have not meant to do any wrong. Your troubles are only another reason in my mind for not taking any advantage of you or deceiving you in the least. Look the truth squarely in the face. I'm bent on keeping my house and getting my living as I have done, and I need a housekeeper that will be true to all my interests. Think how I've been robbed and wronged, and what a dog's life I've lived in my own home. You need a home, a support, and a protector. I couldn't come to you or go to any other woman and say honestly more than this. Isn't it better for people to be united on the ground of truth than to begin by telling a pack of lies ? "

" But—but can people be married with such an understanding by a minister ? Wouldn't it be deceiving him ? "

" I shall not ask you to deceive anyone. Any marriage that either you or I could now make would be practically a business marriage. I should therefore take you, if you were willing, to a justice and have a legal or civil marriage performed, and this would be just as binding as any other in the eye of the law. It is often done. This would be much better to my mind than if people, situated as we are, went to a church or a minister."

" Yes, yes, I couldn't do that."

" Well, now, Alida," he said, with a smile that wonderfully softened his rugged features, " you are free to decide. It may seem to you a strange sort of courtship, but we are both too old for much foolishness. I never was sentimental, and it would be ridiculous to begin now. I'm full of trouble and perplexity, and so are you. Are you willing to be my wife so far as an honest name goes, and help me make a living for us both ? That's all I ask. I, in my turn, would promise to treat you with kindness and respect, and give you a home as long as I lived and to leave you all I have in the world if I died. That's all I could promise. I'm a lonely, quiet man, and like to be by myself. I wouldn't be much society for you. I've said more to-day than I might in a month, for I felt that it was due to you to know just what you were doing."

" Oh, sir," said Alida, trembling, and with tears in her eyes, " you do not ask much and you offer a great deal. If you, a strong man, dread to leave your home and go out into the world you know not where, think how terrible it is for a weak, friendless woman to be worse than homeless. I have lost everything, even my good name."

" No, no ! not in my eyes."

" Oh, I know, I know !" she cried, wringing her hands. " Even these miserable paupers like myself have made me feel it. They have burned the truth into my brain and heart. Indeed, sir, you do not realize what you are doing or asking. It is not fit or meet that I should bear your name. You might be sorry, indeed."

" Alida," said Holcroft gravely, " I've not forgotten

your story, and you shouldn't forget mine. Be sensible now. Don't I look old enough to know what I'm about?"

"Oh, oh, oh!" she cried impetuously, "if I were only sure it was right! It may be business to you, but it seems like life or death to me. It's more than death—I don't fear that—but I do fear life, I do fear the desperate struggle just to maintain a bare, dreary existence. I do dread going out among strangers and seeing their cold curiosity and their scorn. You can't understand a woman's heart. It isn't right for me to die till God takes me, but life has seemed so horrible, meeting suspicion on one side and cruel, significant looks of knowledge on the other. I've been tortured even here by these wretched hags, and I've envied even them, so near to death, yet not ashamed like me. I know, and you should know, that my heart is broken, crushed, trampled into the mire. I had felt that for me even the thought of marriage again would be a mockery, a wicked thing, which I would never have a right to entertain. I never dreamt that anyone would think of such a thing, knowing what you know. Oh, oh! why have you tempted me so if it is not right? I must do right. The feeling that I've not meant to do wrong is all that has kept me from despair. But can it be right to let you take me from the street, the poorhouse, with nothing to give but a blighted name, a broken heart and feeble hands! See, I am but the shadow of what I was, and a dark shadow at that. I could be only a dismal shadow at any man's hearth. Oh, oh! I've thought and suffered until my reason seemed going. You don't realize, you don't know the depths into which I've fallen. It can't be right."

Holcroft was almost appalled at this passionate outburst

in one who thus far had been sad, indeed, yet self-controlled. He looked at her in mingled pity and consternation. His own troubles had seemed heavy enough, but he now caught glimpses of something far beyond trouble—of agony, of mortal dread that bordened on despair. He could scarcely comprehend how terrible to a woman like Alida were the recent events of her life, and how circumstances, with illness, had all tended to create a morbid horror of her situation. Like himself she was naturally reticent in regard to her deeper feelings, patient and undemonstrative. Had not his words evoked this outburst she might have suffered and died in silence, but in this final conflict between conscience and hope, the hot lava of her heart had broken forth. So little was he then able to understand her, that suspicions crossed his mind. Perhaps his friend Watterly had not heard the true story or else not the whole story. But his straightforward simplicity stood him in good stead, and he said gently, "Alida, you say I don't know, I don't realize. I believe you will tell me the truth. You went to a minister and was married to a man that you thought you had a right to marry——"

"You shall know it all from my own lips," she said, interrupting him; "you have a right to know; and then you will see that it cannot be," and with bowed head, and low, rapid, passionate utterance, she poured out her story. "That woman, his wife," she concluded, "made me feel that I was of the scum and offscouring of the earth, and they've made me feel so here, too—even these wretched paupers. So the world will look on me till God takes me to my mother. Oh, thank God! she don't know. Don't you see, now?" she asked, raising her despairing eyes, from which agony had dried all tears.

"Yes, I see you do," she added desperately, "for even you have turned from me."

"Confound it!" cried Holcroft, standing up and searching his pockets for a handkerchief, "I—I—I'd like—like to choke that fellow. If I could get my hands on him, there'd be trouble. Turn away from you, you poor wronged creature! Don't you see I'm so sorry for you that I'm making a fool of myself? I, who couldn't shed a tear over my own troubles—there, there—come now, let us be sensible. Let's get back to business, for I can't stand this kind of thing at all. I'm so confused betwixt rage at him and pity for you—— Let me see; this is where we were: I want someone to take care of my home, and you want a home. That's all there is about it now. If you say so, I'll make you Mrs. Holcroft in an hour."

"I did not mean to work upon your sympathies, only to tell you the truth. God bless you! that the impulses of your heart are so kind and merciful. But let me be true to you as well as to myself. Go away and think it all over calmly and quietly. Even for the sake of being rescued from a life that I dread far more than death, I cannot let you do that which you may regret unspeakably. Do not think I misunderstand your offer. It's the only one I could think of, and I would not have thought of it if you had not spoken. I have no heart to give. I could be a wife only in name, but I could work like a slave for protection from a cruel, jeering world; I could hope for something like peace and respite from suffering if I only had a safe refuge. But I must not have these if it is not right and best. Good to me must not come through wrong to you."

"Tush! tush! you mustn't talk so. I can't stand it at

all. I've heard your story. It's just as I supposed at first, only a great deal more so. Why, of course it's all right. It makes me believe in Providence, it all turns out so entirely for our mutual good. I can do as much to help you as you to help me. Now let's get back on the sensible, solid ground from which we started. The idea of my wanting you to work like a slave! Like enough some people would, and then you'd soon break down and be brought back here again. No, no; I've explained just what I wish and just what I mean. You must get over the notion that I'm a sentimental fool, carried away by my feelings. How Tom Watterly would laugh at the idea! My mind is made up now just as much as it would be a week hence. This is no place for you, and I don't like to think of your being here. My spring work is pressing, too. Don't you see that by doing what I ask you can set me right on my feet and start me uphill again after a year of miserable downhill work? You have only to agree to what I've said, and you will be at home to-night and I'll be quietly at my work to-morrow. Mr. Watterly will go with us to the justice, who has known me all my life. Then, if anyone ever says a word against you he'll have me to settle with. Come, Alida! here's a strong hand that's able to take care of you."

She hesitated a moment, then clasped it like one who is sinking, and before he divined her purpose, she kissed and bedewed it with tears.

CHAPTER XIX.

A BUSINESS MARRIAGE.

WHILE Holcroft's sympathies had been deeply touched by the intense emotion of gratitude which had overpowered Alida, he had also been disturbed and rendered somewhat anxious. He was actually troubled lest the woman he was about to marry should speedily begin to love him, and develop a tendency to manifest her affection in a manner that would seem to him extravagant and certainly disagreeable. Accustomed all his life to repress his feelings, he wondered at himself and could not understand how he had given way so unexpectedly. He was not sufficiently versed in human nature to know that the depth of Alida's distress was the adequate cause. If there had been a false or an affected word, he would have remained cool enough. In his inability to gauge his own nature as well as hers, he feared lest this businesslike marriage was verging toward sentiment on her part. He did not like her kissing his hand. He was profoundly sorry for her, but so he would have been for any other woman suffering under the burden of a great wrong. He felt that it would be embarrassing if she entertained sentiments toward him which he could not reciprocate, and open manifestations of regard would remind him of that horror of his life, Mrs. Mumpson. He was not incapable of quick, strong sympathy in any instance of genuine trouble, but he was one of those men who would shrink in natural recoil from any marked evidence of a woman's preference unless the counterpart of her regard existed in his own breast.

To a woman of Alida's intuition the way in which he withdrew his hand and the expression of his face had a world of meaning. She would not need a second hint. Yet she did not misjudge him; she knew that he meant what he had said and had said all that he meant. She was also aware that he had not and never could understand the depths of fear and suffering from which his hand was lifting her. Her gratitude was akin to that of a lost soul saved, and that was all she had involuntarily expressed. She sat down again and quietly dried her eyes, while in her heart she purposed to show her gratitude by patient assiduity in learning to do what he required.

Holcroft was now bent upon carrying out his plan as quickly as possible and returning home. He therefore asked, "Can you go with me at once, Alida?"

She simply bowed her acquiescence.

"That's sensible. Perhaps you had better get your things ready while I and Mr. Watterly go and arrange with Justice Harkins."

Alida averted her face with a sort of shame which a woman feels who admits such a truth. "I haven't anything, sir, but a hat and cloak to put on. I came away and left everything."

"And I'm glad of it," said Holcroft heartily. "I wouldn't want you to bring anything which that scoundrel gave you." He paced the room thoughtfully a moment or two and then called Watterly in. "It's settled, Tom. Alida will be Mrs. Holcroft as soon as we

can see the justice. Do you think we could persuade him
to come here ? "

" One thing at a time. Mrs. Holcroft,—I may as well
call you so, for when my friend says he'll do a thing he
does it,—I congratulate you. I think you are well out of
your troubles. Since you are to marry my old friend, we
must be friends, too," and he shook her heartily by the
hand.

His words and manner were another ray of light—
a welcome rift in the black pall that had gathered round
her.

" You were the first friend I found, sir, after—what
happened," she said gratefully.

" Well, you've found another and a better one ; and
he'll always be just the same. Any woman might be
glad——"

" Come, Tom, no more of that. I'm a plain old
farmer that does what he agrees, and that's all there is
about it. I've told Alida just what I wished and could
do——"

" I should hope so," interrupted Watterly, laughing.
" You've taken time enough, certainly, and I guess you've
talked more than you have before in a year."

" Yes, I know I'm almost as bad as an oyster about
talking except when I'm with you. Somehow, we've
always had a good deal to say to each other. In this
case, I felt that it was due to Alida that she should know
all about me and understand fully just how I felt concerning this marriage. The very fact that she hasn't friends
to advise her made it all the more needful that I should
be plain and not mislead her in any respect. She has
just as good a right to judge and act for herself as any
woman in the land, and she takes me, and I take her, with

no sentimental lies to start with. Now let's get back to business. I rather think, since Harkins was an old acquaintance of mine, he'll come up here and marry us, don't you? Alida, wouldn't you rather be married here quietly than face a lot of strangers? You can have your own way. I don't care now if half the town was present."

"Oh, yes, indeed, sir! I don't want to meet strangers—and—and—I'm not very strong yet. I thank you for considering my feelings so kindly."

"Why, that's my duty," replied the farmer. "Come, Watterly, the sun is getting low, and we've considerable to do yet before we start home."

"I'm with you. Now, Alida, you go back quietly and act as if nothing had happened till I send for you. Of course this impatient young groom will hurry back with the justice as fast as possible. Still, we may not find him, or he may be so busy that we shall have to come back for you and take you to his office."

As she turned to leave the room, Holcroft gave her his hand and said kindly, "Now don't you be nervous or worried. I see you are not strong, and you shall not be taxed any more than I can help. Good-by for a little while."

Meantime Watterly stepped out a moment and gave his domestic a few orders; then he accompanied Holcroft to the barn, and the horses were soon attached to the market wagon. "You're in for it now, Jim, sure enough," he said, laughing. "What will Angy say to it all?"

"Tell her that I say you've been a mighty good friend to me, yet I hope I may never return any favors of the same kind."

"By jocks! I hope not. I guess it's just as well she

was away. She'll think we've acted just like two harum-scarum men, and will be awfully scandalized over your marrying this woman. Don't you feel a little nervous about it?"

"No! When my mind's made up, I don't worry. Nobody else need lie awake, for it's my affair."

"Well, Jim, you know how I feel about it, but I've got to say something and I might as well say it plain."

"That's the only way you ought to say it."

"Well, you talked long enough to give me plenty of time to think. One thing is clear, Angy won't take to this marriage. You know I'd like to have you both come in and take a meal as you always have done, but then a man must keep peace with his wife, and——"

"I understand, Tom. We won't come till Mrs. Watterly asks us."

"But you won't have hard feelings?"

"No, indeed. Aint you doing your level best as a friend?"

"Well, you know women are so set about these things, and Angy is rather hard on people who don't come up to her mark of respectability. What's more, I suppose you'll find that others will think and act as she does. If you cared about people's opinions I should have been dead against it, but as you feel and are situated, I'm hanged if I don't think she's just the one."

"If it hadn't been this one, I don't believe it would have been anyone. Here we are," and he tied his horses before the office of the justice.

Mr. Harkins greeted Holcroft with a sort of patronizing cordiality, and was good enough to remember that they had been at the little country schoolhouse together. In

Watterly he heartily recognized a brother politician who controlled a goodly number of votes.

When Holcroft briefly made known his errand, the justice gave a great guffaw of laughter and said, " Oh, bring her here! and I'll invite in some of the boys as witnesses."

" I'm not afraid of all the witnesses that you could crowd into a ten-acre lot," said Holcroft somewhat sternly, " but there is no occasion to invite the boys, who-ever they are, or anyone else. She doesn't want to be stared at. I was in hopes, Mr. Harkins, that you'd ride up to the almshouse with us and quietly marry us there."

" Well, I guess you'd better bring her here. I'm pretty busy this afternoon, and—— "

" See here, Ben," said Watterly, taking the justice aside, " Holcroft is my friend, and you know I'm mighty thick with my friends. They count more with me than my wife's relations. Now I want you to do what Holcroft wishes, as a personal favor to me, and the time will come when I can make it up to you."

" Oh, certainly, Watterly! I didn't understand," replied Harkins, who looked upon Holcroft as a close and, as he would phrase it, no-account farmer, from whom he could never expect even a vote. " I'll go with you at once. It's but a short job."

" Well," said Holcroft, " how short can you make it ? "

" Let me get my book," and he took from a shelf the " Justice's Assistant." " You can't want anything shorter than this ? " and he read, " ' By this act of joining hands you do take each other as husband and wife and solemnly engage in the presence of these witnesses to love and honor and comfort and cherish each other as such so long as you both shall live. Therefore, in accordance with the law of the State of New York I do hereby pronounce you husband and wife.' A sailor couldn't tie a knot quicker than that."

"I guess you can, justice," said Holcroft, taking the book. "Suppose you only read this much : ' By this act of joining hands you do take each other as husband and wife. Therefore, in accordance with the law,' etc. Would that be a legal marriage ? "

"Certainly. You'd have to go to a divorce court to get out of that."

"It's my purpose to keep out of courts of all kinds. I'll thank you to read just that much and no more. I don't want to say anything that isn't exactly true."

"You see how it is, Ben. Holcroft hasn't known the woman long, and she's a nice woman, too, if she is boarding at my hotel. Holcroft needs a wife—must have one, in fact, to help run his house and dairy. It wasn't exactly a love match, you know; and he's that kind of a man that a yoke of oxen couldn't draw a word out of him that he didn't mean."

"Yes, yes; I see now," said Harkins. "I'll read just what you say and no more."

"And I'll have a little spread that we can be longer at than the ceremony," added Watterly, who was inclined to be a little hilarious over the affair.

Holcroft, however, maintained his grave manner, and when they reached the almshouse he took Watterly aside and said, "See here, Tom, you've been a good friend to-day and seconded me in everything. Now let the affair pass off just as quietly and seriously as possible. She's too cast down for a gay wedding. Suppose we had a daughter who'd been through such an experience—a nice, good, modest girl. Her heart's too sore for fun and jokes. My marrying her is much the same as pulling her out of deep water in which she was sinking."

"You're right, Jim. I didn't think, and one doesn't have much cause to be so sparing of the feelings of such creatures as come here. But she's out of the common run, and I ought to have remembered it. By jocks you're mighty careful about promising to love, cherish, and obey, and all that, but I guess you'll do a sight more than many who do promise."

"Of course I'm going to be kind. That's my duty. Give Harkins a hint. Tell him that she's lost her mother. He needn't know when the old lady died, but it will kind of solemnize him."

Watterly did as requested, and Harkins, now convinced that his political interests could be furthered by careful compliance with all requirements, put on a grave, official air and was ready for business.

Alida was sent for. She was too agitated to say farewell to any of the poor creatures with whom she had been compelled to associate—even to the few who, though scarcely sane, had manifested tenderness and affection. She had felt that she must reserve all her strength for the coming ordeal, which she both welcomed and feared inexpressibly. She knew how critical was the step she was taking and how much depended on it, yet the more she thought, the more it seemed to her as if Providence had, as by a miracle, given her a refuge. Holcroft's businesslike view of the marriage comforted her greatly, and she asked God to give her health and strength to work faithfully for him many years.

But she had sad misgivings as she followed the messenger, for she felt so weak that she could scarcely walk. It was indeed a pallid, sorrowful, trembling bride that entered Mr. Watterly's parlor. Holcroft met her and, taking her hand, said kindly, "Courage! It will be over in a minute."

She was so pale and agitated that the justice asked, "Do you enter into this marriage freely and without compulsion of any kind?"

"Please let me sit down a moment," she faltered, and Watterly hastened to give her a chair. She fixed her eyes on Holcroft and said anxiously, "You see, sir, how weak I am. I have been sick and—and I fear I am far from being well now. I fear you will be disappointed—that it is not right to you, and that I may not be able——"

"Alida," interrupted Holcroft gravely, "I'm not one to break my word. Home and quiet will soon restore you. Answer the justice and tell him the exact truth."

No elixir could have brought hope and courage like that word "home." She rose at once and said to Harkins, "I have consented to Mr. Holcroft's wishes with feelings of the deepest gratitude."

"Very well. Join hands."

She hesitated and looked for a moment at Holcroft with strange intensity.

"It's all right, Alida," he said with a smile. "Come!"

His perfect honesty and steadfastness of purpose stood him in good stead then, for she came at once to his side and took his hand.

Justice Harkins solemnly opened his big book and read, "'By this act of joining hands you do take each other as husband and wife. Therefore, in accordance with the law of the State of New York, I do hereby pronounce you husband and wife.' That's all."

"I don't think you'll ever be sorry, Alida," said Holcroft, pressing her hand as he led her to a chair. Watterly again bustled up with congratulations, and then said, " You must all come out now to a little supper, and also remember that it was gotten up in a hurry."

The domestic stared at Alida and Holcroft, and then, surmising what had taken place, was so excited that she could scarcely wait on the guests.

Holcroft, with the simple tact which genuine kindness usually suggests, was attentive to his bride, but managed, by no slight effort for him, to engage the two men in general conversation, so that Alida might have time to recover her composure. His quiet, matter-of-fact bearing was reassuring in itself. A cup of strong tea and a little old currant wine, which Watterly insisted on her taking, brightened her up not a little. Indeed her weakness was now largely due to the want of nourishment suited to her feeble condition. Moreover, both nerves and mind found relief and rest in the consciousness that the decisive step had been taken. She was no longer shuddering and recoiling from a past in which each day had revealed more disheartening elements. Her face was now toward a future that promised a refuge, security, and even hope.

The quiet meal was soon over. Holcroft put a five-dollar bill in the hands of the justice, who filled in a certificate and departed, feeling that the afternoon had not been spent in vain.

" Jim," said Watterly, drawing his friend aside, " you'll want to make some purchases. You know she's only what she wears. How are you off for money ? "

" Well, Tom, you know I didn't expect anything of this kind when——"

" Of course I know it. Will fifty answer ? "

"Yes. You're a good friend. I'll return it in a day or two."

"Return it when you're a mind to. I say, Alida, I want you to take this. Jim Holcroft can't get married and his bride not receive a present from me," and he put ten dollars in her hand.

Tears rushed to her eyes as she turned them inquiringly to Holcroft to know what she should do.

"Now see here, Tom, you've done too much for us already."

"Shut up, Jim Holcroft! Don't you end the day by hurting my feelings! It's perfectly right and proper for me to do this. Good-by, Alida. I don't believe you'll ever be sorry you found your way to my hotel."

Alida took his proffered hand, but could only falter, "I—I can never forget."

CHAPTER XX.

"Now, Alida," said Holcroft, as they drove away, "remember that we are two middle-aged, sensible people. At least I'm middle-aged, and fairly sensible, too, I hope. You'll need to buy some things, and I want you to get all you need. Don't stint yourself, and you needn't hurry so as to get tired, for we shall have moonlight, and there's no use trying to get home before dark. Is there any particular store which you'd like to go to?"

"No, sir; only I'd rather go over on the east side of the town where I'm not known."

"That suits me, for it's the side nearest home and I *am* known there."

"Perhaps—perhaps you also would rather go this evening where you are not known," she said hesitatingly.

"It makes no difference to me. In fact I know of a place where you'll have a good choice at reasonable rates."

"I'll go where you wish," she said quietly.

They soon entered a large shop together, and the proprietor said pleasantly, "Good-evening, Mr. Holcroft."

"Good-evening, Mr. Jasper. My wife wants to get some things. If you'll be good enough to wait on her I'll step out to do two or three errands."

The merchant looked curiously at Alida, but was too

polite to ask questions or make comments on her very simple purchases. Her old skill and training were of service now. She knew just what she absolutely needed, and bought no more.

Holcroft laid in a good stock of groceries and some juicy beef and then returned. When Mr. Jasper gave him his bill he went to Alida, who was resting, and said in a low voice, " This won't do at all. You can't have bought half enough."

For the first time something like a smile flitted across her face, as she replied, " It's enough to begin with. I know."

" Really, Mr. Holcroft, I didn't know you were married," said the merchant. " I must congratulate you."

" Well, I am. Thank you. Good-night."

A few moments later he and his wife were bowling out of town toward the hills. Reaching one of these, the horses came down to a walk and Holcroft turned and said, " Are you very tired, Alida ? I'm troubled about you taking this long ride. You have been so sick."

" I'm sorry I'm not stronger, sir, but the fresh air seems to do me good and I think I can stand it."

" You didn't promise to obey me, did you ? " with a rather nervous little laugh.

" No, sir, but I will."

" That's a good beginning. Now see what an old tyrant I am. In the first place, I don't want you to say ' sir ' to me any more. My name is James. In the second place, you must work only as I let you. Your first business is to get strong and well, and you know we agreed to marry on strictly business grounds."

" I understand it well, but I think you are very kind for a business man."

" Oh ! as to that, if I do say it of myself, I don't think it's my nature to be hard on those who treat me square. I think we shall be very good friends in our quiet way, and that's more than can be said of a good many who promise more than they seem to remember afterward."

" I will try to do all you wish, for I am very grateful,"

" If you do, you may find I'm as grateful as you are."

" That can never be. Your need and mine were very different. But I shall try to show my gratitude by learning your ways and wishes and not by many words of thanks."

" Thank the Lord !" mentally ejaculated the farmer, " there's no Mrs. Mumpson in this case ;" but he only said kindly, " I think we understand each other now, Alida. I'm not a man of words either, and I had better show by actions also what I am. The fact is, although we are married, we are scarcely acquainted, and people can't get acquainted in a day."

The first long hill was surmounted and away they bowled again, past cottage and farmhouse, through strips of woodland and between dusky fields from which came the fragrance of the springing grass and the peepings of the hylas. The moon soon rose, full-orbed, above the higher eastern hills, and the mild April evening became luminous and full of beauty.

A healing sense of quiet and security already began to steal into Alida's bruised heart. In turning her back upon the town in which she had suffered so greatly, she felt like one escaping from prison and torture. An increasing assurance of safety came with every mile ; the cool, still radiance of the night appeared typical of her new and most unexpected experience. Light had risen on her shadowed path, but it was not warm, vivifying sunlight, which stimulates and develops. A few hours before she was in darkness which might be felt—yet it was a gloom shot through and through with lurid threatening gleams. It had seemed to her that she had fallen from home, happiness, and honor to unfathomed depths, and yet there had appeared to be deeper and darker abysses on every side. She had shuddered at the thought of going out into the world, feeling that her misfortune would awaken suspicion rather than sympathy, scorn instead of kindness; that she must toil on until death, to sustain a life to which death would come as God's welcome messenger. Then had come this man at her side, with his comparatively trivial troubles and perplexities, and he had asked her help—she who was so helpless. He had banished despair from her earthly future, he had lifted her up and was bearing her away from all which she had so dreaded; nothing had been asked which her crushed spirit was unable to bestow; she was simply expected to aid him in his natural wish to keep his home and to live where he had always dwelt. His very inability to understand her, to see her broken, trampled life and immeasurable need as she saw it, brought quietness of mind. The concentration of his thoughts on a few homely and simple hopes gave her immunity. With quick intuition, she divined that she had not a whimsical, jealous, exacting nature to deal with. He was the plain, matter-of-fact man he seemed; so literal and absolutely truthful that he would appear odd to most people. To her mind, his were the traits which she could now most welcome and value. He knew all about her, she had merely to be herself, to do what she had promised, in order to rest securely on his rock-like truth. He had again touched a deep, grateful chord in speaking of her to the

shopkeeper as his wife ; he showed no disposition whatever to shrink from the relation before the world ; it was
evident that he meant to treat her with respect and kindness, and to exact respect from others. For all this,
while sitting quietly and silently at his side, she thanked
him almost passionately in her heart ; but far more than
for all this she was glad and grateful that he would not
expect what she now felt it would be impossible for her
to give—the love and personal devotion which had been
inseparable from marriage in her girlhood thoughts.
He would make good his words—she should be his wife
in name and be respected as such. He was too simple
and true to himself and his buried love, too considerate
of her, to expect more. She might hope, therefore, as he
had said, that they might be helpful, loyal friends, and
he would have been surprised indeed had he known how
the pale, silent woman beside him was longing and
hoping to fill his home with comfort.

Thoughts like these had inspired and sustained her
while at the same time ministering the balm of hope.
The quiet face of nature, lovely in the moonlight, seemed
to welcome and reassure her. Happy are those who,
when sorely wounded in life, can turn to the natural
world and find in every tree, shrub, and flower a comforting friend that will not turn from them. Such are
not far from God and peace.

The range of Holcroft's thoughts was far simpler and
narrower than Alida's. He turned rather deliberately
from the past, preferring to dwell on the probable con-
summation of his hope. His home, his farm, were far
more to him than the woman he had married. He had
wedded her for their sake, and his thoughts followed
his heart, which was in his hillside acres. It is said that

women often marry for a home; he truly had done so to keep his home. The question which now most occupied him was the prospect of doing this through quiet, prosperous years. He dwelt minutely on Alida's manner, as well as her words, and found nothing to shake his belief that she had been as truthful as himself. Nevertheless, he queried in regard to the future with not a little anxiety. In her present distress and poverty she might naturally be glad of the refuge he had offered; but as time passed, and the poignancy of bitter memories was allayed, might not her life on the farm seem monotonous and dull, might not weariness and discontent come into her eyes in place of gratitude? "Well, well!" he concluded, "this marrying is a risky experiment at best, but Tom Watterly's talk and her manner seemed to shut me up to it. I was made to feel that I couldn't go on in any other way; and I haven't done anything underhanded or wrong, as I see, for the chance of going on. If I hadn't become such a heathen I should say there was a Providence in it, but I don't know what to think about such things any more. Time 'll show, and the prospect is better than it has been yet. She'll never be sorry if she carries out the agreement made to-day, if kindness and good will can repay her."

Thus it may be seen that, although two life currents had become parallel, they were still very distinct.

By the time Holcroft approached the lane leading to his dwelling Alida was growing very weary, and felt that her endurance had almost reached its limit. Her face was so white in the moonlight that he asked solicitously, "You can stand it a little longer, can't you?"

"I 'll try. I'm very sorry I'm not stronger."

"Don't you worry about that! You won't know yourself in a week. Here we are at the lane and there's the house yonder. A moment or two more and you'll be by the fire."

A loud barking startled old Jonathan Johnson out of his doze, and he hastened to replenish the fire and to call off his rather savage dog. He was a little surprised to see Holcroft drive toward the kitchen door with a woman by his side. "He's tried his luck with another of them town gals," he muttered, "but, Jerusalem! she won't stay a week, an' my old woman 'll have the washin' an' mendin' all the same."

He could scarcely believe his ears and eyes when he heard the farmer say, "Alida, you must let me lift you out," and then saw the "town gal" set gently on the ground, her hand placed on Holcroft's arm as she was supported slowly and carefully to the rocking chair beside the fire.

"Jonathan," was the quiet announcement, "this is Mrs. Holcroft, my wife."

"Jeru—beg a pardon. Wasn't 'spectin' jis' sich a turn o' things. Respects, missus! Sorry to see yer enj'yin' poor health."

"Yes, Jonathan, Mrs. Holcroft has been sick, but she's much better and will soon be well. She's very tired now from the long drive, but quiet life and country air will soon make her strong. I'll just step out and care for the horses, Alida, and soon be back again. You come and help me, Jonathan, and keep your dog off, too."

The old man complied with rather poor grace, for he would have preferred to interview the bride, at whom he was staring with all his weak, watery eyes. Holcroft understood his neighbor's peculiarities too well to subject his wife to this ordeal, and was bent on dispatching Jonathan homeward as soon as possible.

"I say, Jim," said the old guardsman, who felt that he was speaking to the boy he had known for thirty odd years, "where on airth did you pick up sich a sickly lookin' critter?"

"I didn't pick her up," replied the farmer laughingly. "I married her fair and square, just as you did your wife a hundred years ago, more or less. Haven't I as good a right to get married as you had?"

"Oh, I aint a-disputin' yer right, but it seems so kind o' suddint that it's taken what little breath I've left."

"How do you know it's sudden? Did you go around telling everyone how you were getting on when you were a-courting?"

"Well, I swan! yer got me. 'Taint so long ago that I disremember we did it on the sly."

"Well now, Uncle Jonathan, you've got nothing to say against me, for I didn't marry on the sly, although I've gone on the principle that my business wasn't everybody's business. When I saw your wife about my washing and mending I didn't know I was going to be lucky so soon. You know you can't marry a woman in this country till she's willing. But tell your wife she shan't lose anything, and the next time I go to town I'll leave that settin' of eggs she wanted. Now, Jonathan, honor bright, do you feel able to walk home if I give you fifty cents extra?"

"Why, sartinly! s'pose I'd take yer away on sich a 'casion? My wife wouldn't let me in if she knowed it."

"Well, you and your wife are good neighbors, and that's more'n I can say for most people in these parts. Here's the money. Mrs. Holcroft isn't strong or well enough to talk any to-night. You got yourself a good supper, didn't you?"

"Yes, yes! helped myself bount'fully. Good-night, and good luck ter yer. I can't help thinkin' it was kind o' suddint though, and then she's sich a sickly lookin' critter. Hope yer haven't been taken in, but then, as you say, the marryin' business, like other kinds o' business, is a man's own business."

"I hope everyone will take your sensible view, Uncle Jonathan. Good-night."

CHAPTER XXI.

AT HOME.

ALIDA was not so cold, weary, and almost faint but that she looked around the old kitchen with the strongest interest. This interest was as unlike Mrs. Mumpson's curiosity as she was unlike the widow. It is true the thought of self was prominent, yet hers were not selfish thoughts. There are some blessed natures in the world that in doing the best for themselves do the best that is possible for others.

The genial warmth of the fire was grateful to her chilled and enfeebled frame; the homely kitchen, with its dresser of china ware, its tin closet and pantry, the doors of which old Jonathan had left open, manlike, after helping himself "bount'fully," all suggested more comfort to this pallid bride, sitting there alone, than wealth of ornament in elegant apartments has brought to many others. She saw her chief domain, not in its coarse and common aspect, but as her vantage ground, from which she could minister to the comforts of the one who had rescued her. Few brides would care to enter the kitchen first, but she was pleased; she who had scarcely hoped to smile again looked smilingly around on the quaint, homelike room.

"And this is to be my home!" she murmured. "How strange, unexpected, yet natural it all is! Just what he led me to expect. The little lonely farmhouse, where I can be safe from staring eyes and unwounded by cruel questionings. Yet that old man had a dozen questions on his tongue. I believe *he* took him away to save my feelings. It's strange that so plain and simple a man in most respects can be so considerate. Oh, pray God that all goes on as it promises! I couldn't have dreamt it this morning, but I have an odd, homelike feeling already. Well, since I *am* at home I may as well take off my hat and cloak."

As she did so, Holcroft entered and said heartily, "That's right, Alida! You are here to stay, you know. You mustn't think it amiss that I left you a few moments alone, for I had to get that talkative old man off home. He's getting a little childish and would fire questions at you point-blank."

"But shouldn't you have taken him home in the wagon? I don't mind being alone."

"Oh, no! he's spry enough to walk twice the distance and often does. It's light as day outside, and I made it right with him. You can leave your things upstairs in your room, and I'll carry up your bundles also, if you are rested enough for the journey."

"Oh, yes!" she replied, "I'm feeling better already."

He led the way to the apartment that Mrs. Mumpson had occupied and said regretfully, "I'm sorry the room looks so bare and comfortless, but that will all be mended in time. When you come down, we'll have some coffee and supper."

She soon reappeared in the kitchen, and he continued, "Now I'll show you that I'm not such a very helpless sort of man. after all; so if you're sick you needn't worry. I'm going to get you a good cup of coffee and broil you a piece of steak."

" Oh ! please let me——" she began.

" No ; can't allow you to do anything to-night but sit in that chair. You promised to mind, you know," and he smiled so genially that she smiled back at him, although tears came into her eyes.

" I can't realize it all," she said in a low voice. " To think how this day began and how it is ending ! "

" It's ending in a poor man's kitchen, Alida. It was rather rough to bring you in here first, but the parlor is cold and comfortless."

" I would rather be brought here. It seems to me that it must be a light and cheerful room."

" Yes, the sun shines in these east windows, and there's another window facing the south, so it's light all day long."

She watched him curiously, and with not a little self-reproach, as he deftly prepared supper. " It's too bad for me to sit idle while you do such things, yet you do everything so well that I fear I shall seem awkward. Still, I think I do at least know how to cook a little."

" If you knew what I've had to put up with for a year or more, you wouldn't worry about satisfying me in this respect. Except when old Mrs. Wiggins was here, I had few decent meals that I didn't get myself," and then, to cheer her up, he laughingly told her of Mrs. Mumpson's essay at making coffee. He had a certain dry humor, and his unwonted effort at mimicry was so droll in itself that Alida was startled to hear her own voice in laughter, and she looked almost frightened, so deeply had she been impressed that it would never be possible or even right for her to laugh again.

The farmer was secretly much pleased at his success. If she would laugh, be cheerful and not brood, he felt sure she would get well and be more contented. The desperate view she had taken of her misfortunes troubled him, and he had thought it possible that she might sink into despondency and something like invalidism; but that involuntary bubble of laughter reassured him. "Quiet, wholesome, cheerful life will restore her to health," he thought, as he put his favorite beverage and the sputtering steak on the table. "Now," he said, placing a chair at the table, "you can pour me a cup of coffee."

"I'm glad I can do something," she answered, "for I can't get over the strangeness of being so waited on. Indeed, everything that was unexpected or undreamt of has happened," and there was just the faintest bit of color on her cheeks as she sat down opposite him.

Few men are insensible to simple, natural, womanly grace, and poor Holcroft, who so long had been compelled to see at his table "perfect terrors," as he called them, was agreeably impressed by the contrast she made with the Mumpson and Malony species. Alida unconsciously had a subtle charm of carriage and action, learned in her long past and happy girlhood when all her associations were good and refined. Still, in its truest explanation, this grace is native and not acquired; it is a personal trait. Incapable of nice analysis or fine definitions, he only thought, "How much pleasanter it is to see at the table a quiet, sensible woman instead of a 'peculiar female'!" and it was not long before he supplemented her remark by saying, "Perhaps things are turning out for both of us better than we expected. I had made up my mind this morning to live here like a hermit, get my own meals, and all that. I actually had the rough draught of an auction bill in my pocket,—yes, here it is now,—and was going to sell my cows, give up my dairy, and try to make my living in a way that wouldn't require any woman help. That's what took me up to Tom Watterly's; I wanted him to help me put the bill in shape. He wouldn't look at it, and talked me right out of trying to live like Robinson Crusoe, as he expressed it. I had been quite cheerful over my prospects; indeed, I was almost happy in being alone again after having such terrors in the house. But, as I said, Watterly talked all the courage and hope right out of me, and made it clear that I couldn't go it alone. You see, Tom and I have been friends since we were boys together, and that's the reason he talks so plain to me."

"He has a good, kind heart," said Alida. "I don't think I could have kept up at all had it not been for his kindness."

"Yes, Tom's a rough diamond. He don't make any pretenses, and looks upon himself as a rather hard case, but I fancy he's doing kind things in his rough way half the time. Well, as we were talking, he remembered you, and he spoke of you so feelingly and told your story with so much honest sympathy that he awoke my sympathy. Now you know how it has all come about. You see it's all natural enough and simple enough, and probably it's the best thing that could have happened for us both. All you have to do is to get strong and well, and then it won't be any one-sided affair, as you've been too much inclined to think. I can go on and keep my farm and home just as my heart is bent on doing. I want you to understand everything, for then your mind will be more satisfied and at rest, and that's half the battle in getting over sickness and trouble like yours."

"I can only thank God and you for the great change in my prospects. This quiet and escape from strangers are just what I most craved, and I am already beginning to hope that if I can learn to do all you wish, I shall find a content that I never hoped for," and the tears that stood in her eyes were witnesses of her sincerity.

"Well, don't expect to learn everything at once. Let me have my way for a while, and then you'll find, as you get strong, and the busy season comes on, that I'll be so taken up with the farm that you'll have your own way. Won't you have some more steak? No? Well, you've enjoyed your supper a little, haven't you?"

"Yes," she replied, smiling, "I actually felt hungry when I sat down, and the coffee has taken away the tired, faint feeling."

"I hope you'll soon be good and hungry three times a day," he said, laughing pleasantly.

"You'll at least let me clear the table?" she asked. "I feel so much better."

"Yes, if you are sure you're strong enough. It may make you feel more at home. But drop everything till to-morrow, when tired. I must go out and do my night work, and it's night work now, sure enough."

"It's too bad!" she said sympathetically.

"What! to go out and feed my stock this clear, bright night? and after a hearty supper, too? Such farming is fun. I feel, too, as if I wanted to go and pat the cows all around in my gladness that I'm not going to sell them. Now remember, let everything go till morning as soon as you feel tired."

She nodded smilingly and set to work. Standing in the shadow of a hemlock, he watched her for a few moments. Her movements were slow, as would be natural to one who had been so reduced by illness, but this very evidence of feebleness touched his feelings. "She is eager to begin—too eager. No nonsense there about 'menial tasks.' Well, it does give one hope to see such a woman as that in the old kitchen," and then the hungry cattle welcomed him.

The traveler feels safe after the fierce Arab of the desert has broken bread with him. It would seem that a deep principle of human nature is involved in this act. More than the restoring power of the nourishment itself was the moral effect for Alida of that first meal in her husband's home. It was another step in what he had said was essential—the forming of his acquaintance. She had seen from the first that he was plain and unpolished—that he had not the veneer of gentility of the man she had so mistakenly married; yet, in his simple truth, he was inspiring a respect which she had never felt for any man before. "What element of real courtesy has been wanting?" she asked herself. "If this is an earnest of the future, thank God for the real. I've found to my cost what a clever imitation of a man means."

It was as sweet as it was strange to think that she, who had trembled at the necessity of becoming almost a slave to unfeeling strangers, had been compelled to rest while a husband performed tasks naturally hers. It was all very homely, yet the significance of the act was chivalrous consideration for her weakness; the place, the nature of the ministry could not degrade the meaning of his action. Then, too, during the meal he had spoken natural, kindly words which gave to their breaking of bread together the true interpretation. Although so feeble and weary, she found a deep satisfaction in beginning her household work. "It does make me feel more at home," she said. " Strange that he should have thought of it ! "

She had finished her task and sat down again when he entered with a pail of milk. Taking a dipper with a strainer on one side of it, he poured out a tumblerful. " Now, take this," he said. " I've always heard that milk fresh from the cow was very strengthening. Then go and sleep till you are thoroughly rested, and don't think of coming down in the morning till you feel like it. I'll make the fire and get breakfast. You have seen how easily I can do it. I have several more cows to milk, and so will say ' Good-night.' "

" Good-night, and may God always bless you for your kindness to me to-day ! "

For the first time since chaos had come into her life Alida slept soundly and refreshingly, unpursued by the fears which had haunted even her dreams. When she awoke she expected to see the gray locks and repulsive features of the woman who had occupied the apartment with her at the almshouse, but she was alone in a small, strange room. Then memory gathered up the threads of the past ; but so strange, so blessed did the truth seem that she hastened to dress and go down to the old kitchen and assure herself that her mind had not become shattered by her troubles and was mocking her with unreal fancies. The scene she looked upon would have soothed and reassured her even had her mind been as disordered as she, for the moment, had been tempted to believe. There was the same homely room which had pictured itself so deeply on her memory the evening before. Now it was more attractive, for the morning sun was shining into it, lighting up its homely details with a wholesome, cheerful reality which made it difficult to believe that

there were tragic experiences in the world. The wood
fire in the stove crackled merrily, and the lid of the
kettle was already bobbing up and down from internal
commotion.

As she opened the door a burst of song entered, securing her attention. She had heard the birds before without recognizing consciousness, as is so often true of our
own condition in regard to the familiar sounds of nature.
It was now almost as if she had received another sense,
so strong, sweet, and cheering was the symphony.
Robins, song-sparrows, blackbirds, seemed to have
gathered in the trees nearby, to give her a jubilant
welcome; but she soon found that the music shaded off
to distant, dreamlike notes, and remembered that it was
a morning chorus of a hemisphere. This universality did
not render the melody less personally grateful. We can
appropriate all that is lovely in Nature, yet leave all for
others. As she stood listening, and inhaling the soft air,
full of the delicious perfume of the grass and expanding
buds, and looking through the misty sunshine on the
half-veiled landscape, she heard Holcroft's voice, chiding
some unruly animal in the barnyard.

This recalled her, and with the elasticity of returning
health and hope she set about getting breakfast.

"It seems to me that I never heard birds sing before,"
she thought, "and their songs this morning are almost
like the music of heaven. They seem as happy and
unconscious of fear and trouble as if they were angels.
Mother and I used to talk about the Garden of Eden, but
could the air have been sweeter, or the sunshine more
tempered to just the right degree of warmth and bright-
ness than here about my home? Oh, thank God again,
again and forever, for a home like this!" and for a few

moments something of the ecstasy of one delivered from
the black thraldom of evil filled her soul. She paused
now and then to listen to the birds, for only their songs
seemed capable of expressing her emotion. It was but
another proof that heavenly thoughts and homely work
may go on together.

CHAPTER XXII.

GETTING ACQUAINTED.

IT was still early, and Holcroft was under the impression that Alida would sleep late after the severe fatigues of the preceding day. He therefore continued his work at the barn sufficiently long to give his wife time for her little surprise. She was not long in finding and laying her hands on the simple materials for breakfast. A ham hung in the pantry and beneath it was a great basket of eggs, while the flour barrel stood in the corner. Biscuits were soon in the oven, eggs conjured into an omelet, and the ham cut into delicate slices, instead of great coarse steaks. Remembering Mrs. Mumpson's failure with the coffee, she made it a trifle strong and boiled the milk that should temper without cooling it. The biscuits rose like her own spirits, the omelet speedily began to take on color like her own flushed face as she busied herself about the stove.

Everything was nearly ready when she saw Holcroft coming toward the house with two pails of milk. He took them to the large dairy room under the parlor and then came briskly to the kitchen. She stood, screened by the door as he entered, then stopped and stared at the table all set and at the inviting breakfast on the stove.

See Alida's half-smiling, half-questioning face, seeking

his approval, he exclaimed, " Well, you *have* stolen a march on me! I supposed you were asleep yet."

" I felt so much stronger and better when I awoke that I thought you wouldn't mind if I came down and made a beginning."

" You call this a beginning do you? such a breakfast as this before seven in the morning? I hope you haven't overtaxed yourself."

" No, only a little of just the right kind of tired feeling."

" Haven't you left anything for me to do?"

" Perhaps. You will know when I've put all on the table. What I've prepared is ready."

" Well, this is famous. I'll go and wash and fix up a little and be right down."

When Holcroft returned, he looked at her curiously, for he felt that he, too, was getting acquainted. Her thin face was made more youthful by color; a pleased look was in her blue eyes, and a certain neatness and trimness about her dress to which he had not been accustomed. He scanned the table wonderingly, for things were not put upon it at haphazard; the light biscuits turned their brown cheeks invitingly toward him,—she had arranged that they should do that,—the ham was crisp, not sodden, and the omelet as russet as a November leaf. " This is a new dish," he said, looking at it closely. " What do you call it?"

" Omelet. Perhaps you won't like it, but mother used to be very fond of it."

" No matter. We'll have it if you like it and it brings you pleasant thoughts of your mother." Then he took a good sip of coffee and set the cup down again as he had before under the Mumpson *régime*, but with a very different expression. She looked anxiously at him, but was quickly reassured. " I thought *I* knew how to make coffee, but I find I don't. I never tasted anything so good as that. How *do* you make it ? "

" Just as mother taught me."

" Well, well! and you call this making a beginning ? I just wish I could give Tom Watterly a cup of this coffee. It would set his mind at rest. ' By jocks ! ' he would say, ' isn't this better than going it alone ? ' "

She looked positively happy under this sweet incense to a housewifely heart. She was being paid in the coin that women love best, and it was all the more precious to her because she had never expected to receive it again.

He did like the omelet ; he liked everything, and, after helping her liberally, cleared the table, then said he felt equal to doing two men's work. Before going out to his work, he lighted a fire on the parlor hearth and left a good supply of fuel beside it. " Now, Alida," he re-marked humorously, " I've already found out that you have one fault that you and I will have to watch against. You are too willing. I fear you've gone beyond your strength this morning. I don't want you to do a thing to-day except to get the meals, and remember, I can help in this if you don't feel well. There is a fire in the parlor, and I've wheeled the lounge up by it. Take it quietly to-day, and perhaps to-morrow I can begin to show you about butter-making."

" I will do as you wish," she replied, " but please show me a little more where things are before you go out."

This he did and added, " You'll find the beef and some other things on a swing-shelf in the cellar. The potato bins are down there, too. But don't try to get up much dinner. What comes quickest and easiest will suit me.

I'm a little backward with my work and must plow al
day for oats. It's time they were in. After such
breakfast, I feel as if I had eaten a bushel myself."

A few moments later she saw him going up the lane
that continued on past the house, with his stout team an
the plow, and she smiled as she heard him whistlin
" Coronation" with levity, as some good people woul
have thought.

Plowing and planting time had come and under hap
pier auspices, apparently, than he had ever imagined pos
sible again. With the lines about his neck, he bega
with a sidehill plow at the bottom of a large, slopin
field which had been in corn the previous year, and th
long, straight furrows increased from a narrow strip to
wide, oblong area. "Ah," said he in tones of stron
satisfaction, "the ground crumbles freely; it's just in th
right condition. I'll quit plowing this afternoon in tim
to harrow and sow all the ground that's ready. Then, s
much 'll be all done and well done. It's curious ho
seed, if it goes into the ground at the right time and i
the right way, comes right along and never gets dis
couraged. I aint much on scientific farming, but I'v
always observed that when I sow or plant as soon as th
ground is ready, I have better luck."

The horses seemed infected by his own brisk spiri
stepping along without urging, and the farmer was swe
speedily into the full, strong current of his habitual in
terests.

One might have supposed the recent events woul
have the uppermost place in his thoughts, but this wa
not true. He rather dwelt upon them as the unexpec
edly fortunate means to the end now attained. This wa
his life, and he was happy in the thought that his ma

riage promised to make this life not merely possible, but prosperous and full of quiet content.

The calling of the born agriculturist, like that of the fisherman, has in it the element of chance and is therefore full of moderate yet lasting excitement. Holcroft knew that, although he did his best, much would depend on the weather and other causes. He had met with disappointments in his crops, and had also achieved what he regarded as fine successes, although they would have seemed meager on a Western prairie. Every spring kindled anew his hopefulness and anticipation. He watched the weather with the interested and careful scrutiny of a sailor, and it must be admitted that his labor and its results depended more on natural causes than upon his skill and the careful use of the fertilizers. He was a farmer of the old school, the traditions received from his father controlled him in the main. Still, his good common sense and long experience stood him fairly well in the place of science and knowledge of improved methods, and he was better equipped than the man who has in his brain all that the books can teach, yet is without experience. Best of all, he had inherited and acquired an abiding love of the soil ; he never could have been content except in its cultivation ; he was therefore in the right condition to assimilate fuller knowledge and make the most of it.

He knew well enough when it was about noon. From long habit he would have known had the sky been overcast, but now his glance at the sun was like looking at a watch. Dusty and begrimed he followed his team to the barn, slipped from them their headstalls and left them to amuse themselves with a little hay while they cooled sufficiently for heartier food. "Well now," he mused,

" I wonder what that little woman has for dinner ? Another new dish, like enough. Hanged if I'm fit to go in the house, and she looking so trim and neat. I think I'll first take a souse in the brook," and he went up behind the house where an unfailing stream gurgled swiftly down from the hills. At the nearest point a small basin had been hollowed out, and as he approached he saw two or three speckled trout darting away through the limpid water.

" Aha ! " he muttered, " glad you reminded me. When *she's* stronger, she may enjoy catching our supper some afternoon. I must think of all the little things I can to liven her up, so she won't get dull. It's curious how interested I am to know how she's got along and what she has for dinner. And to think that, less than a week ago, I used to hate to go near the house ! "

As he entered the hall on his way to his room, that he might make himself more presentable, an appetizing odor greeted him and Alida smiled from the kitchen door as she said, " Dinner's ready."

Apparently she had taken him at his word, as she had prepared little else than an Irish stew, yet when he had partaken of it, he thought he would prefer Irish stews from that time onward indefinitely. " Where did you learn to cook, Alida ? " he asked.

" Mother wasn't very strong and her appetite often failed her. Then, too, we hadn't much to spend on our table, so we tried to make simple things taste nice. Do you like my way of preparing that old-fashioned dish ? "

" I'm going to show you how I like it," he replied, nodding approvingly. " Well, what have you been doing besides tempting me to eat too much ? "

"What you said, resting. You told me not to get up much of a dinner, so I very lazily prepared what you see. I've been lying on the lounge most of the morning."

"Famous ; and you feel better ? "

"Yes, I think I shall soon get well and strong," she replied, looking at him gratefully.

"Well, well ! my luck's turned at last. I once thought it never would, but if this goes on—well, you can't know what a change it is for the better. I can now put my mind on my work."

"You've been plowing all the morning, haven't you ? " she ventured, and there was the pleased look in her eyes that he already liked to see.

"Yes," he replied, "and I must keep at it several days to get in all the oats I mean to sow. If this weather holds I shall be through next week."

"I looked in the milk-room a while ago. Isn't there anything I could do there this afternoon ? "

"No. I'll attend to everything there. It's too damp for you yet. Keep on resting. Why, bless me ! I didn't think you'd be well enough to do anything for a week."

"Indeed," she admitted, "I'm surprised at myself. It seems as if a crushing weight had been lifted off my mind and that I was coming right up. I'm so glad, for I feared I might be feeble and useless a long time."

"Well, Alida, if you had been, or if you ever are, don't think I'll be impatient. The people I can't stand are those who try to take advantage of me, and I tell you I've had to contend with that disposition so long that I feel as if I could do almost anything for one who is simply honest and tries to keep her part of an agreement. But this won't do. I've enjoyed my own dinner so much that I've half forgotten that the horses haven't had theirs yet. Now will you scold if I light my pipe before I go out?"

"Oh, no! I don't mind that."

"No good-natured fibs! Isn't smoke disagreeable?" She shook her head. "I don't mind it at all," she said, but her sudden paleness puzzled him. He could not know that he had involuntarily recalled the many times that she had filled the evening pipe for a man who now haunted her memory like a specter.

"I guess you don't like it very much," he said, as he passed out. "Well, no matter! It's getting so mild that I can smoke out of doors."

With the exception of the episode of dinner the day was chiefly passed by Alida in a health-restoring languor, the natural reaction from the distress and strong excitements of the past. The rest that had been enjoined upon her was a blessed privilege, and still more happy was the truth that she could rest. Reclining on the lounge in the parlor, with a wood fire on one side and the April sun on the other, both creating warmth and good cheer, she felt like those who have just escaped from a wreck and engulfing waves. Her mind was too weary to question either the past or the future, and sometimes a consciousness of safety is happiness in itself. In the afternoon, the crackling of the fire and the calling and singing of the birds without formed a soothing lullaby and she fell asleep.

At last, in a dream, she heard exquisite music which appeared to grow so loud, strong, and triumphant that she started up and looked around bewildered. A moment later, she saw that a robin was singing in a lilac bush by the window and that near the bird was a nest partially constructed. She recalled her hopeless grief when she had last seen the building of one of their little homes; and she fell upon her knees with a gratitude too deep for words, and far more grateful to Heaven than words.

Stepping out on the porch, she saw by the shadows that the sun was low in the west and that Holcroft was coming down the lane with his horses. He nodded pleasantly as he passed on to the barn. Her eyes followed him lingeringly till he disappeared, and then they ranged over the wide valley and the wooded hills in the distance. Not a breath of air was stirring; the lowing of cattle and other rural sounds, softened by distance, came from other farmhouses; the birds were at vespers, and their songs, to her fancy, were imbued with a softer, sweeter melody than in the morning. From the adjacent fields came clear, mellow notes that made her nerves tingle, so ethereal yet penetrating were they. She was sure she had never heard such bird music before. When Holcroft came in to supper she asked, "What birds are those that sing in the field?"

"Meadow larks. Do you like them?"

"I never heard a hymn sung that did me more good."

"Well, I own up, I'd rather hear 'em than much of the singing we used to have down at the meeting-house."

"It seems to me," she remarked, as she sat down at the table, "that I've never heard birds sing as they have to-day,"

"Now I think of it, they have been tuning up wonderfully. Perhaps they've an idea of my good luck," he added smilingly.

"I had thought of that about myself," she ventured. "I took a nap this afternoon, and a robin sang so near the window that he woke me up. It was a pleasant **way** to be waked."

"Took a nap, did you? That's famous! Well, well! this day's gone just to suit me, and I haven't had many such in a good while, I can tell you. I've got in a big strip of oats, and now, when I come in tired, here's a good supper. I certainly shall have to be on the watch to do Tom Watterly good turns for talking me into this business. That taking a nap was a first-rate idea. You ought to keep it up for a month."

"No, indeed! There's no reason why you should work hard and I be idle. I've rested to-day, as you wished, and I feel better than I ever expected to again; but to-morrow I must begin in earnest. What use is there of your keep-.ing your cows, if good butter is not made? Then I must be busy with my needle."

"Yes, that's true enough. See how thoughtless I am! I forgot you hadn't any clothes to speak of, I ought to take you to town to a dressmaker."

"I think you had better get your oats in," she replied, smiling shyly. "Besides, I have a dressmaker that just suits me—one that's made my dresses a good many years."

"If she don't suit you, you're hard to be suited," said he, laughing. "Well, some day, after you are fixed up, I shall have to let you know how dilapidated I am."

"Won't you do me a little favor?"

"Oh, yes! a dozen of 'em, big or little."

"Please bring down this evening something that needs mending. I am so much better——"

"No, no! I wasn't hinting for you to do anything to-night."

"But you've promised me," she urged. "Remember,

I've been resting nearly all day. I'm used to sewing, and earned my living at it. Somehow, it don't seem natural for me to sit with idle hands."

"If I hadn't promised——"

"But you have."

"I suppose I'm fairly caught," and he brought down a little of the most pressing of the mending.

"Now I'll reward you," she said, handing him his pipe, well filled. "You go in the parlor and have a quiet smoke. I won't be long in clearing up the kitchen."

"What! smoke in the parlor?"

"Yes, why not? I assure you I don't mind it."

"Ha! ha! Why didn't I think of it before? I might have kept the parlor and smoked Mrs. Mumpson out."

"It won't be smoke that will keep me out."

"I should hope not, or anything else. I must tell you how I *did* have to smoke Mrs. Mumpson out at last," and he did so with so much drollery that she again yielded to irrepressible laughter.

"Poor thing! I'm sorry for her," she said.

"I'm sorry for Jane—poor little stray cat of a child! I hope we can do something for her some day," and having lighted his pipe, he took up the county paper, left weekly in a hollow tree by the stage driver, and went into the parlor.

After freshening up the fire he sat down to read, but by the time she joined him the tired man was nodding. He tried to brighten up, but his eyes were heavy.

"You've worked hard to-day," she said sympathetically.

"Well, I have," he answered. "I've not done such a good day's work in a year."

"Then why don't you go to sleep at once?"

"It don't seem polite——"

"Please don't talk that way," she interrupted. "I don't mind being alone at all. I shall feel a great deal more at home if you forget all about ceremony."

"Well, Alida, I guess we had both better begin on that basis. If I give up when I'm tired, you must. You mustn't think I'm always such a sleepyhead. The fact is I've been more tired out with worry of late than with work. I can laugh about it now, but I've been so desperate over it that I've felt more like swearing. You'll find out I've become a good deal of a heathen."

"Very well; I'll wait till I find out."

"I think we are getting acquainted famously, don't you?"

"Yes," she nodded, with a smile that meant more than a long speech. "Good-night."

CHAPTER XXIII.

BETWEEN THE PAST AND FUTURE.

HUMAN nature, in common with Mother Nature, has its immutable laws. The people who existed before the flood were, in their primal motives, like those of to-day. The conventionality of highly civilized society does not change the heart, but it puts so much restraint upon it that not a few appear heartless. They march through life and fight its battles like uniformed men, trained in a certain school of tactics. This monotony of character and action is superficial, in most cases, rather than real, and he who fathoms the eyes of others, who catches the subtle quality of tones and interprets the flexible mouth that utters them, will discover that the whole gamut of human nature exists in those that appear only like certain musical instruments, made by machinery to play a few well-known tunes. Conventional restraint often, no doubt, produces dwarfed and defective human nature. I suppose that if souls could be put under a microscope, the undeveloped rudiments of almost everything would be discovered. It is more satisfactory to study the things themselves than their suggestions; this we are usually better able to do among people of simple and untrammeled modes of life, who are not practiced in disguises. Their peculiar traits and their general and dominant laws and impulses are exhibited with less reserve than by those who have learned to be always on their guard. Of course there are commonplace yeomen as truly as commonplace aristocrats, and simple life abounds in simpletons.

When a man in Holcroft's position has decided traits, they are apt to have a somewhat full expression; his rugged nature beside a tamer one outlines itself more vividly, just as a mountain peak is silhouetted against the horizon better than a rounded hill. It probably has been observed that his character possessed much simplicity and directness. He had neither the force nor the ambition to raise him above his circumstances; he was merely decided within the lines of his environment. Perhaps the current of his life was all the stronger for being narrow. His motives were neither complex nor vacillating. He had married to keep his home and to continue in the conditions of life dear from association and the strongest preference, and his heart overflowed with good will and kindness toward Alida because she promised to solve the hard problem of the future satisfactorily. Apart from the sympathy which her misfortune had evoked, he probably could have felt much the same toward any other good, sensible woman, had she rendered him a similar service. It is true, now that Alida was in his home, that she was manifesting agreeable traits which gave him pleasant little surprises. He had not expected that he would have had half so much to say to her, yet felt it his duty to be sociable in order to cheer up and mark the line between even a business marriage and the employment of a domestic. Both his interest and his duty required that he should establish the bonds of strong friendly regard on the basis of perfect equality, and he would have made efforts, similar to those he put forth, in behalf of any woman, if she had consented to marry him with Alida's understanding. Now, however, that his suddenly adopted project of securing a housekeeper and helper had been consummated, he would find that he was not dealing with a business partner in the abstract, but a definite woman, who had already begun to exert over him her natural influence. He had expected more or less constraint and that some time must elapse before his wife would cease to be in a sense company whom he, with conscious and deliberate effort, must entertain. On the contrary she entertained and interested him, although she said so little, and by some subtle power she unloosed his tongue and made it easy for him to talk to her. In the most quiet and unobtrusive way, she was not only making herself at home, but him also; she was very subservient to his wishes, but not servilely so ; she did not assert, but only revealed her superiority, and after even so brief an acquaintance he was ready to indorse Tom Watterly's view, " She's out of the common run."

While all this was true, the farmer's heart was as untouched as that of a child who simply and instinctively likes a person. He was still quietly and unhesitatingly loyal to his former wife. Apart from his involuntary favor, his shrewd, practical reason was definite enough in its grounds of approval. Reason assured him that she promised to do and to be just what he had married her for, but this might have been true of a capable, yet disagreeable woman whom he could not like, to save himself.

Both in regard to himself and Alida, Holcroft accepted the actual facts with the gladness and much of the unquestioning simplicity of a child. This rather risky experiment was turning out well, and for a time he daily became more and more absorbed in his farm and its interests. Alida quietly performed her household tasks and proved that she would not need very much instruction to become a good butter-maker. The short spring of the North required that he should be busy early and late to keep pace with the quickly passing seedtime. His hopefulness, his freedom from household worries, prompted him to sow and plant increased areas of land. In brief, he entered on just the businesslike honeymoon he had hoped for.

Alida was more than content with the conditions of her life. She saw that Holcroft was not only satisfied, but also pleased with her, and that was all she had expected and indeed all that thus far she had wished or hoped. She had many sad hours ; wounds like hers cannot heal readily in a true, sensitive woman's heart. While she gained in cheerfulness and confidence, the terrible and unexpected disaster which had overtaken her rendered impossible the serenity of those with whom all has gone well. Dread of something, she knew not what, haunted her painfully, and memory at times seemed malignantly perverse in recalling one whom she prayed to forget.

Next to her faith and Holcroft's kindness her work was her best solace, and she thanked God for the strength to keep busy.

On the first Sunday morning after their marriage the farmer overslept, and breakfast had been ready some time when he came down. He looked with a little dismay at the clock over the kitchen mantel and asked, " Aren't you going to scold a little ? "

She shook her head, nor did she look the chiding which often might as well be spoken.

"How long have I kept breakfast waiting, or you rather?"

"What difference does it make? You needed the rest. The breakfast may not be so nice," was her smiling answer.

"No matter. You are nice to let a man off in that way." Observing the book in her lap, he continued, "So you were reading the old family Bible to learn lessons of patience and forbearance?"

Again she shook her head. She often oddly reminded him of Jane in her employment of signs instead of speech, but in her case there was a grace, a suggestiveness, and even a piquancy about them which made them like a new language. He understood and interpreted her frankly. "I know, Alida," he said kindly; "you are a good woman. You believe in the Bible and love to read it."

"I was taught to read and love it," she replied simply. Then her eyes dropped and she faltered, "I've reproached myself bitterly that I rushed away so hastily that I forgot the Bible my mother gave me."

"No, no," he said heartily, "don't reproach yourself for that. It was the Bible in your heart that made you act as you did."

She shot him a swift, grateful glance through her tears, but made no other response.

Having returned the Bible to the parlor, she put the breakfast on the table and said quietly, "It looks as if we would have a rainy day."

"Well," said he, laughing, "I'm as bad as the old woman—it seems that women can run farms alone if men can't. Well, this old dame had a big farm and employed several men, and she was always wishing it would rain nights and Sundays. I'm inclined to chuckle over the good this rain will do my oats, instead of being sorry to think how many sinners it'll keep from church. Except in protracted-meeting times, most people of this town would a great deal rather risk their souls than be caught in the rain on Sunday. We don't mind it much week days, but Sunday rain is very dangerous to health."

"I'm afraid I'm as bad as the rest," she said, smiling. "Mother and I usually stayed home when it rained hard."

"Oh, we don't need a hard storm in the country. People say, ' It looks threatening,' and that settles it ; but we often drive to town rainy days to save time."

"Do you usually go to church at the meeting house I see off in the valley ?" she asked.

"I don't go anywhere," and he watched keenly to see how she would take this blunt statement of his practical heathenism.

She only looked at him kindly and accepted the fact.

"Why don't you pitch into me ?" he asked.

"That wouldn't do any good."

"You'd like to go, I suppose ? "

"No, not under the circumstances, unless you wished to. I'm cowardly enough to dread being stared at."

He gave a deep sigh of relief. "This thing has been troubling me," he said. " I feared you would want to go, and if you did, I should feel that you ought to go."

"I fear I'm very weak about it, but I shrink so from meeting strangers. I do thank God for his goodness many times a day and ask for help. I'm not brave enough to do any more, yet."

His rugged features became very somber as he said, " I wish I had as much courage as you have."

"You don't understand me——" she began gently.

" No, I suppose not. It's all become a muddle to me.
I mean this church and religious business."

She looked at him wistfully, as if she wished to say
something, but did not venture to do so. He promptly
gave a different turn to the conversation by quoting Mrs.
Mumpson's tirade on churchgoing the first Sunday after
her arrival. Alida laughed, but not in a wholly mirthful
and satisfied way. " There ! " he concluded, " I'm touching on things a little too sacred for you. I respect your
feelings and beliefs, for they are honest and I wish I
shared in 'em." Then he suddenly laughed again as he
added, " Mrs. Mumpson said there was too much milking
done on Sunday, and it's time I was breaking the Fourth
Commandment, after her notion."

Alida now laughed outright, without reservation.

" ' By jocks ! ' as Watterly says, what a difference there
is in women ! " he soliloquized on his way to the barn.
" Well, the church question is settled for the present, but
if Alida should ask me to go, after her manner this morning, I'd face the whole creation with her."

When at last he came in and threw off his waterproof
coat, the kitchen was in order and his wife was sitting by
the parlor fire with Thomson's " Land and the Book " in
her hand.

" Are you fond of reading ? " he asked.

" Yes, very."

" Well, I am, too, sort of ; but I've let the years slip by
without doing half as much as I ought."

" Light your pipe and I'll read to you, if you wish me
to."

" Oh, come, now ! I at least believe in Sunday as a
day of rest, and you need it. Reading aloud is about as
hard work as I can do."

"But I'm used to it. I read aloud to mother a great deal," and then there passed over her face an expression of deep pain.

"What is it, Alida? Don't you feel well?"

"Yes, oh, yes!" she replied hastily, and her pale face became crimson.

It was another stab of memory recalling the many Sundays she had read to the man who had deceived her. "Shall I read?" she asked.

"Alida," he said very kindly, "it wasn't the thought of your mother that brought that look of pain into your face."

She shook her head sadly, with downcast eyes. After a moment or two, she raised them appealingly to him as she said simply, "There is so much that I wish I could forget."

"Poor child! Yes, I think I know. Be patient with yourself, and remember that you were never to blame."

Again came that quick, grateful glance by which some women express more than others can ever put in words. Her thought was, "I didn't think that even he was capable of that. What a way of assuring me that he'll be patient with me!" Then she quietly read for an hour descriptions of the Holy Land that were not too religious for Holcroft's mind and which satisfied her conscience better than much she had read in former days to satisfy a taste more alien to hers than that of her husband.

Holcroft listened to her correct pronunciation and sweet, natural tones with a sort of pleased wonder. At last he said, "You must stop now."

"Are you tired?" she asked.

"No, but you are, or ought to be. Why, Alida, I didn't know you were so well educated. I'm quite a barbarous old fellow compared with you."

" I hadn't thought of that before," she said with a laugh.

" What a fool I was, then, to put it into your head ! "

" You must be more careful. I'd never have such thoughts if you didn't suggest them."

" How did you come to get such a good education ? "

" I wish I had a better one. Well, I did have good advantages up to the time I was seventeen. After I was old enough I went to school quite steadily, but it seems to me that I learned a little of everything and not much of anything. When father died and we lost our property, we had to take to our needles. I suppose I might have obtained work in a store, or some such place, but I couldn't bear to leave mother alone and I disliked being in public. I certainly didn't know enough to teach, and besides, I was afraid to try."

" Well, well ! you've stumbled into a quiet enough place at last."

" That's what I like most about it, but I don't think I stumbled into it. I think I've been led and helped. That's what I meant when I said you didn't understand me," she added hesitatingly. " It don't take courage for me to go to God. I get courage by believing that he cares for me like a father, as the Bible says. How could I ever have found so kind a friend and good a home myself ? "

" I've been half inclined to believe there's a Providence in it myself—more and more so as I get acquainted with you. Your troubles have made you better, Alida ; mine made me worse. I used to be a Christian ; I aint any more."

She looked at him smilingly as she asked, " How do you know ? "

"Oh! I know well enough," he replied gloomily. "Don't let's talk about it any more," and then he led her on to speak simply and naturally about her childhood home and her father and mother.

"Well," he said heartily, "I wish your mother was living, for nothing would please me better than to have such a good old lady in the house."

She averted her face as she said huskily, "I think it was better she died before——" But she did not finish the sentence.

By the time dinner was over the sun was shining brightly, and he asked her if she would not like to go up the lane to his woodland to see the view. Her pleased look was sufficient answer. "But are you sure you are strong enough?" he persisted.

"Yes, it will do me good to go out, and I may find some wild flowers."

"I guess you can, a million or two."

By the time he was through at the barn she was ready and they started up the lane, now green with late April grass and enlivened with dandelions in which bumble-bees were wallowing. The sun had dried the moisture sufficiently for them to pass on dry-shod, but everything had the fresh, vernal aspect that follows a warm rain. Spring had advanced with a great bound since the day before. The glazed and glutinous cherry buds had expanded with aromatic odors and the white of the blossoms was beginning to show.

"By to-morrow," said Holcroft, "the trees will look as if covered with snow. Let me help you," and he put his hand under her arm, supporting and aiding her steps up the steep places.

Her lips were parted, the pleased look was in her eyes

as they rested on trees and shrubs which lined the half ruinous stone walls on either side. "Everything seems so alive and glad this afternoon," she remarked.

"Yes," replied the matter-of-fact farmer. "A rain such as we had this morning is like turning the water on a big mill-wheel. It starts all the machinery right up. Now the sun's out, and that's the greatest motor power of all. Sun and moisture make the farm go."

"Mustn't the ground be enriched, too?"

"Yes, yes indeed; I suppose that's where we all fail. But it's no easy matter to keep a farm in good heart. That's another reason why I'm so glad I won't have to sell my stock. A farm run without stock is sure to grow poor, and if the farm grows poor, the owner does as a matter of course. But what put enriching the ground into your head? Do you know anything about farming?"

"No, but I want to learn. When I was a girl, father had a garden. He used to take papers about it, and I often read them aloud to him evenings. Now I remember there used to be much in them about enriching the ground. Do you take any such paper?"

"No. I haven't much faith in book-farming."

"I don't know," she ventured. "Seems to me you might get some good ideas out of papers, and your experience would teach you whether they were useful ideas or not. If you'll take one, I'll read it to you."

"I will, then, for the pleasure of hearing you read, if nothing else. That's something I hadn't bargained for," he added, laughing.

She answered in the same spirit by saying, "I'll throw that in and not call it square yet."

"I think I've got the best of you," he chuckled; "and

you know nothing makes a Yankee farmer happier than to get the best of a bargain."

"I hope you'll continue to think so. Can I sit down a few moments?"

"Why, certainly! How forgetful I am! Your talk is too interesting for me to think of anything else," and he placed her on a flat rock by the side of the lane, while he leaned against the wall.

Bees and other insects were humming around them; a butterfly fluttered over the fence and alighted on a dandelion almost at her feet; meadow larks were whistling their limpid notes in the adjoining fields, while from the trees about the house beneath them came the songs of many birds, blending with the babble of the brook which ran not far away.

"Oh, how beautiful, how strangely beautiful it all is!"

"Yes, when you come to think of it, it is real pretty," he replied. "It's a pity we get so used to such things that we don't notice 'em much. I should feel miserable enough, though, if I couldn't live in just such a place. I shouldn't wonder if I was a good deal like that robin yonder. I like to be free and enjoy the spring weather, but I suppose neither he nor I think or know how fine it all is."

"Well, both you and the robin seem a part of it," she said, laughing.

"Oh, no, no!" he replied with a guffaw which sent the the robin off in alarm, "I aint beautiful and never was."

She joined his laugh, but said with a positive little nod, "I'm right, though. The robin isn't a pretty bird, yet everybody likes him."

"Except in cherry time. Then he has an appetite

equal to mine. But everybody don't like me. In fact, *I* think I'm generally disliked in this town."

"If you went among them more they wouldn't dislike you."

"I don't want to go among them."

"They know it, and that's the reason they dislike you."

"Would you like to go out to tea-drinkings, and all that?"

"No, indeed; and I don't suppose I'd be received," she added sadly.

"So much the worse for them, then, blast 'em!" said Holcroft wrathfully.

"Oh no! I don't feel that way and you shouldn't. When they can, people ought to be sociable and kind."

"Of course I'd do any of my neighbors, except Lemuel Weeks, a good turn if it came in my way, but the less I have to do with them the better I'm satisfied."

"I'm rested enough to go on now," said Alida quietly. They were not long in reaching the edge of the woodland, from which there was an extended prospect. For some little time they looked at the wide landscape in silence. Alida gave to it only partial attention, for her mind was very busy with thoughts suggested by her husband's alienation from his neighbors. It would make it easier for her, but the troubled query would arise, "Is it right or best for him? His marrying me will separate him still more."

Holcroft's face grew sad rather than troubled as he looked at the old meeting house and not at the landscape. He was sitting near the spot where he spent that long forenoon a few Sundays before, and the train of thought came back again. In his deep abstraction, he almost forgot the woman near him in memories of the past.

His old love and lost faith were inseparable from that little white spire in the distance.

Alida stole a glance at him and thought, " He's think-ing of her," and she quietly strolled away to look for wild flowers.

" Yes," muttered Holcroft, at last, " I hope Bessie knows. She'd be the first one to say it was right and best for me, and she'd be glad to know that in securing my own home and comfort I had given a home to the homeless and sorrowful—a quiet, good woman, who worships God as she did."

He rose and joined his wife, who held toward him a handful of trailing arbutus, rue anemones, bloodroot, and dicentras. " I didn't know they were so pretty before," he said with a smile.

His smile reassured her, for it seemed kinder than any she had yet received, and his tone was very gentle. " His dead wife will never be my enemy," she murmured. " He has made it right with her in his own thoughts."

CHAPTER XXIV.

GIVEN HER OWN WAY.

ON Monday the absorbing work of the farm was renewed, and every day brought to Holcroft long and exhausting hours of labor. While he was often taciturn, he evidently progressed in cheerfulness and hope. Alida confirmed his good impressions. His meals were prompt and inviting ; the house was taking on an aspect of neatness and order long absent, and his wardrobe was put in as good condition as its rather meager character permitted. He had positively refused to permit his wife to do any washing and ironing. "We will see about it next fall," he said. "If then you are perfectly well and strong, perhaps, but not in the warm weather now coming on." Then he added, with a little nod, "I'm finding out how valuable you are, and I'd rather save you than the small sum I have to pay old Mrs. Johnson."

In this and in other ways he showed kindly consideration, but his mind continually reverted to his work and outdoor plans with the preoccupation of one who finds that he can again give his thoughts to something from which they had been most reluctantly withdrawn. Thus Alida was left alone most of the time. When the dusk of evening came he was too tired to say much, and he retired early that he might be fresh for work again when the sun appeared. She had no regrets, for although she kept busy she was resting and her wounds were healing through the long, quiet days. It was the essential calm after the storm. Caring for the dairy and working the butter into firm, sweet, tempting yellow rolls were the only tasks that troubled her a little, but Holcroft assured her that she was learning these important duties faster than he had expected her to. She had several hours a day in which to ply her needle, and thus was soon enabled to replenish her scanty wardrobe.

One morning at breakfast she appeared in another gown, and although its material was calico, she had the appearance to Holcroft of being unusually well dressed. He looked pleased, but made no comment. When the cherry blossoms were fully out, an old cracked flower vase—the only one in the house—was filled with them, and they were placed in the center of the dinner table. He looked at them and her, then smilingly remarked, "I shouldn't wonder if you enjoyed those cherry blows more than anything else we have for dinner."

"I want something else, though. My appetite almost frightens me."

"That's famous! I needn't be ashamed of mine, then."

One evening, before the week was over, he saw her busy with a rake about the door. Last year's leaves were still scattered about, with twigs and even small boughs wrested by the winds from the trees. He was provoked with himself that he had neglected the usual spring clearing away of litter, and a little irritated that she should have tried to do the work herself. He left the horses at the barn and came forward directly. "Alida," he said gravely, "there's no need of your doing such work; I don't like to see you do it."

" Why," she replied, " I've heard that women in the country often milk and take care of the chickens."

" Yes, but that's very different from this work. I wouldn't like people to think I expected such things of you."

" It's very easy work," she said smilingly, " easier than sweeping a room, though something like it. I used to do it at home when I was a girl. I think it does me good to do something in the open air."

She was persisting, but not in a way that chafed him. Indeed, as he looked into her appealing eyes and face flushed with exercise, he felt that it would be churlish to say another word.

" Well," he said, laughing, " it makes you look so young and rosy I guess it does you good. I suppose you'll have to have your own way."

" You know I wouldn't do this or anything else if you really didn't want me to."

" You are keen," he replied, with his good-nature entirely restored. " You can see that you get me right under your thumb when you talk that way. But we must both be on our guard against your fault, you know, or pretty soon you'll be taking the whole work of the farm off my hands."

" To be serious," she resumed, accompanying him to the barn for the first time, " I think *you* are working too hard. I'm not. Our meals are so simple that it doesn't take me long to get them. I'm through with the hurry in my sewing, the old dog does the churning, and you give me so much help in the dairy that I shall soon have time on my hands. Now it seems to me that I might soon learn to take entire care of the chickens, big and little, and that would be so much less for you to look after. I'm sure I would enjoy it very much, especially the looking after the little chickens."

"Do you really think you'd like to do that?" he asked, as he turned to her from unharnessing the horses.

"Yes, indeed, if you think I'm competent."

"You are more so than I am. Somehow, little chickens don't thrive under a busy man's care. The mother hens mean well, but they are so confoundedly silly. I declare to you that last year I lost half the little chicks that were hatched out."

"Well, then," she replied, laughing, "I won't be afraid to try, for I think I can beat you in raising chickens. Now, show me how much you feed them at night and how much I'm to give them in the morning, and let me take the whole care of them for a month, get the eggs, and all. If they don't do so well, then I'll resign. I can't break you in a month."

"It looks more as if you'd make me. You have a good big bump of order, and I haven't any at all in little things. Tom Watterly was right. If I had tried to live here alone, things would have got into an awful mess. I feel ashamed of myself that I didn't clear up the yard before, but my whole mind's been on the main crops."

"As it should be. Don't you worry about the little things. They belong to me. Now show me about the chickens, or they 'll go to roost while we're talking."

"But I, as well as the chickens, shall want some supper."

"I won't let either of you starve. You'll see."

"Well, you see this little measure? You fill it from this bin with this mixture of corn and wheat screenings. That's the allowance, morning and evening. Then you go out to the barnyard there, and call ' kip, kip, kip.'

That's the way my wife used——" He stopped in a little embarrassment.

"I'd be glad if I could do everything as she did," said Alida gently. "It has grown clearer every day how hard her loss was to you. If you'll tell me what she did and how she did things——" and she hesitated.

"That's good of you, Alida," he replied gratefully. Then, with his directness of speech, he added, "I believe some women are inclined to be jealous even of the dead."

"You need never fear to speak of your wife to me. I respect and honor your feelings—the way you remember her. There's no reason why it should be otherwise. I did not agree to one thing and expect another," and she looked him straight in the eyes.

He dropped them, as he stood leaning against the bin in the shadowy old barn, and said, "I didn't think you or anyone would be so sensible. Of course, one can't forget quickly——"

"You oughtn't to forget," was the firm reply. "Why should you? I should be sorry to think you could forget."

"I fear I'm not like to make you sorry," he replied, sighing. "To tell you the truth——" he added, looking at her almost commiseratingly, and then he hesitated.

"Well, the truth is usually best," she said quietly.

"Well, I'll tell you my thought. We married in haste, we were almost strangers, and your mind was so distracted at the time that I couldn't blame you if you forgot what—what I said. I feared—well, you are carrying out our agreement so sensibly that I want to thank you. It's a relief to find that you're not opposed, even in your heart, that I should remember one that I knew as a little child and married when I was young."

"I remember all you said and what I said," she replied, with the same direct, honest gaze. "Don't let such thoughts trouble you any more. You've been kinder and more considerate than I ever expected. You have only to tell me how she did——"

"No, Alida," he said quietly, obeying a subtle impulse, "I'd rather you would do everything your own way—as it's natural for you. There, we've talked so long that it's too late to feed the chickens to-night. You can begin in the morning."

"Oh!" she cried, "and you have all your other work to do. I've hindered rather than helped you by coming out."

"No," he replied decidedly, "you've helped me. I'll be in before very long."

She returned to the house and busied herself in preparations for supper. She was very thoughtful, and at last concluded: "Yes, he is right. I understand. Although I may do *what* his wife did, he don't wish me to do it *as* she did. There could only be a partial and painful resemblance to his eyes. Both he and I would suffer in comparisons, and he be continually reminded of his loss. She was his wife in reality, and all relating to her is something sacred and past to him. The less I am like her, the better. He married me for the sake of his farm, and I can best satisfy him by carrying out his purpose in my own way. He's through with sentiment and has taken the kindest way he could to tell me that I've nothing to do with his past. He feared, yes, he *feared*, I should forget our businesslike agreement! I didn't know I had given him cause to fear; I certainly won't hereafter!" and the wife felt, with a trace of bitterness and shame, that she had been put on her guard; that he

usband had wished to remind her that she must not
forget his motive in marrying her, or expect anything not
consonance with that motive.   Perhaps she had been
o wifelike in her manner, and therefore he had feared.
he was as sensitive to such a reproach as she would have
been in her girlhood.

For once her intuition was at fault, and she misjudged
olcroft in some respects.   He did think he was through
ith sentiment ; he could not have talked deliberately to
lida or to any other about his old life and love, and he
uly felt that she had no part in that life.   It had
ecome a sad and sacred memory, yet he wished to feel
at he had the right to dwell upon it as he chose.   In
is downright sincerity he wished her to know that he
ould not help dwelling on it ; that for him some things
ere over, and that he was not to blame.   He was pro-
undly grateful to her that she had so clearly accepted
e facts of his past, and of their own present relations.
e *had* feared, it is true, but she had not realized his
ars, and he felt that it was her due that he should
cknowledge her straightforward carrying out of the
ompact made under circumstances which might well
xcuse her from realizing everything fully.

Moreover, direct and matter of fact as he was, he had
elt vaguely the inevitable difficulties of their relation-
hip.   The very word " wife " might suggest to her mind
n affection which he believed it was not in his power to
estow.   They had agreed to give an arbitrary and un-
sual meaning to their marriage, and, while thinking it
ould have no other meaning for him, his mind was
aunted, and he feared that hers might be, by the nat-
ral significance of the rite.   So far from meaning to
int that she had been too wifelike, he had meant to

acknowledge her simple and natural fulfillment of his
wishes in a position far more difficult to fill than even he
imagined. That she succeeded so well was due to the
fact that she entertained for him all the kind feelings
possible except the one supreme regard which, under
ordinary circumstances, would have accounted for the
marriage. The reason that all promised to go so well
in their relationship of mere mutual help was the truth
that this basis of union had satisfied their mutual needs
As the farmer had hoped, they had become excellent
friends, supplementing each other's work in a way that
promised prosperity.

Without the least intention on the part of either,
chance words had been spoken which would not be
without effect. He had told her to do everything in her
own way, because the moment he thought of it he knew
he liked her ways. They possessed a novelty and natural grace which interested him. There are both a natural
and a conventional grace, and the true lady learns to blend
the one with the other so as to make a charming manner
essentially her own—a manner which makes a woman a
lady the world over. Alida had little more than natural
grace and refinement, unmodified by society. This the
plain farmer could understand, and he was already awakening to an appreciation of it. It impressed him agreeably that Alida should be trim and neat while about her
work, and that all her actions were entirely free from the
coarse, slovenly manner, the limp carriage, and slatternly
aspect of the whole tribe which had come and gone during the past year. They had all been so much alike in
possessing disagreeable traits that he felt that Alida was
the only peculiar one among them. He never thought of
instituting comparisons between her and his former wife,

yet he did so unconsciously. Mrs. Holcroft had been too much like himself, matter of fact, materialistic, kind, and good. Devoid of imagination, uneducated in mind, her thoughts had not ranged far from what she touched and saw. She touched them with something of their own heaviness, she saw them as objects—just what they were—and was incapable of obtaining from them much suggestion or enjoyment. She knew when the cherry and plum trees were in blossom just as she knew it was April. The beautiful sounds and changes in nature reminded her that it was time to do certain kinds of work, and with her work was alpha and omega. As her mother had before her, she was inclined to be a house-drudge rather than a housewife. Thrift, neatness, order, marked the limits of her endeavor, and she accomplished her tasks with the awkward, brisk directness learned in her mother's kitchen. Only mind, imagination, and re-finement can embroider the homely details of life. Alida would learn to do all that she had done, but the woman with a finer nature would do it in a different way. Holcroft already knew he liked this way, although he could not define it to himself. Tired as he was when he came home in the evening, his eyes would often kindle with pleasure at some action or remark that interested him from its novelty. In spite of his weariness and pre-occupation, in spite of a still greater obstacle—the inertia of a mind dulled by material life—he had begun to con-sider Alida's personality for its own sake. He liked to watch her, not to see what she did to his advantage, but how she did it. She was awakening an agreeable expectancy, and he sometimes smilingly said to himself, "What next?"

" Oh, no ! " he thought as he was milking the last cow

"I'd much rather she'd take her own natural way i
doing things. It would be easier for her and it's he
right and—and somehow I like her way just as I used t
like Bessie's ways. She isn't Bessie and never can b
and for some reason I'd like her to be as different a
possible."

Unconsciously and unintentionally, however, he ha
given Alida's sensitive nature a slight wound. She fe
that she had been told in effect, "You can help me a
you please, and I would rather you would do this in
way that will not awaken associations, but you must no
think of me or expect me to think of you in any ligh
that was not agreed upon." That he had feared th
possibility of this, that he might have fancied he sa
indications of this, hurt her pride—that pride and del
cacy of feeling which most women shield so instinctivel
She was now consciously on her guard, and so was no
so secure against the thoughts she deprecated as befor
In spite of herself, a restraint would tinge her manne
which he would eventually feel in a vague, uncomfortab
way.

But he came in at last, very tired and thoroughly goo
natured. "I'm going to town to-morrow," he said, "an
I thought of taking a very early start so as to save time
Would you like to go?"

"There's no need of my going."

"I thought perhaps you'd enjoy the drive."

"I would have to meet strangers and I'm so entirel
content in being alone—I won't go this time unless yo
wish it."

"Well, if you don't care about it I'll carry out my fir
plan and take a very early start. I want to sell the butte
and eggs on hand, repay Tom Watterly, and get som

eeds. We need some things from the store, too, I
uppose?"

"Yes, you are such a coffee drinker——" she began,
miling.

"Oh, I know!" he interrupted. "Make out your list.
ou shall say what we want. Isn't there something you
ant for yourself?"

"No, not for myself, but I do want something that
erhaps you would enjoy, too. You may think it a
aste of money, though."

"Well, you've a right to waste some in your way as
ell as I have over my pipe."

"That's good. I hadn't thought of that. You are the
ne that puts notions into my head. I would like three
r four geraniums and a few flower seeds."

He looked as if he was thinking deeply and she felt a
ttle hurt that he should not comply at once with her re-
uest, knowing that the outlay suggested was very slight.

At last he looked up, smiling as he said, "So I put
otions into your head, do I?"

"Oh, well," she replied, flushing in the consciousness
 her thoughts, "if you think it's foolish to spend
oney for such things——"

"Tush, tush, Alida! Of course I'll get what you
ish. But I really am going to put a notion into your
ead, and it's stupid and scarcely fair in me that I hadn't
ought of some such plan before. You want to take
re of the chickens. Well, I put them wholly in your
re and you shall have all you can make off them—
gs, young chickens, and everything."

"That *is* a new notion," she replied, laughing. "I
adn't thought of such a thing and it's more than fair.
hat would I do with so much money?"

"What you please. Buy yourself silk dresses if you want to."

"But I couldn't use a quarter of the money."

"No matter, use what you like and I'll put the rest in the bank for you and in your name. I was a nice kind of a business partner, wasn't I? Expecting you to do nearly half the work and then have you say, 'Will you please get me a few plants and seeds?' and then, 'Oh! if you think it's foolish to spend money for such things.' Why you have as good a right to spend some of the money you help earn as I have. You've shown you'll be sensible in spending it. I don't believe you'll use enough of it. Anyway, it will be yours, as it ought to be."

"Very well," she replied, nodding at him with piquant significance, "I'll always have some to lend you."

"Yes, shouldn't wonder if you were the richest some day. Everything you touch seems to turn out well. shall be wholly dependent on you hereafter for eggs and an occasional fricassee."

"You shall have your share. Yes, I like this notion. It grows on me. I'd like to earn some money to do what I please with. You'll be surprised to see what strange and extravagant tastes I'll develop!"

"I expect to be perfectly dumfoundered, as Mrs. Mumpson used to say. Since you are so willing to lend I'll lend you enough to get all you want to-morrow. Make out your list. You can get a good start to-morrow, for I was too tired and it was too late for me to gather the eggs to-night. I know, too, that a good many of the hens have stolen their nests of late, and I've been too busy to look for 'em. You may find perfect mines of eggs, but, for mercy's sake! don't climb around in dangerous places. I had such bad luck with chicks last year that I've only set a few hens. You can set few or many now, just as you please."

Even as he talked and leisurely finished his supper, his eyes grew heavy with sleep. "What time will you start to-morrow?" she asked.

"Oh, no matter; long before you are up or ought to be. I'll get myself a cup of coffee. I expect to do my morning work and be back by nine or ten o'clock, for I wish to get in some potatoes and other vegetables before Sunday."

"Very well, I'll make out my list and lay it on the table here. Now, why don't you go and sleep at once? You ought, with such an early start in prospect."

"Ought I? Well, I never felt more inclined to do my duty. You must own up I have put one good notion into your head?"

"I have said nothing against any of them. Come, you ought to go at once."

"Can't I smoke my pipe first, please?"

"You'll find it quieter in the parlor."

"But it's pleasanter here where I can watch you."

"Do you think I need watching?"

"Yes, a little, since you don't look after your own interests very sharply."

"It isn't my way to look after anything very sharply."

"No, Alida, thank the Lord! There's nothing sharp about you, not even your tongue. You won't mind being left alone a few hours to-morrow?"

"No, indeed, I like to be alone."

"I thought I did. Most everyone has seemed a crowd to me. I'm glad you've never given me that feeling. Well, good-by till you see me driving up with the geraniums."

CHAPTER XXV.

A CHARIVARI.

THE eastern horizon was aglow with rosy tints the following morning when Holcroft awoke; the stars were but just fading from the sky and the birds were still silent. He knew by these signs that it was very early and that he could carry out his plan of a timely start to town. Dressing very quietly, he stole down stairs, shoes in hand, lest his tread should awaken Alida. The kitchen door leading into the hall was closed. Lifting the latch carefully, he found the lamp burning, the breakfast table set, and the kettle humming over a good fire. "This is her work, but where is she?" he queried in much surprise.

The outer door was ajar; he noiselessly crossed the room, and looking out, he saw her. She had been to the well for a pail of water, but had set it down and was watching the swiftly brightening east. She was so still and her face so white in the faint radiance that he had an odd, uncanny impression. No woman that he had ever known would stop that way to look at the dawn. He could see nothing so peculiar in it as to attract such fixed attention. "Alida," he asked, "what do you see?"

She started slightly and turned to take up the pail; but he had already sprung down the steps and relieved her of the burden.

"Could anything be more lovely than those changing tints? It seems to me I could have stood there an hour," she said quietly. .

"You are not walking or doing all this in your sleep, are you?" he asked, laughing, yet regarding her curiously. "You looked as you stood there like what people call a—what's that big word?"

"I'm not a somnambulist and never was, to my knowledge. You'll find I'm wide enough awake to have a good breakfast soon."

"But I didn't expect you to get up so early. I didn't wish it."

"It's too late now," she said pleasantly, "so I hope you won't find fault with me for doing what I wanted to do."

"Did you mean to be up and have breakfast when I told you last night?"

"Yes. Of course I didn't let you know, for you would have said I mustn't, and then I couldn't. It isn't good for people to get up so early and do as much as you had on your mind without eating. Now you won't be any the worse for it."

"I certainly ought to be the better for so much kindly consideration; but it will cure me of such unearthly hours if you feel that you must conform to them. You look pale this morning, Alida; you're not strong enough to do such things, and there's no need of it when I'm so used to waiting on myself."

"I shall have to remind you," she replied, with a bright look at him over her shoulder, "that you said I could do things my own way."

"Well, it seems odd after a year when everyone who came here appeared to grudge doing a thing for a man's comfort."

"I should hope I was different from them."

"Well, you are. I thought you were different from anyone I ever knew as I saw you *there* looking at the east. You seem wonderfully fond of pretty things."

"I'll own to that. But if you don't hurry you won't do as much as you hoped by getting up early."

The morning was very mild, and she left the outer door open as she went quickly to and fro with elasticity of spirit as well as step. It was pleasant to have her efforts appreciated and almost as grateful to hear the swelling harmony of song from the awakening birds. The slight cloud that had fallen on her thoughts the evening before had lifted. She felt that she understood Holcroft better, and saw that his feeling was only that of honest friendliness and satisfaction. She had merely to recognize and respond to so much only and all would be well. Meantime, she desired nothing more, and he should be thoroughly convinced of this fact. She grew positively light-hearted over the fuller assurance of the truth that although a wife, she was not expected to love—only to be faithful to all his interests. This, and this only, she believed to be within her power.

Holcroft departed in the serenity characteristic of one's mood when the present is so agreeable that neither memories of the past nor misgivings as to the future are obtrusive. He met Watterly in town, and remarked, "This is another piece of good luck. I hadn't time to go out to your place, although I meant to take time."

"A piece of good luck indeed!" Tom mentally echoed, for he would have been greatly embarrassed if Holcroft had called. Mrs. Watterly felt that she had been scandalized by the marriage which had taken place in her absence, and was all the more resentful for the reason that she had spoken to a cousin of uncertain age and still more uncertain temper in behalf of the farmer. In Mrs. Watterly's estimate of action, it was either right, that is, in accordance with her views, or else it was intolerably wrong and without excuse. Poor Tom had been made to feel that he had not only committed an almost unpardonable sin against his wife and her cousin, but also against all the proprieties of life. "The idea of such a wedding taking place in my rooms and with my husband's sanction!" she had said with concentrated bitterness. Then had followed what he was accustomed to characterize as a spell of "zero weather." He discreetly said nothing. "It didn't seem such a bad idea to me," he thought, "but then I suppose women folks know best about such things."

He was too frank in his nature to conceal from Holcroft his misgivings or his wife's scornful and indignant disapproval. "Sorry Angy feels so bad about it, Jim," he said ruefully, "but she says I mustn't buy anything more of you."

"Or have anything more to do with me, I suppose?"

"Oh, come now! You know a man's got to let his women-folks have their say about household matters, but that don't make any difference in my feelings toward you."

"Well, well, Tom! if it did, I should be slow to quarrel with a man who had done me as good a turn as you have. Thank the Lord! I've got a wife that 'll let me have some say about household and all other matters. You, too, are inclined to think that I'm in an awful scrape. I feel less like getting out of it every day. My wife is as respectable as I am and a good sight better than I am. If I'm no longer respectable for having married her, I certainly am better contented than I ever expected to be again. I want it understood, though, that the man who says anything against my wife may have to get me arrested for assault and battery."

"When it comes to that, Jim," replied Watterly, who was meek only in the presence of his wife, "I'd just as lief speak against her as wink if there was anything to say. But I say now, as I said to you at first, she aint one of the common sort. I thought well of her at first, and I think better of her now since she's doing so well by you. But I suppose marrying a woman situated as she was isn't according to regulation. We men are apt to act like the boys we used to be and go for what we want without thinking of the consequences."

"It's the consequences that please me most. If you had been dependent on Mumpsons, Malonys, and Wigginses for your home comfort you wouldn't worry about the talk of people who'd never raise a finger for you. Well, good-by, I'm in a hurry. Your heart's in the right place, Tom, and some day you'll come out and take dinner with me. One dinner, such as she'll give you, will bring you round. One of our steady dishes is a bunch of flowers and I enjoy 'em, too. What do you think of that for a hard-headed old fellow like me?"

Some men are chilled by public disapproval and waver under it, but Holcroft was thereby only the more strongly confirmed in his course. Alida had won his esteem as well as his good will, and it was the instinct of his manhood to protect and champion her. He bought twice as many flowers and seeds as she had asked for, and also selected two simple flower vases; then started on his return with the feeling that he had a home.

Alida entered upon her duties to the poultry with

almost the pleasure of a child. She first fed them, then explored every accessible nook and hiding place in the barn and outbuildings. It was evident that many of the biddies had stolen their nests, and some were brooding upon them with no disposition to be disturbed. Out of the hundred or more fowls on the place, a good many were clucking their maternal instincts, and their new keeper resolved to put eggs under all except the flighty ones that left their nests within two or three days' trial. As the result of her search, the empty egg basket was in a fair way to be full again very soon. She gloated over her spoils as she smilingly assured herself, " I shall take him at his word. I shall spend nearly all I make this year in fixing up the old house within and without, so he'll scarcely know it."

It was eleven o'clock before Holcroft drove to the door with the flowers, and he was amply repaid by her pleasure in receiving them. " Why, I only expected geraniums," she said, " and you've bought half a dozen other kinds."

" And I expected to get my own coffee this morning and a good breakfast was given me instead, so we are quits."

" You're probably ready for your dinner now, if it is an hour earlier than usual. It will be ready in ten minutes."

" Famous! That will give me a good long afternoon. I say, Alida, when do you want the flower-beds made ? "

" No hurry about them. I shall keep the plants in the window for a week or two. It isn't safe to put them outdoors before the last of May. I'll have some slips ready by that time."

" Yes, I know. You'll soon have enough to set out an acre."

The days of another week passed quietly and rapidly away, Alida becoming almost as much absorbed in her interests as he in his. Every hour added to the beauty of the season without. The unplowed fields were taking on a vivid green, and Holcroft said that on the following Monday the cows should go out to pasture. Wholesome, agreeable occupation enabled Alida to put away sad thoughts and memories. Nature and pleasant work are two potent healers, and she was rallying fast under their ministry. Holcroft would have been blind indeed had he not observed changes for the better. Her thin cheeks were becoming fuller, and her exertions, with the increasing warmth of the season, often flushed her face with a charming color. The old sad and troubled expression was passing away from her blue eyes. Every day it seemed easier for her to laugh, and her step grew more elastic. It was all so gradual that he never questioned it, but his eyes followed her with increasing pleasure and he listened, when she spoke, with deepening interest. Sundays had been long and rather dreary days, but now he positively welcomed their coming and looked forward to the hours when, instead of brooding over the past, he should listen to her pleasant voice reading his few and neglected books. There was a new atmosphere in his home—a new influence, under which his mind was awakening in spite of his weariness and absorption in the interests of the farm. Alida was always ready to talk about these, and her questions would soon enable her to talk understandingly. She displayed ignorance enough, and this amused him, but her queries evinced no stupidity. In reading to her father and in the cultivation of flowers, she had obtained hints of vital horticultural principles, and Holcroft said to her laughingly one even-

ing at supper, " You'll soon learn all I know and begin
to teach me."

Her manner of deprecating such remarks was to exag-
gerate them and she replied, " Yes, next week you will
sell my eggs and I shall subscribe for the agricultural
paper my father used to take. Then will begin all the
improvements of book-farming. I shall advise you to
sow oats in June, plant corn in March, and show you
generally that all your experience counts for nothing."

This kind of badinage was new to the farmer, and it
amused him immensely. He did not grow sleepy so
early in the evening, and as he was driving his work
prosperously he shortened his hours of labor slightly.
She also found time to read the county paper and gossip
a little about the news, thus making a beginning in putting him and herself *en rapport* with other interests
than those which centered in the farm. In brief, she had
an active, intelligent mind and a companionable nature.
Her boundless gratitude for her home, which daily grew
more homelike, led her to employ all her tact in adding
to his enjoyment, Yet so fine was her tact that her manner was a simple embodiment of good will, and he was
made to feel that it was nothing more,

While all was passing so genially and satisfactorily to
Holcroft, it may well be supposed that his conduct was
not at all to the mind of his neighbors. News, especially
during the busy spring season, permeates a country neighborhood slowly. The fact of his marriage had soon become known, and eventually, through Justice Harkins, the
circumstances relating to it and something of Alida's
previous history, in a garbled form, came to be discussed
at rural firesides. The majority of the men laughed and
shrugged their shoulders, implying it was none of their

business, but not a few, among whom was Lemuel Weeks, held up their hands and spoke of the event in terms of the severest reprehension. Many of the farmers' wives and their maiden sisters were quite as much scandalized as Mrs. Watterly had been that an unknown woman, of whom strange stories were told, should have been brought into the community from the poorhouse, "and after such a heathenish marriage, too," they said. It was irregular, unprecedented, and therefore utterly wrong and subversive of the morals of the town. They longed to ostracise poor Alida, yet saw no chance of doing so. They could only talk, and talk they did, in a way that would have made her ears tingle had she heard.

The young men and older boys, however, believed that they could do more than talk. Timothy Weeks had said to a group of his familiars, "Let's give old Holcroft and his poorhouse bride a skimelton that will let 'em know what folks think of 'em."

The scheme found favor at once, and Tim Weeks was soon recognized as organizer and leader of the peculiar style of serenade contemplated. After his day's work was over, he rode here and there summoning congenial spirits. The project soon became pretty well known in several families, but the elder members remained discreetly blind and deaf, proposing to wink at what was going on, yet take no compromising part themselves. Lemuel Weeks winked very knowingly and suggestively. He kept within such bounds, however, as would enable him to swear that he knew nothing and had said nothing, but his son had never felt more assured of his father's sympathy. When at last the motley gathering rendezvoused at Tim's house, Weeks, senior, was conveniently making a call on a near neighbor.

It was Saturday evening, and the young May moon would furnish sufficient light without revealing identity too clearly. About a score of young fellows and hired farm-hands of the ruder sort came riding and trudging to Weeks' barn, where there was a barrel of cider on tap. Here they blackened their faces with charcoal and stimulated their courage, for it was well known that Holcroft was anything but lamblike when angered.

"He'll be like a bull in a china shop," remarked Tim, "but then there's enough of us to handle him if he gets too obstrep'rous."

Armed with tin pans and horns which were to furnish the accompaniment to their discordant voices, they started about eight in the evening. As they moved up the road there was a good deal of coarse jesting and bravado, but when they approached the farmhouse silence was enjoined. After passing up the lane they looked rather nervously at the quiet dwelling softly outlined in the moonlight. A lamp illumined the kitchen window, and Tim Weeks whispered excitedly, "He's there. Let's first peek in the window and then give 'em a scorcher."

Knowing that they should have the coming day in which to rest, Holcroft and Alida had busied themselves with outdoor matters until late. She had been planning her flower-beds, cutting out the dead wood from some neglected rosebushes and shrubbery, and had also helped her husband by sowing seed in the kitchen garden back of the house. Then, weary, yet pleased with the labor accomplished, they made a very leisurely supper, talking over garden matters and farm prospects in general. Alida had all her flower seeds on the table beside her, and she gloated over them and expatiated on the kind of blossoms they would produce with so much zest that

Holcroft laughingly remarked, "I never thought that flowers would be one of the most important crops on the place."

"You will think so some day. I can see, from the expression of your eyes, that the cherry blossoms and now the apple blows which I put on the table please you almost as much as the fruit would."

"Well, it's because I notice 'em. I never seemed to notice 'em much before."

"Oh, no! it's more than that," she replied, shaking her head. "Some people would notice them, yet never see how pretty they were."

"Then they'd be blind as moles."

"The worst kind of blindness is that of the mind."

"Well, I think many country people are as stupid and blind as oxen, and I was one of 'em. I've seen more cherry and apple blossoms this year than in all my life before, and I haven't thought only of cherries and apples either."

"The habit of seeing what is pretty grows on one," she resumed. "It seems to me that flowers and such things feed mind and heart. So if one *has* mind and heart, flowers become one of the most useful crops. Isn't that practical common sense?"

"Not very common in Oakville. I'm glad you think I'm in a hopeful frame of mind, as they used to say down at the meeting house. Anyhow, since you wish it, we will have a flower crop as well as a potato crop."

Thus they continued chatting while Alida cleared up the table, and Holcroft, having lighted his pipe, busied himself with peeling a long, slim hickory sapling intended for a whipstock.

Having finished her tasks, Alida was finally drying her

hands on a towel that hung near a window. Suddenly, she caught sight of a dark face peering in. Her startled cry brought Holcroft hastily to his feet. "What's the matter?" he asked.

"I saw——" Then she hesitated from a fear that he would rush into some unknown danger.

The rough crew without perceived that their presence was known, and Tim Weeks cried, "Now, all together!"

A frightful overture began at once, the hooting and yelling almost drowning the instrumental part and sending to Alida's heart that awful chill of fear produced by human voices in any mob-like assemblage. Holcroft understood the affair at once, for he was familiar with the custom, but she did not. He threw open the door with the purpose of sternly expostulating with the disturbers of the peace and of threatening them with the law unless they retired. With an instinct to share his danger she stepped to his side, and this brought a yell of derision. Lurid thoughts swept through her mind. She had brought this danger. Her story had become known. What might they not do to Holcroft? Under the impulse of vague terror and complete self-sacrifice, she stepped forward and cried, "I only am to blame. I will go away forever if you will spare——" But again the scornful clamor rose and drowned her voice.

Her action and words had been so swift that Holcroft could not interfere, but in an instant he was at her side, his arm around her, his square jaw set, and his eyes blazing with his kindling anger. He was not one of those men who fume early under provocation and in words chiefly. His manner and gesture were so impressive that his tormentors paused to listen.

"I know," he said quietly, "all about this old, rude

custom—that it's often little more than a rough lark. Well, now that you've had it, leave at once. I'm in no mood for such attention from my neighbors. This is my wife, and I'll break any man's head who says a word to hurt her feelings—— "

" Oh, yes ! take care of her feelings, now it's your turn. They must 'a' been hurt before," piped up Tim Weeks.

" Good for you, old man, for showin' us your poorhouse bride," said another.

" We don't fancy such grass-widders, and much married, half-married women in Oakville," yelled a third.

" Why didn't yer jump over a broomstick for a weddin' ceremony ? " someone else bawled.

These insults were fired almost in a volley. Alida felt Holcroft's arm grow rigid for a second. " Go in, quick ! " he said. Then she saw him seize the hickory sapling he had leaned against the house, and burst upon the group like a thunderbolt. Cries of pain, yells, and oaths of rage rose above the rain of blows. The older members of the crew sought to close upon him, but he sprung back, and the tough sapling swept about him like a circle of light. It was a terrific weapon in the hands of a strong man, now possessed of almost giant strength in his rage. More than one fellow went down under its stinging cut, and heads and faces were bleeding. The younger portion of the crowd speedily took to their heels, and soon even the most stubborn fled ; the farmer vigorously assisting their ignominious retreat with tremendous downward blows on any within reach. Tim Weeks had managed to keep out of the way till they entered the lane ; then, taking a small stone from the fence, he hurled it at their pursuer and attempted to jump over the wall. This was old, and gave way under him in such a way that he fell on the other side. Holcroft leaped the fence with a bound, but Tim, lying on his back, shrieked and held up his hands. "You won't hit a feller when he's down!"

"No," said Holcroft, arresting his hickory. "I'll send you to jail, Tim Weeks. That stone you fired cut my head. Was your father in that crowd?"

"N-o-o!" blubbered Tim.

"If he was, I'd follow him home and whip him in his own house. Now, clear out, and tell the rest of your rowdy crew that I'll shoot the first one of you that disturbs me again. I'll send the constable for you, and maybe for some of the others."

Dire was the dismay, and dreadful the groaning in Oakville that night. Never before had salves and poultices been in such demand. Not a few would be disfigured for weeks, and wherever Holcroft's blows had fallen welts arose like whipcords. In Lemuel Weeks' dwelling the consternation reached its climax. Tim, bruised from his fall, limped in and told his portentous story. In his spite, he added, "I don't care, I hit him hard. His face was all bloody."

"All bloody!" groaned his father. "Lord 'a mercy! He can send you to jail, sure enough!"

Then Mrs. Weeks sat down and wailed aloud.

CHAPTER XXVI.

" YOU DON'T KNOW."

As Timothy Weeks limped hastily away, Holcroft, with a strong revulsion of feeling, thought of Alida. *He* had been able to answer insults in a way eminently satisfactory to himself, and every blow had relieved his electrical condition. But how about the poor woman who had received worse blows than he had inflicted? As he hastened toward the house he recalled a dim impression of seeing her sink down on the doorstep. Then he remembered her effort to face the marauders alone. "She said she was to blame, poor child! as if there were any blame at all! She said, 'spare him,' as if I was facing a band of murderers instead of a lot of neighborhood scamps, and that she'd go away. I'd fight all Oakville—men, women, and children—before I'd permit that," and he started on a run.

He found Alida on the step, where she had sunk as if struck down by the rough epithets hurled at her. She was sobbing violently, almost hysterically, and at first could not reply to his soothing words. He lifted her up, and half carried her within to a chair. "Oh, oh," she cried, "why did I not realize it more fully before? Selfish woman that I was, to marry you and bring on you all this shame and danger. I should have thought of it all. I ought to have died rather than do you such a wrong."

" Alida, Alida," protested Holcroft, " if it were all to do over again I'd be a thousand times more——— "

"Oh, I know, I know! You are brave and generous and honest. I saw that much when you first spoke to me. I yielded to the temptation to secure such a friend. I was too cowardly to face the world alone. And now see what's happened! You're in danger and disgrace on my account. I must go away—I must do what I should have done at first," and with her face buried in her hands she rocked back and forth, overwhelmed by the bitterness and reproach of her thoughts.

" Alida," he urged, " please be calm and sensible. Let me reason with you and tell you the truth. All that's happened is that the Oakville cubs have received a well-deserved whipping. When you get calm, I can explain everything so it won't seem half so bad. Neither you nor I are in any danger, and as for your going away, look me in the eyes and listen."

His words were almost stern in their earnestness. She raised her streaming eyes to his face, then sprung up, exclaiming, " Oh! you're wounded! "

" What's that, compared with your talk of going away?"

All explanations and reassurances would have been trivial in effect, compared with the truth that he had been hurt in her defense. She dashed her tears right and left, ran for a basin of water, and making him take her chair, began washing away the blood stains.

" Thunder! " he said, laughing, " how quickly we've changed places!"

"Oh, oh!" she moaned, "it's a terrible wound; it might have killed you, and they *will* kill you yet."

He took her hands and held them firmly. " Alida," he said, gravely yet kindly, " be still and listen to me."

For a moment or two longer her bosom heaved with convulsive sobs, and then she grew quiet. "Don't you know you can't go away?" he asked, still retaining her hands and looking in her face.

"I could for your sake," she began.

"No, it wouldn't be for my sake. I don't wish you to go, and wouldn't let you. If you should let the Oakville rabble drive you away I *would* be in danger, and so would others, for I'd be worse on 'em than an earthquake. After the lesson they've had to-night, they'll let us alone, and I'll let them alone. You know I've tried to be honest with you from the first. Believe me, then, the trouble's over, unless we make more for ourselves. Now, promise you'll do as I say and let me manage."

"I'll try," she breathed softly.

"No, no! that won't do. I'm beginning to find you out. You may get some foolish, self-sacrificing notion in your head that it would be best for me, when it would be my ruination. Will you promise?"

"Yes."

"Famous! Now you can bathe my head all you please, for it feels a little queer."

"It's an awful wound," she said in tones of the deepest sympathy. "Oh, I'm so sorry!"

"Pshaw! my head is too hard for that little scamp of a Weeks to break. His turn 'll come next."

She cut away the blood-clotted hair and bound up the rather severe scalp wound with a tenderness and sympathy that expressed itself even in her touch. She was too confused and excited to be conscious of herself, but she had received some tremendously strong impressions. Chief among them was the truth that nothing which had happened made any difference in him—that he was still the same loyal friend, standing between her and the world she dreaded—yes, between her and her own impulses toward self-sacrifice. Sweetest of all was the assurance that he did this for his own sake as well as hers. These facts seemed like a foothold in the mad torrent of feeling and shame which had been sweeping her away. She could think of little more than that she was safe—safe because he was brave and loyal—and yes, safe because he wanted her and would not give her up. The heart of a woman must be callous indeed, and her nature not only trivial but stony, if she is not deeply touched under circumstances like these.

In spite of his laughing contempt of danger, she trembled as she saw him ready to go out again; she wished to accompany him on his round of observation, but he scouted the idea, although it pleased him. Standing in the door, she strained her eyes and listened breathlessly. He soon returned and said, "They've all had enough. We won't be disturbed again."

He saw that her nerves needed quieting, and he set about the task with such simple tact as he possessed. His first step was to light his pipe in the most nonchalant manner, and then he burst out laughing. "I'll hang that hickory up. It has done too good service to be put to common use again. Probably you never heard of a skimelton, Alida. Well, they are not so uncommon in this region. I suppose I'll have to own up to taking part in one myself when I was a young chap. They usually are only rough larks and are taken good-naturedly. I'm not on jesting terms with my neighbors, and they had no business to come here, but I wouldn't have made any row if they hadn't insulted you."

Her head bowed very low as she faltered, " They've heard everything."

He came right to her and took her hand. " Didn't I hear everything before they did ? "

" Yes."

" Well, Alida, I'm not only satisfied with you, but I'm very grateful to you. Why shouldn't I be when you are a good Christian woman ? I guess I'm the one to be suited, not Oakville. I should be as reckless as the devil if you should go away from me. Don't I act like a man who's ready to stand up for and protect you ? "

" Yes, too ready. It would kill me if anything happened to you on my account."

" Well, the worst would happen," he said firmly, " if we don't go right on as we've begun. If we go quietly on about our own affairs, we'll soon be let alone and that's all we ask."

" Yes, yes indeed ! Don't worry, James. I'll do as you wish."

" Famous ! You never said ' James ' to me before. Why haven't you ? "

" I don't know," she faltered, with a sudden rush of color to her pale face.

" Well, that's my name," he resumed, laughing. " I guess it's because we are getting better acquainted."

She looked up and said impetuously, " You don't know how a woman feels when a man stands up for her as you did to-night."

" Well, I know how a man feels when there is a woman so well worth standing up for. It was a lucky thing that I had nothing heavier in my hand than that hickory." All the while he was looking at her curiously ; then he spoke his thought. " You're a quiet little woman, Alida, most times, but you're capable of a thunder gust now and then."

"I'll try to be quiet at all times," she replied, with drooping eyes.

"Oh, I'm not complaining!" he said, laughing. "I like the trait."

He took a small pitcher and went to the dairy. Returning, he poured out two glasses of milk and said, "Here's to your health and happiness, Alida; and when I don't stand up for the woman who started out to save me from a mob of murderers, may the next thing I eat or drink choke me. You didn't know they were merely a lot of Oakville boys, did you?"

"You can't make so light of it," said she. "They tried to close on you, and if that stone had struck you on the temple, it might have killed you. They swore like pirates, and looked like ruffians with their blackened faces. They certainly were not boys in appearance."

"I'm afraid I swore too," he said sadly.

"You had some excuse, but I'm sorry. They would have hurt you if you hadn't kept them off."

"Yes, they'd probably have given me a beating. People do things in hot blood they wish they hadn't afterward. I know this Oakville rough-scuff. Since we've had it out, and they know what to expect, they'll give me a wide berth. Now go and sleep. You were never safer in your life."

She did not trust herself to reply, but the glance she gave him from her tearful eyes was so eloquent with grateful feeling that he was suddenly conscious of some unwonted sensations. He again patrolled the place and tied the dog near the barn.

"It's barely possible that some of these mean cusses might venture to kindle a fire, but a bark from Towser will warn 'em off. She *is* a spirited little woman," he added, with a sharp change in soliloquy. " There's nothing milk-and-water about her. Thunder! I felt like kissing her when she looked at me so. I guess that crack on my skull has made me a little light-headed."

He lay down in his clothes so that he might rush out in case of any alarm, and he intended to keep awake. Then, the first thing he knew, the sun was shining in the windows.

It was long before Alida slept, and the burden of her thoughts confirmed the words that she had spoken so involuntarily. " You don't know how a woman feels when a man stands up for her as you did." It is the nature of her sex to adore hardy, courageous manhood. Beyond all power of expression, Alida felt her need of a champion and protector. She was capable of going away for his sake, but she would go in terror and despair. The words that had smitten her confirmed all her old fears of facing the world alone. Then came the overpowering thought of his loyalty and kindness, of his utter and almost fierce repugnance to the idea of her leaving him. In contrast with the man who had deceived and wronged her, Holcroft's course overwhelmed her very soul with a passion of grateful affection. A new emotion, unlike anything she had ever known, thrilled her heart and covered her face with blushes. " I could die for him!" she murmured.

She awoke late in the morning. When at last she entered the kitchen she stopped in deep chagrin, for Holcroft had almost completed preparations for breakfast. " Ha, ha!" he laughed, " turn about is fair play."

" Well," she sighed, " there's no use of making excuses now."

"There's no occasion for any. Did you ever see such a looking case as I am with this bandage around my head?"

"Does it pain you?" she asked sympathetically.

"Well, it does. It pains like thunder."

"The wound needs dressing again. Let me cleanse and bind it up."

"Yes, after breakfast."

"No, indeed; now. I couldn't eat my breakfast while you were suffering so."

"I'm more unfeeling then than you are, for I could."

She insisted on having her way, and then tore up her handkerchief to supply a soft linen bandage.

"You're extravagant, Alida," but she only shook her head.

"Famous! That feels better. What a touch you have! Now, if you had a broken head, my fingers would be like a pair of tongs."

She only shook her head and smiled.

"You're as bad as Jane used to be. She never said a word when she could shake or nod her meaning."

"I should think you would be glad, after having been half talked to death by her mother."

"As I said before, take your own way of doing things. It seems the right way after it is done."

A faint color came into her face, and she looked positively happy as she sat down to breakfast. "Are you sure your head feels better?" she asked.

"Yes, and you look a hundred per cent. better. Well, I *am* glad you had such a good sleep after all the hubbub."

"I didn't sleep till toward morning," she said, with downcast eyes.

"Pshaw! that's too bad. Well, no matter, you look like a different person from what you did when I first saw you. You've been growing younger every day."

Her face flushed like a girl's under his direct, admiring gaze, making her all the more pretty. She hastened to divert direct attention from herself by asking, "You haven't heard from anyone this morning?"

"No, but I guess the doctor has. Some of those fellows will have to keep shady for a while."

As they were finishing breakfast, Holcroft looked out of the open kitchen door and exclaimed, "By thunder! we're going to hear from some of them now. Here comes Mrs. Weeks, the mother of the fellow who hit me."

"Won't you please receive her in the parlor?"

"Yes, she won't stay long, you may be sure. I'm going to give that Weeks tribe one lesson and pay off the whole score."

He merely bowed coldly to Mrs. Weeks' salutation and offered her a chair. The poor woman took out her handkerchief and began to mop her eyes, but Holcroft was steeled against her, not so much on account of the wound inflicted by her son as for the reason that he saw in her an accomplice with her husband in the fraud of Mrs. Mumpson.

"I hope you're not badly hurt," she began.

"It might be worse."

"Oh, Mr. Holcroft!" she broke out sobbingly, "spare my son. It would kill me if you sent him to prison."

"He took the chance of killing me last night," was the cold reply. "What's far worse, he insulted my wife."

"Oh, Mr. Holcroft! he was young and foolish; he didn't realize——"

"Were you and your husband young and foolish," he

interrupted bitterly, "when you gulled me into employing that crazy cousin of yours?"

This retort was so overwhelming that Mrs. Weeks sobbed speechlessly.

Alida could not help overhearing the conversation, and she now glided into the room and stood by her husband's side.

"James," she said, "won't you do me a favor, a great kindness?"

Mrs. Weeks raised her eyes and looked wonderingly at this dreadful woman, against whom all Oakville was talking.

"I know what you wish, Alida," he replied sternly, "but I can't do it. This is a case for justice. This woman's son was the leader of that vile crowd that insulted you last night. I can forgive his injuring me, but not the words he used about you. Moreover, when I was alone and struggling to keep my home, Mrs. Weeks took part with her husband in imposing on me their fraud of a cousin and in tricking me out of honest money. Any woman with a heart in her breast would have tried to help a man situated as I was. No, it's a clear case of justice, and her son shall go to jail."

Mrs. Weeks wailed afresh at this final sentence. Holcroft was amazed to see his wife drop on her knees beside his chair. He raised her instantly. "Don't do such a thing as that," he said huskily.

Without removing her pleading eyes from his face she asked gently, "Who told us to forgive as we would be forgiven? James, I shall be very unhappy if you don't grant this mother's prayer."

He tried to turn away, but she caught his hand and held his eyes with hers. "Alida," he said in strong agitation, "you heard the vile, false words that Timothy Weeks said last night. They struck you down like a blow. Can you forgive him?"

"Yes, and I plead with you to forgive him. Grant me my wish, James; I shall be so much happier, and so will you."

"Well, Mrs. Weeks, now you know what kind of a woman your son came to insult. You may tell your neighbors that there's one Christian in Oakville. I yield to Mrs. Holcroft, and will take no further action in the affair if we are let alone."

Mrs. Weeks was not a bad woman at heart, and she had received a wholesome lesson. She came and took Alida's hand as she said, "Yes, you are a Christian—a better woman than I've been, but I aint so mean and bad but what, when I see my fault, I am sorry and can ask forgiveness. I do ask your forgiveness, Mr. Holcroft. I've been ashamed of myself ever since you brought my cousin back. I thought she would try, when she had the chance you gave her, but she seems to have no sense."

"There, there! let bygones be bygones," said the farmer in embarrassment. "I've surrendered. Please don't say anything more."

"You've got a kind heart, in spite——"

"Oh, come now! please quit, or I'll begin to swear a little to keep up the reputation my neighbors have given me. Go home and tell Tim to brace up and try to be a man. When I say I'm done with a grudge, I *am* done. You and Mrs. Holcroft can talk all you like, but please excuse me," and with more than most men's horror of a scene, he escaped precipitately.

"Sit down, Mrs. Weeks," said Alida kindly.

" Well, I will. I can't say much to excuse myself or my folks——"

" You've already said everything, Mrs. Weeks," interrupted Alida gently; " you've said you are sorry."

Mrs. Weeks stared a moment, and then resumed sententiously, " Well, I've heard more gospel in that remark than if I'd gone to church. And I couldn't go to church, I could never have gone there again or held my head up anywhere if—if——"

" That's all past and gone," said Alida, smiling. " When Mr. Holcroft says anything, you may depend on it."

" Well, God bless you for intercedin'—you had so much to forgive. Nobody shall ever speak a word against you again while I've got breath to answer. I wish you'd let me come and see you sometimes."

" Whenever you wish, if you care to visit one who has had so much—so much trouble."

" I see now that's all the more reason I should come, for if it hadn't been for you, I'd have been in bitter trouble myself. We've been worse than heathen, standin' off and talking against you. Oh, I've had a lesson I won't forget! Well, I must hurry home, for I left Timothy and Lemuel in a dreadful state."

Seeing the farmer in the barn as she was passing, she rushed to him. " You've got to shake hands with me, Mr. Holcroft. Your wife *is* a good woman, and she's a lady, too. Anyone with half an eye can see she's not one of the common sort."

The farmer shook the poor woman's hand good-naturedly and said heartily, " That's so! All right, Meeting's over. Good-by." Then he turned to his work and chuckled, " That's what Tom Watterly said.

Thank the Lord! she *isn't* of the common sort. I've got to brace up and be more of a man as well as Tim Weeks."

In spite of the pain in his head, Alida's words proved true. He was happier than he had been in many a long day. He had the glow which follows a generous act, and the thought that he had pleased a sweet little woman who somehow seemed very attractive to him that May morning; at the same time the old Adam in his nature led to a sneaking satisfaction that he had laid on the hickory so unsparingly the evening before.

Alida uttered a low, happy laugh as she heard him whistling " Coronation " in jig time, and she hustled away the breakfast things with the eagerness of a girl, that she might be ready to read to him when he came in.

CHAPTER XXVII.

FARM AND FARMER BEWITCHED.

THE day grew warm, and having finished her tasks indoors and cared for the poultry, Alida brought a chair out in the porch. Her eyes were dreamy with a vague, undefined happiness. The landscape in itself was cause for exquisite pleasure, for it was an ideal day of the apple-blossoming period. The old orchard back of the barn looked as if pink-and-white clouds had settled upon it, and scattered trees near and far were exhaling their fragrance. The light breeze which fanned her cheek and bent the growing rye in an adjacent field was perfumed beyond the skill of art. Not only were her favorite meadow larks calling to each other, but the thrushes had come and she felt that she had never heard such hymns as they were singing. A burst of song from the lilac bush under the parlor window drew her eyes thither, and there was the paternal redbreast pouring out the very soul of ecstasy. From the nest beneath him rose the black head and yellow beak of his brooding mate. How, contented and happy she looks!" Alida murmured, " how happy they both are! and the secret of it is *home*. And to think that I, who was a friendless waif, am at home, also! At home with Eden-like beauty and peace before my eyes. But if it hadn't been for him, and if he were not brave, kind, and true to all he

says——" and she shuddered at a contrast that rose
before her fancy.

She could now scarcely satisfy herself that it was only
gratitude which filled her heart with a strange, happy
tumult. She had never been conscious of such exalta-
tion before. It is true, she had learned to cherish a
strong affection for the man whom she had believed to
be her husband, but chiefly because he had seemed kind
and she had an affectionate disposition. Until within
the last few hours, her nature had never been touched
and awakened in its profoundest depths. She had never
known before nor had she idealized the manhood capable
of evoking the feelings which now lighted her eyes and
gave to her face the supreme charm and beauty of
womanhood. In truth, it was a fitting day and time for
the birth of a love like hers, simple, all-absorbing, and
grateful. It contained no element not in harmony with
that May Sunday morning.

Holcroft came and sat on the steps below her. She
kept her eyes on the landscape, for she was conscious
enough on her guard now. "I rather guess you think,
Alida, that you are looking at a better picture than an
artist fellow could paint?" he remarked.

"Yes," she replied hesitatingly, "and the picture
seems all the more lovely and full of light because the
background is so very dark. I've been thinking of what
happened here last night and what might have happened
and how I felt then."

"You feel better—different now, don't you? You certainly look so."

"Yes, you made me very happy by yielding to Mrs.
Weeks."

"Oh! I didn't yield to her at all."

" Very well, have it your own way then."

" I think you had it your way."

" Are you sorry ? "

" Do I look so ? How did you know I'd be happier if I gave in ? "

" Because, as you say, I'm getting better acquainted with you. *You* couldn't help being happier for a generous act."

" I wouldn't have done it, though, if it hadn't been for you."

" I'm not so sure about that."

" I am. You're coming to make me feel confoundedly uncomfortable in my heathenish life."

" I wish I could."

" I never had such a sermon in my life as you gave me this morning. A Christian act like yours is worth a year of religious talk."

She looked at him wistfully for a moment and then asked, a little abruptly, " Mr. Holcroft, have you truly forgiven that Weeks family ? "

" Oh, yes ! I suppose so. I've forgiven the old lady, anyhow. I've shaken hands with her."

" If her husband and son should come and apologize and say they were sorry, would you truly and honestly forgive them ? "

" Certainly ! I couldn't hold a grudge after that. What are you aiming at ? " and he turned and looked inquiringly into her face.

It was flushed and tearful in its eager, earnest interest. Don't you see ? " she faltered.

He shook his head, but was suddenly and strangely moved by her expression.

" Why, Mr. Holcroft, if you can honestly forgive those

who have wronged you, you ought to see how ready God is to forgive."

He fairly started to his feet so vividly the truth came home to him, illumined, as it was, by a recent and personal experience. After a moment, he slowly sat down again and said, with a long breath, "That was a close shot, Alida."

"I only wish you to have the trust and comfort which this truth should bring you," she said. "It seems a pity you should do yourself needless injustice when you are willing to do what is right and kind by others."

"It's all a terrible muddle, Alida. If God is so ready to forgive, how do you account for all the evil and suffering in the world?"

"I don't account for it and can't. I'm only one of his little children; often an erring one, too. You've been able to forgive grown people, your equals, and strangers in a sense. Suppose you had a little boy that had done wrong, but said he was sorry, would you hold a grudge against him?"

"The idea! I'd be a brute."

She laughed softly as she asked again, "Don't you see?"

He sat looking thoughtfully away across the fields for a long time, and finally asked, "Is your idea of becoming a Christian just being forgiven like a child and then trying to do right?"

"Yes. Why not?"

"Well," he remarked, with a grim laugh, "I didn't expect to be cornered in this way."

"You who are truthful should face the truth. It would make you happier. A good deal that was unexpected has happened. When I look out on a scene like this and think that I am safe and at home, I feel that God has been very good to me and that you have, too. I can't bear to think that you have that old trouble on your mind—the feeling that you had been a Christian once, but was not one now. Being sure that there is no need of your continuing to feel so, what sort of return would I be making for all your kindness if I did not try to show you what is as clear to me as this sunshine?"

"You are a good woman, Alida. Believing as you do, you have done right to speak to me, and I never believed mortal lips could speak so to the purpose. I shall think of what you have said, for you have put things in a new light. But say, Alida, what on earth possesses you to call me 'Mr.'? You said James easy enough after the skimelton was over and when old lady Weeks was begging Tim off. You don't need to be scared half to death every time to call me by my first name, do you?"

"Scared? Oh, no!" She was a trifle confused, he thought, but then her tone was completely reassuring.

The day was one long remembered by both. As in nature about them, the conditions of development and rapid change now existed. She did not read aloud very much, and long silences fell between them. They were reaching a higher plane of companionship, in which words are not always essential. Both had much to think about, and their thoughts were like roots which prepare for blossom and fruit.

With Monday, busy life was resumed. The farmer began planting his corn and Alida her flower seeds. Almost every day now added to the brood of little chicks under her care. The cows went out to pasture, Holcroft brought in an increasing number of overflowing pails of milk, and if the labors of the dairy grew more exacting, they also grew more profitable. The tide had turned;

income was larger than outgo, and it truly seemed to the long-harassed man that an era of peace and prosperity had set in.

To a superficial observer things might have appeared to be going on much as before, but there were influences at work which Holcroft did not clearly comprehend.

As Alida had promised herself she spent all the money which the eggs brought in, but Holcroft found pretty muslin curtains at the parlor windows, and shades which excluded the glare from the kitchen. Better china took the place of that which was cracked and unsightly. In brief, a subtle and refining touch was apparent all over the house.

" How fine we are getting ! " he remarked one evening at supper.

" I've only made a beginning," she replied, nodding defiantly at him. "The chickens will paint the house before the year is over."

" Phew ! when do the silk dresses come in ? "

" When your broadcloth does."

" Well, if this goes on, I shall certainly have to wear purple and fine linen to keep pace."

" Fine linen, certainly. When you take the next lot of eggs to town I shall tell you just the number of yards I need to make half a dozen extra fine shirts. Those you have are getting past mending."

" Do you think I'll let you spend your money in that way ? "

" You'll let me spend *my* money just as I please—in the way that will do me the most good ! "

" What a saucy little woman you are becoming ! " he said, looking at her so fondly that she quickly averted her eyes.

"It's a way people fall into when humored," she answered.

"See here, Alida, you're up to some magic. It seems but the other day I brought you here, a pale ghost of a woman. As old Jonathan Johnson said, you were 'enj'yin' poor health.' Do you know what he said when I took him off so he wouldn't put you through the catechism?"

"No," she replied, with a deprecating smile and rising color.

"He said he was 'afeared I'd been taken in, you were such a sickly lookin' critter.' Ha! ha! Wish he might see you now, with that flushed face of yours. I never believed in magic, but I'll have to come to it. You are bewitched, and are being transformed into a pretty young girl right under my eyes; the house is bewitched, and is growing pretty, too, and pleasanter all the time. The cherry and apple trees are bewitched, for they never blossomed so before; the hens are bewitched, they lay as if possessed; the——"

"Oh, stop! or I shall think that you're bewitched yourself."

"I truly begin to think I am."

"Oh, well! since we all and everything are affected in the same way, it don't matter."

"But it does. It's unaccountable. I'm beginning to rub my eyes and pinch myself to wake up."

"If you like it, I wouldn't wake up."

"Suppose I did, and saw Mrs. Mumpson sitting where you do, Jane here, and Mrs. Wiggins smoking her pipe in the corner. The very thought makes me shiver. My first words would be, 'Please pass the cold p'ison.'"

"What nonsense you are talking to-night!" she tried

to say severely, but the pleased, happy look in her eyes betrayed her. He regarded her with the open admiration of a boy, and she sought to divert his attention by asking, " What do you think has become of Jane ? "

" I don't know—stealing around like a strange cat in some relation's house, I suppose."

" You once said you would like to do something for her."

" Well, I would. If I could afford it I'd like to send her to school."

" Would you like her to come here and study lessons part of the time ? "

He shivered visibly. " No, Alida, and you wouldn't either. She'd make you more nervous than she would me, and that's saying a good deal. I do feel very sorry for her, and if Mrs. Weeks comes to see you, we'll find out if something can't be done, but her presence would spoil all our cozy comfort. The fact is, I wouldn't enjoy having anyone here. You and I are just about company enough. Still, if you feel that you'd like to have some help——"

" Oh, no ! I haven't enough to do."

" But you're always a-doing. Well, if you're content, I haven't Christian fortitude enough to make any changes."

She smiled and thought that she was more than content. She had begun to detect symptoms in her husband which her own heart enabled her to interpret. In brief, it looked as if he were drifting on a smooth, swift tide to the same haven in which she was anchored.

One unusually warm morning for the season, rain set in after breakfast. Holcroft did not fret in the least that he could not go to the fields, nor did he, as had

been his custom at first, find rainy-day work at the barn.
The cows, in cropping the lush grass, had so increased
their yield of milk that it was necessary to churn every
other day, and Alida was busy in the dairy. This place
had become inviting by reason of its coolness, and she
had rendered it more so by making it perfectly clean and
sweet. Strange to say, it contained another chair besides
the one she usually occupied. The apartment was large
and stone-flagged. Along one side were shelves filled
with rows of shining milk-pans. In one corner stood
the simple machinery which the old dog put in motion
when tied upon his movable walk, and the churn
was near. An iron pipe, buried deep in the ground,
brought cool spring water from the brook above. This
pipe emptied its contents with a low gurgle into a
shallow, oblong receptacle sunk in the floor, and was
wide and deep enough for two stone crocks of ample
size to stand abreast up to their rims in the water. The
cream was skimmed into these stone jars until they were
full, then Holcroft emptied them into the churn. He
had charged Alida never to attempt this part of the
work, and indeed it was beyond her strength. After
breakfast on churning days, he prepared everything and
set the dog at work. Then he emptied the churn of the
buttermilk when he came in to dinner.

All the associations of the place were pleasant to
Alida. It was here that her husband had shown
patience as well as kindness in teaching her how to
supplement his work until her own experience and judgment gave her a better skill than he possessed. Many
pleasant, laughing words had passed between them in
this cool, shadowy place, and on a former rainy morning he had brought a chair down that he might keep her

company. She had not carried it back, nor was she very greatly surprised to see him saunter in and occupy it on the present occasion. She stood by the churn, her figure outlined clearly in the light from the open door, as she poured in cold water from time to time to hasten and harden the gathering butter. Her right sleeve was rolled well back, revealing a white arm that was becoming beautifully plump and round. An artist would have said that her attitude and action were unconsciously natural and graceful. Holcroft had scarcely the remotest idea of artistic effect, but he had a sensible man's perception of a charming woman when she is charming.

"Mr. Holcroft," she asked very gravely, "will you do something for me?"

"Yes, half a dozen things."

"You promise?"

"Certainly! What's the trouble?"

"I don't mean there shall be any if I can help it," she answered with a light ripple of laughter. "Please go and put on your coat."

"How you've humbugged me! It's too hot."

"Oh, you've got to do it; you promised. You can't stay here unless you do."

"So you are going to take care of me as if I were a small boy?"

"You need care—sometimes."

He soon came back and asked, "Now may I stay?"

"Yes. Please untie the dog. Butter's come."

"I should think it would, or anything else at your coaxing."

"Oh-h, what a speech! Hasn't that a pretty golden hue?" she asked, holding up a mass of the butter she was ladling from the churn into a wooden tray.

"Yes, you are making the gilt-edge article now. I don't have to sell it to Tom Watterly any more."

"I'd like to give him some, though."

He was silent, and something like sudden rage burned in his heart that Mrs. Watterly would not permit the gift. That anyone should frown on his having such a helper as Alida was proving herself to be, made him vindictive. Fortunately her face was turned away, and she did not see his heavy frown. Then, to shield her from a disagreeable fact, he said quickly, "Do you know that for over a year I steadily went behind my expenses, and that your butter-making has turned the tide already? I'm beginning to get ahead again."

"I'm *so* glad," and her face was radiant.

"Yes, I should know that from your looks. It's clearer every day that I got the best of our bargain. I never dreamed, though, that I should enjoy your society as I do—that we should become such very good friends. That wasn't in the bargain, was it?"

"Bargain!" The spirited way with which she echoed the word, as if thereby repudiating anything like a sordid side to their mutual relations, was not lost on her wondering and admiring partner. She checked herself suddenly. "Now let me teach *you* how to make butter," and with the tray in her lap, she began washing the golden product and pressing out the milk.

He laughed in a confused, delighted way at her piquant, half saucy manner as he watched her deft round arm and shapely hand.

"The farmers' wives in Oakville would say your hands were too little to do much."

"They would?" and she raised her blue eyes indignantly to his. "No matter, you are the one to say about that."

"I say they do too much. I shall have to get Jane to help you."

"By all means! Then you'll have more society."

"That was a home shot. You know how I dote on everybody's absence, even Jane's."

"You dote on butter. See how firm and yellow it's getting. You wouldn't think it was milk-white cream a little while ago, would you? Now I'll put in the salt and you must taste it, for you're a connoisseur."

"A what?"

"Judge, then."

"You know a sight more than I do, Alida."

"I'm learning all the time."

"So am I—to appreciate you."

"Listen to the sound of the rain and the water as it runs into the milk-cooler. It's like low music, isn't it?"

Poor Holcroft could make no better answer than a sneeze.

"Oh-h," she exclaimed, "you're catching cold! Come, you must go right upstairs. You can't stay here another minute. I'm nearly through."

"I was never more contented in my life."

"You've no right to worry me. What would I do if you got sick? Come, I'll stop work till you go."

"Well then, little boss, good-by."

With a half suppressed smile at his obedience Alida watched his reluctant departure. She kept on diligently at work, but one might have fancied that her thoughts rather than her exertions were flushing her cheeks.

It seemed to her that but a few moments elapsed before she followed him, but he had gone. Then she saw that the rain had ceased and that the clouds were breaking. His cheerful whistle sounded reassuringly from the barn, and a little later he drove up the lane with a cart.

She sat down in the kitchen and began sewing on the fine linen they had jested about. Before long she heard a light step. Glancing up, she saw the most peculiar and uncanny-looking child that had ever crossed her vision, and with dismal presentiment knew it was Jane.

CHAPTER XXVIII.

ANOTHER WAIF.

IT was indeed poor, forlorn little Jane that had appeared like a specter in the kitchen door. She was as wet and bedraggled as a chicken caught in a shower. A little felt hat hung limp over her ears; her pigtail braid had lost its string and was unraveling at the end, and her torn, sodden shoes were ready to drop from her feet. She looked both curiously and apprehensively at Alida with her little blinking eyes, and then asked in a sort of breathless voice, " Where's him ? "

" Mr. Holcroft ? "

Jane nodded.

" He's gone out to the fields. You are Jane, aren't you ? "

Another nod.

" Oh, *dear !* " groaned Alida mentally ; " I wish she hadn't come." Then with a flush of shame the thought crossed her mind, " She perhaps is as friendless and homeless as I was, and ' him ' is also her only hope. Come in, Jane," she said kindly, " and tell me everything."

" Be you his new girl ? "

" I'm his wife," said Alida, smiling.

Jane stopped ; her mouth opened and her eyes twinkled with dismay. " Then he is married, after all ? " she gasped.

" Yes, why not ? "

" Mother said he'd never get anyone to take him."

" Well, you see she was mistaken."

" She's wrong about everything. Well, it's no use then," and the child turned and sat down on the doorstep.

Alida was perplexed. From the way Jane wiped her eyes with her wet sleeve, she was evidently crying. Coming to her, Alida said, " What is no use, Jane ? Why are you crying ? "

" I thought—he—might—p'raps—let me stay and work for him."

Alida was still more perplexed. What could be said by way of comfort, feeling sure as she did that Holcroft would be bitterly hostile to the idea of keeping the child ? The best she could do was to draw the little waif out and obtain some explanation of her unexpected appearance. But first she asked, " Have you had any breakfast ? "

Jane shook her head.

" Oh, then you must have some right away."

" Don't want any. I want to die. I oughtn' ter been born."

" Tell me your troubles, Jane. Perhaps I can help you."

" No, you'd be like the rest. They all hate me and make me feel I'm in the way. He's the only one that didn't make me feel like a stray cat, and now he's gone and got married," and the child sobbed aloud.

Her grief was pitiful to see, for it was overwhelming. Alida stooped down, and gently lifting the child up, brought her in. Then she took off the wet hat and wiped the tear-stained face with her handkerchief. " Wait a minute, Jane, till I bring you something," and she ran to the dairy for a glass of milk. "You must drink it," she said, kindly but firmly.

The child gulped it down, and with it much of her grief, for this was unprecedented treatment and was winning her attention.

"Say," she faltered, "will you ask him to let me stay?"

"Yes, I'll ask him, but I can't promise that he will."

"You won't ask him 'fore my face and then tell him not to behind my back?" and there was a sly, keen look in her eyes which tears could not conceal.

"No," said Alida gravely, "that's not my way. How did you get here, Jane?"

"Run away."

"From where?"

"Poorhouse."

Alida drew a quick breath and was silent a few moments. "Is—is your mother there?" she asked at length.

"Yes. They wouldn't let us visit round any longer."

"Didn't your mother or anyone know you were coming?"

Jane shook her head.

Alida felt that it would be useless to burden the unhappy child with misgivings as to the result, and her heart softened toward her as one who in her limited way had known the bitterness and dread which in that same almshouse had overwhelmed her own spirit. She could only say gently, "Well, wait till Mr. Holcroft comes, and then we'll see what he says." She herself was both curious and anxious as to his course. "It will be a heavy cross," she thought, "but I should little deserve God's goodness to me if I did not befriend this child."

Every moment added weight to this unexpected burden of duty. Apart from all consideration of Jane's peculiarities, the isolation with Holcroft had been a delight in itself. Their mutual enjoyment of each other's society had been growing from day to day, and she, more truly than he, had shrunk from the presence of another as an unwelcome intrusion. Conscious of her secret, Jane's prying eyes were already beginning to irritate her nerves. Never had she seen a human face that so completely embodied her idea of inquisitiveness as the uncanny visage of this child. She saw that she would be watched with a tireless vigilance. Her recoil, however, was not so much a matter of conscious reasoning and perception as it was an instinctive feeling of repulsion caused by the unfortunate child. It was the same old story. Jane always put the women of a household on pins and needles just as her mother exasperated the men. Alida had to struggle hard during a comparatively silent hour to fight down the hope that Holcroft would not listen to Jane's and her own request.

As she stepped quickly and lightly about in her preparations for dinner, the girl watched her intently. At last she gave voice to her thoughts and said, " If mother'd only worked round smart as you, p'raps she'd hooked him 'stid er you."

Alida's only reply was a slight frown, for the remark suggested disagreeable images and fancies. "Oh, how can I endure it?" she sighed. She determined to let Jane plead her own cause at first, thinking that perhaps this would be the safest way. If necessary, she would use her influence against a hostile decision, let it cost in discomfort what it might.

At a few moments before twelve the farmer came

briskly toward the house, and was evidently in the best of
spirits. When he entered and saw Jane, his countenance
indicated so much dismay that Alida could scarcely
repress a smile. The child rose and stood before him
like a culprit awaiting sentence. She winked hard to
keep the tears back, for there was no welcome in his
manner. She could not know how intensely distasteful
was her presence at this time, nor had Holcroft himself
imagined how unwelcome a third person in his house
could be until he saw the intruder before him. He had
only felt that he was wonderfully contented and happy
in his home, and that Jane would be a constant source of
annoyance and restraint. Moreover, it might lead to
visitation from Mrs. Mumpson, and that was the summing up of earthly ills. But the child's appearance and
manner were so forlorn and deprecating that words of
irritation died upon his lips. He gravely shook hands
with her and then drew out the story which Alida had
learned.

"Why, Jane," he exclaimed, frowning, "Mr. Watterly
will be scouring the country for you. I shall have to
take you back right after dinner."

"I kinder hoped," she sobbed, "that you'd let me stay.
I'd stay in the barn if I couldn't be in the house. I'd
just as soon work outdoors, too."

"I don't think you'd be allowed to stay," said the
farmer, with a sinking heart; "and then—perhaps your
mother would be coming here."

"I can't stand mother no more'n you can," said the
girl, through her set teeth. "I oughtn' ter been born, for
there's no place for me in the world.

Holcroft looked at his wife, his face expressive of the
utmost annoyance, worry, and irresolution. Her glance

was sympathetic, but she said nothing, feeling that if he could make the sacrifice from his own will he should have the chance. " You can't begin to know how much trouble this may lead to, Jane," he resumed. " You remember how your mother threatened to take the law upon me, and it wouldn't be possible for you to stay here without her consent."

" She oughter consent ; I'll make her consent !" cried the child, speaking as if driven to desperation. " What's she ever done for me but teach me mean ways ? Keep me or kill me, for I must be in some place where I've a right to be away from mother. I've found that there's no sense in her talk, and it drives me crazy."

Although Jane's words and utterance were strangely uncouth, they contained a despairing echo which the farmer could not resist. Turning his troubled face to his wife, he began, " If this is possible, Alida, it will be a great deal harder on you than it will on me. I don't feel that I would be doing right by you unless you gave your consent with full knowledge of—— "

" Then please let her stay, if it is possible. She seems to need a friend and home as much as another that you heard about."

" There's no chance of such a blessed reward in this case," he replied, with a grim laugh. Then, perplexed indeed, he continued to Jane, " I'm just as sorry for you as I can be, but there's no use of getting my wife and self in trouble which in the end will do you no good. You are too young to understand all that your staying may lead to."

" It won't lead to mother's comin' here, and that's the worst that could happen. Since she can't do anything for me she's got to let me do for myself."

" Alida, please come with me in the parlor a moment. You stay here, Jane." When they were alone, he resumed, " Somehow, I feel strangely unwilling to have that child live with us. We were enjoying our quiet life so much. Then you don't realize how uncomfortable she will make you, Alida."

" Yes, I do."

" I don't think you can yet. Your sympathies are touched now, but she'll watch you and irritate you in a hundred ways. Don't her very presence make you uncomfortable ? "

" Yes."

" Well, then, she can't stay," he began decidedly. " This is your home, and no one shall make you uncomfortable——"

" But I should be a great deal more uncomfortable if she didn't stay," Alida interrupted. " I should feel that I did not deserve my home. Not long ago my heart was breaking because I was friendless and in trouble. What could I think of myself if I did not entreat you in behalf of this poor child ? "

" Thunder ! " ejaculated Holcroft. " I guess I was rather friendless and troubled myself, and I didn't know the world had in it such a good friend as you've become, Alida. Well, well ! you've put it in such a light that I'd be almost tempted to take the mother, also."

" No," she replied, laughing ; " we'll draw the line at the mother."

" Well, I'll take Jane to town this afternoon, and if her mother will sign an agreement to leave us all in peace, we'll give up our old cozy comfort of being alone. I suppose it must be a good deed, since it's so mighty hard to do it," he concluded with a wry face, leading the way to the kitchen again. She smiled as if his words were already rewarding her self-denial.

"Well, Jane," he resumed, " Mrs. Holcroft has spoken in your behalf, and if we can arrange matters so that you can stay you will have her to thank chiefly. I'll take you back to the poorhouse after dinner, so it may be known what's become of you. Then, if your mother 'll sign an agreement to make no trouble and not come here, we'll give you a home until we can find a better place for you."

There was no outburst of gratitude. The repressed, dwarfed nature of the child was incapable of this, yet there was an unwonted little thrill of hope in her heart. Possibly it was like the beginning of life in a seed under the first spring rays of the sun. She merely nodded to Holcroft as if the matter had been settled as far as it could be, and ignored Alida.

"Why don't you thank Mrs. Holcroft?" he asked.

Then Jane turned and nodded at Alida. Her vocabulary of thanks was undeveloped.

"She's glad," said Alida. "You'll see. Now that it's settled, we hope you're hungry, Jane, aren't you?"

"Yes, I be. Can't I help you put things on the table?"

"Yes."

Holcroft looked at the two for a moment, and then shook his head as he went up to his room. "I thought my wife was nice and pleasant looking before," he thought, "but she's like a picture beside that child. Well, she has behaved handsomely. Tom Watterly didn't tell half the truth when he said she was not of the common run. She's a Christian in deeds, not talk. What's that in Scripture about 'I was hungry'? Well, well! she makes religion kind of natural and plain like, whether it's easy or not. Thunder! what a joke it is to see her so grateful because I've given her a chance to help me out of the worst scrape a man could be in ! As if she hadn't changed everything for the better ! Here I am sure of my home and getting ahead in the world again, and it's all her doing."

In admiration of his wife Holcroft quite forgot that there had been any self-sacrifice on his part, and he concluded that he could endure Jane and almost anything else as long as Alida continued to look after his comfort and interests.

Now that the worst stress of Jane's anxiety was over, she proved that she was half starved. Indeed she had few misgivings now, for her confidence that Holcroft would accomplish what he attempted was almost unbounded. It was a rather silent meal at first, for the farmer and his wife had much to think about and Jane much to do in making up for many limited meals. At last Holcroft smiled so broadly that Alida said, "Something seems to please you."

"Yes, more than one thing. It might be a great deal worse, and was, not long ago. I was thinking of old times."

"How pleasant they must have been, to make you look so happy !"

"They had their uses, and make me think of a picture I saw in a store window in town. It was a picture of a woman, and she took my fancy amazingly. But the point uppermost in my mind was a trick of the fellow who painted her. He had made the background as dark as night and so she stood out as if alive ; and she looked so sweet and good that I felt like shaking hands with her. I now see why the painter made the background so dark."

Alida smiled mischievously as she replied, " That was

his art. He knew that almost anyone would appear well against such a background."

But Holcroft was much too direct to be diverted from his thought or its expression. "The man knew the mighty nice looking woman he had painted would look well," he said, "and I know of another woman who appears better against a darker background. That's enough to make a man smile who has been through what I have."

She could not help a flush of pleasure or disguise the happy light in her eyes, but she looked significantly at Jane, who, mystified and curious, was glancing from one to the other.

"Confound it!" thought the farmer. "That 'll be the way of it now. Here's a little pitcher that's nearly all ears. Well, we're in for it and must do our duty."

Going to town that day involved no slight inconvenience, but Holcroft dropped everything and rapidly made his preparations.

When Alida was left alone with Jane, the latter began clearing the table with alacrity, and, after a few furtive glances at Mrs. Holcroft, yielded to the feeling that she should make some acknowledgment of the intercession in her behalf. "Say," she began, "I thought you wasn't goin' to stand up for me, after all. Women folks are liars, mostly."

"You are mistaken, Jane. If you wish to stay with us, you must tell the truth and drop all sly ways."

"That's what he said when I first come."

"I say it too. You see a good deal, Jane. Try to see what will please people instead of what you can find out about them. It's a much better plan. Now, as a friend, I tell you of one thing you had better not do. You shouldn't watch and listen to Mr. Holcroft unless he speaks to you. He doesn't like to be watched—no one does. It isn't nice ; and if you come to us, I think you will try to do what is nice. Am I not right ? "

"I dunno how," said Jane.

"It will be part of my business to teach you. You ought to understand all about your coming. Mr. Holcroft doesn't take you because he needs your work, but because he's sorry for you, and wishes to give you a chance to do better and learn something. You must make up your mind to lessons, and learning to talk and act nicely, as well as to do such work as is given you. Are you willing to do what I say and mind me pleasantly and promptly ? "

Jane looked askance at the speaker and was vaguely suspicious of some trick. In her previous sojourn at the farmhouse she had concluded that it was her best policy to keep in Holcroft's good graces, even though she had to defy her mother and Mrs. Wiggins, and she was now by no means ready to commit herself to this new domestic power. She had received the impression that the authority and continued residence of females in this household was involved in much uncertainty, and although Alida was in favor now and the farmer's wife, she didn't know what "vicissitudes" (as her mother would denominate them) might occur. Holcroft was the only fixed and certain quantity in her troubled thoughts, and after a little hesitation she replied, " I'll do what he says ; I'm goin' to mind him."

"Suppose he tells you to mind me ? "

"Then I will. That ud be mindin' him. I'm goin' to stick to him, for I made out by it better before than by mindin' mother and Mrs. Wiggins."

Alida now understood the child and laughed aloud. "You are right," she said. "I won't ask you to do anything contrary to his wishes. Now tell me, Jane, what other clothes have you besides those you are wearing?"

It did not take the girl long to inventory her scanty wardrobe, and then Alida rapidly made out a list of what was needed immediately. "Wait here," she said, and putting on a pretty straw hat, one of her recent purchases, she started for the barn.

Holcroft had his wagon and team almost ready when Alida joined him, and led the way to the floor between the sweet-smelling hay-mows.

"One thing leads to another," she began, looking at him a little deprecatingly. "You must have noticed the condition of Jane's clothes."

"She does look like a little scarecrow, now I come to think of it," he admitted.

"Yes, she's not much better off than I was," Alida returned, with downcast eyes and rising color.

Her flushing face was so pretty under the straw hat, and the dark mow as a background brought out her figure so finely that he thought of the picture again and laughed aloud for pleasure. She looked up in questioning surprise, thus adding a new grace.

"I wish that artist fellow was here now," he exclaimed. "He could make another picture that would suit me better than the one I saw in town."

"What nonsense!" she cried, quickly averting her face from his admiring scrutiny. "Come, I'm here to talk business and you've no time to waste. I've made out a list of what the child actually must have to be respectable."

"You're right, Alida," said the farmer, becoming grave at once over a question of dollars and cents. "As you say, one thing leads to another, and if we take the girl we must clothe her decently. But then, I guess she'll earn enough to pay her way. It isn't that I worry about so much," he broke out discontentedly, "but the interference with our quiet, cozy life. Things are going so smoothly and pleasantly that I hate a change of any kind."

"We mustn't be selfish, you know," she replied. "You are doing a kind, generous act, and I respect you all the more for it."

"That settles everything. You'll like me a little better for it, too, won't you?" he asked hesitatingly.

She laughed outright at this question and answered, "It won't do to take too much self-sacrifice out of your act. That's something which does us all good. She ought to have a spelling and a writing book also."

Holcroft was assuredly falling under the sway of the little blind god, for he began at once to misunderstand Alida. "You are very fond of self-sacrifice," he said, rather stiffly. "Yes, I'll get everything on your list," and he took it from her hand. "Now I must be off," he added, "for I wish to get back before night, and it's so warm I can't drive fast. Sorry I have to go, for I can't say I dote on self-sacrifice."

Alida but partially understood his sudden change of mood, nor was the farmer much better enlightened himself in regard to his irritation. He had received an unexpected impression and it seemed to fit in with other things and explain them. She returned slowly and dejectedly to the house, leaving unsaid the words she meant to speak about Jane's relations to her. Now she wished that she had imitated Jane, and merely nodded to the farmer's question. "If he knew how far I am beyond the point of liking, I don't know what he'd do or say," she thought, "and I suppose that's the reason I couldn't answer him frankly, in a way that would have satisfied him. It's a pity I couldn't begin to just *like* a little at first, as he does, and have everything grow as gradually and quietly as one of his cornstalks. That's the way I meant it should be ; but when he stood up for me and defended me from those men, my heart just melted, and in spite of myself, I felt I could die for him. It can't be such an awful thing for a woman to fall in love with her husband, and yet—yet I'd rather put my hand in the fire than let him know how I feel. Oh, dear ! I wish Jane hadn't been born, as she says. Trouble is beginning already, and it was all so nice before she came."

In a few moments Holcroft drove up. Alida stood in the door and looked timidly at him. He thought she appeared a little pale and troubled, but his bad mood prevailed and he only asked briefly, "Can't I get something for you ?"

She shook her head.

"Well, good-by, then," and he drove away with Jane, who was confirmed in her line of policy. "She's afraid of 'im too," thought the child. "Mind her ! guess not, unless he says so." She watched the farmer furtively, and concluded that she had never known him to look more grim or be more silent even under her mother's blandishments. "He's married this one, I s'pose, to keep house for 'im, but he don't like her follerin' 'im up or bein' for'ard any more'n he did mother. Shouldn't wonder if he didn't keep her, either, if she don't suit better. She needn't 'a' put on such airs with me, for I'm goin' to stick to him."

CHAPTER XXIX.

HUSBAND AND WIFE IN TROUBLE.

LIKE many others with simple, strong natures, Holcroft could not be wrong-headed moderately, and his thoughts, once started in a direction, were apt to carry him much farther than the cause warranted. Engrossed in painful and rather bitter musings, he paid no heed to Jane, and almost forgot his errand to town. "I was a fool to ask that question," he thought. "I was getting silly and sentimental with my talk about the picture and all that. She laughed at me and reminded me I was wasting time. Of course she can't like an old, hard-featured man like me. I'm beginning to understand her now. She made a business marriage with me and means to live up to her agreement. She's honest ; she feels I've done her a great kindness in giving her a home, and she's willing to be as self-sacrificing as the day is long to make it up to me. I wish she wasn't so grateful ; there's no occasion for it. I don't want her to feel that every pleasant word and every nice act is so much toward paying a debt. If there was any balance in my favor it was squared up long ago, and I was willing to call it even from the start. She's made me like her for her own sake and not on account of what she does for me, and that's what I had in mind. But she's my superior in every way ; she's growing to be as pretty as a picture, and I suppose I appear like a rather rough customer. Well, I can't help it, but it rather goes against me to have her think, ' I've married him and I'm going to do my duty by him, just as I agreed.' She'll do her duty by this Jane in the same self-sacrificing spirit, and will try to make it pleasant for the child just because it's right and because she herself was taken out of trouble. That's the shape her religion takes. 'Tisn't a common form, I know—this returning good for good with compound interest. But her conscience won't let her rest unless she does everything she can for me, and now she'll begin to do everything for Jane because she feels that self-sacrifice is a duty. Anybody can be self-sacrificing. If I made up my mind, I could ask Mrs. Mumpson to visit us all summer, but I couldn't like her to save my life, and I don't suppose Alida can like me, beyond a certain point, to save her life. But she'll do her duty. She'll be pleasant and self-sacrificing and do all the work she can lay her hands on for my sake ; but when it comes to feeling toward me as I can't help feeling toward her—that wasn't in the bargain," and he startled Jane with a sudden bitter laugh.

"Say," said the child, as if bent on adding another poignant reflection, "if you hadn't married her, I could 'a' come and cooked for you."

"You think I'd been better off if I'd waited for you, eh ? "

"You kinder looked as if yer thought so."

He now made the hills echo with a laugh, excited both by his bitter fancies and the preposterous idea. She looked at him inquiringly and was much perplexed by his unwonted behavior. Indeed, he was slightly astonished at his own strange mood, but he yielded to it almost recklessly. "I say, Jane," he began, "I'm not a very good-looking man, am I ? "

She shook her head in emphatic agreement.

" I'm old and rough and hard-featured ? "

Agan she nodded approvingly.

" Children and some others speak the truth," he growled.

" I never had no teachin', but I'm not a fool," remarked Jane keenly.

" I guess I'm the fool in this case," he added.

" It don't make no difference to me," she said sympathetically. " I'm goin' to mind you and not her. If you ever send her away I'll cook for you."

" Send her away ! " exclaimed the farmer, with a shiver. " God forbid ! There, don't talk any more ! "

For the next half mile he drove in silence, with a heavy frown on his face ; then he broke out sternly, " If you don't promise to mind Mrs. Holcroft and please her in everything, I'll leave you at the poorhouse door and drive home again."

" Course I will, if you tells me to," said the child in trepidation.

" Well, I *do*. People will find that making her trouble is the surest way of making themselves trouble."

" She's got some hold on 'im," concluded Jane, who, in listening to much gossip, had often heard this expression, and now made a practical application of the idea.

Watterly was greatly relieved when he saw Holcroft drive up with the fugitive. " I was just going out to your place," he said, " for the girl's mother insisted that you had enticed the child away," and the man laughed, as if the idea tickled him immensely.

Holcroft frowned, for he was in no mood for his friend's rough jests. ' Go to your mother till I send for you," he said to Jane.

"The fact that you had taken two other females from the house gave some color to Mrs. Mumpson's views," pursued Watterly, who could take only the broadest hint as to his social conduct.

He received one now. "Tom Watterly," said the farmer sternly, "did I ever insult your wife?"

"By jocks! no, you nor no other man. I should say not."

"Well, then, don't you insult mine. Before I'd seen Mrs. Holcroft, you told me she was out of the common run,—how much out, you little know,—and I don't want her mixed up with the common run, even in your thoughts."

"Well, now, I like that," said Watterly, giving Holcroft his hand. "You know I didn't mean any offense, Jim. It was only one of my foolish jokes. You were mighty slow to promise to love, honor, and obey, but hanged if you aint more on that line than any man in town. I can see she's turning out well and keeping her agreement."

"Yes, that's just what she's doing," said the farmer gloomily. "She's a good, capable woman that 'll sacrifice herself to her duty any day. But it wasn't to talk about her I came. She's a sight better than I am, but she's probably not good enough for anybody in this town to speak to."

"Oh, pshaw; now, Jim!"

"Well, I've come on disagreeable business. I didn't know that Mrs. Mumpson and her child were here, and I wish to the Lord they could both stay here! You've found out what the mother is, I suppose?"

"I should say so," replied Tom, laughing. "She's talked several of the old women to death already. The

first day she was here she called on my wife and claimed
social relations, because she's so 'respecterbly connected,'
as she says. I thought Angy'd have a fit. Her respectable connections have got to take her off my hands."

"I'm not one of 'em, thank goodness!" resumed Holcroft. "But I'm willing to take the girl and give her a
chance—at least I'll do it," he corrected himself, in his
strict observance of truth. "You can see she's not a
child to dote on, but I was sorry for her when I sent her
mother away and said I'd try and do something for her.
The first thing I knew she was at the house, begging me
to either take her in or kill her. I couldn't say no,
though I wanted to. Now, you see what kind of a
good Samaritan I am."

"Oh, I know you! You'd hit a man between the eyes
if he charged you with doing a good deed. But what
does your wife say to adopting such a cherub?"

"We're not going to adopt her or bind ourselves. My
wife took the child's part and plead with me in her
behalf, though I could see the young one almost made
her sick. She thinks it's her duty, you know, and that's
enough for her."

"By jocks, Holcroft! she don't feel that way about
you, does she?"

"Why shouldn't she?"

"Why should she? I can take about anything from
Angy, but it wouldn't do for her to let me see that she
disliked me so that I kinder made her sick."

"Oh, thunder, Tom! you're getting a wrong impression. I was never treated better by anybody in my life
than by Mrs. Holcroft. She's a lady, every inch of her.
But there's no reason why she should dote on an old
fellow like me."

"Yes, there is. I have my opinion of a woman who wouldn't dote on a man that's been such a friend as you have."

"Oh, hang it all, Tom! let's talk about business, She's too grateful—that's what worries me. By the way she took hold and filled the house with comfort she made everything even from the start. She's been as good a friend to me as I to her. She's done all she agreed and more, and I'll never hear a word against her. The point I've been trying to get at is this: If Mrs. Mumpson will agree never to come near us or make trouble in any way, we'll take the child. If she won't so agree, I'll have nothing to do with the girl. I don't want to see her mother, and you'd do me one of the kindest turns you ever did a man by stating the case to her."

"If I do," said Watterly, laughing, "you'll have to forgive me everything in the past and the future."

"I will, Tom, for I'd rather have an eye-tooth pulled than face that woman. We're all right—just as we used to be at school, always half quarreling, yet ready to stand up for each other to the last drop. But I must have her promise in black and white."

"Well, come to my office and we'll try to arrange it. The law is on your side, for the county won't support people that anyone will take off its hands. Besides, I'm going to shame the woman's relations into taking her away, **and** they'll be glad there's one less to support."

They drew up a brief, strong agreement, and Watterly took it to the widow to sign. He found her in great excitement and Jane looking at her defiantly. "I told you he was the one who enticed away my offspring," she began, almost hysterically. "He's a cold-blooded villain! If there's law in the land I'll——"

"Stop!" thundered Watterly. His voice was so high and authoritative that she did stop, and with open mouth stared at the superintendent. "Now, be quiet and listen to me," he continued. "Either you are a sane woman and can stop this foolishness, or else you are insane and must be treated as such. You have your choice. You can't tell me anything about Holcroft; I've known him since he was a boy. He doesn't want your girl. She ran away to him, didn't you?" to Jane, who nodded. "But he's willing to take her, to teach her something and give her a chance. His motive is pure kindness, and he has a good wife who'll——"

"I see it all," cried the widow, tragically clasping her hands. "It's his wife's doings! She wishes to triumph over me, and even to usurp my place in ministering to my child. Was there ever such an outrage? Such a bold, vindictive female——"

Here Jane, in a paroxysm of indignant protest, seized her mother and began to shake her so violently that she could not speak.

"Stop that!" said Watterly, repressing laughter with difficulty. "I see you are insane and the law will have to step in and take care of you both."

"What will it do with us?" gasped the widow.

"Well, it ought to put you in strait-jackets, to begin with——"

"I've got some sense if mother aint!" cried Jane, commencing to sob.

"It's plain the law 'll decide your mother's not fit to take care of you. Anyone who can even imagine such silly, ridiculous things as she's just said must be looked after. You *may* take a notion, Mrs. Mumpson, that I'm a murderer or a giraffe. It would be just as sensible as your other talk."

"What does Mr. Holcroft offer?" said the widow, cooling off rapidly. If there was an atom of common sense left in any of his pauper charges, Watterly soon brought it into play, and his vague threatenings of law were always awe-inspiring.

"He makes a very kind offer, that you would jump at if you had sense—a good home for your child. You ought to know she can't stay here and live on charity if anyone is willing to take her."

"Of course I would be permitted to visit my child from time to time? He couldn't be so monstrously hard-hearted as——"

"Oh, nonsense!" cried Watterly impatiently. "The idea of his letting you come to his house after what you've said about him! I've no time to waste in foolishness, or he either. He will let Jane visit you, but you are to sign this paper and keep the agreement not to go near him or make any trouble whatever."

"It's an abominable——"

"Tut! tut! that kind of talk isn't allowed here. If you can't decide like a sane woman the law 'll soon decide for you."

As was always the case when Mrs. Mumpson reached the inevitable, she yielded; the paper was signed, and Jane, who had already made up her small bundle, nodded triumphantly to her mother and followed Watterly. Mrs. Mumpson, on tiptoe, followed also, bent on either pro-pitiating Holcroft and so preparing the way for a visit, or else on giving him once more a "piece of her mind."

"All right, Holcroft!" said Watterly, as he entered the

office, "here's the paper signed. Was there ever such an id——"

"Oh, how do you do, Mr. Holcroft?" cried the widow, bursting in and rushing forward with extended hand.

The farmer turned away and looked as if made of stone.

Changing her tactics instantly, she put her handkerchief to her eyes and moaned, "You never can have the heart to say I can't come and see my child. I've signed writings, 'tis true, under threats and compulsions; but I trust there will be relentings——"

"There won't be one relent!" cried Jane. "I never want to see you again, and a blind post could see that he doesn't."

"Jane," said Holcroft sternly, "don't speak so again. If strangers can be kind and patient with you, you can be so with your mother. She has no claims on me and has said things which make it impossible for me to speak to her again, but I shall insist on your visiting and treating her kindly. Good-by, Watterly. You've proved yourself a friend again," and he went rapidly away, followed by Jane.

Mrs. Mumpson was so taken aback by Holcroft's final words and Watterly's stern manner as he said, "This is my office," that for once in her life she disappeared silently.

Holcroft soon purchased the articles on his list, meanwhile racking his brains to think of something that he could buy for Alida, but the fear of being thought sentimental and of appearing to seek a personal regard for himself, not "nominated in the bond," restrained him.

On his way home he was again sunk in deep abstraction, but the bitterness of his feeling had passed away.

Although as mistaken as before in his apprehension of Alida, his thoughts were kinder and juster. " I've no right to find fault or complain," he said to himself. " She's done all I asked and better than she agreed, and there's no one to blame if she can't do more. It must have been plain enough to her at first that I didn't want anything but a housekeeper—a quiet, friendly body that would look after the house and dairy, and she's done better than I even hoped. That's just the trouble ; she's turned out so different from what I expected, and looks so different from what she did, that I'm just sort of carried away. I'd give half the farm if she was sitting by my side this June evening and I could tell her all I feel and know she was glad. I must be just and fair to her. I asked her to agree to one thing and now I'm beginning to want a tremendous sight more—I want her to like not only her home and work and the quiet life she so longed for, but I want her to like me, to enjoy my society, not only in a friendly, businesslike way, but in another way— yes, confound my slow wits ! somewhat as if she was my wife in reality and not merely in name, as I insisted. It's mighty mean business in me, who have been so proud of standing up to my agreements and so exacting of others to do the same. I went away cold and stiff this afternoon because she wasn't silly and sentimental when I was. I'm to her an unpolished, homely, middle-aged man, and yet I sort of scoffed at the self-sacrifice which has led her to be pleasant and companionable in every way that her feelings allowed. I wish I were younger and better looking, so it wouldn't all be a sense of duty and grati- tude. Gratitude be hanged ! I don't want any more of it. Well, now, James Holcroft, if you're the square man you supposed yourself to be, you'll be just as kind and considerate as you know how, and then you'll leave Alida to the quiet, peaceful life to which she looked forward when she married you. The thing for you to do is to go back to your first ways after you were married and attend to the farm. She doesn't want you hanging around and looking at her as if she was one of her own posies. That's something she wasn't led to expect and it would be mean enough to force it upon her before she shows that she wishes it, and I couldn't complain if she *never* wished it."

During the first hour after Holcroft's departure Alida had been perplexed and worried, but her intuitions soon led to hopefulness, and the beauty and peace of nature without aided in restoring her serenity. The more minutely she dwelt on Holcroft's words and manner, the more true it seemed that he was learning to take an interest in her that was personal and apart from every other consideration. "If I am gentle, patient, and faithful," she thought, "all will come out right. He is so true and straightforward that I need have no fears."

When he returned and greeted her with what seemed his old, friendly, natural manner, and, during a temporary absence of Jane, told her laughingly of the Mumpson episode, she was almost completely reassured. "Suppose the widow breaks through all restraint and appears as did Jane, what would you do?" he asked.

"Whatever you wished," she replied, smiling.

"In other words, what you thought your duty?"

"I suppose that is what one should try to do."

"I guess you are the one that would succeed in doing it, even to Mrs. Mumpson," he said, turning hastily away and going to his room.

She was puzzled again. "I'm sure I don't dote on self-sacrifice and hard duty any more than he does, but I can't tell him that duty is not hard when it's to him."

Jane was given the room over the kitchen which Mrs. Wiggins had occupied, and the farmhouse soon adopted her into its quiet routine. Holcroft's course continued to cause Alida a dissatisfaction which she could scarcely define. He was as kind as ever he had been and even more considerate; he not only gratified her wishes, but tried to anticipate them, while Jane's complete subserviency proved that she had been spoken to very plainly.

One day she missed her spelling lesson for the third time, and Alida told her that she must learn it thoroughly before going out. The child took the book reluctantly, yet without a word. "That's a good girl!" said Alida, wishing to encourage her. "I was afraid at first you wouldn't mind me so readily."

"He told me to. He'd fire me out the window if I didn't mind you."

"Oh, no! I think he's very kind to you."

"Well, he's kind to you, too."

"Yes, he has always been kind to me," said Alida gently and lingeringly, as if the thought were pleasant to dwell upon.

"Say," said Jane, yielding to her curiosity, "how did you make him so afraid of you when he don't like you? He didn't like mother, but he wasn't afraid of her."

"Why do you think he doesn't like me?" Alida faltered, turning very pale.

"Oh! 'cause he looked once jest as he did after mother'd been goin' for——"

"There, be still! You mustn't speak of such things, or talk to me about Mr. Holcroft in such a way," and she hastily left the kitchen. When in the solitude of her own room, she gave way to bitter tears. "Is it so plain," she thought, "that even this ignorant child sees it? And the unhappy change began the day she came, too. I can't understand it. We were so happy before; and he seemed to enjoy being near me and talking to me when his work permitted. He used to look into my eyes in a way that made me hope and, indeed, feel almost sure. I receive no more such looks; he seems only trying to do his duty by me as he promised at first, and acts as if it were all duty, a mere matter of conscience. Could he have discovered how I felt, and so is taking this way to remind me that nothing of the kind was in our agreement? Well, I've no reason to complain; I accepted the relation of my own free will, but it's hard, hard indeed for a woman who loves a man with her whole heart and soul—and he her husband—to go on meeting him day after day, yet act as if she were his mere business partner. But I can't help myself; my very nature, as well as a sense of his rights, prevents me from asking more or even showing that I wish for more. That *would* be asking for it. But can it be true that he is positively learning to dislike me? to shrink from me with that strong repulsion which women feel toward some men? Oh! if that is true, the case is hopeless; it would kill me. Every effort to win him, even the most delicate and unobtrusive, would only drive him farther away; the deepest instincts of his soul would lead him to withdraw —to shun me. If this is true, the time may come when, so far from my filling his home with comfort, I shall make him dread to enter it. Oh, oh! my only course is to remember just what I promised and he expected when he married me, and live up to that."

Thus husband and wife reached the same conclusion and were rendered equally unhappy.

CHAPTER XXX.

HOLCROFT'S BEST HOPE.

WHEN Holcroft came in to dinner that day the view he had adopted was confirmed, yet Alida's manner and appearance began to trouble him. Even to his rather slow perception, she did not seem so happy as she had been. She did not meet his eye with her old frank, friendly, and as he had almost hoped, affectionate, expression; she seemed merely feverishly anxious to do everything and have all as he wished. Instead of acting with natural ease and saying what was in her mind without premeditation, a conscious effort was visible and an apparent solicitude that he should be satisfied. The inevitable result was that he was more dissatisfied. "She's doing her best for me," he growled, as he went back to his work, "and it begins to look as if it might wear her out in time. Confound it! having everything just so isn't of much account when a man's heart-hungry. I'd rather have had one of her old smiles and gone without my dinner. Well, well; how little a man understands himself or knows the future! The day I married her I was in mortal dread lest she should care for me too much and want to be affectionate and all that; and here I am, discontented and moping because everything has turned out as I then wished. Don't see as I'm to blame, either. She had no business to grow so pretty. Then she looked like a ghost, but now when the color comes into her cheeks, and her blue eyes sparkle, a man would be a stupid clod if he didn't look with all his eyes and feel his heart a-thumping. That she should change so wasn't in the bargain; neither was it that she should read aloud in such sweet tones that a fellow'd like to listen to the dictionary; nor that she should make the house and yard look as they never did before, and, strangest of all, open my eyes to the fact that apple trees bear flowers as well as pippins. I can't even go by a wild posy in the lane without thinking she'd like it and see in it a sight more than I once could. I've been taken in, as old Jonathan feared," he muttered, following out his fancy with a sort of grim humor. "She isn't the woman I thought I was marrying at all, and I aint bound by my agreement—not in my thoughts, anyhow, I'd have been in a nice scrape if I'd taken my little affidavit not to think of her or look upon her in any other light than that of housekeeper and butter-maker. It s a scary thing, this getting married with a single eye to business. See where I am now! Hanged if I don't believe I'm in love with my wife, and, like a thundering fool, I had to warn her against falling in love with me! Little need of that, though. She hasn't been taken in, for I'm the same old chap she married, and I'd be a mighty mean cuss if I went to her and said, ' Here, I want you to do twice as much, a hundred-fold as much as you agreed to.' I'd be a fool, too, for she couldn't do it unless something drew her toward me just as I'm drawn toward her."

Late in the afternoon he leaned on the handle of his corn-plow, and, in the consciousness of solitude, said aloud : " Things grow clear if you think of them enough, and the Lord knows I don't think of much else any more. It isn't her good qualities which I say over to myself a hundred times a day, or her education, or anything of the kind, that draws me ; it's she herself. I like her. Why don't I say love her, and be honest ? Well, it's a fact, and I've got to face it. Here I am, plowing out my corn, and it looks splendid for its age. I thought if I could stay on the old place, and plant and cultivate and reap, I'd be more than content, and now I don't seem to care a rap for the corn or the farm either, compared with Alida ; and I care for her just because she is Alida and no one else. But the other side of this fact has an ugly look. Suppose I'm disagreeable to her ! When she married me she felt like a woman drowning ; she was ready to take hold of the first hand reached to her, without knowing much about whose hand it was. Well, she's had time to find out. She isn't drawn. Perhaps she feels toward me somewhat as I did toward Mrs. Mumpson, and she can't help herself either. Well, well, the bare thought of it makes my heart lead. What's a man to do ? What can I do but live up to my agreement and not torment her any more than I can help with my company ? That's the only honest course. Perhaps she'll get more used to me in time. She might get sick, and then I'd be so kind and watchful that she'd think the old fellow wasn't so bad, after all. But I shan't give her the comfort of no end of self-sacrifice in trying to be pleasant and sociable. If she's foolish enough to think she's in my debt she can't pay it in that way. No, sir ! I've got to make the most of it now—I'm bound to—but this business marriage will never suit me until the white arm I saw in the dairy room is around my neck, and she looks in my eyes and says, ' James, I guess I'm ready for a longer marriage ceremony.' "

It was a pity that Alida could not have been among the hazelnut bushes near and heard him.

He resumed his toil, working late and doggedly. At supper he was very attentive to Alida, but taciturn and preoccupied ; and when the meal was over he lighted his pipe and strolled out into the moonlight. She longed to follow him, yet felt it to be more impossible than if she were chained to the floor.

And so the days passed ; Holcroft striving with the whole force of his will to appear absorbed in the farm, and she, with equal effort, to seem occupied and contented with her household and dairy duties. They did everything for each other that they could, and yet each thought that the other was acting from a sense of obligation, and so all the more sedulously veiled their actual thoughts and feelings from each other. Of course, such mistaken effort only led to a more complete misunderstanding.

With people of their simplicity and habit of reticence, little of what was in their hearts appeared on the surface. Neither had time to mope, and their mutual duties were in a large measure a support and refuge. Of these they could still speak freely, for they pertained to business. Alida's devotion to her work was unfeigned, for it seemed now her only avenue of approach to her husband. She watched over the many broods of little chickens with tireless vigilance. If it were yellow gold, she could not have gathered the butter from the churn with greater greed. She kept the house immaculate and sought to develop her cooking into a fine art. She was scrupulous in giving Jane her lessons and trying to correct her vernacular and manners, but the presence of the child grew to be a heavier cross every day. She could not blame the girl, whose misfortune it was to lead incidentally to

the change in Holcroft's manner, yet it was impossible
not to associate her with the beginning of that change.
Jane was making decided improvement, and had Alida
been happy and at rest this fact would have given much
satisfaction in spite of the instinctive repugnance which
the girl seemed to inspire universally. Holcroft recognized this repugnance and the patient effort to disguise it
and be kind.

" Like enough she feels in the same way toward me," he
thought, "and is trying a sight harder not to show it. But
she seems willing enough to talk business and to keep up
her interest in the partnership line. Well, blamed if I
wouldn't rather talk business to her than love to any other
woman ! "

So it gradually came about that they had more and
more to say to each other on matters relating to the
farm. Holcroft showed her the receipts from the dairy,
and her eyes sparkled as if he had brought jewels home
to her. Then she in turn would expatiate on the poultry
interests and assure him that there were already nearly
two hundred little chicks on the place. One afternoon,
during a shower, she ventured to beguile him into listening to the greater part of one of the agricultural journals,
and with much deference made two or three suggestions
about the farm, which he saw were excellent. She little
dreamed that if she were willing to talk of turning the
farm upside down and inside out, he would have listened
with pleasure.

They both began to acquire more serenity and hopefulness, for even this sordid business partnership was growing strangely interesting. The meals grew less and less
silent, and the farmer would smoke his pipe invitingly
near in the evening, so that she could resume their talk

on bucolic subjects without much conscious effort, while at the same time, if she did not wish his society, she could shun it without discourtesy. He soon perceived that she needed some encouragement to talk even of farm matters ; but, having received it, that she showed no further reluctance. He naturally began to console himself with business as unstintedly as he dared. " As long as I keep on this tack all seems well," he muttered. " She don't act as if I was disagreeable to her, but then how can a man tell ? If she thinks it her duty, she'll talk and smile, yet shiver at the very thought of my touching her. Well, well, time will show. We seem to be getting more sociable, anyhow."

They both recognized this fact and tried to disguise it and to relieve themselves from the appearance of making any undue advances by greater formality of address. In Jane's presence he had formed the habit of speaking to his wife as Mrs. Holcroft, and now he was invariably " Mr."

One evening, in the latter part of June, he remarked at supper, " I must give half a day to hoeing the garden to-morrow. I've been so busy working out the corn and potatoes that it seems an age since I've been in the garden."

" She and me," began Jane, " I mean Mrs. Holcroft and I, have been in the garden."

" That's right, Jane, you're coming on. I think your improved talk and manners do Mrs. Holcroft much credit. I'd like to take some lessons myself." Then, as if a little alarmed at his words, he hastened to ask, " What have you been doing in the garden ? "

" You'll see when you go there," replied Jane, her small eyes twinkling with the rudiments of fun.

Holcroft looked at the child as if he had not seen her for some time either. Her hair was neatly combed, braided, and tied with a blue ribbon instead of a string, her gown was as becoming as any dress could be to her, her little brown hands were clean, and they no longer managed the knife and fork in an ill-bred manner. The very expression of the child's face was changing, and now that it was lighted up with mirth at the little surprise awaiting him, it had at least attained the negative grace of being no longer repulsive. He sighed involuntarily as he turned away. " Just see what she's doing for that child that I once thought hideous ! How much she might do for me if she cared as I do ! "

He rose from the table, lighted his pipe, and went out to the doorstep. Alida looked at him wistfully. " He stood there with me once and faced a mob of men," she thought. " Then he put his arm around me. I would face almost any danger for even such a caress again." The memory of that hour lent her unwonted courage, and she approached him timidly and said, " Perhaps you would like to go and look at the garden ? Jane and I may not have done everything right."

" Why, certainly. I forgot about the garden ; but then you'll have to go with me if I'm to tell you."

" I don't mind," she said, leading the way.

The June sun was low in the west, and the air had become deliciously cool and fragrant. The old rose-bushes were in bloom, and as she passed she picked a bud and fastened it on her bosom. Wood thrushes, orioles, and the whole chorus of birds were in full song ; limpid rills of melody from the meadow larks flowed from the fields, and the whistling of the quails added to the harmony.

Holcroft was in a mood of which he had never been
conscious before. These familiar sounds, which had
been unheeded so much of his life, now affected him
strangely, creating an immeasurable sadness and longing.
It seemed as if perceptions which were like new senses
were awakening in his mind. The world was full of
wonderful beauty before unrecognized, and the woman
who walked lightly and gracefully at his side was the
crown of it all. He himself was so old, plain, and unworthy
in contrast. His heart ached with a positive, definite pain
that he was not younger, handsomer, and better equipped
to win the love of his wife. As she stood in the garden,
wearing the rose, her neat dress outlining her graceful
form, the level rays of the sun lighting up her face and
turning her hair to gold, he felt that he had never seen
or imagined such a woman before. She was in harmony
with the June evening and a part of it, while he, in his
working clothes, his rugged, sun-browned features and
hair tinged with gray, was a blot upon the scene. She,
who was so lovely, must be conscious of his rude, clown-
ish appearance. He would have faced any man living
and held his own on the simple basis of his manhood.
Anything like scorn, although veiled, on Alida's part,
would have touched his pride and steeled his will, but
the words and manner of this gentle woman who tried
to act as if blind to all that he was in contrast with herself, to show him deference, kindness, and good-will when
perhaps she felt toward him somewhat as she did toward
Jane, overwhelmed him with humility and grief. It is
the essence of deep, unselfish love to depreciate itself and
exalt its object. There was a superiority in Alida which
Holcroft was learning to recognize more clearly every
day, and he had not a trace of vanity to sustain him.

Now he was in a mood to wrong and undervalue himself without limit.

She showed him how much she and Jane had accomplished, how neat and clean they had kept the rows of growing vegetables, and how good the promise was for an indefinite number of dinners, but she only added to the farmer's depression. He was in no mood for onions. parsnips, and their vegetable kin, yet thought, " She thinks I'm only capable of being interested in such things, and I've been at much pains to give that impression. She picked that rose for *herself*, and now she's showing *me* how soon we may hope to have summer cabbage and squash. She thus shows that she knows the difference between us and that always must be between us, I fear. She is so near in our daily life, yet how can I ever get any nearer? As I feel now, it seems impossible."

She had quickly observed his depressed, abstracted manner, but misinterpreted the causes. Her own face clouded and grew troubled. Perhaps she was revealing too much of her heart, although seeking to disguise it so sedulously, and he was penetrating her motives for doing so much in the garden and in luring him thither now. He was not showing much practical interest in beans and beets, and was evidently oppressed and ill at ease.

" I hope we have done things right ? " she ventured, turning away to hide tears of disappointment.

" Her self-sacrifice is giving out," he thought bitterly. " She finds she can scarcely look at me as I now appear in contrast with this June evening. Well, I don't blame her. It makes me almost sick when I think of myself, and I won't be brute enough to say a harsh word to her. You have done it all far better than I could," he said emphatically. " I would not have believed it if you hadn't shown me. The trouble is, you are trying to do too much. I—I think I'll take a walk."

In fact, he had reached the limit of endurance; he could not look upon her another moment as she appeared that evening and feel that she associated him chiefly with crops and business, and that all her grateful good-will could not prevent his personality from being disagreeable. He must carry his bitterness whither no eye could see him, and as he turned, his self-disgust led him to whirl away his pipe. It struck a tree and fell shattered at its foot. Alida had never seen him do anything of the kind before, and it indicated that he was passing beyond the limits of patience. "Oh, oh," she sobbed, "I fear we are going to drift apart! If he can't endure to talk with me about such things, what chance have I at all? I hoped that the hour, the beauty of the evening, and the evidence that I had been trying so hard to please him would make him more like what he used to be before he seemed to take a dislike. There's only one way to account for it all—he sees how I feel and he don't like it. My very love sets him against me. My heart was over-flowing to-night. How could I help it, as I remembered how he stood up for me? He was brave and kind; he meant well by me, he means well now; but he can't help his feelings. He has gone away now to think of the woman that he did love and loves still, and it angers him that I should think of taking her place. He loved her as a child and girl and woman—he told me so; he warned me and said he could not help thinking of her. If I had not learned to love him so deeply and passionately, and show it in spite of myself, time would gradually have softened the past and all might have gone well. Yet how could I help it when he saved me from so much? I feel

to-night, though, that I only escaped one kind of trouble
to meet another almost as bad and which may become
worse."

She strolled to the farther end of the garden that she
might become calm before meeting Jane's scrutiny. Useless precaution! for the girl had been watching them
both. Her motive had not been unmixed curiosity,
since, having taken some part in the garden work, she
had wished to witness Holcroft's pleasure and hear his
praises. Since the actors in the scene so misunderstood
each other, she certainly would not rightly interpret
them. "She's losin' her hold on 'im," she thought.
"He acted just as if she was mother."

When Jane saw Alida coming toward the house she
whisked from the concealing shrubbery to the kitchen
again and was stolidly washing the dishes when her mistress entered. "You are slow to-night," said Alida,
looking at the child keenly, but the impassive face
revealed nothing. She set about helping the girl, feeling
it would be a relief to keep her hands busy.

Jane's efforts to comfort were always maladroit, yet
the apparent situation so interested her that she yielded
to her inclination to talk. "Say," she began, and Alida
was too dejected and weary to correct the child's vernacular, "Mr. Holcroft's got somethin' on his mind."

"Well, that's not strange."

"No, s'pose not. Hate to see 'im look so, though.
He always used to look so when mother went for 'im
and hung around 'im. At last he cleared mother out,
and just before he looked as black as he did when he
passed the house while ago. You're good to me, an' I'd
like you to stay. 'Fi's you I'd leave 'im alone."

"Jane," said Alida coldly, "I don't wish you ever to

speak to me of such things again," and she hastily left the room.

"Oh, well!" muttered Jane, "I've got eyes in my head. If you're goin' to be foolish, like mother, and keep a-goin' for 'im, it's your lookout. I kin get along with him and he with me, and *I'm* goin' to stay."

Holcroft strode rapidly up the lane to the deep solitude at the edge of his woodland. Beneath him lay the farm and the home that he had married to keep, yet now, without a second's hesitation, he would part with all to call his wife *wife*. How little the name now satisfied him, without the sweet realities of which the word is significant! The term and relation had become a mocking mirage. He almost cursed himself that he had exulted over his increasing bank account and general prosperity, and had complacently assured himself that she was doing just what he had asked, without any sentimental nonsense. "How could I expect it to turn out otherwise?" he thought. "From the first I made her think I hadn't a soul for anything but crops and money. Now that she's getting over her trouble and away from it, she's more able to see just what I am, or at least what she naturally thinks I am. But she doesn't understand me—I scarcely understand myself. I long to be a different man in every way, and not to work and live like an ox. Here are some of my crops almost ready to gather and they never were better, yet I've no heart for the work. Seems to me it 'll wear me out if I have to carry this load of trouble all the time. I thought my old burdens hard to bear; I thought I was lonely before, but it was nothing compared with living near one you love, but from whom you are cut off by something you can't see, yet must feel to the bottom of your heart."

His distraught eyes rested on the church spire, fading in the twilight, and the little adjoining graveyard. "Oh Bessie," he groaned, "why did you die? I was good enough for *you*. Oh! that all had gone on as it was and I had never known——"

He stopped, shook his head, and was silent. At last he sighed, "I *did* love Bessie. I love and respect her memory as much as ever. But somehow I never felt as I do now. All was quiet and matter-of-fact in those days, yet it was real and satisfying. I was content to live on, one day like another, to the end of my days. If I hadn't been so content it would be better for me now. I'd have a better chance if I had read more, thought more, and fitted myself to be more of a companion for a woman like Alida. If I knew a great deal and could talk well, she might forget I'm old and homely. Bessie was so true a friend that she would wish, if she knows, what *I* wish. I thought I needed a housekeeper; I find I need more than all else such a wife as Alida could be—one that could help me to be a man instead of a drudge, a Christian instead of a discontented and uneasy unbe-liever. At one time, it seemed that she was leading me along so naturally and pleasantly that I never was so happy; then all at once it came to me that she was do-ing it from gratitude and a sense of duty, and the duty grows harder for her every day. Well, there seems nothing for it now but to go on as we began and hope that the future will bring us more in sympathy."

CHAPTER XXXI

FOR the next two or three days Jane had no occasion to observe that Alida was in the least degree obtrusive in her attention to the farmer. She was assiduous in her work and more diligent than ever in her conscious efforts to do what she thought he wished; but she was growing pale, constrained, and silent. She struggled heroically to appear as at first, but without much success, for she could not rally from the wound he had given her so unintentionally and which Jane's words had deepened. She almost loathed herself under her association with Mrs. Mumpson, and her morbid thoughts had hit upon a worse reason for Holcroft's apparent repulsion. As she questioned everything in the sleepless hours that followed the interview in the garden, she came to the miserable conclusion that he had discovered her love, and that by suggestion, natural to his mind, it reminded him of her pitiful story. He could be sorry for her and be kind; he could even be her honest friend and protector as a wronged and unhappy woman, but he could not love one with a history like hers and did not wish her to love him. This seemed an adequate explanation of the change in their relations, but she felt that it was one under which her life would wither and her heart break. This promised to be worse than what she had dreaded at the almshouse—the facing the world alone and working till she died among strangers. The fact that they were strangers would enable her to see their averted faces with comparative indifference, but that the man to whom she had yielded her whole heart should turn away was intolerable. She felt that he could not do this willingly but only under the imperious instincts of his nature— that he was virtually helpless in the matter. There was an element in these thoughts which stung her woman's soul, and, as we have said, she could not rally.

Holcroft never suspected her morbid thoughts, and his loyal, loving heart was incapable of dreaming of them. He only grew more unhappy as he saw the changes in her, for he regarded himself as the cause. Yet he was perplexed and unable to account for her rapidly increasing pallor while he continued so kind, considerate, and especially so unobtrusive. He assuredly thought he was showing a disposition to give her all the time she wished to become reconciled to her lot. "Thunder!" he said to himself, "we can't grow old together without getting used to each other."

On Saturday noon, at dinner, he remarked, "I shall have to begin haying on Monday and so I'll take everything to town this afternoon, for I won't be able to go again for some days. Is there anything you'd like me to get, Mrs. Holcroft?"

She shook her head. "I don't need anything," she replied. He looked at her downcast face with troubled eyes and shivered. "She looks as if she were going to be sick," he thought. "Good Lord! I feel as if there was nothing but trouble ahead. Every mouthful I take seems to choke me."

A little later he pushed away almost untasted a piece

of delicious cherry pie, the first of the season. Alida could scarcely keep the tears back as she thought, "There was a time when he would have praised it without stint. I took so much pains with it in the hope he'd notice, for he once said he was very fond of it." Such were the straws that were indicating the deep, dark currents.

As he rose, she said almost apathetically in her dejection, "Mr. Holcroft, Jane and I picked a basket of the early cherries. You may as well sell them, for there are plenty left on the tree for use."

"That was too much for you to do in the hot sun. Well, I'll sell 'em and add what they bring to your egg money in the bank. You'll get rich," he continued, trying to smile, "if you don't spend more."

"I don't wish to spend anything," she said, turning away with the thought, "How can he think I want finery when my heart is breaking?"

Holcroft drove away, looking and feeling as if he were going to a funeral. At last he broke out, "I can't stand this another day. To-morrow's Sunday, and I'll manage to send Jane somewhere or take Alida out to walk and tell her the whole truth. She shall be made to see that I can't help myself and that I'm willing to do anything she wishes. She's married to me and has got to make the best of it, and I'm sure I'm willing to make it as easy as I can."

Jane was a little perplexed at the condition of affairs. Mrs. Holcroft had left her husband alone as far as possible, as she had advised, but apparently it had not helped matters much. But she believed that the trouble she had witnessed boded her no ill and so was inclined to regard it philosophically. "He looks almost as glum, when he's goin' round alone, as if he'd married mother.

She talked too much, and that didn't please him; this one talks less and less, and he don't seem pleased, nuther, but it seems to me he's very foolish to be so fault-findin' when she does everything for him top-notch. I never lived so well in my life, nor he, nuther, I believe. He must be in a bad way when he couldn't eat that cherry pie."

Alida was so weary and felt so ill that she went to the parlor and lay down upon the lounge. "My heart feels as if it were bleeding slowly away," she murmured. "If I'm going to be sick the best thing I can do is to die and end it all," and she gave way to that deep dejection in which there seems no remedy for trouble.

The hours dragged slowly by; Jane finished her household tasks very leisurely, then taking a basket, went out to the garden to pick some early peas. While thus engaged, she saw a man coming up the lane. His manner instantly riveted her attention and awakened her curiosity, and she crouched lower behind the pea vines for concealment. All her furtive, watchful instincts were awake, and her conscience was clear, too, for certainly she had a right to spy upon a stranger.

The man seemed almost as furtive as herself; his eyes were everywhere and his step slow and hesitating. Instead of going directly to the house he cautiously entered the barn, and she heard him a little later call Mr. Holcroft. Of course there was no answer, and, as if reassured, he approached the house, looking here and there on every side, seemingly to see if anyone was about. Jane had associated with men and boys too long to have any childlike timidity, and she also had just confidence in her skulking and running powers. "After all, he don't want nothin' of me and won't hurt me," she reasoned. "He acts mighty queer though, and I'm goin' to hear what he says."

The moment he passed the angle of the house she dodged around to its rear and stole into the dairy room, being well aware that from this position she could over-hear words spoken in ordinary conversational tones in the apartment above. She had barely gained her ambush when she heard Alida half shriek, "Henry Ferguson!"

It was indeed the man who had deceived her that had stolen upon her solitude. His somewhat stealthy approach had been due to the wish and expectation of finding her alone, and he had about convinced himself that she was so by exploring the barn and observing the absence of the horses and wagon. Cunning and un-scrupulous, it was his plan to appear before the woman who had thought herself his wife, without any warning whatever, believing that in the tumult of her surprise and shock she would be off her guard and that her old affection would reassert itself. He passed through the kitchen to the parlor door. Alida, in her deep, painful abstraction, did not hear him until he stood in the door-way, and, with outstretched arms, breathed her name. Then, as if struck a blow, she had sprung to her feet, half shrieked his name and stood panting, regarding him as if he were a specter.

" Your surprise is natural, Alida, dear," he said gently, " but I've a right to come to you, for my wife is dead." and he advanced toward her.

"Stand back!" she cried sternly. "You've no right, and never can have."

"Oh, yes, I have!" he replied in a wheedling tone. "Come, come! your nerves are shaken. Sit down, for I've much to tell you."

"No, I won't sit down, and I tell you to leave me instantly. You've no right here and I no right to listen to you."

"I can soon prove that you have a better right to listen to me than to anyone else. Were we not married by a minister?"

"Yes, but that made no difference. You deceived both him and me."

"It made no difference, perhaps, in the eye of the law, while that woman you saw was living, but she's dead, as I can easily prove. How were you married to this man Holcroft?"

Alida grew dizzy; everything whirled and grew black before her eyes as she sank into a chair. He came to her and took her hand, but his touch was a most effectual restorative. She threw his hand away and said hoarsely, "Do you—do you mean that you have any claim on me?"

"Who has a better claim?" he asked cunningly. "I loved you when I married you and I love you now. Do you think I rested a moment after I was free from the woman I detested? No, indeed; nor did I rest till I found out who took you from the almshouse to be his household drudge, not wife. I've seen the justice who aided in the wedding farce, and learned how this man Holcroft made him cut down even the ceremony of a civil marriage to one sentence. It was positively heathenish, and he only took you because he couldn't get a decent servant to live with him."

"O God!" murmured the stricken woman. "Can such a horrible thing be?"

"So it seems," he resumed, misinterpreting her. "Come now!" he said confidently, and sitting down, "don't look so broken up about it. Even while that woman was living I felt that I was married to you and you only; now that I'm free——"

"But I'm not free and don't wish to be."

"Don't be foolish, Alida. You know this farmer don't care a rap for you. Own up now, does he?"

The answer was a low, half-despairing cry.

"There, I knew it was so. What else could you expect? Don't you see I'm your true refuge and not this hard-hearted, money-grasping farmer?"

"Stop speaking against him!" she cried. "O God!" she wailed, "can the law give this man any claim on me, now his wife is dead?"

"Yes, and one I mean to enforce," he replied doggedly.

"I don't believe she's dead, I don't believe anything you say! You deceived me once."

"I'm not deceiving you now, Alida," he said with much solemnity. "She *is* dead. If you were calmer, I have proofs to convince you in these papers. Here's the newspaper, too, containing the notice of her death," and he handed it to her.

She read it with her frightened eyes, and then the paper dropped from her half-paralyzed hands to the floor. She was so unsophisticated, and her brain was in such a whirl of confusion and terror, that she was led to believe at the moment that he had a legal claim upon her which he could enforce.

"Oh, that Mr. Holcroft were here!" she cried desperately. "He wouldn't deceive me; he never deceived me."

"It is well for him that he isn't here," said Ferguson, assuming a dark look.

"What do you mean?" she gasped.

"Come, come, Alida!" he said, smiling reassuringly. "You are frightened and nervous, and I don't wish to make you any more so. You know how I would naturally regard the man who I feel has my wife; but let us forget about him. Listen to my plan. All I ask of you is to go with me to some distant place where neither of us are known, and——"

"Never!" she interrupted.

"Don't say that," he replied coolly. "Do you think I'm a man to be trifled with after what I've been through?"

"You can't compel me to go against my will," and there was an accent of terror in her words which made them a question.

He saw his vantage more clearly and said quietly, "I don't want to compel you if it can be helped. You know how true I was to you——"

"No, no! you deceived me. I won't believe you now."

"You may have to. At any rate, you know how fond I was of you, and I tell you plainly, I won't give you up now. This man doesn't love you, nor do you love him——"

"I *do* love him, I'd die for him! There now, you know the truth. You wouldn't compel a woman to follow you who shrinks from you in horror, even if you had the right. Although the ceremony was brief it *was* a ceremony; and he was not married then, as you were when you deceived me. He has ever been truth itself, and I won't believe you have any rights till he tells me so himself."

"So you shrink from me with horror, do you?" asked Ferguson, rising, his face growing black with passion.

"Yes, I do. Now leave me and let me never see you again."

" And you are going to ask this stupid old farmer about my rights ? "

" Yes, I'll take proof of them from no other, and even if he confirmed your words I'd never live with you again. I would live alone till I died ! "

" That's all very foolish high tragedy, but if you're not careful there may be some real tragedy. If you care for this Holcroft, as you say, you had better go quietly away with me."

" What do you mean ? " she faltered tremblingly.

" I mean I'm a desperate man whom the world has wronged too much already. You know the old saying, ' Beware of the quiet man ! ' You know how quiet, contented, and happy I was with you, and so I would be again to the end of my days. You are the only one who can save me from becoming a criminal, a vagabond, for with you only have I known happiness. Why should I live or care to live ? If this farmer clod keeps you from me, woe betide him ! My one object in living will be his destruction. I shall hate him only as a man robbed as I am can hate."

" What would you do ? " she could only ask in a horrified whisper.

" I can only tell you that he'd never be safe a moment. I'm not afraid of him. You see I'm armed," and he showed her a revolver. " He can't quietly keep from me what I feel is my own."

" Merciful Heaven ! this is terrible," she gasped.

" Of course it's terrible. I mean it to be so. You can't order me off as if I were a tramp. Your best course for his safety is to go quietly with me at once. I have a carriage waiting near at hand."

" No, no ! I'd rather die than do that, and though he

cannot feel as I do, I believe he'd rather die than have me do it."

"Oh, well! if you think he's so ready to die——"

"No, I don't mean that! Kill me! I want to die."

"Why should I kill you?" he asked with a contemptuous laugh. "That wouldn't do me a particle of good. It will be your own fault if anyone is hurt."

"Was ever a woman put in such a cruel position!"

"Oh, yes! many and many a time. As a rule, though, they are too sensible and kind-hearted to make so much trouble."

"If you have legal rights, why don't you quietly enforce them instead of threatening?"

For a moment he was confused and then said recklessly, "It would come to the same thing in the end. Holcroft would never give you up."

"He'd have to. I wouldn't stay here a moment if I had no right."

"But you said you would not live with me again?"

"Nor would I. I'd go back to the poorhouse and die there, for do you think I could live after another such experience? But my mind has grown clearer. You are deceiving me again, and Mr. Holcroft is incapable of deceiving me. He would never have called me his wife unless I was his wife before God and man."

"I'm not deceiving you in regard to one thing!" he said tragically.

"O God, what shall I do?"

"If you won't go with me you must leave him," he replied, believing that, if this step were taken, others would follow.

"If I leave him—if I go away and live alone, will you promise to do him no harm?"

" I'd have no motive to harm him then, which will be better security than a promise. At the same time I do promise."

" And you will also promise to leave me utterly alone ? "

" If I can."

" You must promise never even to tempt me to think of going away. I'd rather you'd shoot me than ask it. I'm not a weak, timid girl. I'm a broken-hearted woman who fears some things far more than death."

" If you have any fears for Holcroft, they are very rational ones."

" It is for his sake that I would act. I would rather suffer anything and lose everything than have harm come to him."

" All I can say is that, if you will leave him completely and finally, I will let him alone. But you must do it promptly. Everything depends upon this. I'm in too reckless and bitter a mood to be trifled with. Besides, I've plenty of money and could escape from the country in twenty-four hours. You needn't think you can tell this story to Holcroft and that he can protect you and himself. I'm here under an assumed name and have seen no one who knows me. I may have to disappear for a time and be disguised when I come again, but I pledge you my word he'll never be safe as long as you are under his roof."

" Then I will sacrifice myself for him," she said, pallid even to her lips. " I will go away. But never dream that you can come near me again—you who deceived and wronged me, and now, far worse, threaten the man I love."

" We'll see about that," he replied cynically. " At any rate, you will have left him."

"Go!" she said imperiously.

"I'll take a kiss first, sweetheart," he said, advancing with a sardonic smile.

"Jane!" she shrieked. He paused, and she saw evidences of alarm.

The girl ran lightly out of the dairy room, where she had been a greedy listener to all that had been said, and a moment later appeared in the yard before the house. "Yes'm," she answered.

"Be careful now, sir," said Alida sternly. "There's a witness."

"Only a little idiotic-looking girl."

"She's not idiotic, and if you touch me the compact's broken."

"Very well, my time will come. Remember, you've been warned," and he pulled his hat over his eyes and strode away.

"Bah!" said Jane with a snicker, "as if I hadn't seen his ugly mug so I'd know it 'mong a thousand."

With a face full of loathing and dread Alida watched her enemy disappear down the lane, and then, half fainting, sank on the lounge.

"Jane!" she called feebly, but there was no answer.

CHAPTER XXXII.

JANE PLAYS MOUSE TO THE LION.

It can well be understood that Jane had no disposition to return to Mrs. Holcroft and the humdrum duties of the house. There opened before her an exciting line of action which fully accorded with her nature, and she entered upon it at once. Her first impulse was to follow the man of whom she had learned so much. Not only was she spurred to this course by her curiosity, but also by her instinctive loyalty to Holcroft, and, it must be admitted, by her own interests. Poor little Jane had been nurtured in a hard school, and had by this time learned the necessity of looking out for herself. This truth, united with her shrewd, matter-of-fact mind, led her to do the most sensible thing under the circumstances. "I know a lot now that he'll be glad to know, and if I tell him everything he'll keep me always. The first thing he'll want to know is what's become of that threatenin' scamp," and she followed Ferguson with the stealth of an Indian.

Ferguson was not only a scamp, but, like most of his class, a coward. He had been bitterly disappointed in his interview with Alida. As far as his selfish nature permitted, he had a genuine affection for her, and he had thought of little else besides her evident fondness for him. He was so devoid of moral principle that he could not comprehend a nature like hers, and had scarcely believed it possible that she would repulse him so inflexibly. She had always been so gentle, yielding, and subservient to his wishes that he had thought that, having been assured of his wife's death, a little persuasion and perhaps a few threats would induce her to follow him, for he could not imagine her becoming attached to such a man as Holcroft had been described to be. Her uncompromising principle had entered but slightly into his calculations, and so, under the spur of anger and selfishness, he had easily entered upon a game of bluff. He knew well enough that he had no claim upon Alida, yet it was in harmony with his false heart to try to make her think so. He had no serious intention of harming Holcroft—he would be afraid to attempt this—but if he could so work on Alida's fears as to induce her to leave her husband, he believed that the future would be full of possibilities. At any rate, he would find his revenge in making Alida and Holcroft all the trouble possible. Even in the excitement of the interview, however, he realized that he was playing a dangerous game, and when Jane answered so readily to Alida's call he was not a little disturbed. Satisfied that he had accomplished all that he could hope for at present, his purpose now was to get back to town unobserved and await developments. He therefore walked rapidly down the lane and pursued the road for a short distance until he came to an old, disused lane, leading up the hillside into a grove where he had concealed a horse and buggy. Unless there should be necessity, it was his intention to remain in his hiding place until after nightfall.

Jane had merely to skirt the bushy hillside higher up, in order to keep Ferguson in view and discover the spot in which he was lurking. Instead of returning to the house she kept right on, maintaining a sharp eye on the road beneath to make sure that Holcroft did not pass unobserved. By an extended detour, she reached the highway and continued toward town in the hope of meeting the farmer. At last she saw him driving rapidly homeward. He was consumed with anxiety to be at least near to Alida, even if, as he believed, he was no longer welcome in her presence. When Jane stepped out into the road he pulled up his horses and stared at her. She, almost bursting with her great secrets, put her finger on her lips and nodded portentously.

"Well, what is it?" he asked, his heart beating quickly.

"I've got a lot to tell yer, but don't want no one to see us."

"About my wife?"

The girl nodded.

"Good God! speak then. Is she sick?" and he sprung out and caught her arm with a grip that hurt her.

"Please, sir, I'm doin' all I kin for yer and—and you hurt me."

Holcroft saw the tears coming to her eyes and he released his hold as he said, "Forgive me, Jane, I didn't mean to; but for mercy's sake, tell your story."

"It's a long 'un."

"Well, well, give me the gist of it in a word."

"I guess she's goin' to run away."

Holcroft groaned and almost staggered to his horses heads, then led them to the roadside and tied them to a tree. Sitting down, as if too weak to stand, he buried his face in his hands. He could not bear to have Jane see his distress. "Tell your story," he said hoarsely, "quick, for I may have to act quickly."

"Guess yer will. Did yer know she was married?"

"Certainly—to me."

"No, to another man—married by a minister. He's been there with her." She little foresaw the effect of her words, for the farmer bounded to his feet with an oath and sprang to his horses.

"Stop!" cried Jane, tugging at his arm. "If you go rushin' home now, you'll show you've got no more sense than mother. You'll spoil everything. She aint goin' to run away with *him*—she said she wouldn't, though he coaxed and threatened to kill yer if she didn't. 'Fi's a man I wouldn't act like a mad bull. I'd find out how to get ahead of t'other man."

"Well," said Holcroft, in a voice that frightened the child, "she said she wouldn't run away with this scoundrel—of course not—but you say she's going to leave. She'll meet him somewhere—good God!—but how should you understand? Come, let me get home!"

"I understand a sight more'n you do, and you go on so that I can't tell you anything. If you showed sense you'd be glad I was lookin' out for you so I could tell you everything. What's the good of goin' rampaigin' home when, if you'd only listen, you could get even with that scoundrel, as yer call 'im, and make all right," and Jane began to cry.

"Oh, thunder!" exclaimed the chafing man, "tell me your story at once, or you'll drive me mad. You don't half know what you're talking about or how much your words mean—how should you? The thing to do is to get home as soon as possible."

"You aint no reason to be so mad and glum all the while," cried Jane, smarting under a sense of injustice. "Here I'm a-tryin' to do for you, and you'll be sorry

ernuff if you don't stop and listen. And she's been
a-tryin' to do for you all along, and she's been standin' up
for you this afternoon, and is goin' to run away to save
your life."

" Run away to save my life? Are you crazy?"

"No, but you be," cried the girl, excited and exasperated beyond restraint. " If she *is* your wife I'd stand
up for her and take care of her, since she stands up for
you so. 'Stead of that, you go round as glum as a
thundercloud and now want to go ragin' home to her.
Dunno whether she's your wife or not, but I *do* know she
said she loved you and 'ud die for you, and she wouldn't
do a thing that man asked but go away to save your life."

Holcroft looked at the girl as if dazed. " Said she
loved me?" he repeated slowly.

" Of course! You knowed that all 'long—anybody
could see it—an' you don't treat her much better'n you
did mother." Then, with an impatient gesture, she
asked, " Will you sit down and listen?"

"No, I won't!" he cried, springing toward his horses.
" I'll find out if your words are true."

" Oh, yes!" said Jane contemptuously; "run right to
her to find out somethin' as plain as the nose on her
face, and run right by the man that was threatenin' her
and you too."

Wheeling round, he asked, " Where is he?"

" I know, but I won't say 'nuther word till you stop
goin' on. 'Fi's a man I'd find out what to do 'fore I did
anythin'."

Jane had little comprehension of the tempest she had
raised in Holcroft's soul or its causes, and so was in no
mood to make allowances for him. By this time, the first
gust of his passion was passing and reason resuming its

sway. He paced up and down in the road a moment or two, and then sat down as he said, "I don't half understand what you've been talking about and I fear you don't. You've evidently been listening and watching and have got hold of something. Now, I'll be as patient as I can if you'll tell me the whole story quickly," and he turned his flushed, quivering face toward her.

"Then I s'pose you'll scold me for listenin' and watchin' that scamp," said the girl sullenly.

"No, Jane, not in this case. Unless your impressions are all mistaken I may have to thank you all my life. I'm not one to forget those who are true to me. Now, begin at the beginning and go right through to the end; then I may understand better than you can."

Jane did as she was told, and many "says he's" and "says she's" followed in her literal narrative. Holcroft again dropped his face into his hands, and before she was through tears of joy trickled through his fingers. When she finished, he arose, turned away, and hastily wiped his eyes, then gave the girl his hand as he said, "Thank you, Jane. You've tried to be a true friend to me to-day. I'll show you that I don't forget. I was a fool to get in such a rage, but you can't understand and must forgive me. Come, you see I'm quiet now," and he untied the horses and lifted her into his wagon.

"What yer goin' to do?" she asked, as they drove away.

"I'm going to reward you for watching and listening to that scoundrel, but you must not watch me or Mrs. Holcroft, or listen to what we say unless we speak before you. If you do I shall be very angry. Now, you've only one thing more to do and that is, show me where this man is hiding."

"But you won't go near him alone?" inquired Jane in much alarm.

"You must do as I bid you," he replied sternly. "Show me where he's hiding, then stay by the wagon and horses."

"But he same as said he'd kill you."

"You have your orders," was his quiet reply.

She looked scared enough, but remained silent until they reached a shaded spot on the road, then said, "If you don't want him to see you too soon, better tie here. He's around yonder, in a grove up on the hill."

Holcroft drove to a tree by the side of the highway and again tied his horses, then took the whip from the wagon. "Are you afraid to go with me a little way and show me just where he is?" he asked.

"No, but you oughtn' ter go."

"Come on, then! You must mind me if you wish to keep my good will. I know what I'm about." As in his former encounter, his weapon was again a long, tough whipstock with a leather thong attached. This he cut off and put in his pocket, then followed Jane's rapid lead up the hill. Very soon she said, "There's the place I saw 'im in. If you will go, I'd steal up on him."

"Yes. You stay here." She made no reply, but the moment he disappeared she was upon his trail. Her curiosity was much greater than her timidity, and she justly reasoned that she had little to fear.

Holcroft approached from a point whence Ferguson was expecting no danger. The latter was lying on the ground gnawing his nails in vexation, when he first heard the farmer's step. Then he saw a dark-visaged man rushing upon him. In the impulse of his terror, he drew his revolver and fired. The ball hissed near, but did no harm, an before Ferguson could use his weapon again, a blow from the whipstock paralyzed his arm and the pistol dropped to the ground. So also did its owner a moment later, under a vindictive rain of blows, until he shrieked for mercy.

"Don't move!" said Holcroft sternly, and he picked up the revolver. "So you meant to kill me, eh?"

"No, no! I didn't. I wouldn't have fired if it hadn't been in self-defense and because I hadn't time to think." He spoke with difficulty, for his mouth was bleeding and he was terribly bruised.

"A liar, too!" said the farmer, glowering down upon him. "But I knew that before. What did you mean by your threats to my wife?"

"See here, Mr. Holcroft; I'm down and at your mercy. If you'll let me off I'll go away and never trouble you or your wife again."

"Oh, no!" said Holcroft with a bitter laugh. "You'll never, never trouble us again."

"What, do you mean to murder me?" Ferguson half shrieked.

"Would killing such a thing as you be murder? Any jury in the land would acquit me. You ought to be roasted over a slow fire."

The fellow tried to scramble on his knees, but Holcroft hit him another savage blow, and said, "Lie still!"

Ferguson began to wring his hands and beg for mercy. His captor stood over him a moment or two irresolutely in his white-heated anger; then thoughts of his wife began to soften him. He could not go to her with blood on his hands—she who had taught him such lessons of forbearance and forgiveness. He put the pistol in his pocket and giving his enemy a kick, said, "Get up!"

The man rose with difficulty.

"I won't waste time in asking any promises from *you* but if you ever trouble my wife or me again, I'll brea every bone in your body. Go, quick, before my moo changes, and don't say a word."

As the man tremblingly untied his horse, Jane steppe out before him and said, "I'm a little idiotic gir am I?"

He was too thoroughly cowed to make any reply an drove as rapidly away as the ground permitted, guidin his horse with difficulty in his maimed condition.

Jane, in the exuberance of her pleasure, began some thing like a jig on the scene of conflict, and her antic were so ridiculous that Holcroft had to turn away t repress a smile. "You didn't mind me, Jane," he sai gravely.

"Well, sir," she replied, "after showin' you th way to 'im, you oughter not grudge me seein' th fun."

"But it isn't nice for little girls to see such things."

"Never saw anything nicer in my life. You're the kin of man I believe in, you are. Golly! only wished *she* seen you. I've seen many a rough and tumble 'mon farm hands, but never anything like this. It was on his pistol I was 'fraid of."

"Will you do exactly what I say now?" She nodde

"Well, go home across the fields and don't by wor or manner let Mrs. Holcroft know what you've seen o heard, and say nothing about meeting me. Just mak her think you know nothing at all and that you on watched the man out of sight. Do this and I'll give yo a new dress."

"I'd like somethin' else 'sides that."

" Well, what ? "

" I'd like to be sure I could stay right on with you."

" Yes, Jane, after to-day, as long as you're a good girl. Now go, for I must get back to my team before this scamp goes by."

She darted homeward as the farmer returned to his wagon. Ferguson soon appeared and seemed much startled as he saw his Nemesis again. " I'll keep my word," he said, as he drove by.

" You'd better ! " called the farmer. " You know what to expect now."

Alida was so prostrated by the shock of the interview that she rallied slowly. At last she saw that it was getting late and that she soon might expect the return of her husband. She dragged herself to the door and again called Jane, but the place was evidently deserted. Evening was coming on tranquilly, with all its sweet June sounds, but now every bird song was like a knell. She sunk on the porch seat and looked at the landscape, already so dear and familiar, as if she were taking a final farewell of a friend. Then she turned to the homely kitchen to which she had first been brought. " I can do a little more for him," she thought, " before I make the last sacrifice which will soon bring the end. I think I could have lived—lived, perhaps, till I was old, if I had gone among strangers from the almshouse, but I can't now. My heart is broken. Now that I've seen that man again I understand why my husband cannot love me. Even the thought of touching me must make him shudder. But I can't bear up under such a load much longer, and that's my comfort. It's best I should go away now ; I couldn't do otherwise," and the tragedy went on in her soul as she feebly prepared her husband's meal.

At last Jane came in with her basket of peas. Her face was so impassive as to suggest that she had no knowledge of anything except that there had been a visitor, and Alida had sunk into such depths of despairing sorrow that she scarcely noticed the child.

CHAPTER XXXIII.

" SHRINK FROM *YOU?* "

HOLCROFT soon came driving slowly up the lane as if nothing unusual was on his mind. Having tied his horses, he brought in an armful of bundles and said kindly, " Well, Alida, here I am again, and I guess I've brought enough to last well through haying time."

" Yes," she replied with averted face. This did not trouble him any now, but her extreme pallor did and he added, " You don't look well. I wouldn't mind getting much supper to-night. Let Jane do the work."

" I'd rather do it," she replied.

"Oh, well !" laughing pleasantly, " you shall have your own way. Who has a better right than you, I'd like to know ? "

" Don't speak that way," she said almost harshly, under the tension of her feelings. " I—I can't stand it. Speak and look as you did before you went away."

" Jane," said the farmer, " go and gather the eggs."

As soon as they were alone, he began gently, " Alida——"

" Please don't speak so to me to-day. I've endured all I can. I can't keep up another minute unless you let things go on as they were. To-morrow I'll try to tell you all. It's your right."

" I didn't mean to say anything myself till after supper,

and perhaps not till to-morrow, but I think I'd better. It will be better for us both, and our minds will be more at rest. Come with me into the parlor, Alida."

"Well, perhaps the sooner it's over the better," she said faintly and huskily.

She sunk on the lounge and looked at him with such despairing eyes that tears came into his own.

"Alida," he began hesitatingly, "after I left you this noon I felt I must speak with and be frank with you."

"No, no!" she cried, with an imploring gesture, "if it must be said, let me say it. I couldn't endure to hear it from you. Before you went away I understood it all, and this afternoon the truth has been burned into my soul. That horrible man has been here—the man I thought my husband—and he has made it clearer, if possible. I don't blame you that you shrink from me as if I were a leper. I feel as if I were one."

"*I* shrink from *you!*" he exclaimed.

"Yes. Can you think I haven't seen the repugnance growing in spite of yourself? When I thought of that man—especially when he came to-day—I understood *why* too well. I cannot stay here any longer. You'd try to be kind and considerate, but I'd know how you felt all the time. It would not be safe for you and it would not be right for me to stay, either, and that settles it. Be—be as kind to me—as you can a few—a few hours longer, and then let me go quietly." Her self-control gave way, and burying her face in her hands, she sobbed convulsively.

In a moment he was on his knees beside her, with his arm about her waist. "Alida, dear Alida!" he cried, "we've both been in the dark about each other. What I resolved to do, when I started for town, was to tell you that I had learned to love you and to throw myself on your mercy. I thought you saw I was loving you and that you couldn't bear to think of such a thing in an old, homely fellow like me. That was all that was in my mind, so help me God!"

" But—but *he's* been here," she faltered; " you don't realize——"

" I don't believe I do or can, yet, Alida, dear, but that blessed Jane's spying trait has served me the best turn in the world. She heard every brave word you said and I shed tears of joy when she told me; and tears are slow coming to my eyes. You think I shrink from you, do you ? " and he kissed her hands passionately. " See," he cried, " I kneel to you in gratitude for all you've been to me and are to me."

" Oh, James! please rise. It's too much."

" No, not till you promise to go with me to a minister and hear me promise to love, cherish—yes, in your case I'll promise to obey."

She bowed her head upon his shoulder in answer. Springing up, he clasped her close and kissed away her tears as he exclaimed, " No more business marriage for me, if you please. There never was a man so in love with his wife."

Suddenly she looked up and said fearfully, " James, he threatened you. He said you'd never be safe a moment as long as I stayed here."

His answer was a peal of laughter. " I've done more than threaten him. I've whipped him within an inch of his life, and it was the thought of you that led me, in my rage, to spare his life. I'll tell you all—I'm going to tell you everything now. How much trouble I might have saved if I had told you my thoughts! What was there, Alida, in an old fellow like me that led you to care so ? "

Looking up shyly, she replied, " I think it was the *man* in you—and—then you stood up for me so."

" Well, love is blind, I suppose, but it don't seem to me that mine is. There never was a man so taken in at his marriage. You were so different from what I expected that I began loving you before I knew it, but I thought you were good to me just as you were to Jane—from a sense of duty—and that you couldn't abide me personally. So I tried to keep out of your way. And, Alida, dear, I thought at first that I was taken by your good traits and your education and all that, but I found out at last that I had fallen in love with *you*. Now you know all. You feel better now, don't you ? "

" Yes," she breathed softly.

" You've had enough to wear a saint out," he continued kindly. " Lie down on the lounge and I'll bring your supper to you."

" No, please ! It will do me more good to go on and act as if nothing had happened."

" Well, have your own way, little wife. You're boss now, sure enough."

She drew him to the porch, and together they looked upon the June landscape which she had regarded with such despairing eyes an hour before.

" Happiness never kills, after all," she said.

" Shouldn't be alive if it did," he replied. " The birds seem to sing as if they knew."

Jane emerged from the barn door with a basket of eggs, and Alida sped away to meet her. The first thing the child knew the arms of her mistress were about her neck and she was kissed again and again.

" What did you do that for ? " she asked.

" You'll understand some day."

" Say," said Jane in an impulse of good will, " if you're only half married to Mr. Holcroft, I'd go the whole figure, 'fi's you. If you'd 'a' seen him a-thrashin' that scamp you'd know he's the man to take care of you."

" Yes, Jane, I know. He'll take care of me always."

The next morning Holcroft and Alida drove to town and went to the church which she and her mother used to attend. After the service they followed the clergyman home, where Alida again told him her story, though not without much help from the farmer. After some kindly reproach that she had not brought her troubles to him at first, the minister performed a ceremony which found deep echoes in both their hearts.

Time and right, sensible living soon remove prejudice from the hearts of the good and stop the mouths of the cynical and scandal-loving. Alida's influence, and the farmer's broadening and more unselfish views, gradually brought him into a better understanding of his faith, and into a kinder sympathy and charity for his neighbors than he had ever known. His relations to the society of which he was a part became natural and friendly, and his house a pretty and a hospitable home. Even Mrs. Watterly eventually entered its portals. She and others were compelled to agree with Watterly that Alida was not of the " common sort," and that the happiest good fortune which could befall any man had come to Holcroft when he fell in love with his wife.

THE END.